P9-CEM-118

A RISK WORTH TAKING

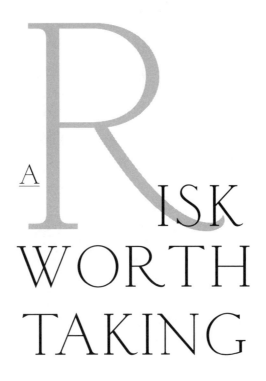

A RISK WORTH TAKING

ROBIN PILCHER

THOMAS DUNNE BOOKS
ST. MARTIN'S PRESS ✠ NEW YORK

THOMAS DUNNE BOOKS.
An imprint of St. Martin's Press.

www.stmartins.com

The song "Little Goldfish" on page 119 is reprinted by permission of Andy Munro, trading as Sprocket Music Publishers, 1986.

Library of Congress Cataloging-in-Publication Data

Pilcher, Robin.
    A risk worth taking / Robin Pilcher.—1st ed.
      p.   cm.
    ISBN 0-312-27002-X
    1. Employees—Dismissal of—Fiction.   2. Risk-taking (Psychology)—Fiction.
    3. Life change events—Fiction.   4. Married people—Fiction.   5. Unemployed—Fiction.   I. Title.

PR6066.I376R57   2004
823'.914—dc22

2003058564

10 9 8 7 6 5 4 3 2

For Oliver, Alice, Hugo, and Florence.
And for Tia Buffy,
who has always been my brilliant first-time reader.

ACKNOWLEDGMENTS

My greatest appreciation goes to Nick Tudor, whose stories inspired the writing of this book.

Thanks also to Pippa and Kirsty, who gave the world the comfort of Tinkers, Pedlars, and Pippers clothing; to Graham and Sandra, who acted as the Railway Children, waving me on along the track to completion; to Flora and Rosannagh, who so tunefully sang to me one of Mr. Boom's greatest hits; to the staff at Fastnet, Fort William; and to Lisa Keany, Caroline Charles, Christo Sharpe, Jim Best, Charlie Cox, and Chris Clyne for keeping me straight on all things technical.

A RISK WORTH TAKING

CHAPTER ONE

THE ALARM CLOCK went off, as it had for the past fourteen months, at seven o'clock. Not at six, as had been the case when he had to get up to go to work. Nevertheless, it was still a shock to the system. Dan Porter groped out an arm from under the duvet and felt for the lever that would stop those infernal bells, but they rang with such vehemence that the clock juddered away from his searching hand and toppled from the bedside table onto the carpeted floor. There it continued its muffled clanging whilst the hand still blindly explored the surface of the table.

"Where the *hell is it?*" Both verbal and physical explosions came simultaneously. The duvet was thrown aside and Dan swung his legs over the bed and sat up. Not a wise act, he thought, as he screwed up his eyes to stop himself from being so completely aware of the oxygen pumping into his brain. As the sensation subsided and his hearing became oriented, he looked down at the clock on the floor, where its fading momentum spun it slower and slower, like a fly in its death throes.

He groaned and keeled forward to pick it up. It was still out of reach. He slid off the bed onto his knees and stretched out for the clock, but he never made it. He watched blearily as it was picked up by a beautiful, slim hand, its fourth finger bearing a band of gold that was held in place by a raised cluster of rubies set around a glinting diamond. A red-painted thumbnail flicked the lever on the clock and put it out of its misery. Dan turned his head to follow up a pinstriped arm, stopping when his eyes came to rest on the gold pendant that hung in the cleavage of her breasts, these being wholesomely accentuated by the way in which she had left open the top three buttons of her white cotton shirt. He turned his head only degrees more and looked up at his wife's face. He had often thought that if ever he had been called upon to write down a full description of her features, he would have sat forever in front of a blank piece of paper because he could never have written all that crap about her eyes being too wide set, or her nose too flat, or her ears too big. Maybe one word was sufficient. PERFECT in big black letters. Jackie always had been, and still was, a complete turn-on. Halfway through their twentieth year of marriage, and she still had that effect on him.

Today, however, it was obvious that the feeling was not reciprocated. Her mouth bore a trace of a smile, but it was one that he could read as meaning "Dan, you really are a sorry sight" rather than "Hullo, my darling, how are you this morning?"

Dan pushed himself to his feet and flopped back on the bed. He lay there with his hand supporting the side of his face and watched as Jackie placed the alarm clock on the dressing table before slipping all her makeup necessities for the day into her handbag.

"Hey," he said, creasing up the corner of his mouth into what he hoped might be taken as an evocative and sexy smile.

"What?" Jackie asked in a clipped voice, without looking in his direction. She walked over to the wardrobe and took a raincoat off one of the hangers.

Dan decided to persevere. "Any chance of you lying back on this bed while I ravish you?"

Flipping the raincoat over her arm, Jackie now turned to look at him. She gave him concentrated appraisal, taking in his regular night-time attire of grey baggy sports shorts and faded blue T-shirt with the moth hole just above the left nipple.

"I wonder if I'm in the least bit tempted," she said, slowly shaking her head.

Dan's hand fell away from his face and he slumped over in feigned dejection. "Well, at least someone makes the suggestion every now and again," he mumbled into the duvet.

"What was that?"

Dan pushed himself to his feet. "Nothing."

"I heard you."

"Yes, well, it was just meant to be a joke."

"And I don't think it was very funny."

Dan let out a deep sigh. "All right, then. Sorry." He pushed his hands into the pockets of his shorts. "Do you want me to make you a cup of coffee?"

Jackie shook her head. "No, I've got to be in the office by eight. There's a finance meeting at nine, but before that I've got to give our set designer a kick up his backside. He was asked at least three months ago to do some modifications on our set for the show in Paris, and so far he hasn't come up with the goods." She scanned the room briefly to make sure she hadn't forgotten anything, then turned and walked towards the door, reaching up and brushing a meaningless kiss onto Dan's cheek as she passed him. He followed on close behind her as she made her way along the narrow landing and down the staircase.

"What are you doing today?" she asked, throwing the question over her shoulder.

"I don't know. I might entertain myself once again with a spot of light housework."

Reaching the bottom of the stairs, Jackie turned to look at him, and once more he realized that his witticism had fallen on a stony face.

"Did you call Ben Appleton?" she asked.

"Yes."

"And?"

"Right now he's firing, not hiring."

Jackie's eyes narrowed, as if trying to detect some evidence of an untruth being told. "Did you really call him?"

"Of course I did." Even though innocent of the apparent crime, he felt his face flush under Jackie's continued stare. "Listen, contrary to what you think, I am still looking for a job."

"Really? Excuse me if I find that rather hard to believe, Dan. There's certainly not much evidence of it up in your office."

Dan's eyes momentarily flickered up the stairwell. "When were you up there?"

"This morning."

"Why?"

Jackie let out a long sigh. "I wasn't actually going to your office, Dan. I went up to fetch the hairdryer from Millie's room. But the door of your office *was* open, and I did happen to notice that your computer didn't have its screensaver on."

"So?"

"It still had an unfinished game of solitaire on it."

Dan laughed. "Oh-oh."

"Don't think it's funny, Dan," Jackie replied sharply. "You cannot go on hiding up there, day after day, doing nothing."

"For heaven's sakes, I'm not doing nothing!"

"But you're not bringing any money into the household, Dan. That's what we need."

"I know we do, but hey, listen, we're not on skid row yet."

"We're not? In that case, I seem to have misunderstood our present circumstances. You've lost your job *and* most of your money on the dot.com fiasco, and because of that, the children have had to change schools, we cannot afford to go on a summer holiday for the first time since Josh was a baby, and you've also been forced to trade in your rather comfortable Mercedes for a fifteen-year-old Saab. Well, forgive me, Dan, if my opinion differs from yours. I would say that we're pretty damned close to being on 'skid row.' You need to get a job, Dan Porter, because my income won't support us forever. I may be the managing director of Rebecca Talworth Design Limited, but the position doesn't carry huge bucks with it, because we're still ploughing profit back into growth."

"I understand all these things, but as I've said countless times before, it'll take a bit of time to find another job."

"We don't have time, Dan!" Jackie cut herself short by glancing at her wristwatch. "And I certainly don't have time to discuss all this now." She walked along the short hallway, avoiding the schoolbags that lay ready for the day, and opened the front door, allowing the warm September sun to flood in across the stripped pine floorboards. Dan followed on behind her into the small front garden. He stood barefoot, his hands still thrust into the pockets of his shorts, as he watched his wife open the gate that led out onto the tree-shadowed pavement of Haleridge Road.

"Could you tell Nina that I will try to make her concert tonight?" she said, closing the gate behind her.

Dan nodded. "See if you can be there this time."

Once again, her expression demonstrated only too well her reaction to the remark. "Not only is my job extremely important to the whole family, Dan, but it also happens to be quite full-on right now."

Dan held up a hand in silent apology. He didn't want her to say any more, having just heard the front door of the adjoining house slam shut. There was no love lost between himself and Mrs. Watt. She was their busybody of a neighbour, and Dan, on more than one occasion, had expressed those exact sentiments to her face. Nothing would give Mrs. Watt more pleasure than to listen in on one of their marital disagreements, even though, over the past few months, she would have every reason to have become bored with their regularity. Her front gate clicked open and Dan watched as Jackie turned to smile a good morning to her. Mrs. Watt appeared from behind the overgrown yew hedge that surrounded their property, and as she passed by Jackie, she slowed down long enough to shoot Dan a tight-mouthed glare of disapproval. He returned the disparaging greeting by thrusting forward his hands in the pockets of his shorts, giving the impression that he was more than a little excited to see her.

"Good morning, Mrs. Watt," he called out in an airy voice.

The woman quickly averted her eyes and, with a loud sucking of teeth, walked quickly on.

Jackie shook her head. "For goodness' sakes, Dan. When will you ever start to take things seriously?" She turned on her heel and disappeared from view behind the yew hedge.

Dan stood for a moment peering up into the cloudless sky as a Boeing 747 roared low overhead on its final approach to Heathrow Airport. He watched it disappear over the roofline of the houses opposite, then walked to the gate and peered over. He was in time to see Jackie's neat figure cross the street and head off down the low-stone-walled alleyway that led to South Clapham tube station. He thought about calling out something like "Have a good day, my sweet!" but knew that she was in no mood for any of his lighthearted banter that morning, so he turned and went back into the house.

As soon as he opened the door into the kitchen, he could tell that one of their recent fosterlings from the Battersea Dogs' Home had done it again. What's more, it took no great powers of detection to work out who the culprit might be. Biggles, the cross collie/spaniel, lay cowering in his basket, whilst his smaller companion, Cruise, made a solid show of proclaiming his innocence by dancing energetically around Dan's feet.

"Bloody hell, Biggles!" Dan exclaimed, pinching his nostrils. "Not again!"

He found the unwelcome evidence of the dog's misdemeanour centre stage in the conservatory extension to the kitchen. He picked up the coal shovel that now resided permanently beside the sliding glass door that led out into the small back garden.

"I don't know how good your geography is, my boy, but I should remind you that the dog home is only a half-hour's brisk walk from here." He gave Biggles a hardened glare just to demonstrate how displeased he was, and the dog reacted by closing his eyes in shame, displaying the dark-ringed "flying goggles" that had given rise to his name.

Having cleaned up the floor and clandestinely discarded the contents of the shovel over the fence into Mrs. Watt's garden (he reckoned that, on that particular morning, she more than deserved it), Dan returned to the kitchen and picked up his mobile phone from the sideboard. As he filled up the kettle, he punched out a joint text message to Millie and Nina, informing them that it was time to get up. It was a ruse that seemed to work much more effectively than a yell up the stairs, his subtlety of thinking being that, even though his daughters were almost one hundred per cent sure that the text was from him at that time in the morning, there was always the slimmest chance that it could have been from someone considerably more exciting than their father.

It never failed to work. Just as the kettle came to the boil, he heard a thump on the floor above. Nina was on the move. He poured himself a cup of instant coffee, waiting for her usual riposte. When it came ringing down the stairs, he mouthed out her words in perfect synchronization. "Dad, stop doing that! It's so unfa-*yer*!"

"Morning, Ni," he called back. "Make sure Millie's up, will you? You've got twenty-five minutes to get out of the house."

"I'm not waking her up. She's a cow." She said it in a crescendo, obviously wanting her sister to hear.

Dan shook his head and walked through to the hall. Nina, still in her pyjamas, sat slumped at the top of the stairs, her feet resting halfway up the banister post.

"She is not a cow, Ni. She is your loving, if not slightly tetchy sixteen-year-old sister who happens to be two years your senior, so I would be grateful if you didn't give her any more excuse than that to splatter your brains against the wall." He took a gulp of coffee. "Okay, tell me. Why is she a cow?"

"She's got my Atomic Kitten CD," Nina replied moodily.

"Ah." Dan paused. "Well, she hasn't actually."

"Yes, she has, Dad. Why do you always have to protect her?"

"I am not always protecting her. I know she hasn't got it because *I've* got it. You'll find it in the CD machine in my office."

Nina's face sneered disapproval. "That's so *sad,*" she said, getting up from the step and stomping off to her bedroom.

"Wake up Mill—" The door slammed shut before Dan could finish. Letting out a long sigh, he returned to the kitchen and pulled out a chair from the table. He sat down, resting his elbows on the table, and began to work his fingers at the throb of anxiety in his head. Biggles, noticing that this might be an opportune moment for reconciliation, crept from his basket and gently laid his muzzle on his master's knee. Dan looked down at the dog and smiled. "Well, thank you, Biggles. At least someone in the world gives me a vague inkling that I'm still loved and appreciated."

CHAPTER TWO

B<small>ACK THEN, HE</small> had always thought that it could have read rather like one of those smart announcements in the social columns of the *Times*; or even printed on a stiff-carded invitation with raised letters, the kind that one might find tucked into the cracked edge of a gilded overmantel mirror in the drawing room of some well-connected household.

Dan Porter and Jackie Entwhistle are pleased to announce their plan for life, formulated whilst consuming two quarter-pounder cheeseburgers and French fries in the Central Park Diner, High Street, Kensington on 3 April 1984. Following their wedding at Chelsea Registry Office on 18 April (which is to be paid for by Jackie's parents who say that it is the last thing that they will ever do, financially speaking, for their daughter) and the arrival of their firstborn on (circa) 8 September of the same year (that being the reason for the breakdown of relationships with Jackie's parents), Dan and Jackie will be moving (when they can afford it) to a large house in (London suburb, south of the river—somewhere) where they will add two more children to their family, plus two dogs—eventually.

Thereafter (when Dan has reached retirement age, having made his fortune in the City, which he is bound to do), they will be moving to a small cottage in the country (South Devon coast preferably) where Dan will sit with a smug smile on his face, knowing that he has not only done his bit to perpetuate the human race, but has achieved it with distinction.

At that time, it all seemed a bit pie-in-the-sky, really. Just the dreams of a young couple, both only two years out of their teens, who were fortified with too much Chardonnay and fizzing with excitement at the prospect of loving, honouring, and cherishing each other until death do us part. Yet for Dan, it could so easily have read something like:

Dan Porter and Sharon Pettigrew or Janice Longshaw or Kathleen Malloney (there were other girls with whom he had clothes-wrestled during midmorning break in the darkened store cupboard of the chemical lab at St. Joseph's Secondary School, Tottenham Hale, North London—but they were the more likely ones to have ended up in the same full-stomached condition that Jackie now found herself to be in) are pleased to announce their plan for life. Following their wedding in St. Mary's Episcopal Church, Tottenham Hale (his mother's local), Dan will take up employment in Baldwin Metals where he will work, on split shifts for £1.50 an hour, alongside his father in the dust-choking, earsplitting environs of the fabrication shed. They will be having only one child (the very same one that's got them into this bloody mess in the first place) because, until a council flat comes up, they will have to live with Dan's parents. Thereafter Sharon/Janice/Kathleen will be getting a job because otherwise they won't be able to afford to go out to the pub together on a Saturday night. Dan would like to take this opportunity to apologize to Tottenham Hotspurs Football Club and to all his mates with whom he goes to matches, because one of the sacrifices that he'll have to make is giving up his season ticket. From now on, he will only be able to watch those matches that are being televised—that is, if Dixon's allows him to buy a television on hire pur-

chase. And finally, once they have reached retirement age, the happy couple plan to . . . live off a state pension for a bit, then die.

To be quite honest, that scenario had been in Dan's mind for a hell of a lot longer than the one that he and Jackie had formulated whilst polishing off the bottle of Chardonnay in the Central Park Diner. It was, in every way, his worst nightmare, and from his early teens had hung over his head like the sword of Damocles, heralding the inevitable progression of his life. He had been born in the wrong place at the wrong time, with neither prospect nor privilege.

So he decided to do his damnedest to avoid ending up like that. He kept his head down at school, both physically and academically, and watched as all his friends opted out as soon as they could with qualifications that suited them better for lives as mobsters rather than businessmen. When he eventually walked out of the gates of St. Joseph's for the last time, he knew that the school's enduring and hard-earned legacy to him was that he was coming away with both these attributes.

University was out—his parents couldn't afford to support him during three years of further education, neither was he willing to burden himself with student loans. So, dressed in his cousin's ill-fitting wedding suit, he headed for the City with his exam certificate, showing his three top-grade A-level passes, carefully folded in his inside pocket. He had no idea what he was doing or where he was going, but he was determined not to catch the tube back to Tottenham Hale without securing some sort of employment for himself.

He would have no doubt been forced to change his mind about that had it not been for the intervention of a kindly commissionaire who had been standing on the steps of a large, gargoyle-fronted building in Cheapside. He had witnessed Dan walk up and down the street four or five times, stopping outside offices, bracing himself to enter, then turning away with a shake of his head.

"You're looking for a job, aren't you, son?" he had said in a voice that would have sounded more fitting on an army parade ground. Dan had nodded meekly, and the commissionaire had given him a wink and flicked his head to motion him into the building. Twenty minutes later, he came out into the late morning sunshine with a photocopied list of stockbroker firms clutched in his hand.

It took exactly four and a half hours and the heavy scoring out of eight names on his list before Dan found himself a job. Walking triumphantly from the lift of the office block in Leadenhall Street, he crossed the reception area, tightly balling up the piece of paper in his fist. As he pushed open the heavy glass doors, he lobbed it into a tall chrome litter bin, then stood outside on the pavement, feeling as if he had reached up to discover that the sword of Damocles was so blunt that it couldn't even cut through butter. Dan Porter, the office trainee from Tottenham Hale, had arrived in the City. From now on, he was going to do nothing but make money for himself.

And he had done just that for three years. No steady girlfriends, not too much excessive boozing. His two greatest expenditures were paying for his share of the rent on the flat that he had moved into with three other work colleagues just off Fulham Broadway, and the occasional sortie down King's Road to buy clothes. And then, one Saturday afternoon, he met Jackie Entwhistle.

Dan had been walking back to his flat when he passed the shop, situated at the unfashionable end of King's Road. It was the name on the sign above the small display window that had at first caught his eye. Rebecca Talworth. He had read about her in some newspaper or magazine. A young dress designer, fresh out of St. Martin's, who they said was destined to make the grade. Dan peered through the window into the shop's crowded interior and almost immediately caught sight of a blonde girl, her face lit with animated humour as she served a customer. Maybe it was the intensity of his stare that had caused a slight tingling on the flawless skin of her cheek, because, for no apparent reason, she turned her head through ninety degrees and looked directly at him, and he was sure, if it was at all possible, that her smile broadened even more. It was on sheer impulse, but he decided not to go any further until he had asked her for a date. He entered the shop and reappeared on the street half an hour later with a grin on his face and a pain in his wallet. The price of the date had been the purchase of a £200 original Rebecca Talworth dress. Of course, Jackie had no idea that it was destined for her. He had said that it was for a friend, but he knew the moment that she held it up against herself to show off the style, that it would be sacrilege for anyone else to own it.

He had given it to her for her twenty-first birthday. Actually, it was four days after her birthday, because she had had to go up north for a big black-tie "do" that her parents were holding in her honour at their golf club near Chester. But Dan had also organized a little celebration of his own. Back to his place, give Jackie the dress, get her to change into it, and then out to dinner at Quaglino's. Trouble was that Jackie never wore the dress and they never made dinner. The truth was that neither of them had worn very much that night.

And that was why they had come to be sitting making plans about their future over a bottle of Chardonnay in the Central Park Diner in Kensington High Street.

CHAPTER THREE

STEPHEN TURNBULL STRODE across the office reception area, a neat cluster of files tucked under his arm, and shot a wink at the young temporary receptionist as he passed by. He kept his eye on her as he walked into his office and smiled to himself when he witnessed through the glass partitioning a slight colour rising to the girl's cheeks. It satisfied him that, at the age of twenty-nine, rising thirty, he still had the charisma and the looks to get that kind of reaction from a girl ten years his junior. He sat down at his desk and clicked the mouse of his computer, and stretching out his long, linen-clad legs, he leaned back in his chair and watched as the screensaver cleared to be replaced by the spreadsheet on which he had been working prior to the meeting.

Stephen had every reason to feel pleased with himself that morning. During the meeting that had finished half an hour ago, he had given a presentation to the company's financial backers demonstrating that everything was going pretty damned well with Rebecca Talworth Design Ltd. After only eighteen months since its inception, the company was performing way ahead of its forecast schedule, and if the spring/summer collection to be shown at Prêt-à-Porter in Paris in three weeks' time proved to be as successful as the previous one, then profit margins might just surpass all expectations.

And Stephen knew that it was he who had been entirely responsible for the whole thing happening. Two years before, whilst working for a small chartered accountancy practice in West Hampstead, he had been assigned a number of "headache" clients, those whose accounting techniques consisted of submitting little or no ledger work and a pile of disordered receipts for reconciliation. Wading through them like an automaton, he had come across Rebecca Talworth's file, and was both surprised and bemused as to why one of the most successful and well-known fashion designers in the country should use such an unprestigious, out-of-the-way company to audit her books. However, having spent an hour scrutinizing her accounts, he had come to realize that the recognition that she had achieved for herself through her creative skills could in no way be complemented by an astute business sense. Rebecca Talworth was, to all intents and purposes, bust. He also surmised that she herself was probably fully aware of the fact and hoped that, by placing her books with a small, unknown firm of chartered accountants, she would be able to cajole them into throwing up a smokescreen to hide her dire financial situation.

It had never been Stephen's plan to become an accountant. When he had left school, he had every intention of going on to art college, having a greater aptitude towards all things creative than to any one thing in the academic field. But his overpowering father had bullied him into altering course, telling him that he expected his only son to take on the eventual running of his own business, and that accountancy was the best grounding with which to accomplish this successfully.

With not one iota of enthusiasm for the work, Stephen had scraped a lowly pass in his final accountancy exams, and consequently had only managed to find employment with the small West Hampstead practice. Every morning, he struggled to get himself out of bed, knowing that the day had little to offer him other than indescribable boredom. But now, as he scrutinized the Talworth file, he began to see a means of escape. He just had to manipulate it correctly.

He laid aside the file that day and went on to sort out the affairs of a self-employed jobbing plumber from Hackney. Then, that night, he took it home and began to put together a proposal for the designer. After a week of working well into the small hours of the morning, he devised a business plan that broadened the parameters of Rebecca Talworth's work into lucrative sidelines, whilst still granting her complete autonomy over designs and products. The control of expenditure and cash flow, however, was to be placed firmly in the hands of a financial director.

It took him five times of asking to arrange a meeting with Rebecca, something which confirmed in his mind that she was fully aware of the fact that her glitzy, jet-setting world was about to crumble around her feet. He was never put off by her complete refusal to speak to him on the telephone, because every time the line went dead, he became more assured that she had little option other than to accept his plan.

They met in her small mews house off Exhibition Road exactly three weeks after he had made his initial attempt to contact her. He handled the meeting with care, always putting across the harder points for her to accept with a generous massaging of her obviously extensive ego. Within an hour, he had struck the deal and was shown to the front door by a smiling, almost ebullient Rebecca Talworth. He left her waving on the doorstep and walked away down the narrow cobbled lane as the newly appointed financial director of Rebecca Talworth Design Ltd., a position that carried a healthy salary increment on the fulfillment of each of his proposed targets. By the time that he had emerged onto Exhibition Road, he had called the chartered accountancy practice in West Hampstead and told them that he was leaving without notice.

As he had imagined, raising the finance on the terms that he had set out in the business plan was plain sailing. In fact, he had managed to better them by narrowing down the offers that he had received from a plethora of financial institutions. They had fallen over themselves to get a foothold in the action, impressed by his proposals to tap into the huge marketing potential behind the goodwill of Rebecca Talworth's name.

Two weeks after the financial package had been finalized, he had negotiated a five-year lease, with an option to buy after that period, on 10,000 square feet of office space in a converted flourmill on the north side of the River Thames, just west of the Wandsworth Bridge. Being on the top floor, it had an abundance of natural light flooding in through the large Velux windows that ran the full length of the roof, and there was ample room for the offices and large studio where the cutting and machining of design samples were to be carried out.

Within three months, Rebecca had closed down her two shops in King's Road, laying off all but two of her sales assistants, and had moved into the new premises. The shops were not part of the business plan. To begin with, retail was to be handled from rented floor space within one of the more prestigious department stores in the West End, depending on which was able to offer the better deal. Once manufacturing was in full swing, then units in similar department stores were to be sought in major cities throughout the world.

And it had worked. The base of the letterheading of Rebecca Talworth Design Ltd. now listed London, New York, Paris, Stockholm, Frankfurt, and Madrid, and if his negotiations proved fruitful, then Tokyo would be added within the next month.

However, from the moment that the new company had started trading, there was one problem that Stephen had found hard to overcome, and that was his working relationship with Rebecca herself. She was still the creative genius, but still hopeless with money, and she displayed a wild extravagance with this new injection of finance. Having been on the receiving end, on a number of occasions, of her quick temper and irrationality of thought, Stephen knew that he had to handle Rebecca with the softest pair of kid gloves in order to maintain a measure of civility between them.

The solution to his problem presented itself in the form of Jackie

Porter, a woman who had been working with Rebecca since she had first started and whom Rebecca had managed to persuade back from her role as mother to a young family to take on public relations for the company. Intelligent, strong-willed, and beautiful, as well as being a good and trusted friend to Rebecca, Jackie had the ideal credentials to run the company and intermediate between Stephen and Rebecca. In a carefully worded address at one of the weekly management meetings, Stephen had proposed that the company should broaden its management base to allow Rebecca more time to expand the design division of the company. He felt that this could best be achieved by the appointment of a managing director.

Stephen did not put forward Jackie's name until the last moment. His timing was perfect. Rebecca agreed without a qualm, and it confirmed in Stephen's mind that she had already been harboring concerns about how best to curb his own powers within the company.

As it turned out, the working relationship between Jackie and himself could not have been more successful. Rebecca allowed them full sanction to get on with the running of her company and, from the day of Jackie's appointment, never bothered to attend another management meeting. Jackie and he travelled to the States and across Europe together, setting up the retail outlets, and because they had to spend many days in each other's company, sometimes under quite tedious and frustrating circumstances, their friendship developed into one of mutual support and respect. At least, that is how Stephen felt that Jackie would read the situation. For him, it was different. He had found himself becoming increasingly attracted to her, even though he knew that she was unattainable. Not only ten years his senior, she was also the mother of three children and the wife of an extremely successful City man. However, there had been considerable changes in Jackie's home life over the past year. Her husband had lost his job and there had been furtive whispers in the office that relationships within her family were becoming increasingly strained. Although it did not seem to affect the way in which she ran the business, Stephen now detected the slightest chink of vulnerability in Jackie's demeanour, one that had never before been apparent.

Stephen broke off his train of thought and glanced over the top of his computer screen. In the office opposite his own, Jackie sat at her desk, raking her fingers repeatedly through her long blonde hair as she wrote quickly on a jotting pad. She looked up to catch her thoughts and their eyes came into contact. He smiled at her and she smiled back, but there was little joy or frivolity in its delivery. She dipped her head and continued to write.

Stephen knocked out a quick rhythm with his hands on the desktop, then pushed himself out of his chair and walked out into the narrow glassed corridor that separated their offices. He gave a token knock on her door and entered.

"All right if I come in?"

Jackie looked up, nodded, then continued to write.

Stephen sat himself down in a chair opposite her. He folded his arms and crossed one foot over the other, but remained silent.

Jackie looked up again. She tilted her head questioningly to the side. "Is anything wrong?"

Stephen shrugged his shoulders. "I was about to ask you the same thing."

Jackie held her pen six inches above the desk and let it go. It clattered down on the dark veneered surface. "Listen, I'm sorry if I didn't seem very communicative at the meeting this morning."

"There's no need to apologize. It couldn't have gone any better. They seemed more than happy with the way things are going."

"As long as things keep going the way we've planned them."

"Meaning?"

"Meaning that if Tom Headwick doesn't come up with the modifications for the set design, then we've got a real problem on our hands."

"But you spoke to him this morning. I was under the impression that he told you they were all but finished."

Jackie scoffed dismissively. "Well, that's what *he* says."

"Have you spoken to Rebecca about it?"

"I haven't been able to get hold of her. She's been with a fabric supplier all morning and has her mobile switched off."

Stephen raised his eyebrows. "What's new?"

"And take a look at this, as well," Jackie said, spinning a sheet of paper across the desk towards him. Stephen bent forward and picked it up.

"It's the schedule."

"Yes. I've just taken it off the Internet."

Stephen studied it for a moment. "What's wrong with it?"

"Quite a lot, actually. We have a slot at one o'clock on Wednesday in the Bourdelle Museum."

Stephen shrugged. "That seems a good time. Means we don't have to get up at sparrowfart."

"Yes, but look who's showing in the Louvre at exactly the same time."

Stephen studied the schedule once more. "Ah. Gaultier."

"Exactly. So where's the press going to be?"

"Oh, hell!" Stephen muttered as he floated the schedule back onto Jackie's desk. "And there's nothing that we can do about it?"

"Not a thing. The Chambre Syndicale set that schedule in stone. Do you want to hear more?"

Stephen groaned and scrunched up his eyes, as if preparing himself for a stinging blow to the face. "If you insist."

"Three of our star models have backed out. I would hazard a guess that they're probably going with him."

"Can they *do* that?"

"I'm afraid so." Jackie smiled. "It's not really a big deal, though. I was half expecting something like this to happen, so I put a provisional booking on six other models from the agency."

Stephen breathed out a sigh of relief. "Thank goodness for that. Well done, you." He pulled his chair forward and leaned his elbows on

Jackie's desk. As he did so, one of his gold cufflinks momentarily caught the sunlight through the full-length window and flashed a brilliant pin-point of light across Jackie's cleavage. "Listen," he said, moving his hand imperceptibly so that the oval reflection played upon the deep split between her breasts, "are you going over to Paris before the show?"

"I had planned to. I don't think that one can tell the organizers too many times how *grateful* we are to be given a slot."

"Right. I'll come with you."

Jackie shook her head. "There's no reason for you to come."

"Oh, but I think I should. Two heads are always better than one, especially if there's a problem to negotiate. Anyway, my workload's pretty clear right up until the Tokyo trip."

Jackie contemplated his offer for a moment, then reached across the desk for her diary. Stephen immediately dropped his hands to his lap in case she caught the positioning of the reflected light from his cufflink. She opened the diary and flipped through the pages. "All right then. What about Saturday?"

"*This* Saturday?"

"I can't do next week. I have meetings every day."

"I don't think that'll be much use then."

"What do you mean?"

"Well, if we hit a problem, we're not going to get it sorted out on a Sunday. What meetings do you have on Monday?"

Jackie glanced back at her diary. "One in the morning, one in the afternoon."

"Are they important or could you put them off to another day?"

Jackie picked up her pen and began to turn it over in her fingers. "You really think it's necessary?"

"As an insurance, yes, I do."

She nodded. "Okay then. I'll get Laurie to change them."

Stephen pushed himself to his feet. "Right. I'll get straight onto Eurostar and book the tickets."

Jackie made no further comment about their arrangement, but swiveled around in her chair and stared out at the panoramic view of the River Thames and the uneven skyline of Wandsworth beyond. Sensing her deep distraction, Stephen stopped halfway to the door and then turned and walked over to the window, arriving in time to see a coxless four glide their boat upriver towards Putney.

"You're really *not* your usual dynamic self this morning, are you?"

"No, not really," she replied quietly.

He turned and sat on the windowsill. "Do you want to talk about it?"

She breathed out a laugh. "No, not really." She turned to look at him. "Anyway, besides being unmarried and without the burden of children, I think you're probably the wrong age and the wrong sex to understand my problem."

Stephen laughed. "I don't know. I've always felt that I've been quite in touch with my feminine side." His remark did not even register a spark of humour on Jackie's face. "Things are a bit difficult at home, are they?"

"Just a little," Jackie murmured. She rested an elbow on the arm of the chair, and closing her eyes, she began to rub a thumb and forefinger up and down the bridge of her nose. "For some reason, it was so much easier to cope with Dan losing his job when it first happened. He was so . . . vulnerable and lost. But now he seems to be so complacent about it all, even happy, and it infuriates me. I don't think that he's making any effort at all to find another job."

"What's he doing at the minute?"

"Not a lot. He does a bit of housework, he takes the dogs for a walk, and most days, he has lunch with one of his friends in the pub. He's also got heavily into cooking, which entails a great deal of watching Jamie Oliver on the television and serving up weird concoctions to me and the kids."

"Well, at least he's doing that. Surely if you were both working, you'd be having to pay someone to look after the house."

"Yes, but you can't count that as a job. Dan was earning close on two hundred thousand pounds a year in the City. That's a pretty expensive housekeeper, wouldn't you say?"

Stephen spread out his hands along the windowsill. "So you are now the family's sole breadwinner."

"Yes, in rather a large nutshell."

"Well, in that case," Stephen said, "I would have thought that the way you're feeling is pretty natural. All your married life, he's been the security for your family—the provider. And now you've had to take over that role. Maybe . . ."—he paused momentarily, being caught in two minds as to whether he should continue—"maybe you've just lost some of your respect for him."

Jackie shot him a steely glance that told him he had overstepped the mark. He immediately tried to backtrack. "Not that you can't rebuild that."

"Damn you."

"I'm sorry. I shouldn't have said that."

"No, I mean damn you for being so intuitive. I was wrong. Maybe age and sex have got nothing to do with it. But what you certainly won't understand is that, in marriage, losing respect for your partner is as bad as infidelity. There is no way that you can ever retrieve that complete, unassailable level of confidence that before existed between you as naturally as . . . the creation of life itself." She turned to look out the window once more. "My word, you've stuck a spear deep into a wound that I was trying my best to ignore."

"I'm sorry."

"Don't be. You've stopped me from fooling myself."

Stephen pushed himself away from the windowsill and moved quickly towards the door. "Come on. You're coming with me."

Jackie's expression was one of puzzlement as she spun around in her chair to track his exit. "Where?"

"Out for lunch."

Jackie shook her head. "No way. I can't. I've got a pile of work to do." She glanced at her wristwatch and laughed. "Anyway, it's only half past eleven."

"I couldn't give a toss. As financial director of Rebecca Talworth Design Limited, I consider it a necessary expense to take the company's managing director out for lunch in order to talk about the extremely successful meeting that we had this morning and . . . to lift her spirits so that she can continue to perform as brilliantly as she has done since taking over at the top." He shot her a wink similar to the one that, half an hour beforehand, had succeeded in turning the young receptionist's knees to jelly. "We'll only be an hour. What's more, you're not the only one who has work to do."

Jackie smiled at him. "All right. We'll have lunch, but let's leave it until midday. That should give you enough time to book those train tickets."

CHAPTER FOUR

Back then, the truth of the matter was that young Mr. and Mrs. Porter had struggled for a bit after they were married. But with the arrival of Josh, a beautiful, healthy nine-pound baby who had threatened to do permanent damage to Jackie's elegantly light frame, they were quite content to live in a state of impecunious bliss in the minute flat that they rented off Baron's Court Road.

Then, in 1986, when Josh was an eighteen-month-old bundle of trouble, all things changed and Dan had to alter his thinking about being born in the wrong place at the wrong time. It was the year of the Big Bang, the deregulation of the stock market, and the staid, formal image of the City took on a new and welcome vibrancy. Dan's firm benefited immediately, being one of the first to be taken over by a large American financial conglomerate, and within three months, he had been plucked from relative obscurity by the company's new senior vice president to be one of their market makers. And from the moment that he started, he thrived on it. His battling days at school had fitted him well for the job. He loved the quick decision, the adrenaline rush of making a deal, the subterfuge in offloading a nonperformer. But above all, he loved making money.

It was probably a much-needed energy release on Dan's part that resulted in Jackie's giving birth to Millie and Nina within the space of the next two years. The flat in Baron's Court had begun to groan with overcrowding, so Dan decided to make the largest personal investment of his lifetime and took out a mortgage on the three-storey, four-bedroom house in Clapham. It was not until they had spent their first few months there, happily throwing themselves about this newly acquired space, that Jackie reminded Dan of their conversation in the Central Park Diner. Three children and a house in a suburb south of the river. They had achieved it all, minus the dogs. Jackie said that the dogs could wait.

Dan had never paid much attention to the letters from headhunting firms that kept turning up in his in-tray. He was quite content to work in a familiar environment with colleagues that he knew and trusted. But there came the time when, at the age of five, Nina joined Millie at Alleyn's School, and with Josh already attending Dulwich College for Boys, Dan suddenly found himself faced with paying three hefty school fees. Having tied up the greater proportion of his extensive savings in long-term investments, the effect on the family's bank balance was immediate, even though Jackie had by now resumed work for three days a week with Rebecca Talworth. Either Dan had to find a better-paid job for himself or else such luxuries as their twice-yearly holidays abroad would have to be forfeited.

Within a month, Dan had been headhunted by a Hong Kong–based investment bank, and thereafter he played the field, never staying with any company for longer than a year. But he found that, no matter for whom he was working, he loved what he did, and he could never quite believe his good fortune in ending up doing a job that made him money and made him smile. It had always been a bit of a laugh, a game, like playing one schoolboy prank after another.

And then he had been badly caught out. Having decided to switch a substantial amount of his investments over to dot.com technology, he moved to another job that paid so well that the cash-in penalties incurred by the change were going to be written off in a year. But five months later, the dot.com bubble burst. Dan had seen it coming and had tried to offload his shares as fast as he could, but traders by now were wary of his techniques and treated them like leprosy. All he could do thereafter was to watch their value drop day by day. And then he had found the internal e-mail on his computer. At first he thought it a mistake that he had received it, obviously just sent out on blanket coverage. Nevertheless, he had read the e-mail through, two pages of corporate jargon, explaining that the company was being forced to shed jobs due to the collapse of the dot.com market. It wasn't until he reached the last paragraph that the true meaning of the e-mail hit him.

"This company has always adopted a policy of last-in, first-out, and for this reason, we find ourselves with no alternative other than to terminate your contract of employment."

There were further remarks and apologies, but Dan hadn't bothered to read them. He picked up the telephone and immediately called the firm of headhunters that had secured his last position. Over the next hour, he tried time and time again to make contact with someone who could give him advice, but he never managed to get past the sweet-talking receptionist. Eventually, he replaced the receiver, and it slowly began to dawn on him that, for the first time in his working life, he was going to be without financial security and without a job.

At first, he had felt furious with himself for investing so recklessly and bitterly resentful at losing his job, but when, over the next few weeks, he received no offers from the headhunting firms that in the past had been falling over themselves to entice him away from one company to another, those feelings compounded to one of pure terror. At night, sleep deserted him and he would more often than not end up in the kitchen in the early hours of the morning drinking endless cups of tea and trying to blank out his thoughts by watching *Open University* or second-rate films on the television.

But those thoughts were all too pervasive, and during his lonely nighttime vigils, he constantly mulled over the effects that his new circumstances would have on the comfortable lifestyle that he and his family had enjoyed up until then. Due to his catastrophic investment in the dot.com market, he no longer had the financial resources to keep the family protected from the consequences of his unemployment; he had only been with the company for two months, so there was to be no substantial redundancy payment; he would have to freeze his pension contributions; the girls were just about to go back to Alleyn's for the start of the autumn term, and he knew that if his unemployment was to be long term, there was no way that he could keep them at the school; it was the start of Millie's sixth form year, so what would be least disruptive to her? Maybe it would be better to move them both to Clapham High School now, rather than halfway through Millie's A-level course.

He couldn't afford to lose the house, either. That was the bedrock of security for his family. At least he had made it a priority to pay off the mortgage, but he couldn't allow the bank to treat it as part of his estate if he were to go completely broke. It would be better to put it immediately into Jackie's name.

And what about Jackie? She was being supportive, but she had other things to think about now, especially with this new high-powered job with Rebecca Talworth. He knew that he disturbed her every time he got out of bed. She would make that aggravated clicking noise with her tongue and turn over to face away from him. They never used to bicker, but it had now become almost a daily occurrence. But he couldn't blame her for that. After all, it was he who had blown away the family's security on a bad investment, and it was he who had been like a bear with a sore head ever since he had lost his job, and everyone in the household had been affected by it.

All, that is, except Josh. He kept his own counsel. He had returned home, having dropped out of Manchester University during his first year, and had immediately set about making himself a stranger to his own family. He found himself a job stacking shelves in Tesco's and then spent every bit of money that he made in the ear-shattering depths of Horace's Inferno, one of Brixton's more notorious clubs. Dan was inwardly enraged that his son should have given up on an opportunity in life that he himself had never been afforded. Yet he'd never sought confrontation over the issue, thinking that it might quite easily result in his son's leaving home and setting himself up in some dive of a flat where he would be completely without parental control.

Always, when morning came and Dan had been woken from his fitful slumber on the kitchen sofa by the sounds of Jackie moving around upstairs, neither one scene from the film nor one equation from the *Open University* course had ever registered in his brain. There had always been too many other things flying around in his head.

CHAPTER FIVE

D
AN ATTEMPTED TO open the door of Josh's bedroom once
more, this time with a dunt of his shoulder, but there appeared
to be some object on the other side that only allowed it to
open a mere six inches. He got down on his knees and put a hand
through the gap, and at a full arm's length, managed to extract a battered
Nike trainer, its toe caved in where it had been acting successfully as a
wedge against his entry. He stood up and opened the door fully, and
the strong, fusty odour of a youth's unventilated lair made him physically reel back. He took a deep inhalation of untainted air before entering, then stepped as gingerly as he would in a minefield over the
disordered piles of clothing that were strewn across every spare inch of
the darkened interior of the room. Having made it across the floor
space without coming into contact with the prostrate body of any one
of Josh's friends, who dossed down with him on an all too regular basis,
Dan drew back the curtains and pushed up the window as wide as it
would go. He then turned to survey the living quarters of his firstborn.

It was almost macabre, like a scene from a film showing the after-
effects of a raid by secret police. Every drawer was open and emptied,

the doors to the fitted cupboard hung wide, the shelves empty except for one sock which drooped forlornly over the edge, as if caught making a valiant effort to join its companion somewhere on the ground. The walls were covered with posters, overlapping, askew, the majority showing the scowling, glary-eyed features of his son's favourite rapper, Eminem. And there, on the bed, completing this scene of violent mayhem, was Josh, lying facedown on the crumpled undersheet, his head hidden beneath a flaccid pillow that happened to be the only form of cover on his otherwise naked body.

Dan cast an eye over the prostrate figure from hidden head to outsized foot—the muscled arms, the wide shoulders, the lean back, the tight buttocks, the cluster of manhood between the dark-haired legs—and he laughed quietly to himself. How was it that such a beautiful, soft-skinned cherub of a little boy could have metamorphosed into this . . . lackadaisical monster?

He took in a breath of nostalgia, realizing immediately that it was the wrong thing to do. He discarded the Nike trainer, the key root to the problem, onto an unused chair, and took hold of Josh's heel and gave it a solid shake.

"Josh?"

He spoke loudly, but his voice sounded deadened in the clothes-padded confines of the room. There was not one twitch of movement from his son's body.

"Come on, Josh. It's time to get up."

He grabbed hold of Josh's ankles and dragged him forcefully down the bed, away from the protection of the pillow. With his body now bent over the edge of the bed, Dan found the target too tempting to ignore and finished off the awakening process by delivering a short, sharp slap to his son's bare buttocks.

Josh turned his head slowly, his long dark curls falling across bleary eyes. "Bugger off, Dad. That was sore."

Dan picked up the sheet that lay at the foot of the bed and threw it over his son. "Drastic action is sometimes called for, I'm afraid."

Josh flumped his head down on the bed again. "I heard you the first time."

"Then you should have made a move earlier, shouldn't you?"

"What time is it?"

"Ten past twelve."

Josh groaned. "But my shift doesn't start until seven o'clock tonight. I don't have to get up yet."

"Oh yes, you do, mate. There's more to life than sticking cans of baked beans on a shelf and head banging in a bloody club all night."

"Like what?"

"Like getting this room tidied up for a start."

Josh swung his legs over the side of the bed and sat up, pulling the sheet across his lap. He surveyed the room through a curtain of hair, and his nose wrinkled in an expression of bewilderment. "Jeez, I only did it two days ago."

"Somehow, I don't think so."

"I did."

"Well, then, you must have worn every article of clothing that you possess over the last two days."

A reluctant smile of acknowledgement creased Josh's mouth. "Yeah, you're right. I must have done."

Dan bent down and picked up a random pair of trousers from the floor. They seemed far too large for his son's lean figure, but that's how he liked them—worn so low on his hips that a vast expanse of knicker elastic was shown above the waistline. A pair of red, cupid-patterned knickers were still inside the trousers. He extracted them and dropped both articles onto the chair occupied by the Nike trainer, then sat down on the bed next to Josh. "So, how was it last night?"

Josh swept a hand through his hair, pulling it away from his face. It was the first time that Dan had seen it uncovered that morning. He studied his son's features, seeing so many similarities to his own. The full eyebrows, the dark brown eyes, the high-bridged nose. The small gold hoop, however, that adorned the upper part of his left earlobe was unique to Josh.

"It was all right. Good DJ anyway."

Feeling little inclination to extract further information about his son's nighttime escapades, Dan turned and picked up a book from the bedside table. It was a copy of Steinbeck's *Grapes of Wrath*. He flicked through the pages. "Are you reading this?" he asked with an element of surprise.

"Yeah. I think he's a great writer. He's brilliantly economic with his words."

Dan replaced the book on the table and let out a deep sigh. "Joshy, my boy, what *are* you going to do with your life? You're too damned intelligent to waste away your time like this."

Josh turned and stared challengingly at his father. "I don't know. What are *you* going to do?"

Dan snorted out a laugh and gave his son's unruly mop of hair a hard ruffle. "Touché! A very good question." He pushed himself to his feet. "The truthful answer is that I don't know, but I'm sure something will turn up."

Josh nodded. "Yeah, that's sort of what I was thinking."

Dan kicked aside the clothing to make a path to the door. "If you take all these down to the kitchen, you can put a load in the washing machine. We'll get them hung out to dry when I get back."

"Where are you off to?"

"I'm meeting Nick Jessop for lunch in the King's Head." Dan turned when he reached the door. "And incidentally, while I'm there, you can take the dogs for a walk around the block for me. And make sure you take a plastic bag with you in case Biggles decides to explode again."

Josh's face expressed acute revulsion. "Thanks a bunch," he murmured, out of earshot of his father. "Dad?"

Dan had left the room by the time Josh called out his name. He returned, leaning a hand against the doorframe. "Yes?"

Josh's mouth was set tight, as if reluctant to speak.

"What is it?" Dan asked again.

"It's just . . . well"—Josh leaned forward on his knees and began flicking at one thumbnail with the other—"things aren't going too well between you and Mum, are they?"

Dan paused briefly before replying. "What makes you think that?"

"I heard you this morning."

"When?"

"This morning. Just before she left for work. You were talking at the bottom of the stairs."

Dan raised his eyebrows. "Hell, I didn't think that we were talking loud enough to wake *you* up."

"I was in the bathroom getting a glass of water."

"Ah, right. Well, I didn't realize."

"They're not, though, are they?"

"What?"

"Things between you and Mum. You seem to be arguing all the time."

"Not all the time."

Josh flicked back his head dismissively, but never raised his eyes. "Who are you trying to kid?"

Obviously only myself, Dan thought to himself. "Everything's all right, Josh. It's just . . . a bit difficult at the minute, what with Mum working every hour of the day and me being out of a job. That kind of pressure is enough to put a strain on even the strongest relationship."

Josh nodded, but Dan could tell that his son was far from convinced. "The girls are being a pain in the arse too," Josh continued. "They haven't been giving you much of a break recently, have they?"

Dan smiled at Josh's unexpected concern. "No, not really. But again, I think it's quite understandable. They're both of an age when life can be, well, fairly traumatic, and I haven't exactly improved their lot by having them move to a new school. They're not particularly happy there . . . and, of course, they blame me for that."

Josh blew out a derisive laugh. "That's such a load of rubbish! You're just too good to them because they're girls. I was never happy at *my* school, but you just kept telling me to knuckle down and get on with it." He reached down and began to collect up some of his clothes. "Or maybe the difference is that now you have *time* to realize that Millie and Nina aren't happy."

Dan scratched a finger repeatedly against the side of his face as his mind fought for an appropriate dismissal to Josh's observation. He couldn't think of one. "You could well be right." He leaned his shoulder against the doorframe. "So, are you saying that it's my fault that you dropped out of university?"

Josh laughed. "No, actually, I'm not. And, to be quite honest, it wouldn't have made a blind bit of difference if you *had* sent me to another school. I've always had a natural aversion to all forms of education."

Dan smiled at his son and walked back into the room and scooped up a pile of clothes from the floor. "I'll put this lot in the washing machine. You bring down the rest."

CHAPTER SIX

It had happened exactly one month and two days after he lost his job. At the precise moment when the first news report broke on the radio, he had been standing in the kitchen, making himself a mug of instant coffee to accompany his lunchtime sandwich. He remembered that he held the spoon brimming with coffee granules hovering above the mug, frozen in his actions, as he listened to the broadcast. By the time that the reporter had signed off, promising to keep listeners up to date with news as it broke, and the incongruously lighthearted music had started once again, only two minute coffee granules had fallen to the base of the mug. In the plethora of reports that filled the newspapers for the next two weeks, it became clear that others throughout the world had also remembered exactly what they were doing, down to the last detail.

He had immediately turned on the television and watched, transfixed at the scenes that were being beamed live from New York. He knew the building so well. He had been in it so many times before, but still he found it impossible to orientate himself, to tell from the shaking, street-level camera shots which tower had actually been hit. When he eventually realized that the one that housed the headquarters of the company for which he had worked for fifteen years still stood, apparently unscathed, he felt a moment's selfish relief that his colleagues would be all right and that they would be able to escape. It could only have been a moment, because as he stood there, no more than three feet away from the television screen, he watched in horror as the second aircraft hit the surviving tower.

Once he had managed to break himself away from the mesmeric images of utter catastrophe, he tried to call his old office in the City. The lines were jammed. He then tried Nick Jessop, an ex-colleague who had coincidentally lost his job at the same time as himself. The domestic help informed him that Mr. Jessop had taken his baby son for a walk. At first, Dan couldn't believe that Nick was able to carry on with such a normal, everyday routine when, twenty minutes before, an occurrence had taken place that was destined to change the world forever. And then he realized that it *had* only happened twenty minutes ago and that Nick wouldn't even know about it. He told the woman to get Nick to turn on the television as soon as he arrived back in the house.

He was now desperate to speak to someone that he knew, someone that he cared about. So he rang Jackie. The receptionist told him that his wife was in a finance meeting and didn't want to be disturbed. Dan had sworn at the girl, really sworn, and within ten seconds he was speaking with Jackie. "Is this really important," she had said, "because I'm in the middle of an extremely tense meeting, and, by the way, don't you dare start calling the office and using the f-word with my receptionist." Dan had said nothing more, other than to tell her to get her ear to a radio or her eyes to a television as soon as her meeting was over.

And then he had remembered that Josh was upstairs in bed. He rushed up the staircase and entered his bedroom with such force that Josh had awoken immediately. Even in his soporific state, Josh could tell that something had happened.

"What's the matter, Dad?" he had asked in a voice that registered real concern. "Why are you crying?"

Until that moment, Dan hadn't realized that he was. "Could you come downstairs, Josh, and watch television with me?" He heard his voice choke as he spoke the words.

"Why?" Josh asked, jumping out of bed and hurriedly pulling on a pair of boxer shorts. "What's happened?"

"I'm not sure, but I think that I might have just witnessed a whole load of my friends being killed."

They had sat on the sofa together for the rest of the afternoon watching the television. They never spoke, except to murmur an occasional expletive at the sheer magnitude of the devastation. Dan tried, on a number of occasions, to contact his old office in the City, but still the lines remained busy. He had never felt so helplessly out of touch in all his life.

When the newspapers eventually managed to compile lists of those who were missing, believed killed, he had counted eight close colleagues and three others whom he had met on a couple of occasions. John Fricker had probably been one of his closest friends, and in the instant that he read his name, he could recall every moment of the beautiful fall weekend that he had spent with John and one of their work colleagues, Debbie Leishman, in upstate New York. It was after that weekend that John and Debbie started to become pretty serious about each other. Dan found their telephone number in his address book, but it took him a full week after reading the name in the newspaper to pluck up the courage to try to make contact with Debbie. When he eventually spoke to her, he found that he couldn't even begin to find adequate words to express the way that he felt, so for a quarter of an hour, he had just listened to the voice of complete incomprehension and desolation at the other end of the line.

It was after he had finished that telephone call, when he was alone in his office at the top of the house in Clapham, that Dan had started to reevaluate his whole life. His own troubles now seemed insignificant.

He thought how lucky he was to have a family, how proud he was to have a seventeen-year-old son who had the sensitivity and strength to sit with a protective arm encircling his father's shoulder as they had watched those scenes from New York. He thought of the girls, miserable at their new school, and he vowed that he would be there for them, to help them through it. It was, after all, only a pinpoint of time in their lives. And he thought how unimportant it was to be without his high-flying job in the City. There were so many other things to cherish, to nurture. From that moment on, he was going to be happy, he was going to be fun, and he was going to be around for a family that needed him.

There was, however, one aspect of that day that Dan had never been able to comprehend. It left a chill where before there had been nothing but the warmth of mutual love and friendship. During those interminably long, dismal hours of September the eleventh, when families throughout the world, totally unconnected with those who had lost their lives, had telephoned each other just to touch base, just to express feelings of togetherness, Jackie had never bothered to call him.

CHAPTER SEVEN

HERE WAS ONLY standing room available when Dan entered the King's Head, many of those who were having lunch being forced to balance plates upon beer glasses in order to free a hand with which to feed themselves. It therefore took Dan a certain amount of time and contortion to push his way to the bar. He tried to catch the attention of Martin, the landlord, but he was busy serving customers at the farthest end of the bar, so he turned his attention to Minty, the New Zealand girl who had been working in the pub for the past few months. She was serving a vociferous young businessman who had divested himself of his suit jacket to reveal a striking pair of red braces worn over a dark blue shirt with white starched cutaway collar. Dan thought how lucky he was that he no longer needed to wear the uniform of the City. He was much happier wearing his jeans and his leather jacket and his loafers. He had come to quite relish the fact that nobody could pigeon-hole him into any one particular job.

He watched as the man leaned across the bar and talked to Minty in a drawling tone of self-assuredness that obviously implied that the barmaid could not help but find him outrageously attractive. As she handed the man his change, Minty beamed him a sweet smile, and then spied Dan.

"Hi, Dan," she said, giving her hands a quick rinse in the basin under the counter and air-flicking them dry. "What can I get you?"

"Pint of Young's, please, Minty."

"Coming right up."

Dan cast an eye around the thronging mass of people. "You haven't seen Nick around, have you?"

Minty was about to answer when they both heard a sound that was quite alien to a busy London pub. Above the roaring cacophony of conversation came a short, gleeful scream that could only be produced by a seriously underaged drinker. It brought an instant hush as heads were turned to source the perpetrator's whereabouts, but the interest was short-lived and the volume in the pub soon crescendoed once more. Dan, however, had no need to work out the origin of the sound. Only one person would be daft enough to bring a five-month-old baby into a smoke-filled pub, and he was sitting somewhere over by the cigarette machine.

Both he and Minty smiled knowingly at each other. "Okay," Dan laughed. "I think I've got him."

Nick Jessop was standing behind his table looking like a distraught kangaroo that had lost its joey. A baby sling hung forlornly empty against his tall frame as he watched with an uneasy smile on his face while young Tarquin's considerable bulk, resplendently dressed in a minute Chelsea Football Club team shirt, was being repeatedly thrown into the air and caught again in the arms of a thin, elderly woman with a squiggly lipsticked mouth and mirrored splodges of rouge on each of her sunken cheeks. Every now and again, she would cease her physical efforts to be fortified by a good slurp of gin and tonic and a deep drag on her cigarette. Then, encouraged by the child's gurning for more, she would again launch him into the air, her knees visibly buckling and a coughing wheeze being forced from her chest every time she clamped her arms around Tarquin's hurtling form. Dan thought it not unlike watching a spider trying to catch a cannonball.

His arrival at the table was enough to break the attention being granted to the circus act, and Nick, with obvious relief, managed to retrieve his only child from the clutches of the woman.

"Thank God you arrived," he breathed out, as he wedged Tarquin into the corner of the velour-covered bench, stopping his protestations by sticking a pacifier in his mouth. "I was just waiting for the moment when she got her timing wrong and took a swig and a drag when Tarquin was still midair."

"Well, I'm afraid that you do slightly ask for it," Dan replied, placing his pint on the table and pulling out the chair that Nick had been saving for him. "You shouldn't keep bringing him in here."

"Not an option, I'm afraid. Laura is working full-time now, and we haven't got any help in the house. Anyway, he likes being gregarious, don't you, my"—he leaned down over his son and blew a raspberry on his nylon-shirted tummy—"cheeky, cheeky chappie!"

"So, how's life treating you?" Dan asked in an attempt to get the conversation back to adult level.

Nick made minor adjustments to Tarquin's position before turning his attention to Dan. "Not bad, actually. In fact, I've got something here that I think might interest you." He reached down under the table and pulled out a battered leather briefcase. He gave Dan a wink as he opened it and extracted a sheet of A4 paper. "Are you ready for this?"

"I can't wait," Dan replied with only a fraction of the enthusiasm being displayed by his friend.

Nick spun the sheet around on the table and sat back against the bench, a broad grin on his face as he watched for Dan's reaction. It was a drawing of something that loosely resembled an oversized banana with what looked like a dead stick insect laid across its top edge. Dan looked up at Nick, cleared his throat, and continued to study the drawing. Maybe it was meant to be the crescent moon, complete with anorexic elf reclining.

Dan shook his head. "No, sorry. You've got me."

Nick frowned. "What do you mean, I've got you?" He spun the drawing around to face him. "It's obvious what it is."

It suddenly dawned on Dan that what was important about the drawing was not so much the content as the artistic prowess. He took back the drawing and studied it with renewed understanding. "It's very good. He's got a very bright future."

"Who has?"

"Tarquin."

Nick snatched the drawing away from Dan. "Okay, that's very funny. Listen, I might not be Van Gogh, but the idea behind it is a real winner."

"Well then, you'd better explain what it is because I don't think that it's obvious at all."

Nick laid the drawing once more in front of Dan and gave it a meaningful thump with his forefinger. "I have designed a child's car seat."

Dan looked back down at the banana and let out a silent sigh. Why the hell is it, he pondered to himself, that whenever men or women have their first offspring at a fairly advanced age, they either act as if theirs was the first household ever to be blessed with infant birth, or that all prior knowledge of rudimentary child care had been compiled by a moron?

"What's wrong with the ones you can get in Mothercare or Halford's?" Dan asked.

"Outdated. This is state-of-the-art technology."

Dan chuckled. "Nick, you're a banker. What the hell do you know about design and technology?"

Nick looked indignant. "I'll have you know I was very good at making Airfix models at my prep school."

Dan stifled a laugh. "Jeez, I don't think those credentials will impress too many would-be users. I mean, you're not planning to *glue* the baby into the seat, are you?"

Nick leaned forward on the table and fixed Dan with a beady eye. "Funny you should mention that."

The smile slid from Dan's face. He slowly shook his head. "Tell me you're not—please."

Nick grinned excitedly. "No. But it is revolutionary."

"All right," Dan said, leaning back in his chair and folding his arms. "Go on then. Hit me with it."

"Okay! What I've come up with is the idea of a seat without any form of retaining straps."

Dan looked a little nonplussed. "Oh?"

"Just wait." Nick began to twist his hands around in the air as if caressing an invisible ball. "Once you've put the child in the seat, you tilt it upwards so that the child's bottom is resting at the lowest point of the structure, and its feet and head at the top, so the only movement it could possibly make is upwards, and that, as you well know, is an impossibility in a car."

"Unless you drive off the side of a motorway and roll ten times down the embankment."

Nick looked peeved at Dan's negativity towards his idea. "No one should be driving that stupidly if they have a child in the car."

Dan let out a resigned laugh. He wasn't even going to bother trying to reason. "All right, you win. I just don't see why you can't put straps on the seat."

"Because they're damned uncomfortable for young babies."

"Well, in that case, you'd be as well sticking their arse in a bucket and wedging them in behind the driver's seat."

Nick shook his head. "Come on, Dan, you've really got to understand what I'm trying to achieve here, because"—he aimed his forefinger at the centre of Dan's chest—"I want *you* to handle the product marketing."

Dan looked aghast. "You've got to be joking! I'd be better trying to sell Kalashnikov rifles to Toys 'R' Us!"

"You'd be getting paid for it."

"Oh, yeah?"

"On commission. And don't tell me that a bit of income wouldn't come in useful."

Dan's grin showed affection for his friend. Maybe he had been a bit cynical. Nick was only trying to help. "Well, that is very kind and thoughtful of you, Nick. I'll tell you what, let's talk about it again once you've found a manufacturer."

Nick balled his fist enthusiastically. "Good idea." He swept the drawing off the table and replaced it in his briefcase. He shot a glance of self-reassurance at Tarquin's now-slumbering form before leaning back on the table. "Listen, I've got a plan for you and me tomorrow."

"Really? And what might that be?"

"Well, how about heading up to Curzon Street and having a relaxed haircut and shave in Trumpers? It would be just like old times!"

Dan laughed. "A good thought, Nick, but firstly, I don't need a haircut; secondly, I couldn't afford it anyway; and thirdly, just in case you've forgotten, tomorrow is our 'brew' day. We can't go without our unemployment benefit now, can we?"

"Ah," Nick replied quietly through clenched teeth. "That was the other thing I wanted to talk to you about. The trip to Trumpers was meant to be, well, a sort of celebration."

"Was it? Celebrating what?"

"The fact that I signed off the brew yesterday. I've got a new job."

"Where?"

"In the City. With Broughton's."

Dan raised his eyebrows. "Well done, you. Congratulations. When do you start?"

"Two weeks on Monday. I hope to hell that I can find someone to look after Tarquin by then. I don't think that I'd be too popular if I turned up at work with him strapped to my front." He paused. "I don't suppose you'd consider . . ."

"No, Nick, I would not."

"Right. Of course not. Well, it was just a thought."

"So you're obviously not going to be relying on the child seat to make your fortune."

"No. I was just planning for it to be a sideline."

Dan laughed. "Probably just as well."

For the first time, Nick saw the funny side of Dan's ribbing. "Yes, maybe you're right." He drained the remainder of his pint, put the glass on the table, and began to spin it round with his fingers. "Listen, Dan, once I've been with Broughton's for a bit, I'll put in a good word for you."

Dan shook his head. "Don't bother. I'm not going back to the City."

"Come on, Dan!" Nick exclaimed. "You're too damned good not to go back. I just don't understand why you haven't had any job offers since September eleventh."

Dan shot him a wink. "Ah, but I have, Nick. I just haven't told you about them. Six, maybe seven, actually, but I declined every one of them."

"But why, for God's sake? You have to work, Dan." There was almost a hint of desperation in Nick's voice.

"I will, but not in the City. I think I've probably mellowed too much to get involved in the cut and thrust of high finance again. Anyway, I had my fair share of the pot of gold over the years. Maybe it's time to put something back."

Nick's mouth dropped open. "That sounds a bit dangerous. You're not contemplating going into the church, are you?"

"Bloody hell, no! Could you see me in a dog collar?"

Nick visibly shuddered. "No, you're quite right. Stupid suggestion. So, what *are* you thinking of doing?"

"I don't know, but I'm sure something will turn up." His words struck a familiar chord, and he smiled to himself as he remembered Josh's clever riposte a couple of hours before.

On the bench, Tarquin made a gurgling noise and fluttered his eyelashes, threatening to wake up, but then he just turned his head and settled back into a deep sleep. Nick took his jacket off the back of the chair next to Dan and laid it gently over his son.

"When was the last time you heard from Debbie Leishman?" he asked.

"I got an e-mail from her two days ago," Dan replied.

"How is she?"

"She's coping. Did you know that she'd had a baby?"

"Never. When was that?"

"In June."

"How amazing!" Nick furrowed his brow. "Could it have been John's child?"

"Of course it was John's child. She didn't even know that she was pregnant when he was killed on nine-eleven."

Nick clicked his tongue. "What a bugger, eh? On the other hand, it's pretty marvelous that she has something of his for always, if you get my meaning."

"It would have been better still if they had been married. Then she would have got some compensation."

"Are you still sending her money?"

"As much as I can, yes. I don't think Jackie would be too pleased if she found out that I was keeping another woman."

Nick swept away a long string of blonde hair from his face. "Are things going any better with you and Jackie, or is she still being a bit frosty?"

Dan snorted out a laugh. "No, the girls are now the frosty ones. Jackie has turned into the ice maiden." He let out a long sigh. "But I keep smiling through it all and cooking them semidelicious meals and coming out with jovial remarks that no one finds particularly funny, in the hope that my infectious happiness will lead us all to a better life."

"And is there any sign of that happening?" Nick asked.

Dan chuckled. "No. I just irritate the hell out of them all."

Nick became thoughtful and began tapping his fingers on the table.

"Listen, Dan, why don't you try getting out of London for a bit? I mean, there's nothing to stop you from taking the whole family away somewhere for a week."

Dan shook his head. "The school term's just started, Nick. You can't just whip the kids away when you feel like it." He glanced at Tarquin on the bench. "Maybe you don't know about that kind of thing yet. Anyway, Jackie has Paris Fashion Week coming up soon, so there's no way that she would want to go."

"Well, go over to Paris with her. Get Battersea Gran to look after the kids."

The remark made Dan smile. When his father had died two years before, he had moved his mother from her council house in Tottenham Hale to a small flat in a high-rise block overlooking the River Thames in Battersea. It had never ceased to amuse him that she was now universally known as Battersea Gran. "Yeah, I could, I suppose. I'll have a word with Jackie tonight when she gets home."

Nick gave a quick nod of his head as if to finalize the point. "Good." He leaned over his son and carefully extracted a newspaper from the pocket of his jacket. "Now, let's move on to more important matters. How about coming to Stamford Bridge on Saturday?"

"Who's playing?"

"Chelsea versus Spurs—their first clash of the season," Nick replied, folding the paper across the back page and handing it over to Dan. "Thought you'd like to come to support your old team."

Dan glanced quickly at the prematch report before pushing the paper back across the table. "I don't know. I can't really make any plans until I know what Jackie is doing."

"Come on!" Nick cajoled. "It would be just like old times."

"Old times!" Dan laughed. "Nick, whenever we've been to a match together, we've ended up sitting at opposite ends of the pitch, yelling tribal abuse at one another."

"Okay, then, bring an extra Tottenham scarf with you. I don't mind being a Spurs fan for a day."

Dan raised his eyebrows in surprise. "My word, I think you mean it."

"Of course I do. Anything for an old mate."

"Well, that certainly would be the supreme sacrifice." He paused. "How many tickets could you lay your hands on?"

"How many extra are you looking for?"

"Just the one. For Josh."

Nick gave him a thumbs-up. "I'll see what I can do." He picked up his empty beer glass and got to his feet. "Right, keep an eye on Tarquin and I'll get another couple of pints in. Do you want anything to eat?"

"Not really. I'll share a ham sandwich with you, if you want."

"Right, coming up!" He slapped Dan's shoulder as he passed him by. "And while I'm away, think about how we can improve on the design of the car seat."

CHAPTER EIGHT

A$_S$ HE SAT in his office at the top of the house that evening, desperately seeking an e-mail that had vanished from the screen of his laptop, strong evidence came to Dan's nostrils that his carefully prepared gourmet meal was fast becoming a burnt offering. He jumped up from his desk, squirting the screen arrow off to oblivion, and bolted down the stairs, two at a time. He raced into the kitchen and threw open the oven door, reeling back as the scorching fumes hit his face. He picked up an oven glove from the work surface and waved it about to clear the air, then gingerly extracted the smouldering roasting pan from the oven and hurried out through the French doors into the garden. As the heat from the pan began to penetrate through the flimsy glove, he looked around in desperation to try to find a suitable surface on which to put it. He opted, more out of necessity than choice, for the bird table.

Pulling off the glove, he blew hard on his seared fingers to relieve them, and despondently viewed the blackened lump that was to have been Nigella Lawson's Loin of Pork with Bay Leaves.

"Bugger it!" he said quietly to himself, and turned and walked back into the kitchen.

The fumes had now risen to the ceiling and hung above his head like a swirling sea mist, and for the first time he became aware that he had not been alone in the kitchen when he had attempted his rescue. Millie sat with her chin resting on her hands at one end of the long pine table, her homework spread out in front of her. There was not much indication, however, of any great learning taking place, unless she had found a way of indoctrinating her brain with an enormous pair of Sony earphones clamped about her head, whilst her eyes feasted on a video recording of that day's episode of *Eastenders*.

Dan kicked the oven door closed and lobbed the oven glove onto the work surface. "Millie, you twit, you might have called me. The whole house could have caught on fire."

Millie made no move, except to pull a long string of chewing gum from her mouth and then reel it back in again with her tongue. Dan moved up behind her and lifted the earphones off her head. "Millie!"

His daughter jumped round in her chair. "What?"

"Your dinner is cremated. It is burnt to a frazzle."

"So? You can't blame me for that."

"I'm not blaming you for anything, but didn't you happen to notice that it was nigh on impossible to see the television for smoke?"

Millie once again resumed her chin-in-hands position and fixed her eyes on the television. "How was I to know that it wasn't *meant* to be like that?"

"Well, I would have thought that the smell might have given you just the smallest indication that something was burning."

"I didn't notice the smell."

"Millie! Come on, pull the other one!"

She twisted round again, her hands outstretched to accentuate her blamelessness. "I didn't! How could I? I was listening to music."

Dan was left speechless by the reply. He shifted his baffled gaze from the earphones in his hand, which were still linked to the portable CD on the table and still blaring out music, to Millie's ears, wondering if there was some appalling defect in his daughter's sensory organs about which he had not previously known. He eventually accepted it for what it was, a complete non sequitur to stop him from pestering her during her nightly vigil with *Eastenders*.

Dan let out a sigh. "Right then, where's Nina?"

"Upstairs, practicing her flute," Millie replied, without dragging her eyes away from the sight of pint-sized Barbara Windsor pulling yet another man-sized pint in the Queen Vic.

"For heaven's sakes, she's just had a concert! Hasn't she played enough for one day?"

"She thinks she played rubbish."

"Oh? I thought it all sounded pretty good. Who put that idea into her head?"

Millie looked at Dan out of the side of her eyes. "Probably every-body in the orchestra, if not the school."

Dan shook his head. "Come on, Millie, surely things aren't that bad, are they?"

"Don't you believe it!" she mumbled in reply.

Dan put down the earphones on the table. "Right, well, let's cheer everybody up. Seeing that the dinner's burnt, I'll have to get a takeaway. What do you want? Indian or Chinese?"

Millie's eyes suddenly brightened. "Can we have sushi?"

"No, Millie, we can't."

"Why not?"

Dan leaned one hand on the worktop, the other on his hip, as he gave overplayed thought to Millie's question. "Two reasons, mainly. One, because the nearest sushi bar is in Victoria, and two, because the car is being extremely fickle and has decided not to start. Therefore, we have no way of getting sushi."

Millie despondently slumped her face back into her hands. "Couldn't you get Mum to pick some up on the way home?"

"Indian or Chinese, Millie?"

Millie fixed her eyes on the television once more. "Don't mind. Whatever."

Dan flipped open the rubbish bin and dropped in the three cardboard lids. "Right, on the menu this evening we have chicken rogan mush, chicken pathia, and pilau rice." He took a serving spoon from the drawer and stood with it hovering above the tinfoil containers. "What's it going to be? Ni, you can have first choice."

Both Millie and Nina remained transfixed in front of the television, as they had done since he had walked back into the kitchen bearing the two anaemically blue plastic bags.

"Listen, can we have the television off for a bit?"

It was like talking to a brick wall. Dan walked over to the table and stretched across Millie's shoulder and took the remote from her grasp. The television clicked and died. To his surprise, there were no vociferous complaints, both girls seeming to accept it with bland indifference.

"I've got to go to the loo," Millie said, sliding off her chair.

"Come on! You could have done that while I was out."

"Didn't need to go then," Millie retorted as she left the room.

Dan let out a resigned sigh. "Right then, Ni, what do you want?"

Nina walked over to the sideboard and eyed the contents of the containers with an expression that registered supreme distaste. "What is that?"

"Well, for the second time, it's chicken rogan josh, chicken pathia, and pilau rice."

"Haven't you got any poppadoms?"

"Yes, I have. They're in the oven keeping warm."

"Which is the mildest?"

"I think the rogan josh."

"Could I just have rice and poppadoms?"

Dan stood with the spoon still poised. "No, you have to have a bit of one or the other."

"Why?"

"Because . . . I bought it for you, that's why."

"You could always put my share in the fridge for Josh. He doesn't mind what he eats."

Dan decided that he had reasoned enough. He spooned out some rice and a small amount of rogan josh onto a plate and handed it to Nina. "If you get the poppadoms out of the oven, you can have mine if you like."

As Nina carried her plate over to the table, Millie came back into the kitchen. Dan gave her a plate already filled with food. He wasn't going to go through the same rigmarole with her.

"Can we put the television back on?" Millie asked.

"No, we can't," Dan replied, putting the containers into the oven before taking his own plate over to the table.

Millie groaned at the same time that Nina asked, "Why not?"

Dan handed a fork to each of his daughters. "Because I thought that we might talk instead."

"What about?" Nina asked halfheartedly, sticking the fork into her rice and letting it dribble back onto her plate.

"I don't know. What would you like to talk about?"

His question was met by silence. Dan took a mouthful of food, hoping that one of the girls might have said something by the time he had finished it. It didn't work. "All right, then. Ni, I thought your concert went very well tonight."

"Dad, you fool!" Millie hissed through clenched teeth. "I *told* you about that."

Dan ignored his elder daughter. "I thought you played really well."

"I did not," Nina mumbled.

"Well, I disagree with you and I know for a fact that Mrs. Partridge does as well."

Millie and Nina turned to look at Dan simultaneously, both with questioning frowns creasing their foreheads. "Who is Mrs. Partridge?" Millie asked.

"Come on, Millie," Dan exclaimed. "You know as well as I do who Mrs. Partridge is. Nina's music teacher."

For a moment, both girls stared open-mouthed at him before bursting out laughing, Nina managing to spray her mouthful of food across the table in the process.

"Nina!" Dan exclaimed, reaching over to wipe the splattering of pilau rice off the television screen. "Okay then, what have I said that's so funny?"

Millie swung around in her chair to face Dan, her eyes sparkling with intrigue—or maybe it was humour—Dan couldn't work out which, but it was certainly the most animated that he had seen his elder daughter all evening.

"So what did you say to Mrs. *Partridge,* then, Dad?" she asked. "Was it something like 'My word, Mrs. *Partridge,* didn't the orchestra play well tonight? Do you think Nina has any chance of getting an A in her GSCE's, Mrs. *Partridge?*"

Dan was bemused by all the hilarity, but nevertheless pleased that he had at least succeeded in making his daughters laugh. It didn't happen very often. "Maybe not those exact words, but something like that, yes."

Nina was laughing so much now that she fell forward and thumped her forehead on the table. The blow obviously caused her pain because she immediately straightened up, her only reaction to the blow being a silent, round-mouthed "Ow."

Millie took in a deep breath to control herself. "Her name, Dad, is Miss Peacock, not Mrs. Partridge."

Dan smacked his hand against his mouth. "It's not."

Millie nodded, then burst out laughing again.

"Oh, hell," Dan said quietly.

"Have you always called her Mrs. Partridge, Dad?" Nina eventually managed to ask.

"Yes, I'm pretty sure I have," Dan replied, looking as if he had just sucked on a sour lemon.

As the kitchen filled with laughter once more, the door opened and Jackie walked in. She surveyed the scene of conviviality as she shrugged off her raincoat. "My word," she said flatly. "You all seem very happy this evening."

"You'll never guess what, Mum," Nina said, using her mother's entrance as a diversionary tactic to jettison the remainder of her rogan mush into the rubbish bin.

"No, I probably won't," Jackie replied distractedly as she walked across to the telephone to check the notepad for messages.

"Dad has been calling Miss Peacock, my music teacher, Mrs. Partridge."

Jackie gave Nina a half-smile and ran a hand over her daughter's long dark hair. "Sorry I didn't make the concert, darling. I just couldn't get away from work."

The humorous twinkle vanished from Nina's eyes. "That's all right," she replied quietly.

Millie pushed back her chair and got to her feet. "Can we go upstairs to watch television, Mum?"

"Sure you can."

"Thanks. Come on, Ni."

As the two girls left the kitchen, Jackie slumped down onto the chair that Millie had just vacated. Dan cleared the dirty plates off the table and carried them across to the sink.

"How's your day been?" he asked, rinsing them off under the tap.

"Exhausting," Jackie replied.

Dan took the containers from the oven and put them on the worktop. "I'm afraid we're on takeaway tonight. I had a bit of a disaster with the loin of pork."

Jackie held up a hand. "Thanks, but I really couldn't eat a thing. I had a huge lunch."

"Right." He scrutinized the contents of the three containers. "Well, I don't think I'll risk giving it to the dogs," he said, mainly for the benefit of himself. "That might just be tempting providence." He discarded everything into the rubbish bin and rubbed his hands clean on a dishtowel. "Can I get you a glass of wine, then?"

Jackie shook her head. "No, don't bother. I thought that I might just have a bath and go straight to bed."

Dan sat down on the chair next to her. "So, how did you get on with the set designer?"

"Oh," Jackie replied. "So you remembered."

"Of course I remembered. What makes you think I wouldn't remember?"

"Well, I just thought . . . Look, don't let's get started into another argument. I'm too tired."

"We're not having an argument! I was just asking!"

"All right! I'm sorry." Jackie leaned her elbows on the table and covered her face with her hands. "I really do feel exhausted."

Dan reached across and gave her arm a gentle pat. "It's not surprising. You're working bloody hard." He got to his feet and walked over to the fridge. "Are you sure you don't want to have a glass of wine? I'm going to have one."

"All right then, but just half a glass."

Dan poured out the wine and handed her the glass. He sat down again. "Listen, when is Prêt á Porter?"

"In three weeks' time."

"Do you have to go over beforehand?"

Jackie turned to look at him. She paused before replying. "Yes, actually. I do."

"Good. In that case, I thought that I'd come with you."

Jackie's eyes opened wide. "What?"

"Well, I just thought that we needed a bit of time together. It would be the perfect opportunity."

Jackie bit at her lip. "Dan, I've got to go over this weekend. I was going to tell you tonight."

"Oh. Right. Well, I could try to get Battersea Gran to come over, but it's a bit short notice."

"Dan, I'm going with Stephen."

Dan's eyes shifted around the room as he tried to work out who the hell Stephen was. "Stephen?"

"Who might that be?"

"Our financial director."

"Ah."

"It's business, Dan. I've got some serious negotiations to do with the organizers. Stephen said that he would come over and give me a hand."

Dan pulled a long face. "Well, I hope you're only speaking metaphorically."

"Don't be so bloody stupid. You know as well as I do what I mean."

"Right. So when will you be back?"

"Probably Monday or Tuesday. Stephen thought it better to spill the visit over into a weekday, just in case we hit problems at the weekend."

Dan scratched a finger across his forehead. "Why is it that I haven't heard of this Stephen before?"

Jackie let out a long sigh. "Maybe because you've never been interested in what I do before."

"Jackie, that's nonsense and you know it."

"Well, if you were so well up to speed, you would know that it was Stephen who is wholly responsible for setting up Rebecca Talworth Design Limited, and I think probably wholly responsible for getting me the job as managing director."

Dan cocked his head to the side and winked. "Sounds like some guy, this Stephen."

Jackie drained her wine glass in one gulp. "Right, I'm going upstairs." She pushed back her chair and stood up.

"I was only joking, you know."

"That's your problem, Dan. You're always joking. Maybe you should think about trying to take life a little more seriously and get yourself a bloody job!"

She grabbed her raincoat from the back of the chair and stormed out of the kitchen, slamming the door behind her. In the silence that ensued, Biggles crept out of hiding from his basket in the conservatory and came over and laid his head on Dan's knee.

Dan gave the dog a solid pat on his large black-and-white head. "Biggles, my boy, your timing seems to be a hell of a lot better than mine."

CHAPTER NINE

DAN SAT IN the ageing Saab outside St. Bartholomew's Church in Battersea, killing time until his mother appeared by attempting to fit the convertible hood flush with the top of the windscreen so that they wouldn't have to make the journey back to Clapham with frozen scalps. He had never really been aware of the draught himself until the day before when he had whisked Jackie up to Waterloo Station and had dropped her outside the Eurostar terminal with her woollen scarf tied Russian-peasant-style around her head. He had secretly hoped that wonderboy Stephen could have seen her like that, but as he watched her walk into the building, she had pulled off the scarf, given her head a quick shake, and once more looked immaculate. Well, from the rear view at any rate. She hadn't actually bothered to turn round, not even for a final goodbye.

Two young children, clutching crayoned drawings in their hands, came running out through the doors of the church, heralding the end of the service. Dan watched as they hid behind one of the stone pillars, whispering excitedly to one another, and then jumped out when their parents appeared. Neither mother nor father showed any reaction to their children's sudden appearance. Go on, Dan thought, do something! At least clutch a hand to the heart or stagger back in feigned shock. But no, they just pushed their children on in front of them and headed up the street in animated and godly conversation with each other.

Dan watched the procession of worshippers stream out of the church and shake hands with the storklike vicar at the door; there were a couple of ex-military types who stood ramrod straight and threw back their heads in laughter at the punchline of the story their wives simpered out to the vicar; there was a bevy of Born Agains, with their nonexistent dress code and their smiles of sheer goodness and radiant sincerity; there was an old woman with a woolly hat pulled down over her tangle of matted hair who shuffled past the vicar without a word and went off down the street, muttering to herself as she carried her worldly belongings in several plastic bags, their handles entwined in her grubby, mitted fingers; and then there were the stalwarts—the ladies who cleaned the floors, polished the brasses, arranged the flowers, and organized midweek fund-raising coffee mornings to which only they turned up. They were dressed in drab Sunday best coats done up to the neck, carrying handbags on their forearms and gloves in hand, and they wore hats that appeared to have been beaten into submission with cudgels before adorning their tightly permed white hair.

Dan could never quite fathom why it was that, as long as he could remember, old ladies always seemed to have dressed in exactly the same way. Was there never a time in their lives when they favoured bright figure-hugging clothes and glossed their mouths with devil-red lipstick? Had those pink-spectacled eyes never flashed a "Come on, try your luck with me" to some cool young dude on the other side of the dance floor? It was hard to imagine. Maybe they all went through some bizarre metamorphic process as they approached their golden years, entering into some weird extrusion plant dressed as butterflies and coming out the other end as mothy pensioners.

Thank God for Mum, Dan thought to himself. There she was, rounded and wholesome, dressed in a fuschia pink raincoat, her grey, loose-curled hair blowing free in the breeze, standing amongst them like a rose in a cabbage patch. It didn't take much to imagine her still as that young, vibrant teenage girl, dressed in flared skirt and bobby socks, who had walked away with every jive competition held at the Metropole Dance Hall in Tottenham Hale.

Dan got out of the car and went around to the passenger door and held it open for his mother. She gave him a little wave but remained on the pavement talking with one of her fellow church slaves, no doubt fixing up the next scintillating meeting of the Scrape-Your-Knuckles-to-the-Bone-for-the-Welfare-of-the-Church Club. A nod and a gentle pat on the arm confirmed the arrangement and Battersea Gran crossed over the road to the car.

"Hullo, dear," she trilled, offering up her cheek for a kiss. Dan obliged. "My word, hasn't it got cold all of a sudden? What's happened to the Indian summer that nice Mr. Fish promised us on the telly?" She reached up and gave the lapel of his leather jacket a shake. "And look at you without a jersey. You may think you look sexy in that thing, but it's not going to keep out the chill."

"I'm fine, Mum," Dan replied, wrestling his jacket from her grip. "In fact, I'm feeling quite hot." For heaven's sakes, Dan thought to himself, nearly forty-one years old and you're still rising to her over-protective quips.

"Oh, well, if you say so," his mother sighed as she reversed her bottom onto the car seat and pulled her raincoat around her. Shutting the door more carefully than usual, Dan walked around to the other side of the car and got in.

"My word, this is very nice," his mother cooed as she rubbed a hand along the wood veneer finish of the dashboard. "Very plush in-deed. Is it new?"

"Is what new?" Dan asked, clipping in his seat belt.

"The car."

"Mum, it's fifteen years old," Dan replied, wondering how his mother could have possibly missed the fact that the interior of the car looked as if it had been used for carting livestock at some time in its past.

"Well, you wouldn't think it, would you?" She nosed the fetid air in the car and her mouth pursed with disgust. "Have you been smoking?" she asked tartly.

"No, I haven't. It must have been the last owner."

Battersea Gran sucked her teeth. "Probably died of lung cancer. Why else would anyone want to get rid of a nice car like this?"

"Right, Mum. Pull over your seat belt and I'll do it up for you."

Dan clipped in the belt and started the car on the third time of asking. He executed a five-point turn in the middle of the narrow street, much to the annoyance of a taxi driver and a motorcyclist who were forced to wait while he carried out the manoeuvre. "Okay, then," he said, holding up a hand in apology and accelerating the car towards Battersea Park Road, "Clapham next stop."

"I think that I should go back to the flat first, dear."

"Do you really need to? It's just that I've left the roast in the oven and the girls won't have the sense to take a look at it."

"Nature calls, I'm afraid. I don't think that I'd make it to Haleridge Road."

"Wasn't there a loo in the church?"

"Oh, yes, but I wouldn't dream of using that one."

"Why not?"

"Because . . . well, you know . . . going to the toilet in church. Just doesn't seem right."

"Mum, even Jesus had to have a pee sometimes."

"Of course he did, dear, but I'm sure that he would have taken himself off somewhere very discreet to do it."

Dan suppressed a laugh. "What? Like the desert?"

"Probably."

"A bit of overkill, though, wasn't it?"

"What do you mean?"

"Forty days and forty nights."

Battersea Gran narrowed her eyes at her son, but it was insufficient to mask a sparkle of humour. "No need to be irreverent now, Daniel Porter."

The block of flats, situated overlooking Battersea Reach Wharf, was typical of uninspired sixties architecture. Originally council flats, it had been bought for a song in the early nineties by some property developer who saw the potential in its riverside location. Having refurbished the building from leaky top to graffitied bottom, he stuck a uniformed concierge in the hallway, gave the block a smart new name, and flogged the flats off as "exclusive residences." The building had been inhabited in the main by retired gentlefolk, and when Dan had moved his mother there after the death of his father, he had had grave misgivings about whether it would be for the best, taking her away from her simple lifestyle in Tottenham Hale and placing her in this somewhat up-market environment.

But his doubts proved to be unfounded. His mother treated the place as if it were an outpost of her own little street in North London, and single-handedly went about developing a community spirit in the building that had never existed before her arrival. She forced greetings from her reticent fellow residents in the lift and went around knocking on doors and inviting her somewhat surprised and lonely neighbours around to her little flat for cups of tea and mountains of her own homemade scones. Even the grumpy old concierge was soon won over by her open friendliness and hospitality. Flat 10F2 in Cavendish Rise soon became the focal point for residents' meetings and fund-raising campaigns to pay for pot-plants in the foyer and Christmas parties for the few children who lived in the block. Not that Battersea Gran was much good at constitutional matters, or discussing things like plumbing problems and rent reviews, but she put herself in charge of refreshments, and that proved an excellent rallying call to all those with empty stomachs and infinitely greater discussion skills than her own.

"I'll only be a moment, dear," she said as she let herself into the flat and hurried off down the narrow passage to the lavatory. "Just go into the lounge and I'll be with you in a minute."

The furniture in the small room was set out exactly as it had been in the front room of the Porters' little terraced council house in Tottenham Hale. Dan had offered to buy her new furniture from Habitat, but she didn't want "that rubbish" and insisted on moving everything from the old house. The ducks still flew up the wall, the picture of the Siamese girl with tear in eye still hung opposite the black-and-white photograph of his mother as an excited young teenager, standing on-stage at the Metropole with Bill Haley and the Comets, and the brown velour suite was still set around the fireplace (albeit now a false one) and angled towards the television. The only real difference was that, where the netted window in the front room of the old house looked out onto a line of parked cars and the dirt-engrained façade of the houses opposite, the view from the full-width window on the tenth floor of the block was unimpeded, taking in the curve of the River Thames from Wandsworth Bridge to Battersea Bridge and a broad panorama across Fulham and Chelsea, stretching on out to the White City Stadium and beyond.

Dan glanced at his watch and began worrying about yet another roast ending up on the bird table. He walked across to the door. "How are you doing, Mum?" he called down the passage.

"Just a minute, dear." Her voice came from the bedroom. "I'm just slipping into a thermal. I'm feeling the cold a bit."

"Be as quick as you can, then."

She appeared at the door of the bedroom with only one arm slipped into a sleeve of her vest, revealing an ample frontage encased in a flesh-coloured brassiere. "I am, Dan. Just be patient."

"Okay. It's just the—"

"The roast. I know, dear. And while your mind is on cooking, you should have a look at that recipe I found for you in *Woman's Weekly*. I left it open on the coffee table." She eventually managed to struggle into her vest. "I thought it looked rather good."

I'm sure it will be, Dan thought, as he went back into the lounge and walked over to the table. Her idea of a good recipe was cheesy chicken or spiced meatballs in gravy. He picked up the magazine. Yes, that would be about the norm. An exciting lamb stew with kidney beans. He dropped the magazine back on the table.

His mother appeared, doing up the buttons of her overcoat. "Right, that's me ready."

"Good. Let's go then."

"Don't forget the magazine."

Dan blew out a resigned sigh and scooped up the *Woman's Weekly.*

A S IT TURNED out, lunch happened to be a great success. Apart from the roast beef appearing from the oven in a state of readiness that Dan had always strived to achieve—a crispy coating of fat on the outside and succulently red in the middle—the meal was, as far as Dan could remember, the first for many a moon that had been conducted without one cross or needling word being fired across the table. That was, of course, the doing of Battersea Gran. When she had been married to Dan's father, she had considered it her role in life to lavish him with praise and undying devotion (or "devoshun," as she would pronounce it when warbling out one of her favorite songs, Johnny Tillotson's "Poetry in Moshun"). However, since his death, that instinct had now been shifted onto her grandchildren, and in her simple, down-to-earth way, she always seemed able to extract from them the best of their characters. No matter what they did, it was always right by Battersea Gran—and they loved her for it. She was delighted by Josh's ability to stack shelves in Tesco's and intrigued by his visits to Horace's Inferno; she became tearful with pride when, after lunch, she sat listening to Nina as she stuttered through the *Braveheart* theme on her flute; and, even though Dan had tried to admonish her for it, she roared with laughter at Millie's stories of how she had been caught standing on top of the lavatory cistern in the school cloakrooms, blowing cigarette smoke up towards the Xpelair fan, or how she had given a one-fingered reply to the class geek when he asked her to go out with him.

As well as being a listener, Battersea Gran also had infinite knowledge of all things that interested the children, gleaned from the television in her flat. She knew more than either Dan or Josh about how Tottenham Hotspurs were doing in the league table, who scored the goals during their last match, and who the manager was lining up for his next multimillion-pound signing; she watched *Top of the Pops* every week so that she could baffle the girls with her knowledge of rappers and heavy metal bands and the endless stream of manufactured boy groups, girl groups, and mixed groups; and when Josh went to Manchester University (the first Porter ever to achieve this distinction), she would wake herself at five o'clock every morning to watch *Open University.* She even began to achieve a vague understanding of some of the complex mathematical problems that the ginger-moustached lecturer was writing down on his flipchart. But then she discovered that Josh was studying English, so thereafter she decided to give up her early morning vigils and just stick to the less erudite information that daytime television afforded her.

Every birthday and every Christmas, the children received expensive, jaw-dropping presents from their grandparents in Chester, but during their visits to London (which thankfully for Dan were both brief and scarce), neither of Jackie's parents showed themselves capable of any degree of spontaneity or fun with the children. But then, Josh, Millie, and Nina had Battersea Gran to provide that, and they had an instinctive understanding that having her constantly in their lives was worth much more than the material goods bestowed upon them by *the others*. If there was ever to be a battle of loyalties, then Battersea Gran was always going to win hands down. Josh spoke for them all when he once described her as being the *ultimate* Gran.

That evening, the weather had displayed typically fickle British ten-
dencies and changed from winter back to the Indian summer that Mr.
Fish, the television weatherman, had promised. As Dan drove home
after taking Battersea Gran back to her flat, he had to make use of the
visor to shield his eyes from the watery rays of the setting sun, and the
freezing draught that had earlier blown in through the gap at the top
of the windscreen had now become a warm and comforting blast. Even
though it was just before seven o'clock in the evening, Clapham Common was now awash with people who had been lured from their homes
by the rise in temperature. As he sat in the queue for the traffic lights,
Dan watched the walkers, the joggers, the footballers, the Frisbee
throwers, and the kite flyers, as well as the bedlam of unruly dogs that
joined in with any game that would accommodate them.

All was quiet when he entered the house. There was a note on the
third step of the stairs that explained the silence. Jessica Napier, one of
Millie's closest friends from her previous school, had rung to ask Millie
and Nina around to her house for the evening. Dan scrumpled up the
paper in his fist and walked through to the kitchen. He was pleased
about that. Millie had had little contact with Jessica since she left Alleyn's. Maybe this heralded a new beginning to their relationship.

He briefly considered taking Biggles and Cruise out to join the
hordes on Clapham Common, but then decided that, for once, they
could make do with their nightly traipse around the block. It was a
better idea to enjoy the tranquility while it lasted. He took a beer from
the fridge, picked up a Sunday magazine from the table, and made his
way out into the back garden.

He flicked the ring pull on the can and sucked away the froth, then
pulled a lichen-covered garden seat from under an untamed honeysuckle at the bottom of the garden and positioned it in the sun, giving
the seat a perfunctory sweep with his hand before sitting down. He
opened the magazine at a page that showed the unappetizing image of
a lamb stew with kidney beans floating like drowned beetles on its
grease-bubbled surface. He turned back to the front cover and swore

quietly to himself, realizing that he had picked up his mother's *Woman's Weekly* by mistake. He took a long pull from his beer can and spun the magazine onto the seat beside him. It fell to the ground and lay with its pages flapping over in the breeze.

Dan sat with eyes closed and head tilted back until he sensed the sun's warming rays leave his face. He watched as its fiery tip sank behind the rooftops of the houses at the end of the street, taking with it what little heat had been afforded the day. Feeling a shiver run through his body, he decided that it was time to head indoors.

As he leaned forward to pick up the magazine, he noticed a spider crawling its way across the page, perfectly dissecting the face of a woman with high cheekbones and bright blue eyes that caught the blinding glint of a camera flash. As it continued on its way, the spider was momentarily lost against a background of spiky brown hair before appearing once more on the cold grey of the rain-clouded sky. And then, with a few tentative steps, it descended from the magazine and scuttled away across the bricked patio to the sanctuary of the weed-infested flower border.

Dan picked up the magazine and studied the photograph. The woman was standing with her arms around the shoulders of two small children whose impish grins would seem to indicate that her loving envelopment was probably more a necessary entrapment for the benefit of the photographer. Behind the three figures, dark, colourless hills ran down into the dull, glassy waters of some kind of lake or reservoir. Against this background, the multicoloured plaid trousers that the woman and two children were wearing contrasted brightly.

Dan stood up from the bench, beer can in hand, and made his way across to the French doors that led into the house. As he walked, he read the headline that was written below the photograph. "Too Good Boss Decides to Sell Business."

He deposited the empty can in the rubbish bin as he passed, and then sat down at the table, laying the magazine open in front of him. The headline intrigued him. Surely this homely looking woman, with not a trace of makeup on her face, wasn't the one being described as a "too good boss"? Dammit, if she was, she was a far cry from any of the high-powered businesswomen that he had ever come across. He knew for a fact that Jackie would never set foot in *her* workplace with features that looked as if they had been scrubbed clean with a pumice stone. What the hell did she do to be described as a "too good boss"? He leaned forward on the table and began to read the article.

Twelve years ago, Katie Trenchard (42) had everything set out for what she thought would be a peaceful and comfortable life. She and her husband Patrick (45) lived in a handsome detached house in the village of Cloveden, five miles from Plymouth, where Patrick worked as a lecturer in marine biology at the university. There were shops, cinemas, and theatres within easy reach, they entertained on a regular basis, and they were able to make use of the many facilities that the university had to offer. And then, in one crazy month, they made a decision that would change their lives forever. They sold their beloved house, said goodbye to their friends, and moved to Fort William in the northwest of Scotland where they ploughed every last penny into the purchase of Seascape, a small prawn-processing factory.

"It was Patrick's fault," says Katie, narrowing her strikingly blue eyes. "It had always been his lifetime ambition to run a business of his own. He had carried out a number of small research projects for Seascape and heard through the grapevine that it was for sale. He knew that it was an opportunity he couldn't let slip."

Dan raised his eyebrows. Bloody fools, he thought to himself. What a madcap thing to do.

Within three months of taking over the business, the Trenchards had set up new agencies in France, Italy, and Spain, and very soon found that demand for their product outstripped supply. However, any profit that was being made had to be ploughed straight back into the business to upgrade its ageing equipment and meet the stringent regulations laid down by the Health and Safety Office of the Highland Regional Council. Consequently, there were no funds available for sumptuous accommodation, and for the first two years, they lived in only just bearable comfort in a three-room crofter's cottage on the shores of Loch Eil.

"Mind you, we very rarely seemed to be at home," says Katie. "The workers started at seven o'clock every morning and Patrick and I were always there half an hour before they arrived. During the high season, when the prawns were coming in thick and fast, the packers were producing over 10 tonnes a day, which meant that we all had to work on into the night just to keep up with our intake. Patrick and I would walk around like zombies for about four months of the year!"

Bloody fools, Dan repeated to himself. Fancy having to work hours like that and not make any money.

Katie's involvement in the company, however, ended on the eve that Max (now 10 and pictured left) was born. Her duties then changed from office administration to child care, a task that included trying to stop the little baby from freezing to death.

"Scotland was hit by one of the severest winters ever experienced for about twenty years," says Katie. "The only source of heat in the cottage was an ancient wood-burning range in the kitchen, which filled the room with smoke if there was even a hint of dampness on the logs. It was pure hell. I think Max spent the first six weeks of his life, day and night, cocooned in an old sleeping bag that, judging from the smell, had been at one time occupied by a family of mice. I think that was when I reached my lowest point. I just longed to be back in our old life in Plymouth."

I bet you did, thought Dan.

A year and a half later Sooty (8, pictured right) was born, making her first appearance into the world with a mass of jet black curly hair. Although christened Sacha, the nickname that Patrick gave her on first seeing his new daughter in the hospital has stuck. "Sooty's arrival spurred Patrick into action," says Katie. "He knew that if I was to go through yet another freezing winter with two children, let alone one, then he ran the risk of losing his whole family. By this time, we were beginning to see the light at the end of the tunnel with Seascape, so Patrick managed to persuade the bank to let him take out a mortgage on a nearby farmhouse that was being sold by the estate from which we rented the cottage. The house was pretty run-down, but at least it had an oil-fired Rayburn and central heating, so my days of shifting around armfuls of wood thankfully came to an end!"

Getting up from the table, Dan walked over to the fridge and took out another can of beer. He flicked the ring pull and took a drink. He was beginning to have a certain amount of admiration for this family stuck away up in the north of Scotland. They may have been mad, but by God, they were resilient. He sat back down and found his place in the article.

Living on the breadline, however, continued to be the name of the game for the Trenchard family. One of the ways in which Katie embraced this culture was by starting to make clothes for her children, using off-cut fabrics that she bought from the local drapery store in Fort William. Her design principle was based on what her children seemed to be comfortable wearing. Baggy trousers in brightly coloured brushed cotton with elasticated waists, and big pockets in which useful things like toy tractors and crumbling biscuits could be stored. The design for her skirts followed a similar vein. Next came sweaters with wide, easily rolled up sleeves, and made out of a polar fleece material that Katie sourced from a factory in Inverness which specialized in clothes for hillwalkers and mountaineers.

"What I hadn't bargained for," continues Katie, "was the demand from mothers at Max's playschool for me to make similar clothes for their own children. At the time, we needed every bit of spare cash that we could

lay our hands on, so the kitchen became like the Tailor of Gloucester's workroom!"

One of her greatest aficionados, however, just happened to be the nine-year-old son of the chief executive of the Local Enterprise Company, a burly red-bearded Highlander called Rhuraidh MacLeod. Rhuraidh was a good friend of Patrick's, having helped him on a feasibility study for an expansion plan for Seascape, so there seemed nothing unusual in his visiting their house one evening with a clump of papers stuck under his arm.

"He wasn't there to talk about Seascape, though," says Katie. "He wanted to talk to me about my clothes."

Over a glass of whisky, Rhuraidh explained that there was a small clothes manufacturing unit on the same industrial estate where Patrick's plant was based that had just lost its main customer, a large retail chain in the south that had decided to cut costs by moving its manufacturing base to Eastern Europe.

Quite right too, Dan thought to himself. I'd have done the same. He turned the page. There was another photograph, this time of a brooding young male model with thick brown hair worn fashionably messy and a crucifix dangling from his left earlobe. He was wearing a black T-shirt that fell well below the waistline of his open bomber jacket and a pair of trousers cut like army fatigues, their cuffs caught up on the padded tops of his Nike trainers. The image took up the whole page with the typeset of the article wedging the young man in from all sides. It was large enough for Dan to be able to make out a label with the name Vagabonds sewn onto the right-hand side pocket of the trousers.

"Rhuraidh said that the twenty jobs that were to be lost at the factory might not seem that much, but it would be felt like a hammer blow in such a small community as Fort William. He felt, however, that it could be saved, and before he took his leave of us that evening, he presented Patrick and me with a brief, three-page document which outlined his plans."

Rhuraidh MacLeod had given the company a working title, Vagabonds, a word that Katie had heard him use quite often to describe his young, hyperactive son. He envisaged the new company to be mail order, so that manufacturing, ordering, and packaging could all be handled from the same unit, and payment for articles would be up front. Rhuraidh's idea was that the workforce should be laid off for two months during which time he had set Katie the monumental task of sourcing fabrics, producing samples, and photographing the catalogue while he would use the expertise in his office to set up the computer system and buy in mailing lists.

"It was pretty daunting," admits Katie, "but the carrot that Rhuraidh cleverly dangled in front of my nose was that, for the first six months, manufacturing costs would be borne jointly by the Local Enterprise Company and the District Council.

"So I decided to take on the challenge—not so much because I wanted to do it, but more out of a sense of loyalty to Rhuraidh. If he had taken this much trouble to save twenty jobs, then it had to mean a great deal to him. So Vagabonds became the name of the company, and exactly two months after Rhuraidh's visit, the first little pair of baggy trousers with elasticated waist and oversized pockets rolled off the production line and were sent off to our first mail order customer. It was a very exciting moment!"

Two years later, when demand for Vagabonds was spreading right across Europe, Katie was approached by the headmaster of Fort William High School to help their final-year Art and Design students with design technique and manufacture.

"I agreed to do it, although somewhat reluctantly," says Katie. "I really felt that I couldn't spare the time. But thank goodness I did. Those kids were so much more in tune with what everyone was wearing, and from that first year onwards, I incorporated many of their ideas into the Vagabonds range of clothes. I always credited their names in the catalogue under the heading 'Designers,' which I think made them feel that they had hit the big time!"

Almost six years to the day since the company started, Katie has decided that the time has come to sell up.

"The company is now in the position to be taken to a worldwide market," says Katie, "and it needs someone with a greater business brain than I to be able to accomplish that! What's more, I have been so occupied with Vagabonds over the years that I feel that I have missed out on a great chunk of my children's lives. I just want to spend more time with them."

Dan looked up as the door of the kitchen opened and Josh walked in.

"Hi there. Where have you sprung from?"

"Upstairs," Josh replied, pulling the flex from the kettle and filling it up from the tap.

"Really? I thought I was alone in the house. Aren't you working tonight?"

"No. I couldn't be bothered. I rang in and said I was ill."

"Oh," Dan murmured before turning back to the magazine to read the final paragraph of the article.

"Vagabonds is not only a niche market, but our products would seem to be considered a classic, judging by our ever-escalating order book. It will quite simply run and run."

"Hey, Vaggas. Awesome wear."

Dan turned to find Josh looking over his shoulder at the magazine. "What?"

"Those trousers. They're called Vaggas."

Dan frowned quizzically at his son, then shot a glance back at the photograph of the young male model. "You mean you *know* about them?"

"Of course I do. They're Vaggas."

"Which I suppose has to be an abbreviation of Vagabonds, the name of the company that makes them."

"Whatever," Josh said, moving over to the sideboard to make himself a cup of coffee. "I just know them as Vaggas."

"But how on earth do *you* know about them?"

"I've seen them worn in the Inferno. They're great for clubbing, being loose-fitting and all that."

"Are you telling me that these trousers are considered 'cool wear'?"

Josh laughed. "No, I'm not telling you that because I wouldn't use a phrase like that. Maybe . . . um . . . 'ultimate' wear would be better."

"For heaven's sakes," Dan murmured incredulously, knowing that Josh's use of that word was reserved for only the best things in life.

"They're pretty difficult to get hold of, though. All I've ever managed to lay my hands on is one of their baseball caps, and that's because I nicked it off a friend. You know the one. It's got a *V* on the front with sort of squiggly bits at the side."

Dan nodded slowly. "Yes, that does ring a bell."

"I've tried to find the company on the Internet, but I don't think they've got a website. From what I gather, you can only buy them on mail order."

Dan flipped over the page to study once more the unassuming, countrified woman who had obviously stumbled upon a style phenomenon. "If these trousers are such a success, why has nobody ever tried to copy them?"

"I'm not sure—but if I was going to buy a pair, I'd only want them to be the genuine article. It's like you buying a pair of Levi's, isn't it? You wouldn't want to walk around in a pair of denims with the name of a supermarket stuck on your backside."

Dan took Josh's point with a flick of his head. "Probably not. So, in your opinion, the market for Vaggas, as you call them, could grow?"

"And how!" Josh replied, taking a swallow of his coffee and pulling out a chair for himself next to Dan. "I wouldn't think they're even scratching the surface yet. I'm not the only one who's been trying to get hold of a catalogue. Nobody even knows where the wretched company is based! I mean, whoever's running the business at present has no idea what a huge market he's missing out on."

"Seemingly, it's all run from the north of Scotland."

"Is it? Well, maybe the boss should lay down his bagpipes and get down here and do some marketing."

Dan slid the magazine across the table to Josh. "That's the 'boss' there," he said, stabbing his finger on the face of the woman. He could tell from Josh's expression that he was unimpressed, almost disappointed.

"Doesn't look particularly dynamic, does she?" Josh remarked.

Dan smiled. "Not really. But give her her due, she did start the company as a hobby. She's obviously done bloody well to get it to where it is now."

Josh drummed his fingers on the table. "Maybe, but what they need to do is find someone who really *knows* how to run a business like that. Like Mum, for instance. If she took it over, she'd just make the whole thing explode."

Dan bit thoughtfully at the side of his cheek. "I wonder. I mean, I don't doubt your mother's capabilities, but this really is a completely different kettle of fish. Rebecca Talworth's name was pretty well established before Jackie started building up the company."

"Dad," Josh replied, shaking his head, "go into any club that has a name for itself south of the river and ask if either the names Rebecca Talworth or Vaggas mean anything to them. I know what the answer would be."

"You're going to tell me Vaggas, aren't you?"

"Probably ninety per cent?" Josh hazarded a guess.

"This is unreal!" Dan stated incredulously. "I can't believe that something started from sewing scraps of cloth together in the north of Scotland should become sort of cult wear."

"Well, it seems to have worked." Josh drained his coffee. "Hey, that article doesn't give a contact number, does it?"

Dan flipped over to the end of the article. "No. Nothing. I suppose you could get it through directory enquiries."

"Yeah, I suppose." Josh rinsed out his mug under the tap. "Don't think I'll bother, though. I'm a bit skint at the minute. I'd just get tempted."

"They don't cost *that* much, do they?"

"About fifty quid, which is more than I can afford at the minute."

"Fifty quid! Bloody hell!"

"Well, they don't seem to have any difficulty shifting them at that price." Josh got up from the table, walked across the kitchen, and opened the door that led into the hall. "Listen, I'm going to have a quick bath, and then go around to see Phil Neilson. We were supposed to meet over the weekend, but we never got our acts together and he's heading back to university tonight."

Dan pushed himself to his feet. "Okay. Maybe see you later, then."

Josh nodded. "Are the girls not here?"

"No. They're spending the evening with one of Millie's friends."

"Right. Are you okay by yourself, then?"

Dan smiled at his son's unnecessary but kindly concern. He shot him a wink. "I'm fine. Thanks."

As he heard Josh's footsteps ascend the staircase at speed, Dan picked up the Sunday magazine that he had initially sought out and took it over to the table. He pushed the *Woman's Weekly* to the far side of the table and sat down. He read one paragraph of an article about some high-flying interior designer in London, but his mind was elsewhere. His eyes went back to Battersea Gran's magazine. He reached over the table and drew it towards him, opening it once more at the photograph of Katie Trenchard and her two children.

If Josh was really right about this, then maybe it was worth finding out a little more about the company. If there was this huge untapped market, then maybe it could be a winner. He'd always gone on about something turning up. He'd never believed in omens, but nevertheless, the way that this had come to light was all pretty strange. A woman's magazine given to him by his mother for some ghastly recipe, the article, the company for sale, and then Josh telling him that their product was one of the hottest things around. Maybe he was right about Jackie's expertise. Of course, she had her job with Rebecca Talworth, but if he were to take on the management of the company, they could work on the marketing together. In fact, doing something in which they both had a common interest might be the stimulation their relationship needed at that precise moment.

Dan pushed back his chair and pulled out the drawer in the table. After a bit of rummaging, he found a blunt pencil and one of Nina's old exercise books. He creased it open at a blank page. Right, he thought to himself, let's give this a bit of thought.

I. Source a manufacturer in Eastern Europe. Cheaper production costs.

II. Mail order *and* Internet sales. Spread the market worldwide.

III. No need to live in Scotland. Could run everything from Haleridge Road.

IV. Not stock, though. Need to rent a small industrial unit nearby.

V. Fabrics, designs, etc. No knowledge of that. Maybe have to keep Katie Trenchard on as design consultant for a year. On second thought, maybe not. Contention between her and Jackie?

VI. Funding. Mortgage house? Idea dismissed. Telephone Nick Jessop to see if he could wangle a short-term loan without collateral through Broughton's.

Nick. Of course. That was exactly to whom he should be talking. Dan got up from the table and walked over to the telephone. He dialed his number from memory.

"Nick?"

"Hi, Dan."

Dan heard a loud splash of water in the background. "Sorry, have I caught you at a bad time?"

"Sort of. I'm just giving Tarquin his bath. Hang on a minute while I get him out."

Dan waited, hearing Nick's muffled voice talking away to his son.

"Right," Nick said eventually. "That's him sorted. I hope you're not ringing up to do more gloating about that result yesterday."

Dan laughed. "Now would I do a thing like that?"

"Yes, too bloody right you would!"

"Well, you have to admit, it *was* a pretty good match. Anyway, thanks, Nick, for getting me those tickets."

"No problem."

"Listen, that isn't actually the reason for the call. You're a wealth of information about all things to do with young children, and I just wondered if you had ever heard of a mail order company called Vagabonds?"

"Yes, sure I have."

Dan was momentarily struck dumb by Nick's instantaneous reply. "What? You *know* of them?"

"Of course I do. It's a pretty well-known company. I think Laura came across them about a year ago. She gave a pair of their trousers to one of her godchildren, and we've been getting their catalogues ever since. In fact, Laura was thinking of ordering up pairs for both herself and Tarquin." Nick's voice went distant. "Weren't we, my little man?" His mouth came back to the receiver. "So, why this sudden interest in Vagabonds?"

"Oh, no particular reason," Dan replied airily. "It's just that I read an article about the woman who started it." He paused for a moment. "So, do you know others who buy from Vagabonds?"

"Sure. I couldn't tell you right now who they are, but yeah, I've seen adults and kids of all ages wear the trousers."

"Right. And you think it's probably quite a well-run company."

"I've no idea, Dan, but I reckon it would be more successful than many of the other mail order companies. For a start, their catalogue is brilliant."

"Do you have one there?"

"Not right beside me. I'm actually in the bathroom, Dan."

"You wouldn't be able to give me a telephone number, would you?"

Dan heard Nick let out a long sigh. "Well, you'll have to hang on a minute. The catalogue is downstairs somewhere."

"Okay. Sorry about this."

The LCD readout on Dan's portable telephone registered a further three minutes before Nick came back on the line. "Right. Are you ready for this?"

"Fire away," Dan replied, hovering his pencil over Nina's exercise book.

"Telephone number is 01397 890000 and fax is 01397 890110. There doesn't appear to be an e-mail number."

"No, that's fine. Many thanks, Nick."

"Okay. Can I return to the peace of my Sunday evening routine now?"

"Of course you can, my son. With my blessing."

Dan didn't even bother to hang up the receiver. He pressed the button to disconnect the line and then immediately dialed the number that Nick had given him. He just planned to leave a message on the Ansaphone and get them to send off a catalogue to him. He never imagined for one moment that, on a Sunday night, his call would be answered.

"Hullo?" It was a woman's voice, shrill and questioning, and it gave Dan the immediate impression that his telephone call was not particularly welcome. In the background, there seemed to be a steady, rhythmic thrumming that was loud enough to make Dan hold the receiver an inch or two away from his ear.

"I'm sorry," Dan said. "I'm not sure if I've got the right number. I was trying to get hold of a company called Vagabonds."

"What?" the voice shouted. It was then that Dan realized that her shrill tone was probably only a consequence of the background noise.

"Vagabonds. Is that Vagabonds?" Dan asked distinctly.

"Yes. Sorry. I should have said that, shouldn't I? It's just that we're a bit hectic here."

"Well, I was expecting to talk to an Ansaphone. I didn't think that anyone would be working on a Sunday night."

"Sorry, I didn't catch that. I'm afraid that I'm in the workshop and all the machines are going."

Dan decided then that it wasn't going to be worth asking for a catalogue. Better all round if he called back in the morning. On the other hand, he couldn't just hang up.

"Am I talking to Katie Trenchard?" Dan asked, stepping up the volume of his voice.

"Yes. Who's that?"

"You don't know me, but my name is Dan Porter. I live in London."

"Yes. Excuse me, can you hold the line for a moment, please?" Dan heard a muted question being asked and the woman replying, "No, just finish off the XLs tonight. We can put out the Ls tomorrow evening." She returned to the receiver. "I'm sorry. How can I help you?"

"Right, well, I've just read this article about you in a magazine."

"Magazine, yes." Another machine seemed to have been added to the general cacophony of background noise, this one being situated not very far from Katie Trenchard's mouthpiece.

"And there were a couple of photographs too."

"So you'll want to come up to see me."

"What?" Dan asked, taken aback by the woman's directness.

"When do you want to come up, then?"

Dan felt strangely bemused. My word, he thought, it's not a wonder this woman has made a success of her company if she's able to catch people off guard like this. "Hold on, I wasn't thinking exactly . . ."

"What?"

Dan took a deep breath to steady himself. "I just wanted to ask a few questions."

"That's fine. I'm quite happy to do that. How about sometime this week then?"

Dan now began to laugh to himself. Katie Trenchard was obviously a born seller. All he had been meaning to do was to ring up for a catalogue, and here he was, on a Sunday night, being invited up to the wilds of Scotland as a prospective buyer of her company. He, Dan Porter, who had never been north of Manchester in his life!

"Erm," he muttered, trying to think of some way of stalling her for a moment. "Right; just let me have a look in my diary." He clamped his hand over the receiver. What the hell was he doing? Just say "Thanks, but no thanks" and end the call. He stared down at the notes he had made in Nina's exercise book. Come on, you fool, he thought to himself, there *is* an opportunity here. You know that. If you just say you're not going to go, you'll regret it in the long run. And anyway, why the hell suddenly be so cautious? You were never that way in the City.

Dan made a quick surmise of his present domestic situation. Jackie was in Paris, back on Tuesday; the kids were at school for the week; Battersea Gran would probably be able to come round and look after them and the dogs. So why should he not just go? It would probably do him a load of good to get away from the house and from London for a couple of days. What's more, even if nothing came of it, it would at least give Jackie the impression that he was actively pursuing some form of gainful employment.

He took his hand away from the receiver and held it to his ear. The background noise seemed to have increased in volume. "When could I come up?" he asked.

"What? Listen, I'm sorry. I'm going to go outside the building." Dan heard a door slam and immediately the noise became a distant hum. "That's better. Now, what did you ask me?"

"When would it be suitable for me to come up?"

"Well, the earlier part of the week would be best. I'm going to be away all day tomorrow, but Tuesday would be good."

"Right. And what's the best way of getting to where you are?"

"Did you say you were based in London?"

"Yes."

"Well, there's an overnight sleeper that goes direct from Euston to Fort William. That gets you here at about a quarter to ten in the morning. Or you could fly to Glasgow, and then take the train. Either way, if you call this number when you get to the station, I could get someone to meet you."

"Okay." Dan took a deep breath. "So Tuesday's fine with you?"

"Absolutely. I look forward to meeting you . . . er . . . sorry, what was your name again?"

"Dan Porter."

"Right . . . Dan. And, as a matter of interest, what was the magazine again?"

Dan walked over to the table and flipped it over to the front cover. *"Woman's Weekly."*

"Oh, all right then." Her reply seemed flat, almost registering a slight air of disappointment. "I'll see you Tuesday, then."

THE TELEPHONE CALL to Battersea Gran was brief. She was quite happy to look after the children for a couple of days, but for once she kept the conversation brief, being engrossed in her regular Sunday night viewing of *Monarch of the Glen.* Dan put down the receiver with a wry smile on his face. If she had but known that he was heading off to a place that had to be similar in many ways to the untamed wilds of Glen Bogle, then she would have gleaned from him every last bit of information about his motives for going—as well as asking him to get Susan Hampshire's autograph while he was there.

Dan left the kitchen and ran up the two flights of stairs to his office. He pressed the START button on his computer before returning to the landing.

"Josh?" he called down the stairwell.

He heard a splash from the bathroom.

"What?"

"Come up to my office when you're finished, would you?"

He went back into his office and sat down at his desk, simultaneously clicking the mouse on the Internet icon. By the time Josh appeared, still dripping wet with a towel wrapped around his lower torso, Dan had the train schedule from Euston to Fort William up on the screen.

"Yeah?" Josh asked.

"Listen, I'm going up to Scotland for a couple of days," Dan said, without taking his eyes away from the screen.

"You're what?"

Dan laughed. "I'll be back on Wednesday or Thursday, depending on train times. I've called Battersea Gran and she's coming over to look after you all until Mum gets back."

"Why on earth have you decided to go up to *Scotland*?"

Dan bit on his lip, then turned to Josh. "I'll tell you only if you promise that it won't go any further."

Josh raised his eyebrows. "In-trigue."

A new page had come up on the screen. Dan made a selection before continuing. "I'm going to take a look at that company, Vagabonds."

"*Vagabonds*?" Josh asked. "For what reason?"

"Because it's up for sale."

Josh let out a short, derisive laugh. "Hang on, you've lost me. You're not saying that you're thinking of buying it—are you?"

"Well, let's just see, shall we? You said yourself that the market has hardly been scratched. I think it's worth finding out a bit more about them."

"Wow!" Josh exclaimed in quiet incredulity. Dan felt a light punch on his left shoulder, and he turned to look at his son who was slowly nodding, a grin of "ree-spect" on his face. "Nice one, Dad. Go for it."

"Keep it to yourself, though."

Josh gave him a wink and tapped the side of his nose with a forefinger. "Mum's the word."

Dan smiled and shook his head. "No, Josh, that is definitely *not* the word."

CHAPTER TEN

As JACKIE ENTERED her hotel bedroom that evening, a soft wedge of reddened sunlight flooded across the thick patterned carpet, eventually trapping itself under the footwell of the small leather-inlaid desk that stood against the wall. Throwing her hand-bag onto the bed, she took a coat hanger from the wardrobe and hung up her suit jacket, then walked across to the full-length window and opened it. She leaned her hands on the wrought iron guardrail and breathed in the warm air, filled with the rich aromatic smells of the city, as she looked out over the glinting skyline of Paris from her vantage point on the heights of Montmartre. The incessant traffic hummed busily below her on the Boulevard de Clichy, broken now by the melodious bells of Sacré Coeur calling out the evening mass.

A smile of contentment brushed across her mouth. Everything had gone to plan over the weekend—the meeting with the Chambre Syndicale, the suitability of their venue in the Bourdelle Museum. And what's more, she had received e-mails both from the agency in London confirming the model bookings and from the set designer saying that all would be completed by the time that she returned to London.

Back to London. The mere thought of it immediately replaced her calm with a stomach-knot of agitation. She loved having her own space, being able to return to her hotel bedroom every evening and relish the successes of each day. She couldn't do that in London. Every evening was the same when she returned to the house in Clapham. No matter what her mood, the oppressive atmosphere of gloom and despondency that emanated throughout the place would envelop her and she would almost physically sense her own character being overpowered by ill-feeling and contempt. And she knew that it was Dan who was wholly to blame for bringing about that change in her.

Taking in a long, steadying breath, Jackie closed her eyes and concentrated on locking those bad thoughts away. She cast her mind back over the past few days and realized that since boarding the Eurostar at Waterloo Station, she had neither been stressed nor bad-tempered. She had had no reason to be, or what was maybe more accurate, nobody had given her reason to be.

Yet she hadn't been by herself, had she? When Stephen had first suggested that he come with her to Paris, her immediate reaction had been to put him off the idea. She had wanted to be free from male company, to do her own thing without having to make the effort of conversing with another man. But she had realized soon after their arrival in Paris that the disruption at home and the possible problems that she thought might arise during her visit had left her feeling quite vulnerable and unsure as to whether she would be able to cope. Over the course of the weekend, Stephen had proved himself to be a true friend and a wonderful support, and being in the company of someone so much younger than herself and without having the burden of her family weighing constantly on her mind had made her feel enlivened and youthful and carefree.

That day, having wrapped up their workload by noon, they had enjoyed a prolonged lunch together in one of the small restaurants below the steps of Sacré Coeur, where cars rattled at speed along the cobbled street. The waiter, dressed in a starched white ankle-length apron, served the six tables with an unquestioning attentiveness, and although Jackie had tried to banish the idea from her mind, she could not help but sense a notion of illicit romance about them being together, tucked away in the little backstreet restaurant, with the warming flow of red wine in her throat and the lingering tang of garlic on her tastebuds. As she and Stephen had laughed together across the table, she had had a momentary pang of guilt, thinking that if she *had* made the trip with Dan, maybe it would have been beneficial to their relationship. But even that one fleeting thought had pervaded her being with a shivering anxiety and she had dismissed it immediately, determined to free herself of reality for as long as their trip lasted.

A rhythmic knock on her bedroom door broke her away from her thoughts. She closed the window and walked across to the door and opened it. Stephen stood outside in the corridor, a grin on his face and a bottle of champagne and two glasses in his hands. He raised them up, a questioning slant on his mouth.

"How about a bit of a celebration?"

Jackie leaned a hand against the door, a barrier against his entry. "I thought that's what we were doing at lunchtime."

"This one's on me," he said, sidling his way past her into the bedroom.

"I really think that I've had enough," Jackie stated without moving away from the door. It could have been taken as a flat refusal, had she not followed it with a bubble of laughter as she watched Stephen disregard her opinion entirely, untwisting the wire and exploding the cork from the bottle. He poured a froth of champagne into each glass, waiting for it to settle before topping both up. He held out a glass at arm's length towards her, leaving Jackie no option other than to shut the door and walk over to take her glass.

"Here's to you, then," Stephen said, clinking his glass against hers.

"And to you, too. I think we've both done a pretty good job sewing up all the loose ends." Jackie took a mouthful of champagne, feeling it pierce the sides of her mouth like icy needles before slipping in a cold cascade down her throat. "Ooh, that is delicious."

She would have put her hand over the top of her glass, but Stephen moved too fast for her. He filled it to the brim once more. "I don't think that *we've* done a pretty good job. It was entirely you. I've never felt such a spare prick in all my life. I admit that, on this occasion, I was wrong. One head turned out to be infinitely better than two."

"That's not true. I'm really glad you came."

Stephen paused. "Are you?"

"Yes. I know now that I did need the moral support."

Stephen moved towards her. "Listen, I hope you don't mind me doing this, but I find it rather disconcerting talking to you with that speck of dirt on your face." He reached up and brushed the side of her cheek gently with his thumb. The particle disappeared, but Stephen kept his hand inches away from her face, trying to judge what her reaction had been to his touch. He felt butterflies rise in his stomach when Jackie made no attempt to move away from his outstretched hand.

"Must have got there when I was at the window," she said. "Has it gone?"

"Yes," he replied. "Your face returns once more to its usual perfect flawlessness." He inched his hand back and rested it against the peach-smoothness of her skin. Then he felt the pressure as her head tilted to his touch. That was enough. He didn't need to know any more right now. She had showed willingness by that one almost imperceptible action. But he had to play this game so carefully. Everything depended on it—his job, the future. He dropped his hand to his side, noticing as he did so a momentary look of surprise on Jackie's face. He smiled at her, knowing that she would probably take it as one of affection. Only he knew that it was indeed one of satisfaction.

"I'm sorry," he said, placing the offending hand in the small of his back. "That was uncalled for. I shouldn't have done that."

Jackie shook her head. "There was no harm in it." She smiled. "At least we're both adult enough to know that it couldn't have been taken any further."

"Of course not." He filled up his champagne glass and took a swig. "What would you have done, though?"

"What do you mean?"

"If I had tried to take it further."

Jackie shifted her glance away from Stephen. He noticed a pinky glow rise to her cheeks, but he had an idea that it was embarrassment, or maybe a flush of excitement that had caused it, rather than anger at his suggestion. "I'm a married woman, Stephen, with three teenage children. You shouldn't ask me that kind of question."

Stephen shrugged his shoulders. "Maybe you're right. I do know, however, that you have been in better form over these past few days than I have ever witnessed in all the time that I've known you. The trouble is that I *know* the reason for that, because you've told me—on more than one occasion. When we walked into that restaurant today, I saw men stop eating and turn to look at you, and I can tell you that to be able to draw a Frenchman's attention away from his food takes some doing. I bet that if you had stopped to tell *them* that you were the mother of three teenage children, you would have been met by a chorus of *'Mais ce n'est pas possible!'* I tell you, I was proud to be with you, even though it was under slightly, well, false pretences."

Jackie smiled at him. "That's a very kind thing to say."

"For heaven's sakes, I'm not being *kind*! Don't demean yourself! I'm being 'kind' when I go to visit my granny in her sheltered accommodation in Welwyn Garden City. I'm being 'kind' when I scratch the tummy of the smelly old spaniel that my parents dote on, even though I'd rather guide it out of the house with a boot. You've got a long way to go before I start being *kind* to you."

Jackie said nothing and looked away.

Stephen drained his glass. "I can take a hint." He moved close to Jackie, and placing his hands on her shoulders, planted a loud, brotherly kiss on her forehead. She closed her eyes and Stephen could sense by the way her head tilted back that she would probably be a willing recipient for something a little more intimate. But he left it there. If anyone was to make the first move, it had to be her. He turned and walked across to the door and opened it. "Use your days here well, Jackie. While you're happy and relaxed, which I know you are, just try to work out exactly what it is that you want to do. You're a beautiful, clever woman with a wonderful sense of humour, and I love being with you—as would any man. So please don't spend the rest of your life in discontent and bitterness. It would be such a waste."

Jackie stood where he had left her, her arms crossed as she looked down at the floor and traced the point of her shoe around the pattern of the carpet.

"I'll give you a call, say about nine o'clock, and we can go out to get something to eat, all right?" Jackie seemed not to have heard him. "All right?" he repeated.

She looked up at him and nodded.

Closing the door behind him, Stephen thrust his hands deep into his pockets. Dammit, maybe he had pushed it too far at the end. There was no way of knowing whether her silence was out of contempt for his forthrightness, or whether she was already considering what he had said. He felt a momentary frisson of guilt, knowing that he had been playing an uncompromising game with her own deep vulnerability. He let out a sigh and started off along the corridor towards the lift. He pressed the button and watched as the lift lumbered its way down towards him. As it pinged to a halt, he heard a door open at the end of the corridor.

"Stephen?"

Jackie stood in the open doorway, her arms still crossed, and he felt the butterflies rise once more in his stomach when he noticed that it enhanced the deep cleft of her breasts into which he had played the reflected light of his cufflink days before.

"Yes?"

She did not reply immediately, but raked back her blond hair with her fingers.

"You don't need to go yet."

She turned and walked back into her room, leaving the door open and ready for him.

CHAPTER ELEVEN

D URING THE PAST twenty years, the life of a banker had taken
Dan to many far corners of the world. He liked to think of
himself as a seasoned traveler, flying in the relative comfort of
business class to America and Europe, to Russia and Australia, to the
Middle East and the Far East. Over the years, he had worked out how
to combat jetlag so that he was able to get off a plane and go straight
into a meeting without feeling that his brain was swimming in syrup.
But never, in all the time that he had been circumnavigating the globe,
had he experienced quite such an uncomfortable journey as the one
that he was undertaking now, as the overnight sleeper from Euston
rocked and juddered its way northwards towards Scotland.

By three o'clock in the morning, he had all but given up trying to
get any sleep. The coarse linen sheet and meagre woollen blanket that
were his allotted coverings for the night seemed to be drawn magnet-
ically towards the floor, and he had had to get up at least five times
(twice thumping his head on the extremely hard wooden edging of the
upper bunk) to try to work out yet another way of getting the bloody
things to stay on his bed. If the stifling heat in the compartment had

been consistent, then he wouldn't have bothered, but every now and again the heating system would go into reverse thrust and the temperature would drop sharply to a level that would render a sealskin-clad Eskimo incapacitated with frostbite.

His traveling companion, a rotund tractor salesman from some market town just outside Glasgow, was having no such problems in sleeping. He had engaged Dan in lively conversation from the moment that he had entered their shoebox-sized compartment and Dan had understood absolutely nothing of the guttural soliloquy that had been imparted to him. It had been even more disconcerting when the man had started to undress himself in an area that only allowed for one foot to come into contact with the floor at any one time. Dan had wedged himself into the corner of his bunk, watching in trepidation as the man's huge, boxer-shorted backside came ever closer to him. It reminded him too much of a film in which an unfortunate Mafia victim came to a grisly end inside a giant hydraulic scrap metal press. The man had then heaved himself up the ladder to his bunk (Dan had averted his eyes at that point as the boxer shorts left nothing to the imagination), turned off his light, thumped his pillow twice, broke wind loudly, and immediately fell into a deep and sonorous sleep.

Having eventually sorted out his cover problem by wrapping both sheet and blanket tightly around him, Dan had contorted himself back onto the bunk and eventually fallen into a fitful sleep. It seemed like only ten minutes before there was a sharp rap at the door. The tractor salesman slept peacefully on, so it was left to Dan to reach up and open the door to the attendant.

"Glasgow in half an hour," the thin, waistcoated man said, his breath staled by cigarettes, as he thrust a small tea tray into Dan's hand.

"It's not for—"

But the attendant was obviously working to a tight schedule because he was already banging on the next door before Dan could finish his dozy remonstration.

There could be few more awkward situations in life than to be starved of sleep, then handed a tray that contained boiling hot tea whilst lying prostrate on the bottom of two shelves and wrapped in swaddling clothes. Fixing his sandpapered eyes on the level of the tray, Dan first tried sitting up, but his upper body had only reached an angle of forty-five degrees before his head came into contact with the top bunk. He then tried lifting his legs but only managed to hold the position of a bent banana for a few seconds. After a moment's intensive thought, he decided to attempt a rolling action, but again was thwarted when the teapot slid precariously to the edge of the tray. It was only that near disaster that shot a bolt of adrenaline into his befuddled mind and enabled him to engage a small measure of lateral thought. He found beside him the small shelf that was specifically designed for the purpose of holding the tray, and having rid himself of the element of danger, he was able to unravel himself from his bedclothes and stand up.

Dan gave the man a friendly shove. "Excuse me, but it's time for you to get up."

The tractor salesman grunted and somehow managed to turn his overweight body around on the plank-sized bunk. Had Dan not ducked to retrieve the tray at that precise moment, he would probably have been knocked senseless because the man's arm flailed out across the open floor space.

"Whassamatter?"

That was when Dan lost his cool. He stood on the bottom rung of the ladder, unclipped the shelf above the man's head, and thrust the tray upon it. "It's time for you to get your fat arse out of that bed, mate. The train will be stopping in Glasgow in five minutes."

The man woke immediately and stared wide-eyed at Dan. "All right, laddie. Keep your hair on," he whined defensively.

Those were the last words that passed between them. Dan lay on his bunk, head turned towards the wall, as he listened to the man hurriedly wheeze his way through his dressing routine. He then thumped his suitcase off the luggage shelf, opened the door, and was gone. Dan reckoned that it was a good twenty minutes before the train eventually stopped in Glasgow, and with a satisfied grin on his face, he fell into a deep sleep.

"Fort William in half an hour."

Dan had been ready for the attendant this time. He had swung his legs off the bed and stood up as the door was opened so that when he received the tray, he was able to place it straightaway onto the tractor salesman's bunk. He closed the door and stretched out his cramped limbs, then turning around, flipped up the blind on the window. He blinked twice. "Bloody hell!"

The sky was the colour of dirty washing-up water and the dark hills were only just visible through a curtain of sleety rain. There didn't appear to be any sign of life forms. No roads, no houses, no animals. Nothing. It was a complete wilderness. This train was taking him to the ends of the world. For at least five minutes, he kept looking out the window, hoping, almost praying that he could find solace in seeing one twinkling light, one smoking fire, one moving car. But all that he witnessed were the hills getting higher and the day getting darker. Just before he turned away, he did manage to spot a huddle of sheep, crammed up tight together in the shelter of a stone wall, and he thought that their expressions of abject misery must have matched his own.

"You girls should all move to London," he muttered to himself as he turned away from the window. He let out a short, manic laugh. God, he thought, is this what happens when you come up to Scotland? You start talking to *sheep*?

Dan was quite heartened, yet somewhat amazed when at least thirty other fellow passengers disembarked from the train at Fort William. He also noticed that every one of them was much better equipped than he for the current weather. A jolly group of climbers, dressed in hooded anoraks and breeches and gaudy coloured socks, strode towards him along the platform, making light of their weighty rucksacks, and even less of the freezing sleet that blew about the unsheltered station. As they passed by, they shot amused smiles at each other as they saw Dan struggle with already numbed fingers to do up the zip of his trendy but totally inadequate leather bomber jacket. He was glad that they weren't around to witness his next move. He started out towards the station exit, with head bowed against the icy blast, and immediately stepped into a puddle that was deep enough to fill one of his Gucci loafers with congealed water. It was at that point that he almost felt like crying with frustration and misery. He stood on the platform, holdall in hand and leather shoulders sagging, wondering to himself what the hell he was doing there and wishing that he was back in the warm, familiar surroundings of good old Clapham.

He found a moderately sheltered bench in the lee of the ticket office and there took off his shoe and poured a rivulet of slush from its soft tan interior. He dried it out as best he could and then changed into his only spare pair of socks. By the time that he had finished, he was the only person on the platform, save for one extraordinary figure that stood by the exit, looking in his direction. He or she was dressed in a pair of black Wellington boots and a long red anorak with an attached hood, the drawstrings of which were pulled so tight about the face that it looked as if all necessary sensory functions were carried out by means of one rather large, red nose. Dan picked up his holdall and walked along the deserted platform towards the figure, and it was then that he was suddenly struck by its uncanny resemblance to the murderous Venetian dwarf in the film *Don't Look Now.*

"Are you Dan Porter?" a voice mumbled deep within the hood.

"Yes."

"Come on quickly, then. The van's outside."

There were no introductions, no pleasantries passed on how he had fared on the journey, no lighthearted apology for the state of the weather. At that precise moment, he almost felt like walking in completely the opposite direction to the obtuse, red-coated figure, seeking out a good hostelry, and staying there until such time as he could crawl, pissed out of his tiny mind, back onto the train for London.

He found consolation in the fact that the van was a brand-new Ford Transit with the word *Vagabonds* written in a wavy, multicoloured line along its side. At least that reassured him that he wasn't going to be taken off to some dank hovel on a remote hillside and tortuously cut into little pieces with a blunt bread knife. He waited at the side of the passenger door while the figure got into the driver's side and reached over to unlock it for him. He climbed in and felt immediately the comforting warmth of its interior. The engine was started and then the figure undid the drawstrings of the hood and pushed it back. For the first time, Dan was assured that his driver was a woman, and as she ruffled her spiky brown hair, he recognized her features from the photograph in Battersea Gran's magazine.

She turned to him, a smile on her bright, scrubbed face. "Hullo, Dan. I'm Katie Trenchard," she said, holding out a hand. "The weather's so bad that I thought I'd come to meet you rather than wait for your telephone call."

"Pleased to meet you," he replied. Shaking her hand was like gripping an icicle.

"I'm sorry that I didn't introduce myself earlier. You just looked so cold and miserable standing on the platform that I thought it would be best to get you into the heat before we started having any conversation. Anyway, how was your journey?"

"Interesting."

"Let me guess. You got no sleep, the heating blew hot and cold, and you shared your compartment with someone who snored."

Dan was amazed. "That's a bit *too* accurate. You didn't arrange it, by any chance, did you?"

Katie laughed. "No. It's just par for the course. The secret is to slip a tenner into the attendant's hand before you set off. They're usually very good at juggling around with the berths."

"Thanks for the tip. I'll make sure I do that on the way home."

Katie revved up the engine, engaged gear, and moved off towards the exit of the station car park. "Are you returning to London tonight?"

"Probably. I left the return open in case I needed more time up here." As they turned out onto the street, he looked out of the window at the people scurrying from shop to shop with their umbrellas angled in protection against the driving sleet. He let out a rueful laugh. "But I think that I'll try to get back there as soon as I can."

"So you don't think much of our wonderful weather, then?" Katie asked, her voice lilting with amusement.

"I can't believe that there could be such a change over five hundred miles. It was like summer when I left London last night. Is September always like this up here?"

"No, not at all. This is just a bit of a freak. The forecast is quite good for tomorrow." She glanced across at him. "So if you do stick around for another day, you won't be needing to invest in an unglamorous article like my anorak."

Dan looked down at his attire. The sodden leather jacket was now beginning to steam in the heat of the van and his damp jeans felt warm against his skin. Only his foot inside its greasy loafer refused to give any indication that it was thawing out. "I had no idea what to expect," he said quietly.

"Obviously not," Katie laughed.

Dan bit at his lip. "Okay, point taken."

"Sorry. I shouldn't laugh. It was just that you did look quite out of place on the platform back there."

"Just as you would have done if you had arrived at Euston with nothing but your nose revealed to the world."

"Maybe. I could have been taken for some eccentric Muslim woman, though."

Katie accelerated the van towards a set of traffic lights that had just changed from green to amber. She thought about crossing them, but at the last moment slammed her foot on the brakes, skidding the van to a halt. Dan felt a crashing blow on the back of his head and a millisecond later found himself hemmed in by long rolls of brightly coloured fabric.

"Heavens, are you all right?" Katie asked with concern as she pushed back the rolls into the rear of the van. "I hadn't realized that they were still there. They should have been taken into the factory last night."

Dan decided against passing comment about how his head felt. The dull thumping simply blended itself into his overall feeling of sheer discomfort. "Are we going there now?"

"Yes. It's on a small industrial estate just outside town. It's not very far away."

Ten minutes later, they crossed over an unmanned level crossing and drove through a set of gates beside which stood a large white sign announcing that they were entering the Cruach Industrial Estate. The road weaved through a line of long, low prefabricated units, the majority of which had untidy stacks of fish boxes and pallets outside their large blue doors. These were slid closed against the bite of the wind blowing in across the choppy waters of the sea loch, on the exposed shores of which the industrial estate was situated.

Katie pulled the van to a halt outside an unmarked building and switched off the engine. "This is it then. Home to my empire."

"Looks good," Dan replied, trying to sound enthusiastic as he surveyed the rusting pillars that supported the ineffectual porch above the glass-paneled entrance door, its paintwork weathered and peeling.

"Come on, then. We'll go inside and I'll make you a warming cup of coffee." She picked up a large canvas bag from the floor of the van and opened the door. She stopped halfway out and turned to him. "Heavens, it's just occurred to me that you've probably not had anything to eat. Would you like me to get you a bacon sandwich?"

"That would be great—if it's not too much bother."

"Not at all. I'll get Hilary to go round to the café for one."

As soon as Dan opened the door of the van, his nostrils were invaded by the overpowering smell of fish. Even though the wind was blowing in fresh across the loch, the odour had an irrepressible permanence about it as if it were deep-set into the fabric of the buildings and exuded through every warped crevice. Katie led Dan through the entrance door and into an open-plan work area, and immediately he could hear the hum of sewing machines from beyond the room. He spied, through the glass panel of an adjoining door, a line of women sitting intently at work.

The room in which he was standing was cluttered but businesslike with multipinned progress charts and Vagabond photographs lining every wall. The reception desk was manned by a young girl who had smiled broadly at him as he entered. Behind her, two women clicked away on the keyboards of their computers, talking as they did into hands-free mouthpieces. He heard one say in a lilting, friendly voice, "Good *morrrning!* Vagabonds. This is Maggie speaking. How can I help you?"

"Hilary," Katie said to the girl behind the reception desk, "this is Mr. Porter from London." The girl stood up and forthrightly shook Dan's hand. "Could you do me a great favour and pop round to the Greasy Spoon and get him a bacon sandwich?"

"Of course," she replied keenly, immediately retrieving her raincoat from the stand beside her desk.

Dan thrust his hand into his pocket for change. "Listen, I must—"

"No, don't be silly," Katie interjected. "I think the least we can do after your desperate trip to the frozen north is stand you to a bacon sandwich." She took off her anorak and hung it up on the coat stand, then pulled off her Wellington boots and kicked her feet into a pair of old brown sailing shoes with broken backs, an indication that changing her footwear was a pretty regular occurrence. It was the first time that Dan had seen her free from her somewhat unflattering rainwear and he was impressed with what he saw. He watched her as she walked over to where the electric kettle teetered rather precariously on one of the windowsills. She gave it a shake to check that there was sufficient water in it and switched it on. Although no taller than five and a half feet, she had a figure that was totally in proportion to her height. Her hips were slim, her bust was full but firm inside her blue cashmere polo-necked jersey, and although she was wearing a brightly coloured pair of Vagabonds, the generous cut of which would no doubt have delayed many a "heavier set" woman from going on a crash diet, he could tell that, in Katie's case, they were hiding from view a pert bottom and a shapely pair of legs.

"Right," she said, returning to where he stood at the reception desk. "While we're waiting for that to boil, would you like me to explain what's happening in here?"

Dan took off his leather jacket, which had begun to steam in the heat of the office and give off a smell like a bullock with a personal hygiene problem. "Could I hang this somewhere to dry? It's soaked right through."

"Of course," Katie said, taking the jacket from him. "I'm sorry. I should have thought."

She walked to the far end of the room and spread the garment over a radiator at the back of an unoccupied desk that Dan reckoned to be her own. "That should do it."

"Are you sure it'll be all right like that?" Dan asked, eyeing his precious jacket with concern.

"I would think so. It won't harm the leather, if that's what you mean."

Dan decided to trust her judgment. She, of all people, must know about that kind of thing.

"Okay, then," she said, stopping behind the two women who sat at the computer screens, talking incessantly into their mouthpieces. She put a hand on a shoulder of each. They turned to give her a brief smile without faltering in their conversations. "These two lovely ladies are Heather and Maggie. Come over here and I'll explain what they're doing."

Dan moved around the side of the reception desk and walked over to stand beside her.

"Best to look at Maggie's screen. She's just started to take an order." She paused as Maggie typed in the name of a Mrs. Catherine Swift. Dan watched as the screen immediately filled with Mrs. Swift's address, telephone number, and banking details. "That's what I like to see,"

Katie whispered to him. "A satisfied customer returning for more." She reached over Maggie's shoulder and pointed to one of the field boxes near to the bottom of the screen. "That shows that Mrs. Swift has already spent five hundred and eighty pounds with us this year."

Dan was impressed. "Are there many customers like her?"

"Oh, yes," she replied quite assuredly. "Once Maggie has finished this order, I'll ask her to bring up our Top Ten list. I'm pretty certain that you won't find Mrs. Swift's name on it."

Maggie pressed a key, and the address and banking details were re-placed by another screen format. She started to type in the order that was being given to her over the telephone.

"This is the stock handling format now," Katie explained. "Maggie types in what's required and then checks it against stock. If we have what the customer wants, then she reserves it and that's knocked off the stock list. If we don't have it, then it goes into a pending file. After each order is taken, it gets transferred to the monitor in the stockroom and, if all goes well, it should be in the post by the end of the day. If there is some part of the order that is pending, it gets printed out onto a manufacturing list, and along with stock update sheets, goes through to the girls in the workshop who then know what they have to pro-duce."

"Why do you bother printing out hard copy for them?" Dan asked. "Why don't you have a monitor in the workshop like you do in the stockroom?"

Katie smiled. "Because the girls in there don't like computers. We tried it once but it nearly ended in a walkout." She walked over to the kettle, which Dan had heard click off a minute before. "They much prefer good old-fashioned pieces of paper." She spooned instant coffee into a mug and poured in the water. "How do you like it?"

"Black's just fine."

As Katie handed him the mug, Hilary walked in through the front door of the office, the shoulders of her raincoat damp with rain and her long dark hair plastered against the sides of her face. She placed a silver foil package on the top of the reception desk, took off her coat, and then shook her head from side to side, spraying out water like a shaking dog. "My word, that's *horrible* out there," she exclaimed, tousling her hair with her fingers. She walked over to Dan and handed him the warm package before replacing her raincoat on its peg.

"I'm sorry about that, Hilary," Katie said. "I should have stopped by on the way here. I'm afraid my mind is a bit full of other things at the minute."

"Not to worry," the girl said brightly.

Dan smiled his appreciation at the young receptionist before she resumed her seat.

"What would you like to do?" Katie asked. "We could either sit down and have a chat now, or we could continue with the tour?"

"If it's all the same to you," Dan replied, "I think it might be best to leave questions to the end." Holding his coffee mug between arm and chest, he took the silver wrapper off the bacon sandwich and threw it in a wastepaper bin. "As long as you don't mind me having breakfast as we go."

"Not at all. Come on then, we'll start in the workshop."

Katie led Dan through the windowed door at the back of the office and immediately he was hit by the whirring discord of the sewing machines and the blare of pop music from the speakers that were suspended from the metal rafters above the shop floor. Dan counted twelve machinists, all bent in concentration over their work, running the brightly coloured fabric through their machines, working foot pedal and hands in complete synchronization. Beside each workstation was positioned a stack of plastic boxes on the sides of which were written a series of numbers, preceded by two letters. Dan noticed that no two boxes were the same.

Katie saw him studying them. "Those are the manufacturing codes," she shouted into his ear. "Different fabrics, different size garments, and different panels. Everything gets started at the back beside the cutting table and then moves forward, so that the finished article comes off over there by the door. Elsie here"—Elsie glanced up when she heard her name being mentioned, took one look at Dan, and went puce with embarrassment—"is doing pockets, and once she's finished this batch, she'll push her boxes on to Karen in front there who'll put in the elastic."

Katie led the way through the row of machinists to the back of the shop floor. As they walked, a shrill wolf whistle pierced the air and Dan turned to see the girl next to Elsie lean over and give her a teasing punch on the arm. Elsie's embarrassment was so intensified that her head almost disappeared into her lap.

Katie laughed. "Don't worry. They give that treatment to any man who walks in here. You actually got off quite lightly." She rested her hands on the edge of the large cutting table, and both she and Dan watched as a well-built girl wearing a baseball cap back to front deftly steered an electric cutting knife around a pattern that was laid upon a layer of fabric almost a foot deep.

"This is a pretty skilled job," Katie boomed out. "One slip of the knife and that whole lay of material may well have to be junked."

"Has that happened before?" Dan asked.

Katie smiled at him and moved close to the baseball cap. "Morag, he's asking if we've ever had to scrap a lay before?"

The girl's head jerked up to look at him, and Dan was quite taken aback by the obvious affront that flashed in her eyes. She shook her head once before resuming her work.

Dan could tell that Katie was suppressing a laugh. "There's your answer." She turned and made her way back towards the door. "It is without doubt these girls that have made this company, not me. They think nothing of working over the weekend or well into the night if we fall behind on manufacturing. I seem to remember that when you called on Sunday night, it was pretty late, wasn't it?"

Dan nodded.

"Well, there you are then. In a way, you've already been witness to it. They all take pride in what they do, and what makes it even better is that they're all my friends. We're just one big happy family."

Dan couldn't help but notice that there was almost a heaviness of heart in the way that Katie adulated her workers. As they returned to the office area, it came to him that of course she would feel that way. She was selling the business, after all, and the uncertainties regarding the future employment of her "family" had to be weighing heavily on her mind.

By the time that Dan had finished off his bacon sandwich and drunk his cup of coffee, they had completed the tour, having passed quickly through the high-shelved stockroom, with its neatly folded rows of trousers and jerseys, and the dispatch room, stacked with packets of tissue paper and smart blue boxes with *Vagabonds* written in gold italics across their lids. Returning to the reception area, Dan collected his holdall and followed Katie to the rear of the office. She pulled a chair away from the wall for him before sitting down at her desk.

"Right, then," she said. "Let's get to the questions. What would you like to ask me?"

Unzipping his holdall, Dan dug around to retrieve Nina's battered exercise book. "May I?" he asked, reaching across and taking a biro from the wicker pen tray on Katie's desk. He sat down on the chair and crossed his legs. "Well, let's start with the most important question. Can I ask you what your turnover is?"

Katie raised her eyebrows, seemingly startled by the forthrightness of the question. "Right." She hesitated briefly. "Well, I think that last year we were at about the half-million mark, but I reckon that the company will surpass it this year."

For a moment, Dan hovered pen above pad. He hadn't been expecting anything close to that. His mind raced back to what he and Josh had discussed in the kitchen in Clapham. If Vagabonds wasn't yet "scratching the market," then, by hell, it wasn't doing badly as it was. Still, he found it hard to believe that a business such as this was housed in what looked like a Nissan hut in one of the farthest outposts of the United Kingdom could ever be capable of achieving such a turnover.

"And your profit margin?"

Again Katie seemed perplexed by the question. She let out a sigh. "I couldn't give you an exact answer to that. You would have to speak to our accountant. Our manufacturing costs are pretty high, but I would never think of changing the way we work. Last year, I think we cleared about twenty-five thousand after wages, but most of that went into paying off a medium-term bank loan." She leaned forward on her desk. "Can I ask *you* a question?"

"Sure," Dan replied.

"Why would anyone reading *Woman's Weekly* be at all interested in profit margins?"

"I'm sorry?"

Katie sat back in her chair. "Well, surely they'd be more interested in, well, less mundane matters. In fact, I was rather surprised that you wanted to do an article about me so soon after the last one."

Dan frowned. "I'm afraid you've lost me."

Katie stared at him for a moment. "You're wanting to write an article on me, aren't you? For *Woman's Weekly*?"

Dan laughed. "No. What on earth gave you that idea?"

"But that's what you said on the telephone."

"I never said anything of the sort."

"But you are a journalist?"

"No, I certainly am not."

Katie's fresh-faced complexion seemed to drain of colour. "You're not from the Inland Revenue, are you? Because if you are, you'll have to—"

"Listen," Dan interrupted her, beginning to feel an itch of irritation niggle at his sleep-starved mind. "I saw an article about you in a copy of *Woman's Weekly* that my mother had given me"—that was a good start, he thought—"for some recipe or other, and I read it. I then rang you up and said that I wanted to speak to you about your company, and you told me to come up. So I have done exactly that."

"But why?"

"Because," Dan replied, his voice rising in frustration, "you said that you were selling your business and I thought that I might be interested in buying it."

Katie thumped a hand to her mouth. "Oh, no," she mumbled.

"What do you mean, 'oh no'?"

"I didn't hear you say that." She paused for a moment, biting at her bottom lip. "Oh my goodness, I think that I must have picked up the wrong end of the stick altogether."

Dan shook his head dismissively. "Oh well, there's no harm done."

"But there is," Katie replied quietly. "I've brought you all the way up here to Scotland for no reason."

"Well, let *me* be the judge of that."

"There's nothing to judge!" Katie exclaimed. "I sold the business two weeks ago!"

For a moment, Dan was rendered speechless. He sat staring at her as her words sank into his brain. "What do you mean? It can't be . . . I mean, so soon?" he stuttered. "I'd only just read about it in the magazine."

"Didn't you look at the date?"

"What?"

"The date on the *Woman's Weekly*. That article was published about four months ago."

Dan screwed up his eyes in disbelief. "You've got to be joking!" He leaned back in his chair and smacked his hands on his forehead. "For heaven's sake, I never even thought to look."

"I really am so sorry. If I'd known that—"

"No, no, it's entirely my own fault. I should have checked. It just never occurred to me."

Katie made a brave attempt at a smile. "Would you like another cup of coffee?"

"No . . . thank you." Jeez, he thought to himself, being out of work must have stagnated your brain. If someone in the bank had carried out such an appalling research job, he would have been out on his bloody ear! Moreover, what a waste of time! What a damned waste of *money*! "Can I ask who bought the business?"

"A young couple who wanted to downshift from London. I had three offers, one of them being higher than theirs, but they were the only ones prepared to keep the factory running up here."

Dan let out a deep sigh, and leaning forward, replaced the biro in the pen tray. "Well, that's that, then," he said, dropping Nina's exercise book back into the holdall.

"I feel awful about this," Katie declared, her teeth clenched in embarrassment.

"There's no need to. It can all be blamed on my own stupidity." Zipping up the holdall, he got to his feet and took his jacket off the radiator behind Katie's desk. He was pleased at least that it had dried out. "Well, I won't take up any more of your time," he said, putting on the jacket.

"I really am sorry that your trip was so abortive."

"As I said, it was my own fault entirely." He picked up his holdall. "Listen, you should maybe tell the new owners of the company that there is a huge untapped market for Vagabonds in London. My son told me that all his friends are after them. They are apparently the ideal wear for clubbing."

"Really?"

"That's what he says. They're supposedly deemed to be '*ultimate*' wear, and believe me, that's some praise coming from my son."

Katie rose to her feet. "In that case, I certainly will tell them." She pushed her hands into the pockets of her trousers. "What are you going to do now?"

Dan remembered his thoughts of earlier that morning about going into a local pub and anaesthetizing his chilly discomfort with drink. The idea of it had suddenly increased its appeal by at least the power of ten. "I'll just head back to town and kill time until this evening."

Katie started towards the entrance door. "I'll give you a lift, then."

"No, don't bother. I feel that I've wasted enough of your time already. I'd be grateful, though, if you could ask Hilary to call me a taxi."

Katie sucked her teeth loudly. "This is ridiculous," she said, marching across to the coat stand and taking down her anorak.

"What's ridiculous?" Dan asked as he followed on.

"I can't have you waiting in Fort William all day for your train."

"Look, please don't bother about—"

"Well, I'm sorry, but I do bother." She turned to Hilary. "I'm going to take Mr. Porter back to Auchnacerie, so if anything urgent crops up, you can get hold of me there." She dug her hand in the pocket of her anorak and took out a bunch of keys. "Right, come on then. Let's go."

"Where exactly are we going?"

"Back to my house."

Dan sighed quietly. Under the circumstances, he would much rather be alone in his own company with a large drink in hand. "I don't suppose it would do any good to raise an objection?"

"None at all. No matter what you say, I feel responsible for bringing you all the way up here under false pretences. It's the least I can do."

Dan shrugged his shoulders. "Okay. I'm in your hands, then."

Two minutes later, they were out of the industrial estate and heading westward at speed in Katie's bright red Volkswagen Golf GTI, having thankfully (for Dan's head) by-passed the Vagabonds van in the car park. The day had got no brighter, but at least the dark clouds that shrouded the surrounding hills were valiantly holding back the sleet.

"Nice car," Dan commented, not really wishing to make conversation, but thinking it would be rude if he just sat ruminating over his own incompetence.

"My little perk," Katie replied. "Vagabonds has literally taken over my life the past few years, so I felt I deserved some sort of reward for all the effort."

"I would have thought that you'd all have four-wheel drives up here."

"They're not necessary. If there's a bit of snow, a normal car will cope just as well, as long as you drive carefully." Katie smiled at him. "Is it not true that there are more four-wheel drives in London than there are in any other part of the country?"

Dan laughed. "I wouldn't know the statistics, but yes, there do seem to be quite a number of them around."

"Probably quite useful for getting over zebra crossings without getting stuck on pedestrians."

Dan sucked in a breath through his teeth. "Do I detect a hint of sarcasm in your tone?"

Katie chuckled. "Maybe just a little." She swung the car to the right and drove up a steep tarmacked gradient and pulled to a halt in front of a drystone wall, behind which Dan could spot every now and again the bobbing head of a child.

"Thank goodness! It's break time," Katie said as she turned off the engine. "Listen, I won't be a moment. I'm just going to pick up my daughter, Sooty. She wasn't feeling very well this morning, so I think a half-day off school might do her some good."

"As long as Max doesn't catch sight of you taking her away."

Katie frowned. "What?"

"Or maybe he's not at the same school."

Her eyes suddenly lit with understanding. She pointed a finger at him. "Of course. The magazine. You know it all." She pushed open the door. "You're right. Max is here, but he can get the bus back later. I will endeavour to spirit Sooty away without causing a scene."

Dan watched as she jogged across to the gates of the school and entered the playground. Finding himself alone for the first time since being given the news about the company, Dan now felt able to vent the pent-up rage at his own stupidity. He screwed up his eyes and knocked hard on his forehead with a clenched fist. "Shit. Shit. *SHIT!*" He thwacked a hand down on the plastic fascia, his voice resounding around the confines of the car. As he continued to rebuke himself under his breath, he witnessed a small pair of hands grasp the top of the playground wall and a carrot-topped head came into view, peering quiz-zically around. The boy caught sight of Dan, and then dropped behind the wall. Five seconds later, he appeared again, this time as if catapulted upwards. He swung his legs over the wall and sat staring at Dan, non-chalantly twiddling his thumbs.

At first Dan thought it best to ignore the boy. He pretended to play around with the catch of the glove compartment for a few seconds, but when he looked up, he still found himself fixed in the boy's beady gaze. Maybe he should say something to him. He tried the electric windows, but they didn't work without the ignition being switched on, so he opened the door a fraction, eager to keep the heat in the car.

"Hullo," he said, trying to sound bright and friendly.

The boy nodded once.

"What's your name, then?"

"Murdoch," the boy answered in a drawn-out monotone.

"So how old are you, Murdoch?"

"Eleven," the boy replied without altering the pitch of his voice.

"Right." Dan heaved out a sigh at the effort of trying to continue this stilted conversation. "And do you enjoy school?"

The boy shrugged his shoulders. "S'all right." He tilted his head slightly to the side. "Was that you?"

"What do you mean?"

"Was that you who called out 'shit'?"

Dan bit at his lip in embarrassment. "Ah, well, yes, I'm afraid it was. Sorry about that."

Murdoch thumped a fist down on the fingers of some unfortunate schoolmate who was grappling at the wall in an attempt to join him in his lofty position. "My dad never says 'shit.' "

"Quite right too. It's not a good thing to say."

"He says 'shite.' "

Dan cleared his throat. "Well, neither are very good words," he said, his voice sounding oddly schoolmasterly. "Better not to say them at all."

"No, probably not," Murdoch replied quietly, slipping back into his monotone.

Dan gave the boy a wink, feeling quite pleased with himself that his short lesson in the avoidance of bad language had obviously penetrated the carrot-topped head.

Murdoch, however, looked menacingly questioning again. "What about 'bugger'? Do you think that's a good word?"

Dan was mercifully spared from answering the question by a male voice that boomed out from the other side of the wall. "Murdoch! Get yourself down from there and into your classroom." The boy disappeared like a coconut that had been knocked off its perch in a fairground stall.

Dan was still staring at the vacant space when Katie, clutching the hand of a skipping girl with tousled dark hair, walked towards the car. She opened the door and pushed forward the seat, and the little girl clambered into the back.

"Sorry about that," Katie said, as she got into the car. "You were right. There was a bit of a showdown with Max."

"Not to worry. I was pleasantly entertained by a young man called Murdoch."

The little girl in the back of the car made a noise that sounded as if she was being violently sick. "Murdoch is *revolting!*" she cried out. "He picks his nose and *flicks* it at people."

"All right, Sooty," Katie protested as she reversed the car. "I don't think that we need to know that. Anyway, you haven't said hullo to Mr. Porter yet."

"Dan, please." Dan turned around and smiled at the young girl who was struggling with the buckle of her seat belt. "Hullo, Sooty. Nice to meet you."

"Where are you from?" Sooty asked without making eye contact with him.

"London."

"I fought so."

"Really? Now, how would you know that?"

"'Cos you sound as if you are off *Eastenders*."

"Sooty!" Katie exclaimed reproachfully. "You mustn't be so forward."

"But he does."

Dan laughed. "You're right too. Mind you, my accent used to be a lot stronger than it is now."

"Why has it changed?" Sooty asked.

"Probably working in the City all my life."

"Why does that change your accent?"

"Well, in the City, you work with different people from all over the world, and sometimes they don't speak very good English, so you have to make yourself understood as best you can. That means knocking out the accent a bit."

"Do I have an accent, Mummy?"

"I'm not sure," Katie replied. "Maybe you should ask Dan if you do."

"Do I, Dan?"

"Well, yes, I can tell that you're from Scotland. Your accent's not nearly as strong as Murdoch's, though."

"*Pleeease* don't talk about Murdoch," Sooty moaned. "He makes me feel ill!"

Dan shot a grimace at Katie who returned a similar expression. "Murdoch's father is a gamekeeper on one of the estates here," Katie said. "The whole family's a bit . . . well, how can I put it? A bit undisciplined."

Dan nodded. "That would seem to figure."

Katie stuck the car into third gear and edged out into the centre of the road to see if it was safe to overtake a large articulated lorry with foreign number plates and a logo of a fish on its tailgate. "So you work in the City, then?" she asked, accelerating past the lorry.

"I did, yes, for twenty years."

"Doing what?"

"For most of the time, investment banking."

"And now?"

"Nothing . . . at present. Just waiting for the right opportunity to come along."

Katie let out a sigh. "And you thought that Vagabonds might have fit the bill."

"It might have done."

"God, I feel so awful about that."

"Well, you don't have to. It was just a misunderstanding on both our parts."

"Mummy," Sooty piped up from the back of the car, "can you put on the tape?"

"No, angel, Dan and I are talking."

"But it's so *boring*! You can talk when you get home."

"Sooty!"

"I don't mind," Dan cut in, feeling that he too would like an excuse not to hear any more of Katie's heartfelt apologies.

"You haven't heard the tape yet," Katie murmured out of the side of her mouth.

She pressed the button on the stereo, and immediately the car was filled with the nasal tones of a man who sang in a Scottish accent far exceeding the bounds of wee Murdoch's humble offering.

There was a little girl who had one little goldfish, one little goldfish, one little goldfish,
There was a little girl who had one little goldfish, and the goldfish's name was Doris.

There was a little boy who had two little goldfish, two little goldfish, two little goldfish,
There was a little boy who had two little goldfish, and the goldfishes' names were Doris . . . and Horace.

The road meandered gently as it ran eastwards alongside a single-track railway line that followed the rocky shoreline of a dark-watered loch. As the little girl in the song acquired another goldfish called Clovis, Katie pointed a finger in front of Dan's chest.

"Our house is somewhere over there in the mist on the other side of the loch. I'm afraid that we have to go right up to the end and then back again to get to it."

"How far are you from Fort William?" Dan asked.

"About twenty miles."

"And you do the journey every day?"

"Not just once. I come home every day for lunch."

"That's eighty miles a day!"

"And more. I have to pick up the children from the school bus as well. It's probably nearer ninety." Katie glanced across at him. "Different from living in London, isn't it?"

"Just a little. On the other hand, one leg of your journey would most likely take less time than it would take me to travel from Clapham up to the City."

Katie changed up a gear once more and zipped past a slow-moving car. "Most likely."

Dan gave the fascia of the dashboard an appreciating pat. "And much more fun too."

By the time that they pulled off the road and drove through a pair of rough stone pillars, they had listened to Sooty's song three times. The tune now hung in Dan's brain like a constant taunt, and he had begun to make up names for the bloody goldfish that could never be mentioned, other than maybe at a rugby club dinner. The short drive led up past an unkempt garden with overgrown flowerbeds bordering a lawn that was in desperate need of mowing. In the centre of this hayfield, a large round trampoline with a gaping hole in the centre of its bouncing mat dripped inconsolably. The stone-built farmhouse, on the other hand, which was situated at the top of the garden, looked comforting and happy, its white-astricaled windows smiling out across the loch, despite the fact that its view was significantly curtailed by the low-lying mist.

Katie drove around to the back of the house and parked the car in one of a series of arched openings in a long, barnlike building, next to an ageing Mercedes estate car. She retrieved her canvas bag from the well at Dan's feet and got out of the car, pulling the seat forward for Sooty.

Dan squeezed himself out of the passenger door, trying to avoid bumping the lurid purple mountain bike that leaned against one of the heavy wooden beams supporting the floor of the loft above.

"Take care you don't slip on these flagstones," Katie said as she stepped deliberately across the courtyard to the back door. "They're an absolute deathtrap."

Dan brought up the rear as they entered the house and walked through a small glory hole, filled with gumboots and fishing rods and shelves stacked with DIY paraphernalia. Another door led into a large kitchen, which, despite its size, seemed equally as cluttered. A drying pulley, lined with clothes, hung above the Rayburn cooker, and the round leafed table that was pushed in against the curved window seat was piled with books and files and fabric samples. A large ginger cat, with its front feet tucked under its chest, sat upon the closed lid of a laptop computer and ignored their arrival entirely. Dan wondered why it had chosen that resting place in preference to the obvious comfort of the old sofa, with its plaid rug covering and piles of colourful cushions, situated against the wall next to the television.

"Would you excuse me for a moment?" Katie said, dumping her canvas bag on the table. "I just have to go upstairs." She walked across to a door wedged into the corner of the room by a large pine Welsh dresser. "Sooty will keep you company until I get back, won't you, Sooty?"

As soon as she had left the room, Sooty jumped onto the sofa, reached for the television remote, and switched it on. Hands on chin, elbows resting on the arm of the sofa, she became immediately absorbed in the antics of a cartoon dog that was frantically trying to bury a smouldering stick of dynamite. Dan glanced around at the countless examples of children's artwork that adorned most parts of the yellow walls, then as the television boomed out the demise of the unfortunate dog, he walked across to the window and stared out into the cold, grey shroud of mist that seemed to be balking any chance of brightness from the day.

He couldn't even begin to live with this kind of weather. Not day after day. Especially being stuck out in the middle of nowhere, with neither sight nor sound of another person for miles around. It began to dawn on him that the most thankful thing that had happened to him all day was that Vagabonds *had* been sold, and the best of British luck to the young couple from London who had bought it. If they weren't both clawing at the doors of the sleeper train within the next few months, then, more than likely, they were already flying pretty high over the cuckoo's nest.

Dan heard the sound of Katie's footsteps come down the stairs. She opened the door and walked in. "Right. What time is it?" She glanced up at the kitchen clock above the Rayburn. "A quarter to twelve. I suppose it's a bit early, but let's have some lunch anyway." She pulled open the door of the fridge. "Would you like a beer?"

"If you have one, that would be great," Dan replied.

Katie took out a can and lobbed it over to Dan.

"Now, what have we got?" she said, peering into the fridge. "Not a lot, I'm afraid. Tomorrow's usually the big shopping day, so we're pretty low on supplies. How about . . . cheese on toast and tomato soup?"

Dan pulled the ring off the can. "Sounds good to me."

Sooty had her lunch in front of the television while Dan and Katie sat on the window seat eating theirs. Katie resumed her questioning of Dan, and by the time that she had stacked the dishwasher with their bowls and plates and they had finished off their mugs of coffee, he had told her about the house in Clapham, about Jackie and her high-flying and demanding job, about Josh and his low-flying and undemanding job, and about Millie and Nina and their supreme wish that Dad would get another job so that they could return to their old school and be with their friends. Battersea Gran's name was explained in full, both Biggles and Cruise were discussed, and even his old mate Nick and doted-upon son Tarquin got a mention.

"Heaven's above!" exclaimed Katie, glancing at the clock and jumping to her feet. "It's half past two! I was meant to get Patrick at two o'clock."

Dan slid off the bench. "Can I be of any help?"

Katie cleared the two mugs from the table and put them in the washing machine. "No, it's all right. I can manage."

"Are you sure? I know that his factory is quite close to your workshop. I could easily find my way back there. My own insurance probably covers me for driving your car."

Katie slowly straightened up from the washing machine and stood staring at him, biting her lip. "Ah," she said quietly.

"Daddy's not at work, Dan," Sooty said, breaking herself away from the television. Still leaning on the arm of the sofa, she bounced up and down on her knees. "He's upstairs, isn't he, Mummy?"

Katie smiled forlornly at her daughter. "Yes, angel, he is."

Dan pushed his hands into the pockets of his unzipped bomber jacket. "Sorry. I didn't realize that. I thought that when you said you had to get him, you meant from—"

"I think that I should maybe explain something," Katie cut in. She glanced over to where Sooty was once more engrossed in yet another television programme. She crossed her arms and leaned against the towel rail of the Rayburn. "There *was* a slight untruth told in that magazine article about me. I said that the reason I had decided to sell Vagabonds was that I wanted to spend more time with the children."

"And that you felt it could expand to a worldwide market," Dan added.

"Exactly." Katie paused, twisting up the side of her mouth, as if steeling herself to continue. "The real reason, however, is that I don't want to be away from the house much anymore." Dan watched her intently as she once again gathered her thoughts. "You obviously know that Patrick runs his own prawn-processing business."

"Yes. Seascape."

"Right. Well, five years ago, in June I think it was, Patrick had been up in Mallaig picking up a load of prawns from the boats, and he was driving back to Fort William in the lorry when he had an accident. It wasn't too serious. He just drove rather slowly into a ditch. However, when I eventually managed to drag out of him the reason for it happening, he said that he had suddenly got a really bad attack of pins and needles all the way down his right side, and that he had lost control of the lorry. I told him to go straight to the doctor, but he wouldn't. At that time of year, the factory is at its busiest, and he said that he couldn't afford to start getting all namby-pamby about his health. Anyway, about two weeks later, it happened again, but this time he lost all feeling in his right leg. Thankfully, he was in the office at the time, because he fell over quite heavily and thumped his head against the side of a desk. The whole episode gave him quite a shock, so he was more than willing to go to see the doctor after that. The consultation lasted five minutes and Patrick was immediately hustled off to Inverness for tests. And the long and the short of it is that he was confirmed as having multiple sclerosis."

"For heaven's sakes," Dan muttered.

"The specialist said that it was early days and there was no way of knowing how fast the disease would develop. However, taking Patrick's age into account, he said that it was more likely to be the progressive form of the disease rather than the relapsing remitting form, especially as he had already experienced some numbness in his limbs. Having said that, he felt that Patrick would have periods of remission at this stage and saw no reason why he shouldn't just keep on working as normal. That, of course, came as music to Patrick's ears. After that, he kept going harder than ever. I never tried to stop him, because I knew it was his release."

"How did it affect him?"

"Once he was in remission, it didn't at all, except that he would be exhausted at the end of a working day, but I was never sure whether that was a symptom of the disease or just because he was going at it all hours."

"Has he had a relapse?"

"Yes, one about three months after the initial bout. That lasted for about three weeks, but again it didn't seem to leave any permanent damage, so he just kept going on as normal. Then there was this brilliantly long period of remission when we almost forgot that he had the wretched disease."

"And that came to an end?"

Katie nodded. "About five months ago, and this time, I'm afraid, he was left with acute weakness in both legs."

"Is there any chance that that'll improve?"

"The specialist didn't say anything to Patrick, but he told me that I should expect that to be the norm from now on."

"Is he still working?"

"Oh, yes. There's nothing wrong with his brain. It's just his body that doesn't work too well. He *has* had to delegate a lot more work now, but I still take him into the office about three times a week, depending on how he's feeling. But at other times"—she pointed over to the table in the window—"that's where he works."

"Is there no treatment he can get?"

Katie smiled. "Yes, but it's all fairly unorthodox. He is in constant contact with this strange little lady who lives up near Spean Bridge. She's a faith healer. The funny thing is that Patrick was such a sceptic before all this happened, but now he dotes on her every word." Her smile faded. "Also, one of the boys from the factory drives him up to Inverness every fortnight where he goes into a hyperbaric chamber for about an hour."

"What's that?"

"It's like a diving bell. I'm not entirely sure how it all works, but I know that it's pressurized to a certain depth and then pure oxygen is pumped into it, and Patrick sits there like a goldfish, getting extremely bored." She pushed herself away from the towel rail. "In fact, that's where he's been this morning. He feels absolutely knackered when it's all over, so, more often than not, he goes to bed when he gets home. That's why I went upstairs when we arrived. He gave me strict instructions to wake him at two o'clock."

Dan blew out a long breath. "What a hell of a pressure *you* must have on you at the moment."

"Well, life is certainly not as easy as it was. I've had to juggle my time as best I can, keeping Vagabonds going and trying to look after Patrick and getting the children to and from school. But it really wasn't working, and that's why I decided to sell my business. And then, of course, Patrick is a completely different person."

"In what way?"

"Oh, he can be morose, insufferably bad-tempered, and he gets extremely frustrated at his inability to carry out even the simplest tasks. I'm sure you can understand that."

"Of course," Dan replied, wishing that he hadn't asked such a blatantly stupid question. He glanced across at Sooty on her sofa. "What about the children? How have they reacted to it all?"

"Max, I think, understands that Patrick is quite ill. He hasn't really changed in any way towards his father, which is a good thing, but he has become very tactile and loving towards me. I think he's just trying to lend his support in the best way that he can."

"And Sooty?"

"I don't think that she's really taken it in. The innocence of youth, no doubt. She just calls her father Mr. Wibbly Wobbly."

"It's that bad, is it?"

Katie walked towards the door that led to the stairs. "You'll soon see for yourself."

"Can I do anything to help?"

Katie smiled back at him as she opened the door. "No thanks. We've got a good routine going."

CHAPTER TWELVE

J ACKIE STOOD, SUITCASE in hand, on the pavement outside the house in Haleridge Road and watched until the taxi had reached the bottom of the avenue, turned the corner, and disappeared from sight. She turned her gaze to the house and let out a deep sigh. She couldn't remember feeling this way since the days when she had had to go back to boarding school after a long, carefree holiday. The journey back from Paris had been wonderful, but the stone of foreboding had been sitting heavily in her stomach from the moment that she had got out of bed that morning. And now she was here. Back to reality.

She took in a nervous breath and opened the gate, and taking the house key from her pocket as she walked up the short path, she pushed it into the lock and opened the door. She was relieved that the house seemed quiet. She didn't bother to call out, but dropped her suitcase in the hall and walked along the passage to the kitchen.

Battersea Gran was standing at the sink when she entered, scrubbing away at a pot with a Brillo pad, unaware of Jackie's presence. The dogs, however, caught sight of her and Biggles let out a deep throaty bark before sidling over to greet her. The pot clattered into the sink and

Battersea Gran turned quickly, a look of fright on her face. She clasped a pink rubber-gloved hand to her bosom. "Oh, Jackie, it's you! What a terrible shock that dog gave me!"

Jackie shot her the thinnest of smiles. "Are you all right?"

Battersea Gran leaned a hand against the sink. "Yes, I'll be fine. Just set the old ticker thumping a bit."

"Why not have a seat for a moment?"

"No, no, that's not necessary," she replied, returning to her cleaning duties on the pot. "I'll just get this all cleared away for you."

Jackie took off her coat and dropped it over the back of one of the kitchen chairs.

"So, how was Paris?" Battersea Gran asked.

Jackie immediately felt the guilt well up from some hidden place in her subconscious and prickle at her cheeks. She turned and pretended to sift through some unopened letters on the table. "Fine."

"That's nice, then," her mother-in-law replied, bending with a degree of effort to put the pot away in the cupboard below the sink.

Jackie brought herself under control. "Is Dan not here?"

"No, dear, he's away at the minute."

Jackie frowned. "What do you mean, 'away'?"

"He's in Scotland, dear," Battersea Gran replied, pulling off her rubber gloves. "He went up there last night."

"*Scotland*? What on *earth* is he doing in Scotland?"

"I've no idea. He just rang me on Sunday night and asked if I could come over and look after the kids because he had to go to Scotland."

"But he doesn't *know* anybody in Scotland."

"I wouldn't know about that, dear, but he must have gone up there for some good reason." She cast a quick glance around the kitchen before walking through to the hallway.

"When is he going to be back?" Jackie called after her.

"Tomorrow, or maybe the next day. He wasn't very sure."

Letting out a sigh of incomprehension, Jackie leaned her bottom against the kitchen table and folded her arms. Battersea Gran came back into the kitchen, tucking in a scarf at the neck of her pink raincoat.

"Where are you going?" Jackie asked.

"Home, dear." She took a pair of gloves from her pocket and pulled them on. "I've made a nice steak pie for the girls, and—"

"But you can't go home yet," Jackie cut in, her voice rising in agitation.

"I beg your pardon?"

"I mean, what about tomorrow?"

"Well, you're back from your travels now. You'll surely be able to look after the place now."

"But I can't! I've got to go to work."

Battersea Gran gave her a broad smile. "Oh, I'm sure you can phone in to say you're going to be a little bit late."

"Gran, I cannot afford to be late," Jackie snapped at her. "This is probably the busiest time of the year for me. You simply cannot go."

"Well, I'm very sorry, dear, but I *am* going."

"But . . . what about the dogs?"

Battersea Gran eyed the two dogs, both of whom had skulked away to their baskets the moment that Jackie had raised her voice. "Ah, yes. I can see that they might be a bit of a problem. Well, never mind"— she reached up and gave Jackie a peck on the cheek—"I'm sure that you'll be able to work something out." She turned and made her way towards the door, only to have her exit blocked by Jackie.

"Please, Gran, you can't go."

"But I must, dear. I have to make tea for a residents' meeting to-night."

Jackie stood in the kitchen doorway and watched her mother-in-law bustle along the passage to the hall. "Did Dan put you up to this?"

Battersea Gran turned, a questioning frown on her brow. "Now, what could you mean by that?"

"It was Dan, wasn't it? He said to you that I would be home tonight and that I would be able to look after the kids."

"No, that's not right, dear. I don't think you told him *when* you were going to be home."

"I did tell him!"

"Well, in that case, he never told me." There was more than a sense of finality in Battersea Gran's reply. She picked up her handbag from the hall table, opened the front door, and left the house.

Still standing with arms folded, Jackie leaned her head against the doorframe and closed her eyes. "You bastard, Dan Porter. You damned *bastard*!"

She turned and walked back into the kitchen, and the dogs cringed when she glowered in their direction. She went over to the fridge, tugged open the door, and took out the cellophane-wrapped steak pie of Battersea Gran's making. As she thrust it into the oven and turned on the dial, the telephone rang. She sprang to it and picked it up.

"Hullo?" she asked irately. She moderated her tone as soon as she heard the voice. "Oh, hi, it's you. . . . Yes, I know, I'm sorry. I've just been left up the creek without a paddle by my mother-in-law. . . . Because Dan's gone off to Scotland for some reason and I've been left to deal with the kids and the dogs. . . . No, I can't. Millie and Nina will be back at any minute. . . . I know, I would like that too. . . . It was great. I really enjoyed myself. Thank you for everything, Stephen."

She put down the telephone, and for the first time since entering the house, a broad smile spread across her face.

CHAPTER THIRTEEN

HE ENTERED THE kitchen slowly, his weight resting heavily on two walking sticks. He shuffled painstakingly past Katie, who stood holding the door open for him, and drew his arm sharply away from the touch of her outstretched hand. Dan could tell by the look on her face that it had always intended to be more a caring gesture than a supportive grip. He was a couple of inches shorter than Dan, but built as powerfully as a rugby prop forward, and the rolled-up sleeves of his checked shirt showed off muscles that bulged at the effort of keeping himself on his legs. His features were pallid, but bore signs of having been, at one time, healthily weather-beaten, and although his unbrushed mop of brown hair was thinning on the crown, Dan could not detect one hint of it going grey.

It was his eyes, however, that struck Dan as fascinating. There was an incredible brightness about them, and he could read in them a spirit of adventure, a sparkle of wicked humour, and a wildness at the injustice of being struck down in his prime by such a disabling disease.

Katie moved between them. "Patrick, this is Dan Porter from London."

"All right, just hang on a minute. Let me just get myself organized before I say hullo." It came out as an irascible retort, making Dan turn instinctively to watch for Katie's reaction. But she never broke her gaze away from her husband, and Dan could read only love and concern in her expression.

Patrick moved slowly over to the window seat and leaned heavily on the table while he hooked the sticks onto the back of a wooden chair. He edged himself round and sat down heavily. Blowing out with the effort, he ran his fingers through his hair and smiled up at Dan.

"Nice to meet you, Dan," he said, offering a hand. "Sorry about the delay in introductions."

Dan stepped forward and shook his hand, and immediately noticed that the zip on his faded yellow corduroy trousers was undone.

"Good to meet you too, Patrick." He shook the hand as gently as he could without it seeming that he was making allowances for the man's condition. "Maybe I should tell you confidentially that your shop's open."

Patrick glanced down into his lap and let out a disparaging guffaw. "Oh, bugger, I'm always doing that." He began to struggle with the zip. "It's a damned good thing that I don't get out of the house much nowadays. No doubt living in this bloody politically correct country of ours, I'd have been arrested for public indecency about eight times by now." He seemed to be making no headway with the zip. "Oh, bloody hell, Kate, can you do it?"

Katie stepped forward and slid up the zip. "Watch the language, Patrick," she murmured quietly, her face inches away from his. "Sooty's over there on the sofa."

"Oops! Never saw her," he said, smirking like a naughty schoolboy. "Hi, Soots, how've you been? Feeling any better?"

Sooty ended her afternoon's television watching with a long stretch. "Yes, fanks." She climbed off the sofa and came over to her father and began to climb onto his knee.

"Can you cope?" Katie asked her husband.

"Of course we can, can't we, Soots? As long as you don't start bouncing."

Sooty leaned her curly black head against her father's chest. "Have you been diving today, Wibbly?"

"I certainly have. All the way down to forty feet, my girl. We're only a stone's throw from that wreck now, so it won't be long before I bring up all that treasure and we'll all be multimillionaires."

Patrick tickled his daughter's tummy and she squealed with laughter. "Can we make Dan a multimillionaire too?" she asked her father.

Patrick pushed Sooty gently off his knee. He looked up at Dan, a smiling glint in his eye. "Of course not! We don't know him nearly well enough."

"Oh, *please*, Wibbly!"

"Okay, well, let me interrogate him first and see if he's a trustworthy sort of a bloke." He pointed to the other side of the curved window bench. "Have a seat, Dan. I don't like people standing in front of me. It makes me feel inferior."

"Come on, Sooty," Katie said as Dan slid onto the bench. "Let's put the kettle on."

Patrick shifted awkwardly around on his bottom and rested his elbows on the table. "So, I hear that your trip up here has been a bit abortive."

"You could say that. It was my fault entirely, though."

"Well, from what Kate says, it doesn't sound like it. I think it's high time that she had her ears syringed." Katie turned from filling the kettle at the sink and stuck out her tongue at her husband, to which he reciprocated in similar fashion. "So, you worked in the City, then?"

"Yes, for about twenty years."

"So you were there through the Big Bang."

"I certainly was. That's when everything took off."

"And were you one of the infamous Dagenham boys that took the trading floor by storm?"

Dan grinned. He liked the directness of this man. "No. I was from

Tottenham Hale, but I suppose my background was pretty similar to theirs."

Patrick seemed impressed. "Good for you. Nothing like taking the bull by the horns."

"We were lucky to be given the opportunity. I could quite easily have ended up working with my father in a north London metal works."

"But you didn't, did you."

"No."

Patrick used both hands to shift a leg to a more comfortable position. "I've always thought that it must have been a pretty hairy business, trading on the floor. I mean, you must have been fairly young at the time, weren't you?"

"Early twenties." Dan paused. "I suppose the best way I could describe it is like having one huge but permanent adrenaline rush. We worked hard and played hard. Well, most of the other guys did. I was more concerned with making as much money as I could and keeping hold of it so that I'd never have to return to Tottenham Hale again."

"If you enjoyed it that much, why give it up, then?"

"Well, I never really gave it up. It gave *me* up. I was made redundant about fourteen months ago."

"But surely, with *your* experience, you could have got another job?"

"Yes, you're right."

Patrick cocked his head to the side, waiting for Dan to continue. "So? Why not?"

Dan let out a deep breath. "Because of nine-eleven. I lost one of my best mates in the building, as well as a good number of work colleagues. I just decided then that there were more important things in life other than trying to make piles of money."

Patrick nodded slowly. "I can understand that." He leaned forward on the table and fixed Dan with an intense stare. "But you miss it, don't you?"

Dan smiled. "Yes, I do. Every day. If you've had a pretty tough upbringing without any of the niceties of life, then you have to fight to survive. You have to be one step ahead of the gang on the street, otherwise you're going to end up lying facedown in the gutter nursing four broken ribs . . . or worse. The job was made for me, like it was made for every other boy and girl who started from nothing and ended up dealing in the City. We all sailed pretty close to the wind, but we knew instinctively how to handle a situation that was as volatile and as unpredictable as our backgrounds in life. It was just . . . the survival of the fittest. Cowboy country, really."

"Hah!" Patrick exclaimed, slamming his hand down on the table. A fierce excitement suddenly burned in his eyes as he turned to his wife. "Kate, did you hear that?"

Katie grinned broadly at him and nodded as she poured hot water into the teapot.

"You . . ." Patrick continued, pointing his finger at Dan, "have just come out with my expression. I could almost have taken a bet that you would too."

Dan laughed. "Why?"

"Because"—Patrick clenched his fists and waved them about in the air, trying to find the right words—"because that kind of business is so vibrant, so cut and thrust, so . . . basic that it puts a fire in your belly and you know that if you don't just go out there and grab every opportunity that arises, you're going to . . . shrivel up and die."

"And you reckon that your business is like that too, do you?"

"Exactly."

"In that case, it must have been a hell of a change from being a lecturer at a university."

He seemed surprised. "How did you know about that?"

"Dan knows everything about us," Katie said, placing two mugs of tea in front of them on the table. "He gleans all his information from *Woman's Weekly,* don't you, Dan?"

Dan twisted his mouth to the side at the teasing remark. "Not always, but on this occasion, yes." He turned his attention back to Patrick. "So how did it come about?"

"Do you really want to hear it?" Patrick asked, casting a challenging look at Dan.

"If you could be bothered."

Patrick took a drink from his mug. "Okay then. Well, you're right, I was a lecturer—in marine biology at Plymouth University. The department there also used to carry out research projects for fish farming businesses and the like, and that was how I first came across Seascape. But anyway, that part of the story is quite a bit down the line. What really happened first was that an old mate of mine from London came down to stay with us for the weekend. He was running a successful wholesale business, supplying fresh fish and scallops and the like to restaurants throughout the West End, and he just happened to mention that he was on his way down to Penzance to find a new buyer." He paused to take another gulp of tea. "Anyway, all the students were away on holiday at the time and there was no ongoing research in the department, so I asked him what it entailed. He said that it was pretty simple. One just had to go into the buying shed and buy the right quality at the right price." He looked over to Katie who was watching Sooty busily colour in a picture on a large piece of paper that she had spread out on the floor in front of the Rayburn. "It was just twice a week, wasn't it, Kate?"

Katie looked over and nodded.

"So I asked him if there was any reason why I shouldn't be able to do it. He wasn't too sure to begin with, because he was concerned that once the university started up again, I wouldn't have the time. Anyway, I suggested that if he paid for my fuel, I'd work without commission for the duration of the holidays, and then if it didn't work out or I proved completely inept at the job, he hadn't lost out too much. So, at about four-thirty on the Monday morning, we both headed down to Penzance. We did a bit of buying and—well, if you'll excuse the horrible pun—I got hooked."

"So you did continue doing it?"

"Yes. It all worked in very well. Just before the beginning of the next semester, I juggled around with the timetable and made sure that I wasn't giving lectures on the mornings that I went off buying."

"How long did you do that for?"

"Oh, now," Patrick drawled, scratching at the unshaven stubble on his chin, "I took over Seascape in 'ninety-one, so . . . maybe, two years?"

"And then Seascape came on the market."

"Yes. Well, to be quite honest, it never actually *came* on the market. I knew Archie Brannon, the owner of Seascape, quite well, and I'd been up to Fort William a number of times to see him. He had started a really good business, processing langoustines and prawns for the European markets, primarily Spain, Italy, and France. He found out that when all the fishing boats came into harbour up here, they were just dumping the small catch over the side. So he decided to capitalize on it and he made a bloody good job of it too. The only trouble with Archie was that he had one appalling failing. He couldn't keep his pants on. Eventually, his wife ran out of patience and dragged him through the divorce courts, and she came out with a hefty settlement. Archie was already heavily borrowed at the bank, so he was left with no alternative other than to sell the business."

"How did you find out about it?"

"We were working on some research for Seascape at the time, and I got a telephone call from Archie saying that we had to stop everything. He told me the whole story, and that night I went home and discussed it with Kate."

"What do you mean? Buying the business?"

"Exactly. I wasn't going to hang around. At the time, we'd only been married a couple of years. We had no children, no animals, no commitment to anyone else but ourselves. Kate was working as a secretary in some law firm in Plymouth and was bored out of her skull, and I would much rather have been working full-time around the harbours in Falmouth and Penzance than teaching hungover and apathetic students in the classroom. So we grasped the opportunity. I negotiated a price with Archie, we sold the house in Plymouth for a packet, and then moved up here, the proud owners of Seascape."

"And how did you cope with the change?"

Patrick smiled at Katie. "Oh, we managed, didn't we? It *was* completely different, though. I had never come across xenophobia before, but by God, it hit us in the face when we got here. I was known universally as 'the Englishman' at every harbour in Scotland. Seascape had been in business for five years, but when I started buying, it was always 'sold to the Englishman!' " He smiled and shook his head. "But, my word, it was fun. I remember going up to Ullapool for the first time, and driving down the hill into the town. There were all these boats in the harbour, nearly every one of them was flying a different national flag, and sitting out in the bay were these bloody great Russian trawlers. When I got down to the harbour, I couldn't believe my eyes. It wasn't just fish that was being traded. It was everything! The Russians were bartering with their vodka and caviar, and the Scottish fishermen were dealing in Levi jeans and whisky, and the Spanish were in there too. It was just one big international, free-for-all market." Patrick let out a scoffing laugh. "In Ullapool of all places! Stuck right up there in the northwest of Scotland!"

Dan smiled. He was beginning to warm to this man more with every moment that he was in his company.

"But it was hard to start off with, I have to admit," Patrick continued, "especially for Kate. We'd sunk every last penny into the purchase of Seascape, so we were forced to live pretty much hand-to-mouth for a couple of years before we really got it going. And to do that, we had to expand the business, and that meant buying from other harbours. It was then that we came up against some pretty shady characters who didn't like us butting in on their market." He settled his elbows on the table. "I remember one time returning from the East Neuk of Fife with the refrigerated lorry stuffed full of prawns, and about twenty miles into the journey, the bloody thing just stopped dead. Now, what you've got to realize is that if the lorry stops, then the refrigeration unit packs up as well. So I was desperately looking around under the bonnet, but I just couldn't work out what the hell the matter was with the damned thing. Anyway, having checked absolutely everything else, I eventually took the cap off the fuel tank and it sort of grated as I turned it. There was still sand stuck in the neck of the tank."

"Someone had put *sand* in it?" Dan asked incredulously.

Patrick shrugged. "It was a warning. 'Don't come back here, Englishman.' That sort of thing."

"What about the load of prawns?"

"Oh, we unloaded this oozing, smelly load of pulp when I got back to Fort William."

"You lost the lot?"

"Yes. About three thousand pounds' worth."

"Did you ever go back to buy in Fife?"

Patrick held up his hands defensively. "No way. Those guys meant it. I didn't want to end up floating in the harbour."

Katie came across with a mug of tea and slid herself onto the bench beside Dan. "There *was* one time when you nearly got killed in the line of duty."

Patrick shot her a quizzical look. "When was that, Kate?"

"In Italy."

"Jeez, yes. Now that wasn't funny."

"What happened?" Dan asked.

Patrick contorted his face. "I had a new customer in Pisa. I didn't know much about him, but he'd put in a big order and he insisted that I go over there with the shipment. Anyway, I'm pretty convinced now that he was Mafia. I arrived at his place in the evening, and he took one look at the prawns and said that I was trying to swindle him. 'They are all *deefferent* sizes,' he said. So he and two of his henchmen pushed me into the cold store, threw in a lightweight anorak, and locked me in with two pallet loads of prawns. 'I want them *sorrted* out by the *morrning*!"

"Don't tell me you were left in there overnight?"

"Too bloody right I was."

"How on earth did you survive that ordeal?"

"Not very well. I returned back here with double pneumonia and my bank balance about five thousand pounds short."

Dan laughed. "This is unreal! I wouldn't have thought that running a prawn business could prove to be such a dangerous occupation."

Patrick shot him a wink. "Ah, but that's what makes it so much fun. You're dealing in"—he clicked his fingers and pointed at Dan—"well, you said it. Cowboy country."

"Yes, but my line of business was pretty tame compared with that," said Dan, leaning back against the window and pushing his hands into the pockets of his jacket. "You don't get into those kinds of situations in the City."

"I bet *you* did. I bet you laid your life on the line every time you made a deal."

"Not literally."

"All right then, your livelihood. Weren't there times when you thought, If this deal doesn't go through, then that's me finished?"

Dan smiled. "Yes, constantly."

"Well, there you go then." Patrick thumped his fists on the table. "I think there are great similarities between us, Dan. Neither you nor I have ever had anything handed to us on a plate. We've both had to fight hard to succeed in businesses that were never our absolute destiny. And that's what makes success all the sweeter." He glanced round at the kitchen clock. "Listen, Kate said that you were catching a train this evening. What time does it leave Fort William?"

"Just before eight o'clock."

"Great! That gives us just under four hours," Patrick replied excitedly, as he grabbed the two sticks off the chair and began preparing himself for a move to his feet. "How would you like to see around the factory?"

Katie broke her silence. "Wait a minute, Patrick."

"What's wrong?" Patrick asked, a questioning scowl on his face.

"Do you really think you should?"

"Of course I should!" he retorted, pushing himself with a great deal of effort to his feet. "There's nothing wrong with me!"

"How will you get to Fort William? I can't take you. I've got to pick up Max."

"That's no problem. Dan can drive the Merc and I'll get Pete Jackson to bring me back."

Katie shrugged her shoulders. "Well, if you're sure. Just don't overdo it."

Patrick gave her a sweet, innocent smile. "I shall be a model of tranquility and calm."

"Oh yeah? That'll be the day!" Katie laughed.

Even though Dan had reversed the car out of the barn and parked close to the back door, it was still a full ten minutes before Patrick managed to heave himself into the passenger seat. Despite having to negotiate the lethal flagstones in the courtyard, he dismissed any offer of help, and there was nothing that Katie or Dan could do other than to stand watching in fearful trepidation as he laboriously wobbled his way around the car, the rubber tips on his walking sticks losing their grip on more than one occasion. Once he was settled in the car with his sticks tucked in around his feet, Katie leaned in and gave him a kiss on his cheek before closing the door.

Dan walked round and met her at the rear of the car. "Thanks for the hospitality, Katie," he said, "and probably the best idea would be to draw a thick black line through our meeting this morning."

"Agreed," replied Katie, "but nevertheless, it's been a pleasure to meet you, and I have to say, selfishly speaking, that I am delighted that you made the trip. You've been a real tonic for Patrick. He doesn't get to meet many kindred spirits up here, and I haven't seen him so stimulated for ages."

"He's a great man—and a survivor, too."

"I sincerely hope so." She surprised Dan by reaching up and giving him a kiss on his cheek. "You must give Patrick your telephone number in London. He'd love to speak to you every now and again."

"Of course. I'd like that too."

"What are you lot doing?" Patrick's muffled voice boomed in the car.

Katie smiled. "You'd better go. Have a good trip back to London."

"I will," Dan replied, walking to the driver's door and opening it, "and I'll remember your tip about giving the backhander to the steward."

"You do that."

"And please say goodbye to Sooty for me."

"Of course." She shooed him away with her hands. "Now *go,* before he starts getting hopelessly agitated."

K ATIE HAD BEEN right about the weather, only she had been a good twelve hours out with her prediction. As they pulled out onto the main road at the head of the loch, Dan suddenly realized that the mist had dispersed, and the sun beamed through the broken clouds as they scudded westwards towards the dark, towering presence of Ben Nevis. The waters of Loch Eil had turned from murky brown to muted blue and the hills on the far side were transformed to purple and green in their newly acquired light. Even though the ground rose steeply to one side of the road, Dan was now made aware of the vastness of the countryside that surrounded him. There was a mysticism about it, a power in its complete emptiness that seemed to diminish even the need for human existence. Yet, for some reason, he didn't feel uncomfortable with it. It was as if every stone, every tree, every shadow-filled crevice on the hills was saying, "Don't be frightened. Don't run away. You are quite welcome to be part of our world."

"You haven't been listening to anything I've been saying, have you?"

Dan turned to look at Patrick. "Sorry?"

"I was just attempting to point out to you that that's our house over there on the other side of the loch." Patrick smiled. "Ah! I see you've got that look in your eye."

"And what look might that be?"

"The same one that I had when I first came up here. This country-side has a hell of a draw, doesn't it?"

Dan laughed. "I'm a Londoner, Patrick, right to the core."

"So was I."

"Really?"

"Well, southwest London. Wimbledon, actually."

"Ah," Dan said with a smirk on his face. "Home of the well-heeled. Educated at public school, were you?"

Patrick cleared his throat. "As a matter of fact, yes. You wouldn't hold that against me, would you?"

Dan shook his head. "No. As a matter of fact, I don't think that I hold many things against anybody. I feel that if you end up being content with your own existence, then you take everyone at face value."

"And my face fits?"

Dan shot him a wry smile. "It'll do."

Patrick laughed and slapped a hand on Dan's arm. "I like you, Dan. You're a man after my own heart."

The factory was situated on the north side of the small industrial estate through which Dan and Katie had driven earlier in the day. It was longer than most of the other buildings but still constructed in similar prefabricated fashion. At one end of the shed, next to the main road, a paling fence did rather an ineffectual job of hiding from view a motley line of rusty containers that were jacked up on metal supports, and most of the car parking space was taken up with stacks of empty pallets and blue plastic boxes. Dan waited for a small forklift truck to buzz backwards at speed across the forecourt before pulling into a parking space in front of an insignificant door marked Office. He switched off the engine and got out of the car, and immediately could tell that Patrick's factory was partly responsible for the all-pervading smell of fish that emanated throughout the area.

Dan walked around to the passenger side and held the door open for Patrick. "Can you manage?"

Patrick replied as Dan thought he might. "No problem." He shifted his legs manually out of the car. "Listen, I'll tell you what you can do. See that shed over there?" He pointed to a wooden building wedged in between the paling fence and the nearest container. "You'll find a wheelchair in there. I hate using the bloody thing, but the floor in the factory is always soaking wet, and that's lethal for me."

Dan made his way over to the building, located the wheelchair, and brought it back. Once more Patrick refused his help as he shifted around on his sticks and thumped himself down into the chair.

"Right!" he said. "I'll start the explanation here. The lorries pull in right where we are now and the prawns are off-loaded in twenty-kilogram boxes, and usually they go straight into the factory." He pointed to the row of containers. "If, however, we get a backlog to process, we use those for chilling. That's more likely to happen in the high season, which is about May to September, but it mostly depends on how much is coming in from the boats. There's a monitor in the office that gives a readout of the temperature in each container. You'll understand from the story I told you about the sand in the fuel tank that it's vital that they're kept at exactly the right temperature." He glanced up at Dan. "Any questions yet?"

"No. Brilliantly explained so far."

Patrick pointed to the open bay at the end of the shed. "Okay, then. Wagons roll!"

Dan pushed the wheelchair across the car park and entered the building.

"Stop!" Patrick ordered, holding up his hand. "Get yourself a white coat and a hat from the hook over there, and stick a pair of wellies on your feet. You'd better get the same for me." As Dan walked over to the line of hooks, Patrick added, "Minus the wellies, of course."

Over the next hour, Dan was once more fully indoctrinated into yet another thriving Trenchard business. He walked beside Patrick as he guided his wheelchair slowly through the prawn washing area, the packing room, and on into the bay where the prawns, packed neatly into polystyrene boxes, were cryogenically frozen in a vast, stainless steel chamber. They stood for barely a minute in the dispatch freezer, where the temperature was kept controlled at -25 degrees Centigrade, as they watched the well-muffled storeman scoot back and forth on his forklift, shifting around shrink-wrapped pallets loaded with the polystyrene boxes. As they went, Patrick talked with incessant enthusiasm about the business, while Dan broke in with questions that he hoped would not show himself up as a complete ignoramus.

"How many people do you have working here?"

"Fifty-five maximum, but that goes down to about forty in the low season."

"And what's the output of the place?"

"Again, it depends on the time of year, and what the weather's like. After a storm, for instance, it can take three days for the seabed to settle, so it can be feast or famine quite often. But generally speaking, in the winter months we can process about six tonnes per day, but that can go up to ten tonnes a day, no problem, in the high season."

"So summer is when you put in the hours, then?"

"Do we not! We start at seven o'clock every morning regardless, and sometimes we don't get away until about two o'clock the following morning. That's why most of our workforce comes from abroad— Spain, Russia, those kinds of places. For most of the year, we work pretty antisocial hours, and the locals aren't too keen on that."

"And your principal markets are France, Spain, and Italy?"

"That's right. We pack the prawns according to the requirement of each country. For France, it's one-kilo boxes for the frozen market and three-kilo boxes for fresh. The latter get sent down to Glasgow and are being sold in the market next morning in Paris. For Italy, it's eight hundred grams frozen, and Spain, one and a half kilograms frozen. The quality specifications differ as well. The French and the Italians, for instance, love greensacks, but the Spanish won't touch them."

"What's a greensack?"

"A prawn that is carrying its eggs. They show up on the neck and give a sort of greeny tinge to the overall colouring of the prawn. Greensacks are only caught in June and July, though."

"So, which harbours are you buying from now?"

"Campbeltown, Oban, Mull, Mallaig, Peterhead, Buckie, Fraserburgh. All over the north and west of Scotland, really. However, it's only from Campbeltown and Mull that we buy for the fresh market. Campbeltown is renowned for landing the best prawns. Clonkers, we call them."

"Surely you can't get around to all these places yourself?"

"No way. I use agents now. They call the office in the morning and tell us what the catches are. There are a couple of small boats that come into Mallaig with whom we deal direct, but that's only because I've built up a good relationship with them over the years. We still buy on the stone weight for everything, even though everything goes out of here on metric weight. Fishermen aren't too keen on change, if you know what I mean."

THE QUESTIONS AND answers went on into the evening as they sat together in a pub in Fort William, drinking beer and eating wholesome plates of homemade steak pie and chips. At seven-fifteen, Pete Jackson, Patrick's production manager, was dropped off to drive him home.

"We'll give you a lift to the station," Patrick said.

"No need to bother," replied Dan, getting up from the table and picking up his holdall. "I'll just walk along there. It's not far, and I need a bit of fresh air."

Patrick held out a hand. "It's been good meeting you, Dan."

"I've enjoyed it too, Patrick." He shook his hand. "Thanks for showing me around the plant. You really have built up a pretty good business here."

"Yes, I know it." He gripped his two sticks in one hand and brandished them at Dan. "Let's just hope I can keep it going."

Dan smiled at him. "I have no doubt in my mind that you will. Give my regards to Katie, won't you? Oh, hang on!" He put the holdall on the table, unzipped it, and took out Nina's exercise book. "I told her that I'd give you my telephone number in London." He wrote down the number, ripped the page out of the book, and gave it to Patrick.

"Anytime you feel like a chat, give me a call."

Patrick folded up the piece of paper and put it in the top pocket of his shirt. "I will do. I'd like that very much."

Dan zipped up the holdall once more and slid it off the table. "Best of luck, Patrick, with everything."

Patrick nodded slowly. "Thanks. I'll be needing plenty of that."

CHAPTER FOURTEEN

As Jackie opened the door of the house, the dogs burst past her, nearly taking her legs from underneath her, and disappeared at speed along the passage into the kitchen. She threw the leads onto the hall table and glanced at her watch. It was nearly ten past nine. She felt a tremor of panic run through her as she hurried after the dogs.

"Millie! Nina!" she yelled as she walked past the bottom of the stairs. "For goodness' sakes, get your acts together! You're ten minutes late for school already."

Millie appeared at the kitchen door with a half-eaten piece of toast in her hand. "We're just having our breakfast."

"Well, eat it on the way to school," Jackie snapped as she pushed past her into the kitchen. Her eyes fixed on Nina who was hunched over a bowl of cereal, her eyes glued to the television. "Nina! What the hell are you doing?" She picked up the remote from the table and zapped the television. "Would you two stop moving like dead turtles and get out of this house?"

Millie pulled a face at her sister. "Chill out, Mum," she murmured.

Jackie turned and glared at her. "What do you mean, 'chill out'? I was meant to be in the office at eight o'clock this morning, and I'm still here at ten past nine because I've had to walk the damned dogs and try to get you two off to school."

"Wasn't our fault," Nina grumbled. "You didn't wake us up in time."

"That is not true, Nina. I woke you both at seven-thirty. If you'd have got up then, *you* could have taken the dogs for a walk and we wouldn't be running round in circles now."

"Dad always wakes us twice," Millie said.

"Yes," Nina agreed. "First with a knock and then, half an hour later, with a text."

Jackie unplugged her mobile phone from the charger and put it in her handbag. "I really do not feel like speaking about your father right now. I don't know where the hell he is, but he should be here. He *knows* that this is probably my busiest time of the year." She picked up her coat from the back of a chair and put it over her arm. She took in a deep, settling breath. "Right. I'm off. Make sure you double-lock the door, okay?"

She looked curiously at Nina who had turned slowly in her chair, her nose wrinkled and a sneer of disgust on her face.

"What's that smell?" Nina said, getting to her feet and walking around the work island. "Eeeugh! Biggles has done a poo."

"You cannot be seri . . ." Jackie came over and witnessed the mess on the floor. "Oh, you bloody dogs," she whimpered. "What's the point in my taking you for a walk? That's what you're supposed to do *then*!" She skirted gingerly around the affected area and threw open the French door. "Get out! Get out, you revolting animals!" she screamed at the dogs. Biggles, who had pressed himself into the farthest corner of the room, moved like lightning out into the garden as if expecting a boot to help him on his way, while Cruise trotted nonchalantly after him.

Both Millie and Nina hurriedly picked up their schoolbags and made a break for the door. "We'd better get off to school, Mum," Millie said, a sudden urgency in her manner.

"You can't go yet!" Jackie howled. "What am I going to do with *this*?"

"You could always leave it for Josh," Nina suggested as she pushed her sister out of the door in front of her. "He doesn't mind smelly things." She giggled. "He is one himself."

As Jackie stared with abhorrance at the task that faced her, she heard the girls laugh their way along the passageway and slam the front door on their departure from the house. Letting out a choking sob, she dumped her handbag on the work island, threw her coat back over the chair, and went to retrieve the pink rubber gloves, last used by Battersea Gran for a much more pleasant task than the one that faced her.

She was standing with a dumbstruck expression on her face, a cloth held between thumb and forefinger over a bucket filled with dirty brown water, when Dan walked into the kitchen.

"Hi," he said airily, as he dropped his holdall to the ground. "I didn't expect to find *you* here."

He walked towards her with the intention of giving her a kiss, but Jackie backed away from him.

"Don't you come near me," she croaked in anger.

Dan stopped in his tracks. "Why? Have you got the flu or something? Come to think of it, you don't look too good. You're as white as a sheet."

Jackie was speechless with rage.

"Look, why not have a seat while I make you a cup of coffee? You shouldn't be doing housework if you're not feeling well."

"Where have you been?" Jackie asked quietly, her teeth clenched.

"Me?" Dan said brightly, filling the kettle up with water. "I've been up to Scotland for a couple of days."

"I know," Jackie replied in the same tone of voice.

"Oh?" Dan turned, a perplexed expression on his face. "Why ask, then?"

"Because I want to know what the *hell you've been doing up there*?" Her voice crescendoed to a scream.

"All right, all right. What's all the aggro about?"

Jackie dropped the cloth into the bucket with a splosh and started tugging the rubber gloves off her hand. "Aggro? I'll tell you what the aggro's about. I come back here yesterday from Paris, having had an appallingly hard weekend's worth of business to deal with, only to find your mother looking after the place because you've decided on a whim to swan off to Scotland."

"It wasn't on a wh—"

Jackie held up a hand. "Let me finish, please. Despite an inordinate amount of pleading on my part, your mother then puts on her wretched pink raincoat and leaves, saying that I can look after the place, the children, and the dogs." She moved slowly towards Dan, swinging the plastic gloves from side to side. "But the one itsy-bitsy problem with that, Dan, is that I can't. Why, you might ask yourself? Because I have a job, an extremely important job both to me and to this family, and right at this wonderful moment in time, it just happens to be the busiest time of the year for the company for which I work. You, on the other hand, do *not* work, therefore your input to this family at the best of times is fairly useless. So I think it not wholly unreasonable for me to ask what the *hell you were doing in Scotland*!"

Dan handed her a mug of coffee, but she never broke her anger-filled eyes away from him. He placed it on the work island beside her and walked over to the table and sat down on a chair. "I went up there to have a look at a company."

Jackie was silent for a moment. She began drumming her red-painted fingernails on the top of the island. "What kind of company?" she asked, her voice now sounding more controlled.

"A clothing mail order company."

"Why?"

"Because it was for sale."

Jackie frowned. "And you were looking to *buy* it?"

"Well, I certainly wanted to have a look at it before making up my mind one way or the other."

"And?"

"It had been sold two weeks ago."

"Hah!" Jackie scoffed loudly, placing clenched fists on hips. "You went all the way up to Scotland to look at a business that had been sold two weeks ago?"

"It happened to be quite an understandable mistake."

"Oh, I'm sure. Pray tell me, Dan, how were you supposing to fund this purchase?"

"Well, my thoughts were that if I felt that the company was a goer, then we could maybe have remortgaged the house—"

"Wait a minute," Jackie cut in. "What do you mean 'we'?"

Dan let out a sigh. "I wanted to talk to you properly about all this."

"We are talking properly about it. What do you mean 'we'?"

Dan slid his coffee cup across the table. "Okay. I thought that if this company looked good, then, with your skills in the fashion business and mine on the financial side, we could grow it into a worldwide business on the Internet." He paused. "I just thought that it would be good for both our . . . relationships if we did something together, you know, jointly, and made a bit of money at the same time."

Jackie rolled her eyes. "And you took it upon yourself to presume that I would give up my job as managing director of Rebecca Talworth to come and help you run some poxy little mail order company that you'd just happened to unearth somewhere up in Scotland?"

"Actually, it happens *not* to be a poxy little company, and anyway, I didn't presume anything of the kind. I just thought that you could have helped sort of part-time."

"Part-time! Dan, I don't have time for part-time! I work all hours of the day as it is. You could not find a job that is more demanding than mine right now." She shook her head. "I can't believe this. I really can't believe what you're telling me." She looked around and, for lack of something better to do, took a large gulp of coffee that was still far too hot to consume in that fashion. She rushed over to the sink, threw away the remainder of the coffee, filled up the mug with cold water from the tap, and drank copiously.

"For God's sakes, Jackie, it was only an idea."

Jackie took in a few deep breaths before replying. "Really? And I suppose that if it *had* been for sale and you liked what you saw, you would have asked me to give up my work, sell up my house— remember that, Dan—*my* house, and move lock, stock, and barrel up to some heathen part of Scotland."

"That was not what I thought. The business could quite easily have been run from here."

"Oh, Dan, get a grip on your bloody senses!"

"Oh, piss off! Just because you think you're so bloody wonderful."

The door was pushed open and slammed against the wall. Josh stood in the doorway like a gunslinger entering a saloon bar. He was wearing nothing except a pair of boxer shorts. "What—the—hell—is—going— on—here?" he drawled out.

"Keep out of this, Josh," Jackie snapped at him.

"I'm sorry?" he said, entering the room slowly. "I thought by the volume of your voices that you were intending for the whole street to be involved in your little discussion. What the hell has got into you two? You seem to have become incapable of saying one civil word to each other."

"Your father—" "Your mother—" Dan and Jackie started in unison, then both stopped abruptly and stared at one another with foolish em- barrassment.

Jackie spoke first, her voice deliberate. "We were just discussing your father's trip up to Scotland. It seems that he went up there to look at a small mail order company with the intention of buying it."

Josh's face brightened. He turned to Dan. "Oh, yeah! How did you get on?"

Dan looked daggers at him.

"Wait a minute," Jackie said, looking from one to the other. "You knew about this?"

"Yes. I thought it was a great idea. Vagabonds is a terrific company. They make brilliant clothes." He smiled excitedly at his father. "What's the story, then?"

"The company has already been sold," Dan replied quietly.

Josh sighed. "Oh, what a bummer."

Jackie spluttered in disbelief. "You two are as bad as each other. You're just two bloody wasters, ruining your lives and ruining everybody else's at the same time."

Josh held up his hands defensively. "Wait on, now! That's a bit heavy. I don't like being called a waster, and I certainly am not involved with anybody else's life other than my own."

The tension in the room was broken by the sound of the telephone ringing. Jackie walked over and picked it up. She turned and held the receiver out to Dan. "It's for you," she said curtly.

"Hullo . . . Who? . . . Oh, hullo, Patrick, how are you?" Dan held up his hand to stop either Jackie or Josh from leaving the room. "Yes, thanks, it was a good journey. I managed to get a compartment to myself, thanks to Katie's advice. . . . Sure, go ahead." He held up his hand once more to reaffirm his request for them to stay put, and then turned and stared out into the garden as he listened.

"Dan, I can't wait any longer," Jackie said as Dan put down the receiver five minutes later. "I *have* to get to work."

"Please—if you could just wait a minute." He walked back to the table and pulled out two chairs for Jackie and Josh. "Sit down, would you?"

"Dan, I can't—"

"Please."

Jackie let out a loud sigh as both she and Josh sat down at the table. "So? What is it?"

"I've been offered a job . . . for four months."

Jackie raised her eyebrows. "Well, I suppose that's better than nothing. After all, it's a foot in the door and if it all goes well, you might be kept on for longer."

"No. It's only for four months."

"Right. Where is it? In the City?"

Dan shook his head and looked directly at Jackie, anticipating already her reaction to his answer. "Scotland."

Jackie placed her elbows on the table and slowly keeled her head forward into her hands. "Who has offered you a job in Scotland? Not this . . . mail order company?"

"No. It's another one, but it does belong to the husband of the woman who has just sold that company." He paused. "Listen, please don't say anything until I've explained it all to you."

Over the next ten minutes, Dan told them everything that he knew about the Trenchards. Josh sat staring at Dan throughout, enthralled and captivated by the story, whilst Jackie never lifted her head from her hands.

"What an amazing guy," Josh said when Dan had eventually finished.

"Yes, he is."

"So," Jackie sighed, sitting back in her chair. "I suppose that means that you're going to take the job."

"I don't know," Dan replied. "I thought we might discuss it."

"Why did he not ask you yesterday? Why wait for you to come all the way down to London before asking you?"

"Because yesterday he had someone lined up to help him run the business. The chap telephoned him this morning to say that the company that currently employed him had changed their tune and were now insisting that he serve out his contract."

"And that just happens to be four months," Jackie stated slowly.

"Exactly. Patrick is now desperate. He can't really cope by himself, not after his last relapse. It was his wife who made him call me."

"I think you should do it," Josh said forthrightly.

"Wait a minute," Jackie exclaimed, holding up her hands. "Don't let's be too hasty here. Maybe this guy can't cope up in Scotland, but how on earth am *I* going to be able to cope down here? I haven't got the time to look after the place and the girls and you, Josh. I'm having to go back over to Paris in a couple of weeks."

"Maybe Battersea Gran wouldn't mind coming round to stay," Josh suggested.

Jackie shook her head. "This is all going too fast," she sang out in a desperate voice. "Listen, there's no way that Battersea Gran can manage for that length of time. Damn it, she proved that over the weekend. She was out of here like a bullet."

"That's because you were back here," Dan said. He looked around the kitchen. "And you have to admit that there's not much sign of the fact that she wasn't able to manage."

"Well . . . what about the dogs? They can't be left all day in the house. Battersea Gran won't be here *all* the time."

"Could you do without the car?" Dan asked.

"I don't drive it anyway, Dan," Jackie answered tersely.

"Well, in that case, I could take the dogs with me."

Jackie bit at her lip as she watched him silently. "You're going to take the job, aren't you?"

Dan nodded slowly. "If Battersea Gran can help out, then, yes, I think I will take it. I'm not doing anything else, and the man is desperate for help."

Jackie took in a deep breath and got to her feet. "Well, that's that, then. End of discussion."

"It's only for four months, Jackie," Dan said.

She picked up her handbag and her coat. "Yes. Of course. Only four months." She walked towards the door. "By the way, your dog shat on the other side of the island this morning. Maybe you could finish clearing it up before you go."

Dan pushed himself to his feet. "Jackie, don't be unreasonable. I wasn't thinking of going *today.*"

Jackie walked towards the door and opened it. "Well, I would if I were you, Dan. For all our sakes, I think you should." She walked out of the kitchen, and a moment later the front door slammed behind her.

"Oh, for God's sakes," Dan murmured under his breath.

"Don't worry about it," Josh said quietly. "She's just a bit cranky at the minute." He got up from the table, picked up Nina's cereal bowl and Dan's mug, and walked over to the sink. "So, what are you going to do?"

"I don't know."

Josh picked up the telephone and pushed in a quick-dial code. He held the receiver out to his father. "Have a word with Battersea Gran and explain the situation. Knowing her, she'll be more than happy to help out, especially if she knows about your friend's circumstances."

"What about the girls?" Dan asked, taking the receiver from Josh.

"They'll be fine, Dad. They're a unit on their own. Just leave a note for them. They'll understand."

An hour later, Dan had a large suitcase in the boot of the car and the dogs sitting looking rather puzzled on the backseat. He was pretty sure Biggles was thinking that his misdemeanor that morning had been the final straw, and that now he was being returned to the dog home. Dan walked back into the house, licking the envelope in which he had put the note for the girls. He placed it on the hall table, next to the one that bore Jackie's name, and then went to the bottom of the stairs.

"Josh?"

"Hang on, I'll be down in a minute," Josh's voice rang out from his bedroom.

"I'm heading off, Josh."

"I heard you. Just give me a minute."

Dan leaned against the banister rail. He heard Josh's footsteps coming along the passageway. He appeared at the top of the stairs, fully dressed in a pair of his bum-showing jeans and a blue parka, a beanie pulled hard onto his black, curly head. On his back was an overstuffed rucksack with a white T-shirt streaming out its side.

Dan looked questioningly at him. "Where are *you* off to?" he asked as Josh came down the stairs.

"Scotland," Josh replied with a broad grin on his face.

Dan couldn't help but laugh. "Josh, you can't come."

"Why not?"

"Because . . . it's totally different up there. You wouldn't enjoy it. There aren't any nightclubs or venues or things like that. I don't even know if there's a Tesco's."

Josh blew out derisively. "Oh, what the hell! Listen, Dad, I'm in a rut here. You said it in so many words the other day in my bedroom. I'm going noplace. I'm sick of my dead-end job and I'm sick of life in London. Even Horace's Inferno has been taken over by West End posers." He shrugged the haversack higher onto his back and adjusted the shoulder straps. "I've been trying to think of something else to do for the past few months, but I just came up blank every time. I know this is impulsive, but what the hell, you're doing something pretty impulsive as well. So come on, man, I'm quite willing to do something adventurous if you are."

Dan felt the unaccustomed prickle of emotion in his eyes. "All right, Josh. Come on, we'll do something impulsive together." He put an arm around his son's shoulder and held him tight. "Nothing ventured, nothing gained, eh?"

Josh grinned at his father. "Let's hit the road, then."

CHAPTER FIFTEEN

IT WAS ONLY a short distance, barely a mile, between the Trenchards' house and the cottage. Dan drove hard on the heels of the red Golf as it sped along the narrow road that followed the south shore of Loch Eil. He was almost taken unawares when Katie's brake lights suddenly shone red. She swung the car to the right through a rusting gate that hung askew from one hinge, and drove up a short, rutted track, the grass in its centre brushing heavily on the underside of her car.

"Oh, gawd," Josh muttered as they followed the Golf up the track. "I saw this place from back there, and I was going to make some stupid joke about it being our new home in the Highlands."

The low, corrugated iron–roofed cottage was situated thirty yards back from the road on a small hillock, its three front windows giving out to a view across the loch. That was its only plus point. Sections of the wooden fence that surrounded its small, overgrown garden had fallen victim to the wind and those that still stood were covered with greeny-black lichen. A nondescript climbing plant, devoid of much of its foliage despite it being only September, grew in a tangled heap up the rough stone wall and hung like an unkempt fringe over the drab brown front door. At the back of the cottage, there was a flat-roofed harled extension with a small metal window that was, in architectural terms, utterly discordant with the rest of the building.

"Still pleased you came?" Dan laughed, as he creaked open the Saab door.

Josh leaped enthusiastically from the car. "Wouldn't miss it for the world."

They had arrived late the previous night after a drive that had included numerous stops for the dogs and at least three completely unnecessary excursions, thanks to Josh's appalling map-reading skills. Due to his fraught exchange of words with Jackie and the subsequent speedy departure from London, it had completely slipped Dan's mind to telephone Patrick and Katie to say that he was on the way north, so they were amazed at his quick response to their cry for assistance, and even more so when they saw his extraordinary entourage. It was decided over a beef sandwich and a couple of restoring glasses of Glendurnich malt whisky that Dan and Josh should stay the night in the small downstairs spare bedroom, but Katie had told Dan out of earshot of Patrick that the room had to be kept free for him, as there were times when he couldn't make it up the stairs to their own bedroom. It was at that point that the Trenchards' former home, about which Dan had already read Katie's gruelling account of damp discomfort, was mentioned.

"We had a holiday let in July," Katie said, as she ducked under the sparsely leaved vine and put an enormous key in the door lock, "but that was the last time it was used, so please don't expect too much." She shouldered open the door and Dan and Josh followed her in.

There was a distinctly musty smell about the place, and dust, highlighted by the sun that glanced through smeared windows, showed up on every surface. The front door led straight into a kitchen-cum-sitting room, this being made apparent by the presence of a cream-coloured stove, with scoured chrome tops and hardened dribbles of brown grease below its oven door, at one end of the room, and a moth-eaten three-piece suite in a nice shade of dung at the other end. Other than that, the room was sparsely furnished, save for a small fridge next to the stove, an old sideboard with a glass-fronted cabinet above it, both painted in gaudy green to make them look as if they were one unit, and four plastic-seated chairs pushed in around a small table that was covered by a faded oilcloth, and upon which sat two bottles that flowed with candlewax.

"For heaven's sakes!" Katie exclaimed, holding a hand to her mouth. "You know, I think I must have forgotten to come in to clear up the place after they'd gone." She let out a sigh and shook her head. "That's what happens when you have other things on your mind."

Dan shrugged. "It doesn't seem too bad." He turned to Josh. "What do you think?"

"Does the telly work?" Josh asked, pointing to an enormous television set that dwarfed the three-legged table on which it rested in the corner of the sitting area. Judging from its antiquity, Dan thought it highly unlikely that it had been switched on since Muffin the Mule graced the screen.

"I think so," Katie replied. "I seem to remember that it's quite like viewing through a snowstorm, though." She walked across to a door at the back of the room. "I hardly dare look in here," she said, pushing it open. She shuddered as she entered the bathroom, built into the flat-roofed block at the back of the house. "Well, it's freezing, but it's clean enough."

Dan and Josh peered through the doorway. There was an old cast-iron bath with sticky-out feet and peculiarly bulbous taps, a basin with a mirrored cupboard above it, and a lavatory with a wooden seat.

"How is the water heated?" Dan asked.

Katie smiled as she walked past them into the main room. "Ah, well, now that's another thing. The stove does it all. The water, the radiators in the bathroom and the bedrooms, and, of course, the cooking too."

Dan was pleasantly impressed. "That sounds quite efficient."

"Quite," said Katie, biting at her bottom lip. "The trouble is that the stove burns solid fuel."

"Oh yes," Dan chuckled. "I remember now. It takes whole forests to feed it."

"Actually, it's not that bad. It's a bit of a pig to get started, but once it's going well, you can close it right down and it just burns slowly."

"What about getting the wood?"

"I'm sure there'll be some logs in the lean-to at the back of the cottage, but if not, I can get Patrick to order you up a load."

She threaded her way through the three-piece suite and opened up a door at the east end of the cottage. "That's one of the bedrooms. It's got a double bed." She opened the door next to it. "And there's a single bed in there." She turned to Dan and Josh. "That's it, I'm afraid. Not quite the Ritz, but it's all we have. What do you think?"

Dan blew out a breath that was visible in the cold of the room. "Well, it's the right size for us both."

Katie took that as a noncommitment. "I'm sorry. It's not brilliant, is it? I suppose we could try and find some lodgings for you, but it's just the dogs that—"

"I think it's great!" cut in Josh. He turned to his father. "Come on, Dad, it'll do us all right."

"No, I wasn't meaning . . ." He paused to get his words right. "Yes, it's absolutely fine for us. We'll get it cleaned up and heated in no time. It's . . . perfect."

Katie's eyes expressed relief. "That's great, then!" She walked across to the kitchen sink, which was situated in front of the window nearest the stove, and opened up the cupboard beneath it. "There's some cleaning stuff in there, and"—she got down on her hands and knees and put her head into the cupboard, and there was an immediate sound of trickling water above in the roof space—"that's your water turned on." She got to her feet and pulled open a door next to the stove. "And there's a mop and bucket and a vacuum cleaner in there."

"Okay," said Dan. "Just leave us to it, then."

"Would you mind if I did?" Katie asked. "I really have to make sure that Patrick's all right before I go to work."

"Of course. We can easily cope here."

"Good. And then you must both come over to the house for lunch, say about half-past one? I think Patrick is pretty eager to take you into Seascape this afternoon, so maybe after that you could go to the supermarket in Fort William and buy some provisions for yourselves." She turned to Josh. "I don't know what plans you have, Josh, but Patrick said that, if you wanted, he could give you a job in the factory."

"Nice one!" replied Josh enthusiastically. "That would be sound."

"Right then. Well, best of luck and we'll see you at lunch."

Having pulled the Saab up onto the side of the track to allow Katie to reverse down to the road, both Dan and Josh watched as she accelerated away, giving a short blast on the horn before disappearing around a bend in the road. Dan shot a sideways glance at Josh and snorted out a laugh. "Bit of a change of lifestyle, eh?"

Josh turned and surveyed their new abode. "They should film us for the next episode of *Survivor.*" He let out a resigned sigh. "Could be character-building, I suppose."

Dan reached over and pulled his son's beanie down over his eyes. "I'm glad you came, Josh. I think I'd be near suicide by now if you hadn't." He gave him a macho slap on the shoulder. "Come on. Let's get started."

As they walked up the track, Dan opened the back door of the Saab to let out the dogs. Cruise came out like a bullet and stood looking around, ears cocked and nosing the air, as if already getting himself in tune with the whereabouts of interesting females. No scent was carried on the chilly wind, so he lost interest and headed off to cock his leg against a large stone at the side of the track. Biggles, on the other hand, was reluctant to get out. After the long journey, and still not totally convinced that he wasn't being taken back to the dog home, he regarded the car as his refuge. He lay on the backseat, feet skywards, with his upper lip curled back to give the best view of his curved white teeth.

"All right, I'm not going to force you to get out," Dan said, leaving the door open for him. "You just don't know what you're missing, though."

IF THERE HAD been a passing stranger that morning inquisitive enough to find out who now dwelled in this remote cottage, it would have become immediately apparent to him that the new occupants had survived their years without once putting a match to an open fire. For an hour, Dan and Josh knelt in front of the stove, trying to coax some form of incendiary reaction from a six-month-old edition of the *Press & Journal* that they had found lining a cupboard, a roll of lavatory paper, five unpaid parking tickets issued by the London Borough of Chelsea (courtesy of the glove compartment of the Saab), a flier announcing the impending visit of a celebrated DJ called JamHamFister to Horace's Inferno (plucked in desperation from the pocket of Josh's parka), and a pile of damp twigs. It was the plastic sheaths on the parking tickets that eventually got it going, but the whoops of delight that met this monumental achievement immediately turned to choking coughs of asphyxiation as the damp chimney refused to draw away the dense blue smoke. Instead, it regurgitated it out, along with a good dollop of soot, into the joyous faces of Dan and Josh.

"Bloody hell!" exclaimed Dan, jumping back from the stove and wiping his blackened hands down the front of his leather jacket before he knew what he was doing. "Shit!"

"Don't worry! It's going to go. Look!"

The smoke was now curling back into the stove, like someone exhaling cigarette smoke from his mouth and sucking it up through his nose.

"Put more wood on it, then!" Dan cried out urgently.

Josh stuffed the remainder of the pile of twigs into the fire. "Should I close the door?"

"No, just leave it for a moment."

They stood back and watched mesmerically as the flames slowly crept up through the twigs and then began to curl up the chimney. Thirty seconds later, there was a healthy roar from the stove.

"Right," said Dan. "I think that's cracked it. We'll stick a couple of logs in there too, and pray that it doesn't go out." He glanced at the watch on his sooty wrist. "God, it's eleven o'clock and we haven't even started yet."

"How are we going to wash?" Josh asked, staring at his filthy hands. "The water will still be freezing."

"Hell's teeth, Josh! What's the point of cleaning ourselves up now?" He swept a hand around the dust-covered room. "We've got this to do yet." Josh looked suitably despondent. "Never mind, by the time we've finished, the water should be hot." He walked over to the cupboard and took out the mop and bucket and handed them to Josh. "Right, now for the real work."

An hour and a half later, they had the place cleaned from Ajaxed bath to Flash-sparkled floor. By that time, the stove had managed to heat the water to a bearable tepidity, and they were able to wash off the worst of their engrained dirt before taking their belongings in from the car and starting to unpack them.

Dan was shoving a pile of shirts into his small chest of drawers when Josh entered the bedroom, frowning quizzically at his mobile phone.

"This thing's broken," he said, giving it a shake. "The battery's full, but all it does is bleep at me."

"Probably because there's no reception here."

"What do you mean, no reception? Mobile phones work everywhere, don't they?"

"Not in a tube train, they don't."

"We're not *in* a tube train, Dad."

"I know, but the principle's the same. If you're out of range of a signal, then you don't get reception."

"Do you mean to say that we're out of range up *here*?"

"Probably."

"But this is mainland Britain. I thought the whole place was covered."

"Obviously not."

"Well, how am I meant to text my mates?"

Dan laughed as he threw a handful of socks into a drawer. "I don't know. Try walking up the hill at the back of the cottage. You might get lucky up there."

With a discontented groan, Josh slipped the mobile into the pocket of his trousers. His eye caught the contents of Dan's suitcase on the bed. "What on earth is *that*?"

"What on earth is what?" Dan asked, following Josh's baffled gaze.

"That beige thing."

"It's my skiing outfit."

"Why have you brought that?"

"Because, Josh, it can get like the Arctic up here, and I don't possess any other clothes that suit extreme weather conditions."

Josh laughed. "Maybe, but you *can't* walk around in a pair of sludge-coloured salopettes. It's just . . . geeksville." He pulled the bulky outfit out of the suitcase and threw it onto the bed. "What else have you got in here?" He flicked through Dan's clothes. "Dad, you've brought at least three of your Armani suits! When are you thinking of wearing them?"

Dan gave his son's hand a slap to get him away from his suitcase. "All right, mastermind. Just because your daily attire makes you look as if you're about to muck out a pigsty."

"Oooh!" Josh sang out. "That's a bit acid."

Dan smiled. "Okay, point taken. We'll go find a shop in Fort William this afternoon and I'll get myself kitted out in some appallingly countrified attire. How would that suit you?"

"I'm sure whatever you wear, Dad, you won't forego your usual sartorial elegance."

Dan blew a raspberry. "My word, you are an eloquent little devil today, aren't you?"

At twenty past one, having shared the peaty-brown water of a deep and luxuriously hot bath, they left a warming cottage and drove to the Trenchards' house for lunch. It turned out to be a hurried affair, mostly because Patrick was champing at the bit to get to the factory and start showing Dan and Josh the ropes. By a quarter to three, he had both father and son standing in the packing room, wearing identical garb of a blue boiler suit with matching peaked cap, a pair of Wellington boots, a long plastic apron, and a pair of bright yellow rubber gloves. Both looked awesomely surprised at the speed of their incumbency and at the task that Patrick had set for them.

"Best way to learn about this business is from the grass roots up- wards," he said, pushing himself in his wheelchair over to one of the long, stainless steel packing tables. "Maria José! Could you come over here for a minute?"

A young Spanish girl with flawless sallow skin and dark brown eyes walked across from the far side of the packing room. Her black hair was gathered in a ponytail and pulled through the adjusting band at the back of her cap, and even though she was dressed in the similarly unsexy style of both Dan and Josh, it did nothing to diminish her obvious Latin good looks.

"Right," Patrick continued. "Maria José, this is Dan and Josh." Sticky rubber-gloved handshakes ensued between them. "Maria José is in charge of both our packer training and quality control. She's going to show you everything you need to know about prawns; how to grade them, how to pack them, how to tell a bad one from a good one. By the end of a week, you should both know instinctively the source of a consignment by its quality, as well as the destination of each of the boxes you have packed." He laughed out loud at the expression of horror on Dan's face. "Don't look so worried, Dan. You'll manage fine."

"Talk about being thrown in at the deep end," Dan groaned. "I'm not the most practical of people, you know."

"Neither was I when I started in here. In fact, it took me about two months to get to grips with it all." He reached out and gave Dan's arm a shove. "It's important that you do this, Dan, not only to help you understand the business, but also it shows the others that you can work alongside them. It's only for a week, and Maria José will be looking after you the whole time. She won't let you make a mistake. Anyway, look at Josh." Dan turned to see that Josh had already started to sift through a large yellow box of prawns that stood beside the packing table, listening attentively to what the Spanish girl had to say about them in her husky, broken English accent. "He seems to be enthusiastic enough."

"I'm not sure if the enthusiasm stems from the sorting of the prawns," Dan said out of the corner of his mouth.

Patrick laughed. "In that case, he'll learn fast." He backed his wheelchair away from the table. "Kate said that you'll be wanting to buy some provisions?"

"Yes, and I've also got to find myself something a little more suitable to wear for your unpredictable Scottish weather."

"Probably not a bad idea. Well, we're only going to be working until four o'clock this afternoon, so we'll head into Fort William after we've finished up here. Then tomorrow morning, it would be best if you both started with the rest of the gang at seven o'clock. Reckon you're up to that?"

"It'll be just like old times."

"Good." He turned his wheelchair towards the door that led through to the office, and then glanced back over his shoulder. "Oh, and another thing. Does Josh drive?"

Dan sucked in a breath. "He's passed his test, but he's hardly been behind the wheel since then. He always used public transport in London."

"Well, this is probably the best place for him to get back into it again. The reason why I mentioned it is that, eventually, you and I will be away from the factory quite a bit, and he'll need to have a way of getting to and from work."

"In that case, we can both take our lives in our hands and let him start this afternoon."

"Okay. And then maybe in a couple of days when he's got back into the way of it, you can stop by our house on your way into work and drive me here in the Merc."

Dan looked uncertain. "Well, let's just see how Josh gets on, shall we?"

"What's the matter? Don't think I can manage it?"

"I'm sure you can, Patrick, but maybe Katie might think differently."

"Don't worry. I know my limitations—and that's all that matters, right?"

The remark was not made as a lighthearted quip, but more as a firm directive. It took Dan by surprise.

"If you say so," he replied, determined not to show outright acceptance of the idea. He watched as Patrick negotiated the shallow ramp that had been built for him at the door, then turned to find that Josh had two boxes of neatly packed prawns already sitting on the table in front of him. Dan guessed that the expression of delight on his face was not so much due to the successful completion of the task as with the fact that Maria José was standing close to him and bathing him in brown-eyed congratulations.

CHAPTER SIXTEEN

THAT'S YOUR FULL fry-up, Ronnie," said Eck, the proprietor of the Cormorant Café, as he slid a plate brimming with eggs, bacon, sausage, black pudding, and tomatoes across the table.

Ronnie Macaskill held a hand to the edge of the Formica top to stop the plate from overshooting and ending up in his lap. He rolled his copy of the *Daily Record* into a tube and placed it at the side of the table next to the battered black notebook and mobile phone. "Thanks, Eck," he said, glancing up at the man as he sidled back to his place behind the counter, wiping his hands on his stained white apron.

He took a large mouthful of his breakfast just as his mobile rang. He pulled a small paper napkin from the dispenser on the table and wiped his hands, and then picked up the phone, checking the source of the call on the screen before hitting the SPEAK button. "Good morning, Betty," he said, gulping down his food. "How are things with you in Fort William?"

"Oh, it's a fine day here now, Ronnie," the office manager at Seascape replied in her euphonious voice. "That wretched cold weather seems to have moved on, so maybe we'll be getting that Indian summer after all."

"Aye, that would be suiting us now, would it not?" Ronnie replied, before taking a swig of hot, sweet tea from his mug.

"And what like is it in Oban?" Betty asked.

"Much the same." He looked out of the window, catching sight of a seagull settling itself awkwardly on the top of the winch drum of one of the trawlers. "There's quite a stiff breeze down here at the harbour, but the sky seems settled enough."

"So have you been buying for us today?"

"Aye, I have." He reached over for his notebook, opened it, and flicked through the pages. "I gave you a call earlier, but your phone was engaged."

"Och, I can well believe that. It's been havoc here this morning. Jimmy called in from Buckie, and then Patrick from Mallaig, so the line has been red hot."

"Patrick's up in Mallaig, is he? Now, how would he be managing that?"

"He went up with this new chappie from London. Did you not know about him working for us?"

"No. Never heard a word. How long has he been with Seascape?"

"Just over a week now. Dan Porter's his name. He came up with his son Josh, and they've both been working in the packing house to get the feel of the place. This is the first morning that Patrick and he have been off buying together."

"And what's this Dan Porter from London like?"

"He seems to be a pleasant enough man. He's managed to put Patrick in a better mood, at any rate."

"And does he know anything about the prawn?"

"He knows more now than he did a week ago. He's been a banker in his life—not a fisherman or the like."

"A banker, eh? So what happened to the lad that we were to be getting from Ocean Produce in Aberdeen?" Ronnie broke the yoke of his second fried egg with a piece of bread and put it in his mouth.

"The company's not letting him away for the next four months. Dan Porter is only here temporary-like, just to give Patrick a hand."

"And how does Patrick seem to be keeping?"

Betty's voice seemed to hush. "I wouldn't say he's that good, Ronnie. When did you last see him?"

"Not for a couple of months or so."

"Well, you'd see a big change. He's still walking around on sticks, but to my mind, it's awful dangerous for him. He's fallen over in the office a number of times now."

"Aye, it's truly a bad thing, especially for a man so active as himself."

"If he wasn't so active, it might be a great saving to him. Since Dan Porter has started in the job, Patrick has been coming into the factory at seven o'clock every morning."

"That's Patrick for you, though. He'll keep going to the end."

"Which could well be hastened, Ronnie, if he goes on like this." Betty rustled some papers. "Look here, I've been speaking too long again. You'd better be letting me know what you have for us."

Ronnie ran a stubby finger down the page as he gave Betty the names of the boats, the number of boxes that were coming off each, and the price paid. He read slowly, knowing that Betty would be entering them in the database as he spoke. *Bonnie Maud,* 4 boxes, £14 per stone; *Misty Blue,* 5 boxes, £16 per stone; *Minch Hunter,* 6 boxes, £18 per stone. They weren't the best, having been caught by deep-sea trawlers working the inky depths of the Minch. He much preferred to buy off the small fishing boats that set their creels close into the rocky shoreline of the Mull of Kintyre. That was where the clonkers were caught.

"And that's it for the day," Ronnie said, holding the mobile between his cheek and shoulder and slipping the elastic band over the notebook.

"Thanks, Ronnie. Will you be buying from Oban tomorrow as well?"

"I'll have to find out if there are any boats due in. If not, I might just take a ride down to Campbeltown and see if I can pick up some clonkers for you."

"Well, we certainly could do with some. Mercamadrid were on the phone this morning from Spain looking for some big ones."

"I'll do my best, Betty. Speak to you tomorrow."

He pressed the button on his mobile and put it down on the notebook, and went back to enjoying his breakfast.

"Mind if I join you?"

Ronnie looked up to see Billy Inglis, the buyer for one of Seascape's rival companies, standing in front of him. He glanced over to the table that Billy had been occupying up until a moment ago, and wondered why he wanted to come over to his table. Besides being rivals at the bid, Ronnie never felt that he had much in common with the lanky East Coast man.

"Aye, if you wish," Ronnie said, pointing to a chair with a fork laden with bacon and black pudding.

Billy pulled out the chair and sat down, and immediately leaned forward on his elbows and blinkered his eyes with his hands.

"Is something wrong, Billy?" Ronnie asked, his brow creased questioningly.

"Have ye no' seen the car that's just pulled up ootside?"

"No."

"Well, hae a look."

Letting out a sigh, Ronnie laid down his knife and fork, got to his feet, and went over to the window. He angled his vision so that he could see farther up the pier, and caught sight of the ageing BMW, lovingly polished as always so that its bright red paintwork gleamed in the morning sun.

"Och, for heaven's sakes," he mumbled to himself. "It's the bloody politician." He returned to the table, where Billy continued to shield his face. "Aye, I see what you mean. What the hell's he doing down here?"

"Probably bored a'body else on the West Coast."

"Did he see you?"

"I canna be sure aboot that. I'm takin' no risks, though."

The door of the café opened and a large man in his early thirties with a bull neck and a supercilious smile on his florid face heaved himself up the steep step. His football-sized head was prematurely balding and those few strands of hair that still survived were splayed out across his scalp like parched rhizome roots in a desert. He pulled off a pair of string-backed driving gloves, finger by finger, before unbuttoning his blue serge overcoat to reveal an enormous belly that overhung the trousers of his charcoal grey suit.

"God's sake," Ronnie murmured, sliding lower in his chair so that he could use Billy as a screen. "Imagine getting that stuck in your fishing net."

"Is it him?" Billy asked, darting his eyes from side to side, trying to use his peripheral vision to catch a glimpse at what lay behind him.

"Who else? He's not seen us yet, though."

Ronnie noticed that Eck, the owner of the Cormorant Café, had done his utmost to avoid catching the eye of the man, but eventually had to turn from the grease-splattered cooker to thump yet another full fry-up on the counter. The man greeted him loudly, and did a jumpy little dance as he tucked his thumbs into the waistband of his trousers and pulled them up. He had called Eck by name and followed it by casting his piggy eyes around those tables closest to the counter to see if anyone had noticed that he had done so. But no one took a blind bit of notice of him. It was clear that others felt the same as Ronnie and Billy—that being acquainted with the man would do nothing to enrich one's life.

Unfortunately, Ronnie was acquainted with him. It wasn't that Maxwell Borthwick had ever done him any harm or injustice. It was just that he was one of those self-opinionated, thick-skinned, conniving individuals that Ronnie had done his best to avoid most of his life. He came from Inverness and spoke in a thin, whining accent, and Ronnie had always imagined him as the kind of young boy who either would have been dragged off into some teacher-free corner of the school playground to get beaten up quite regularly or, if he was ever lucky enough to be involved in a game with the other boys, would have been made to play the role of "the enemy." That was probably the reason why he had gone into politics—to give back a little of what he had received, and to give himself the power that he knew he had so blatantly lacked in his earlier days.

Not that his chosen career had been as successful as he would have liked. When the new Scottish Parliament had been formed, he had put himself forward as a Scottish Socialist Party candidate for the Highlands and Islands. He wanted to see a Democratic Scotland—power to the people and not allegiance to the Crown. He wanted Scotland for the Scots and he wanted to rid the country of the parasitic presence of its landowners, no matter if they were English, Dutch, Danish, Swedish, or whatever, those who lived privileged existences, in many cases in absenteeism, off the struggling labours of those unfortunate enough to work for them or live as tenants on their vast estates. Absolute partition was the only way forward.

It was a simplistic manifesto, yet an emotive one, and during the run-up to the election, Maxwell's words were seldom out of the local press, his high-pitched voice constantly heard on Moray Firth Radio, expounding his views with such nationalistic vehemence that it appeared that he was not going to be satisfied until he had seen every haw-haw–speaking toff living in Scotland lose his head on the guillotine. He wanted a new pecking order in *his* country, and he wanted to be at the top of it.

Maxwell felt that nothing could stop him from taking his seat in the Assembly Rooms in Edinburgh, and he therefore adopted for himself an image that he thought reflected the importance of his new status. He bought his clothes from Austin Reed, joined a new golf club on the outskirts of Glasgow that was frequented by some of the hierarchy of Scottish politics (even though it was a good four-hour drive from

his home in Inverness and he barely knew the difference between a
driver and a putter). He made sure he was seen at all the events that
would be featured in *Caledonia* magazine, and to transport himself from
Inverness to his place of work in Edinburgh, he had purchased the
second-hand BMW 525i.

However, it was all to no avail. Five weeks before the election, he
had had to undergo an operation on a delicate part of his anatomy, and
even though he craved notoriety and publicity for himself, he was mor-
tified when some Conservative-voting doctor or money-grabbing porter in the hospital had leaked it to the newspapers. Most of the tabloids
had picked it up, but the most humiliating for Maxwell was the *Daily
Star,* which printed a short, four-line paragraph directly opposite the
right nipple of the Page 3 girl under the headline "Borthwick Drops a
Ball." It was assured that everyone was going to read it.

Maxwell had thereafter gone to ground, or to be more precise, had
hidden himself for a week beneath the stiff white sheets of his hospital
bed before leaving the scene of his betrayal in sunglasses and a broad-
rimmed hat to return, tail between legs, to the neat little council house
of his doting mother in Inverness. There, he had been able to unleash
the full power of his political authority by banning her from reading a
newspaper or watching any programme on the television. Not that anyone in the media was remotely interested in Maxwell Borthwick anymore.

But then he had bounced back, still fired by his convictions, and
found himself a job as a junior councillor with the Highland Regional
Council. It was only a stepping-stone, in Maxwell's view, until the
realms of Holyrood opened up their arms and welcomed him as a key
figure in the development of the New Scotland. Until then, he made
sure that he was going to be seen in all the places where he felt there
were ardent, "grass-roots" feelings for his policies. Places like the Cormorant Café in Oban.

He took the cup of coffee that Eck had banged down on the

counter, and having poured the contents of the saucer back into the cup, he gently stirred it with the bent teaspoon as he glanced around the place.

"My wordie, he's seen us," Ronnie said, rubbing his fingers across his forehead.

"Good morning, gentlemen," Maxwell said brightly, his voice sounding like an over-revving chainsaw. "Would you mind if I have a seat at your table?"

"Ye can have mine, if ye like," Billy said, getting up from his chair.

"I'm sure that Mr. Borthwick can quite easily pull one over from another table," Ronnie responded, giving Billy a look that dared him to leave at his peril.

"Of course I can. No need to move, Billy." He put his cup down on the table, and as he turned his back on them to retrieve a chair, Billy shot Ronnie a sneering thanks and sat down again.

"So," said Maxwell, spilling his bulk over the edges of the red plastic chair, "what's the trade been like?"

"Above average," Ronnie replied, knowing that the man's understanding of the fish trade was below minimal and that he could have said anything. Billy, however, had decided not to be so forgiving.

"Prawns the size of elephants this morning. It's aye good when the boats are fishin' aff the Azores."

Maxwell nodded understandingly. "Yes, so I have been told."

The two buyers caught each other's eye across the table. Ronnie took a drink of tea to stop himself from laughing and Billy dug frantically in his pocket for a handkerchief and gave his nose a prolonged blow.

"So who have you been buying for today, Ronnie?"

"Seascape."

"Ah, right. I hear that the Englishman is not keeping so well."

Ronnie glowered at the man. "Now, would that be Patrick you're talking about, MacSwell?" He always liked to get the accent wrong on his name. He felt that it was more fitting for the bumptious blimp of a man.

"Of course. There's no other Englishman that works for Seascape."

Ronnie cocked his head to the side. "Well, that's where you're wrong, MacSwell. Seemingly, Patrick has just hired another man to help him. From London, I believe. A banker, no less."

Maxwell stared at Ronnie, unaware of the dribble of coffee that ran down the deep, podgy cleft at the side of his mouth. He placed his cup with a clatter onto its saucer. "Now, that's just typical, isn't it?"

Billy drummed his fingers on the table. "Whit dae ye mean by that?"

Maxwell clasped his sausage fingers together and rested them on his stomach. "Well, it just seems to me that there are plenty of good men up here looking for jobs. Why give priority to someone coming up from the south?"

Ronnie let out a quiet sigh. He was a Scotsman through and through, yet he didn't like these "us and them" ideas that Maxwell had spouted so readily to the media. His own father had been a forester all his days, working on an estate up near Lochcarron in Wester Ross. Ten years ago, it had been bought by a Danish industrialist who had ploughed money into the place to improve its infrastructure. He employed thirty staff where before there had only been ten, and had funded the building of the new community hall, which thereafter became the main focal point of the area, being the venue for the various local council meetings and for the Saturday night *ceilidhs*. His father had always maintained that the Dane would have got a poor return on the capital that he had invested in the property.

"So what brings you down to these parts, MacSwell? You're a long way from your jurisdiction, are you not?"

"Always good to get out and meet the people," Maxwell replied with a smug smile.

"Does yer boss ken that ye're doon here?" Billy asked, narrowing his eyes at the man.

Maxwell drew himself up in his chair. "I am my own boss, Billy. I have been for some time now. I am one of two coordinators of business development for the Highland Regional Council."

Billy scratched his head quite theatrically, giving the impression that he was totally perplexed. "Aye, that may be so, but are we not in Argyll at the minute?"

"Well, yes, but . . ." Maxwell spluttered.

"Maybe he was just wanting to give the car a wee bit of a run," Ronnie said to Billy, a wry smile on his face. "It's still going well, I suppose?"

"Like a dream," Maxwell replied, glad that the direction of the conversation had changed. "I had it tuned the other day by Frangalini Motors in Inverness."

"Tuned, eh?" Ronnie sang out as he drained the last of the tea from his mug. "Well, there's a thing."

Maxwell glanced over both shoulders, and then leaned forward in his chair. "I got it up to a hundred and fifteen miles an hour on the A9 this morning."

Billy had taken a tin of tobacco from his pocket and was busy rolling an anorexic cigarette. "In that case, ye'd better watch oot for yersel', boy." He licked the paper, squeezed the cigarette, and put it in his mouth. "Itherwise ye'll soon be withoot yer precious car."

Maxwell flumped back in his chair. "Oh, I don't worry about that kind of thing. I've got a radar detector fitted."

"Aye, I reckon you would have," said Ronnie, picking up his notebook and mobile phone. "Well, gentlemen, it'll do me no good sitting around gossiping all day." He pushed back his chair and got to his feet. "So if you will both excuse me."

"Aye," said Billy, hurriedly getting to his feet. "And I've got tae see a man aboot a dog."

Maxwell watched the two men as they hurriedly paid Eck at the counter and then jostled with each other to get to the door. He turned back to the table and finished off his cup of coffee with a smack of his lips. So the trip had been worth it. He had found out about this new Englishman working for Seascape. That was not good news. That bloody man Trenchard had always got up his nose. Maybe the time would be right to have a quick word in the ear of Allan Duguid in Buckie. His prawn business had been suffering from the day that Trenchard took over Seascape. A little leverage on his part in Allan's favour might well be rewarded quite handsomely.

As Maxwell pushed himself to his feet, pulling the folds of his overcoat around his stomach, a mobile sounded in his pocket. He extracted it from the depths and pressed the button.

"Hullo? . . . Oh, yes, good morning, Cyril. . . . Where am I? Oh, well, at the minute, I'm in, er, Dingwall. . . . Yes, Cyril, as soon as I can. . . . Well, I can't be there that soon because my, er, car is in the garage. . . . No, I can't take the bus, because the garage is here in Dingwall, and I couldn't then . . . all right, Cyril, I'll get there as soon as possible. Thank you, Cyril. . . . Goodbye."

Maxwell's face had changed from ruddy red to deep purple. He waddled quickly over to the counter and paid his bill, then left the café at speed. It would be that creep Cyril Bentwood, he thought to himself, as he pressed the key fob to open the doors of the BMW. He had always seen it as the final insult, having an Englishman as a boss.

CHAPTER SEVENTEEN

As BETTY, THE office manager at Seascape, had hoped, the weather settled into the warmth of a prolonged Indian summer that spilled over from September into the first few weeks of October. The garden at the cottage, which had been a colourless wilderness when Dan and Josh had arrived, took on a new lease of life, bursting forth in resurgence with hollyhocks, larkspur, and foxgloves that splashed pink and blue and purple along the narrow border of the property. Even the dormant honeysuckle that had clung so miserably to the front wall of the cottage responded by producing a thin covering of dark green leaves and even the occasional small but heavily scented flower.

Although Josh was working most days in the factory, he found time to plunder Patrick's tool shed for the necessary hardware to restore order to the garden. He pulled free the wind-blown sections of the fence from the tangled matt of overgrown grass and hammer-and-nailed them back into place with a volley of missed blows and wind-absorbed expletives. He then put to use his teenage ingenuity by enticing an itinerant Blackface ewe into this now secure palisade to eat down the grass, but her gourmet tastes turned out to be more for the sweet stalks of the flowers than the rank, tasteless roughage. Consequently, Josh had to hurriedly dispense with her services by wrestling her reluctant form from the garden, during which exercise he was given little creditable assistance from the dogs. Biggles sat cowering by the front door of the cottage, having never before encountered on his jaunts around Clapham Common anything quite so weird as this long-haired, violent creature, while Cruise, who had not scented one decent bitch in all the time that he had been in Scotland, sniffed hopefully at the ewe's backside. The unfortunate result of this failed experiment was three hours' hard labour on Josh's part, kneeling on damp ground with a pair of rusty garden shears, to get the grass to a height that could be managed by Patrick's mower. Having discarded the raked-up piles over the fence to the ex-pectant Blackface ewe, who was now content with any slim pickings, Josh had steered the groaning mower up and down, and at the end of a further hour, stood back with pride as he surveyed his new, perfectly striped and perfectly yellow front lawn.

The interior of the cottage had also been restored to full working order. Dan had managed to conquer the temperamental idiosyncrasies of the cooking stove, his success being such that even with the vents shut right down and with the wood barely glowing, he was forced to throw open the front windows to allow out the heat generated both by the stove and by the hot water tank that gurgled as dangerously as a capped geyser. The walls throughout the cottage had been given a fresh coat of white paint, courtesy of Patrick and the odd-job man at Sea-scape, the kitchen table adorned with a new oilcloth, while the three-piece suite, now swathed in a mass of brightly coloured bothy rugs, had been rearranged so that each seat commanded an excellent view of the new television-cum-video that Dan had rented from a small elec-trical store in Fort William.

Not that their new daily routine allowed much time for watching it. They would set out each morning at six-fifteen, leaving the front door wedged open to allow the dogs the run of both the house and the garden, and then drive along the narrow road to Auchnacerie, the headlights of the car beaming forth bravely into the soulless black void of the surrounding countryside. At first, Dan had felt his skin creep with uneasiness at the eerie desolation that enfolded him, having never before driven without a set of headlights blasting into his rearview mirror and the red taillights of the preceding car only yards in front of him. But now, he had come to find it exhilarating, as if every day he and Josh were setting out on a new voyage of discovery, "going where no man had gone before." Josh would then drop him off at the end of the road leading up to the Trenchards' house, where Dan would stand watching as the lights of the car twisted through the bends in the road, like the sweeping beams of a lighthouse, until they disappeared around the edge of the hill that dropped sharply down into the depths of Loch Eil.

After the first few weeks of this routine, Dan had tried his best to change it. At the outset, he had always found Patrick in the kitchen, sitting expectantly at the table and beginning his slow ascent to his feet as soon as Dan walked into the room. But soon, it was Dan who had to wait while he listened to the frustrated oaths that rang down the stairwell from the Trenchards' bedroom above. Later still, both he and Katie would sit in the kitchen discussing how best they could persuade Patrick to take things easier while he slept on, undisturbed by the blast of his alarm radio. On such mornings, it was always Katie who bore the brunt of Patrick's fury as he castigated her for not making sure that he was awakened when the alarm went off.

Yet Patrick was not for persuasion. Dan suggested that he could quite easily handle the buying at Mallaig by himself, but this was met with that steely glint of determination in Patrick's eyes. "Nothing wrong with me, Dan," he had said. "Body may be a bit tired, but the brain's still active. Anyway, you've still got a lot to learn."

And so they had continued to head off on their buying trips to-gether, Patrick more often than not falling fast asleep in the passenger seat as soon as Dan had the old Mercedes in motion. As he drove, Dan would study the slumbering form of the man, every day seeing visible changes in his features. His face had lost its weather-beaten glow and the skin on his sunken cheeks had now taken on the colour and texture of putty, whilst the sheer effort of concentrating on the movement of his limbs had produced lines on his forehead that were as deep as plough furrows. Witnessing this decline in Patrick's health, Dan now had mixed feelings as to whether his decision to come up to Scotland had been the correct one. Patrick would have continued to use a buyer at Mallaig and would not have been capable of getting into the office so much. He would have had to stay at home, using the kitchen table as his workplace, taking it easy, pacing himself, and no doubt every day getting more and more frustrated and angry with the world. So it was a no-win situation. Yet what really upset Dan was to have met this man with whom he had such an immediate and powerful rapport and to be able to do absolutely nothing but watch as this deterioration took place. And if he felt that way after such a short space of time, he could not begin to quantify the emotional turmoil that Katie had to be suffering.

There was, however, an up side to it all. Dan hadn't felt as exhilarated in a job since the days when he had worked as a money broker on the Stock Exchange floor. He loved the atmosphere of the auction, the wry smiles and cutting banter that were exchanged when he and Patrick had caught out a rival bidder. He loved the postmortems in the harbour café afterwards when they would sit with the other buyers, discussing over a gargantuan and totally unhealthy breakfast the quality of the day's catch. He loved dealing directly with the fishermen in the smaller boats, watching with incomprehension as the spokesmen for their buying cartel gathered lobster creels into a circle on the quayside and sat in a waft of cigarette smoke while they discussed in Gaelic the various offers for their prawns. A man would eventually turn from the group, there would be a click of fingers, and simultaneously he would point to the purchaser and call out his name in an accent that was as foreign to Dan's ears as any that he had heard before. "*Meester Trrenchard, ye can tek eet feer Seascape the day.*"

And then, of course, bringing Josh had been the best thing that he could have done. With every day that passed, Dan realized how little he had known about his son before. Josh was certainly not the useless layabout that Jackie had accused him of being. Over the weeks that he had been in the factory, he had proved himself to be a hard worker, determined to do the job well, if not better than anyone else in the packing room. And that was not Dan's own judgment of the boy's capabilities. That was Patrick's.

Dan also loved having his company in the cottage. Josh turned out to be surprisingly house-proud, something that Dan found most odd, remembering only too well the orderless upheaval of his son's bedroom in London, and his enthusiasm for their home diminished any small feeling of sparseness and discomfort that Dan might have secretly harboured about the place. On those evenings when Dan arrived back at the cottage earlier than usual and Josh was working overtime in the factory, he missed having him around. He loved their new man-to-man relationship, feet up in front of the television, beer in hand, watching a football match or a film that Dan had picked up at the local video store on the way home. He therefore felt a momentary pang of resentment, before giving instant and laddish congratulations, when Josh broke the news to him that, on some occasions, the reason for his delayed return had been due to Maria José, the young Spanish girl in the factory, with whom he had either been going for a drink in the Nevisview Inn or seeing a film at the local cinema.

Besides this unexpected but pleasing revelation, there were other hidden depths to Josh's character that took Dan completely by surprise. After his success with the cottage lawn, which he had managed to transform to a deep and healthy shade of green following nightly floodings with buckets of water, Josh had become quite passionate about gardening, so much so that when all was in order, and when work and Maria José allowed, he turned his attentions to the much greater challenge of restoring the Trenchards' garden to some degree of horticultural sanity. It was because of this and because Dan and Katie had eventually managed to cut a deal with Patrick, being that he could continue going on the early morning jaunts to Mallaig as long as he carried out his office work at home, that the two Porters began to spend most of their weekends at Auchnacerie. It was not long, therefore, before they were considered a welcome extension to the family. Josh took on the role of hero and surrogate elder brother to Max, the two of them heading off up into the hills together on mountain bikes, with the dogs keeping pace, where they would tackle long and, to all accounts, dangerously harebrained journeys of exploration. Dan, meanwhile, found that he could combine his work with Patrick with taking over the weekend cooking duties from Katie, and having become used to the hit-and-miss technique of cooking on a traditional heat-storage stove, he was pleasantly surprised at the way his culinary concoctions were devoured with relish, even by the children. Thereafter, not only was he given the title of resident chef to the "Auchnacerie House Hotel," he also became known to one and all as "Dan the Man," thanks to a short and quite erudite poem written by Sooty.

There was a man called Dan
Who sat in a frying pan
It gave him a brown suntan
Poor old Dan

Katie told Dan later that the problems encountered by Sooty over the meter of the last line had resulted in much sighing and pencil chewing at the kitchen table, until quite suddenly, inspiration had struck.

It gave him a brown suntan
Poor old Dan the Man

There had been little improvement, however, in Dan's popularity on the home front. Communication with Jackie had been nonexistent, even though Josh had found a place next to a lone, windswept silver birch a hundred yards straight up the hill from the back of the cottage where three blips of reception could be achieved on a mobile phone. Every night, Dan would walk the dogs up to the tree and call the house in Clapham. Sometimes he spoke to Battersea Gran, with whom he had long and informative conversations; sometimes it was Millie or Nina, both of whom displayed little interest at hearing their father's voice at the other end of the line. But he never got to speak to Jackie. He had tried to call her at work, but she was never there, the first week being out at business meetings and the second week in Paris. He left voicemail messages on her mobile that she never answered, although she did eventually reply to a text. It read only *Taking Josh with you was a clever move.*

The message upset him greatly. He hadn't realized until then that there was this measure of vindictiveness about their relationship. Okay, they had had their disagreements and arguments, but that kind of statement was more in tune with a couple getting a divorce and wrangling over the custody of their children. He sent her another text saying that it had been Josh's decision to come with him, that Josh was now working in a good job and making good money, and that she would be extremely proud of him, because *he* certainly was. Dan decided to leave it at that, hoping that she would now be satisfied that there had been no scheming rationale behind the move to take Josh.

Thereafter, he did continue to call her every second night, but it was always Battersea Gran, Millie, or Nina who answered the telephone. Then, one evening, as he picked his way down the hill in the dark, following the winding sheep track through the heather, it dawned on him that, in all their years of marriage, he had never gone so long without speaking to his wife.

CHAPTER EIGHTEEN

D AN HAD NO idea that the Seascape refrigerated van was parked at the back of the Trenchards' house. He had become used to measuring his steps in the darkness of the early morning—up the road, into the courtyard, and across to the back door—but on this occasion, it was only a sixth sense that stopped him from slamming his face into the rear door of the vehicle. He skirted around it and entered the house. Katie was standing by the Rayburn, her mouth stretched open in a long, shuddering yawn.

"Everything all right?" Dan asked, sensing that there was something amiss.

Katie pushed the heels of her hands deep into the sockets of her eyes. "Not really, no. Patrick had an appalling night. He was sleeping downstairs and got up to go to the loo, and then fell over. I couldn't move him and he couldn't move himself, so I had to put a mattress on the bathroom floor and roll him onto it."

"Is he still there?"

"No, Pete arrived about half an hour ago with the van and he carried him back to his bed before heading back to the factory in Patrick's car."

Dan had no doubt that Pete Jackson would be able to manage such a Herculean task. The factory manager at Seascape was built like an ox and had an awesome reputation in the heavy events at Highland Games throughout Scotland.

"What time did this happen?"

"About three o'clock."

"You should have got hold of me. I would have come straight over."

Katie lifted the lid of the Rayburn and put on the kettle. "I did try. I left a message on your mobile."

"Hell, I'm sorry about that. The wretched thing doesn't work in the cottage. We have to yomp up the hill to get a line."

"That's what I thought."

"And I don't suppose you could have left him for a minute and come over in the car."

Katie shook her head. "No. For all Patrick's bluster and bravado, he is absolutely terrified of what's happening to him. As I was putting the duvet over him, he grabbed hold of my hand, and he wouldn't let go."

"Do you mean you spent the whole night with him in the bathroom?"

"I hadn't much option. It was bloody cold and extremely uncomfortable as well. I must remember to put a rug down on those tiles in case it happens again."

"You must be feeling exhausted."

Katie poured boiling water into two cups of instant coffee and gave one to Dan. "You get used to it. Most nights, there's something going on. Not usually as bad as that, though."

"What happens now, then?"

"Well, much against Patrick's wishes, I've told him to stay in bed and I've called the doctor. He's on his way out from Fort William."

Dan took his coffee over to the table and sat down on the window seat. "In that case, why don't you let me deal with the children today?

I can easily drop them off at school and pick them up later. That'll give you time to catch up on some sleep."

Katie shook her head, using the opportunity to dispel some of the fatigue from her brain. "No, I'll be fine. Anyway, I'm afraid that you've got *your* work cut out for the day."

"Oh?"

Katie came over and sat down opposite him. "Patrick wants you to take the refrigerated van down to Oban. There was a lorry scheduled to pick up this morning's catch, but it's been redirected over to the East Coast." She dug into the pockets of her Vagabonds and brought out a piece of paper. "That's the mobile number of Ronnie Macaskill, our buyer in Oban. Give him a call when you arrive there and he'll arrange a meeting place with you down at the harbour."

Dan scratched the side of his face and laughed. "Right. So which way is Oban?"

"Pete has written out directions for you and left them on the passenger seat in the van," Katie replied. "He says that it should take you no more than two hours at this time of the morning. It's only about sixty miles."

"And then I head straight back to the factory?"

"Yes, as quickly as you can. There's a shipment meant to be going out tonight to Mercabarna and there's a shortfall in the order, so Pete wants you back as soon as possible."

Dan drained his coffee. "Well, I'd better be going then." He rinsed out his cup under the tap and placed it on the draining board. "Listen, if you want anything, give me a call on the mobile. I'll bring Patrick's car back from the factory, so I could easily pick up Max and Sooty on the way home."

Katie nodded appreciatively. "Thanks. I'll let you know. It really depends on what the doctor says."

"Okay." He waggled a finger at her. "You just take it easy, do you hear? You've got backup now."

Dan made Oban in exactly two hours. He reckoned that he would be able to do it in less time on the way back to Fort William because it had taken him a good half hour to get used to the van's hefty gearbox and more than an hour to judge the width of the vehicle on the tight-bending road that wound its way down the eastern side of Loch Linnhe. He telephoned Ronnie Macaskill when he was three miles from Oban, stopping off to make the call at the entrance to the Dunstaffnage Yacht Marina.

The harbour was not difficult to find. As he drove down the hill into Oban, he could see the boats clustered together beyond the buildings that lined the promenade, above them protruding the distinctive red and black funnel of a Caledonian MacBrayne ferry. He followed the mainstream of traffic and found himself quite unexpectedly driving out onto the pier.

The Cormorant Café was an insubstantial pale blue clapboard edifice resting on a pile of railway sleepers and tucked in protectively against the harbour wall. There was a gap of about two feet between the ground and the door, and therefore an upturned fish box had become a permanent fixture in front of the café to act as a step. Dan entered the establishment and looked around for his contact, and immediately saw a slightly built man wearing a pair of brown corduroy jeans, a dark blue donkey jacket, and a wise look on his agreeable face rise to his feet at the far end of the café. He picked up a notebook and mobile phone from the table and walked towards him with easy strides.

"Mr. Porter, I believe," he said in a slow, deliberate voice, holding out a hand.

"Dan," he replied, shaking the hand.

"Good to meet you, Dan. I'm Ronnie Macaskill." He flicked a thumb towards the counter. "Are you wanting to get yourself a cup of coffee?"

"No, I won't bother. I've got to get this load back to the factory as quickly as I can."

Ronnie nodded slowly. "So Pete told me this morning. We do, however, have a slight complication."

Dan frowned at the man. "Being?"

"Being that I have four boxes of clonkers on their way up from Campbeltown and Pete Jackson wants you to take those back with you as well. The lorry is heading on to Glasgow, so I'm going to be meeting him in Lochgilphead in about three quarters of an hour."

"That's going to make me pretty tight for time."

"Aye, I realize that, so I'm thinking that it would be best if we met up again outside of the town so that you can get away up the road as quickly as possible. Now, would you be knowing any landmarks around here?"

Dan scratched at the back of his head. "Not really. Oh, except that yacht marina about three miles north from here."

"Dunstaffnage. That would do just grand. If you get yourself there in about an hour and a quarter, I'll see if I can drive like the wind and get to you as soon as I can."

"Right. So where do I get loaded up here?"

Ronnie pushed open the door of the café. "I'll show you." He stepped down onto the fish box and Dan made to follow him, but the man turned around quickly and pushed Dan back into the café, closing the door behind him.

"Oh, damn the world!" he muttered, as he walked over to the window and peered out at the side. "What the hell is he doing down here again?"

"What's the matter?" Dan asked.

Ronnie beckoned him over. "Have a look here." He moved out of the way to give Dan his space. "You see that red BMW there?"

Dan saw the distinctive badge above the grill of the car, its nose just visible at the far side of the Seascape van. As he watched, a hugely overweight man with a head like a turnip and dressed in a billowing blue serge overcoat appeared from the back of the van and walked slowly along its side, casting a furtive glance into the cab as he passed by.

"Is that the owner of the car?" Dan asked.

Ronnie stepped forward and glanced out the window. "Aye, that's Maxwell Borthwick, our self-styled Robin Hood of the Highlands."

"What do you mean by that?"

"He's all for taking from the rich and giving to the poor, excepting that he's got his wires a wee bit crossed over what he's trying to achieve."

"Which is?"

Ronnie twisted his mouth into a wry smile. "To put it in a nutshell, he would be a happy man if he were to be given credit for ridding this land of all those who spoke with anything other than a Scots accent."

Dan grimaced. "In other words, he wouldn't be very pleased to meet me."

"Oh, he'd like to meet you all right. He knows all about you, but I'm thinking that we won't give him the pleasure. He's a dangerous man, that Maxwell Borthwick. Like all quasi politicians, he has friends in all the wrong places, and his number one enemy just happens to be Patrick Trenchard."

"How did that come about?"

"Patrick had a head-to-head with him once during a political discussion on the local radio station and he succeeded in leaving the man spluttering for answers. Unfortunately for Maxwell, the programme was heard by a journalist who wrote a scathing report on the man's inability for debate. It was printed in most of the national newspapers the following day. Now, Maxwell is the type of man who doesn't take kindly to being made to look a fool. He'd certainly like to get his pound of flesh off Patrick." Ronnie pulled back from the window. "Right, that's him away now. I don't know where he's headed off to, but hopefully, it will give you time to get loaded up and away out of here before he finds out that it was you who was driving the van." He opened the door of the café and jumped down to the ground without using the step. "I'd better be getting myself off to Lochgilphead." He pointed to a large shed two hundred yards away at the town end of the quay. "If you take the van round the back of that shed there and ask for Tommy, he'll get you loaded up. He's expecting you. And take care going in through the gate. It's awful narrow."

"Right, and I'll see you at Dun"—his mind went blank—"at the yacht marina in about an hour and a quarter."

"Aye, that'll be fine." He walked over to a small white Peugeot van parked at one end of the Cormorant Café and got in, and there hardly seemed time for him to start the engine before he sped off along the quay.

There were two other lorries waiting to be loaded when Dan arrived at the shed. He negotiated the tight entrance gate with care, pulled the van into the line, and then went off in search of Tommy. He was informed by one of the lorry drivers that it was Tommy himself who was negotiating the restricted loading space at speed on a forklift truck. When he caught sight of Dan and the Seascape logo on the side of the van, he held up his hands, fingers outspread, to indicate that he was going to be no longer than ten minutes.

In typical West Coast fashion, it was three quarters of an hour before the second lorry was finished being loaded. Dan pulled the van hard against the wall of the loading area to allow the lorry to reverse out past him, and then drove into the shed.

"Sorry about that," Tommy said as he jumped off his forklift and started to manhandle the prawn boxes off the pallet and into the back of the van. "You'll be Dan Porter then."

"That's right," Dan replied, pulling on a pair of leather gloves that he had found in the cab's cubbyhole. He went to pick up three boxes from the pallet, realized that he wasn't going to manage them, and settled for two.

"And how's Patrick keeping?" Tommy asked as he collected his next load.

"Not so good, I'm afraid. He had a bad night last night."

Tommy rested his hands on top of the boxes. "It's a real bastard, that kind of thing happening to a man like Patrick. He's such an active man." He heaved up the boxes and walked around to the back of the van. "He's awful well liked in these parts, you know," he called out.

"I can well see why. He's a great man."

Tommy came back to his forklift and rested once more on his next load of prawn boxes. "I'll agree with you entirely on that. Now, I mind the time when . . ."

The story took all of ten minutes to recount, and Dan began to cast surreptitious glances at his wristwatch. He was meant to be up at the yacht marina in fifteen minutes. He realized now why the lorries had taken so long to load. Tommy was a born storyteller. Dan wanted to grab the boxes on which the forklift driver rested his hands and get on with the loading, but he knew that it would be taken as an unfriendly action, so he resigned himself to listening to the whole drawn-out account.

"Aye, he's a fine man," Tommy concluded eventually, picking up the boxes and thus allowing Dan to dive in for his next load. "Right, just one more pallet after this one."

Dan groaned quietly.

Exactly at the time of his rendezvous with Ronnie, Dan slammed shut the backdoor of the van and pulled down the heavy levers on the airtight doors. Pulling off his gloves, he glanced toward the narrow entrance gates, just to get a judgment on their width before he reversed out. "Oh for God's sake!" he exclaimed, throwing his gloves to the ground in frustrated fury. "What the hell is he doing parked there?"

The red BMW, which he had seen earlier down at the harbour, was drawn up perfectly into the gateway, leaving no more than six inches' gap between each of its bumpers and the gate pillars. Dan ran over to the entrance, squeezed his way past the car, and looked up and down the street. He saw the bulky figure of the man waddling his way jauntily up the street.

"Hey, mate!" Dan yelled out.

The man turned and looked back towards him. "Are you, by any chance, addressing me?" he asked in an aggravatingly high-pitched voice.

"Too right I am. What the hell are you doing parking your car there? It's a bloody gateway."

"Well, that may be so, but there's no sign of a yellow line. I'm quite within my legal rights to park there."

"Come on, that's being bloody obtuse. There are no lines at all on this street. You could have parked anywhere."

"And I choose to park exactly there."

Dan realized that being rude to the man wasn't going to help matters. "All right, then. Would you mind *please* moving your car? I happen to have a pretty valuable load of prawns on that van, and I have to get them back to Fort William as soon as possible."

The man's flabby features spread wide into an ingratiating smile and he took a few steps back towards Dan. "Do I have the pleasure of meeting Mr. Dan Porter?"

Dan breathed a sigh of relief, thinking that his diplomacy was working. "You do. And you must be Mr. Maxwell Borthwick."

The man stopped. "That's right." He pulled up the sleeve of his overcoat and studied his watch. "Well, Mr. Porter, I have an extremely important meeting to attend, and I'm afraid that I'm late as it is"—he turned and waved his hand in the air—"but it should take no more than an hour." With that, he hurried away with the grace of a seal making for water.

Dan thought about running after the man and laying into him, but realized that it would be a pointless exercise. As he squeezed past the car again, he felt like turning and sinking a foot into its highly polished side, but again knew that it would only lead to trouble.

He was walking back to the van to get his mobile to call Ronnie when he saw the pile of pallets at the side of the load yard. They were stacked three deep and to a height of at least eight feet. He studied them for a moment, then walked over and gave them a shake. They were as solid as a rock. He glanced back at the car, his head to the side as he studied the miniscule gaps at either end. Then he turned and went off to find Tommy, the forklift driver.

Tommy was a complete artist with his truck. Having coupled on fork extensions, he edged them carefully under the BMW and jammed some old sacks and a couple of blankets between the bodywork and the retaining frame so that there would be no possibility of damaging the car. Then he lifted the car effortlessly off the ground and slowly moved backwards, his eyes darting from one end of the car to the other as he negotiated it through the gateway. Once clear, he picked up a little more speed, reversing back and twisting the forklift round so that it sat directly opposite the pallets.

"Are you sure they'll take the load?" Dan asked, having second thoughts as to whether his idea had been such a good one after all.

"Without a doubt. They could hold a lorry up there."

He drove the forklift forward until the car was inches from the pallets and then continued to lift it until the wheels were exactly level with the top of the stack. He once again edged forward, working his lift, tilt, and sideshift levers as quickly and as accurately as a touch typist, until he had the car exactly where he wanted it. Then he settled it down, without so much as a scuff mark on its shiny red bodywork, high up in its new parking place.

As he reversed the forklift back, Tommy turned to Dan and shot him a wicked grin. "Aye, and there are no yellow lines up there either. He can park on my pallets as long as he likes, which is just as well, because I'm going off for the day now."

As he sped away into the shed, there was a squeal of tyres and Ronnie's little Peugeot came careering into the yard. He pulled to a halt and emerged slowly from the van, his eyes fixed on the BMW teetering up on its perch, his mouth bearing the expression of a surprised goldfish. "Now what, may I ask, is going on here?" he asked in a voice that trilled with laughter.

"Sorry for not making the rendezvous, Ronnie. I had a bit of a run-in with our friend Mr. Borthwick. He parked his car right in front of the gates so that I couldn't get the van out."

Ronnie's shoulders had begun to shake with silent mirth. "Oh, boy," he said, still staring at the car, "wait until Patrick hears about this. He will surely laugh himself clean out of his bed." With a click of his fingers, Ronnie hurried round to the back of his van. "I think we should get you away from here before the local constabulary hear about your wee escapade."

Less than a minute later, the Campbeltown consignment was loaded into the refrigerated van. Dan slammed shut the back door, pulled hard on the levers, and turned with his hand outstretched to the still-chuckling buyer.

"Good to meet you, Ronnie."

"Aye, and it's been a pleasure meeting you too, Dan Porter. You're a man after Patrick's heart, and I dare say that you'll be making a good few friends while you're up here in Scotland as well."

Dan raised his eyebrows. "And probably one or two enemies as well."

Ronnie glanced up at the BMW. "Aye, that is probably quite an understatement of fact." He gave Dan a friendly slap on the arm. "But no doubt you'll be able to cope with that."

Dan walked around to the driver's door and pulled it open. "I've coped with worse in my time."

Ronnie shot an index finger at him and winked. "I'm sure you have, Dan Porter. I'm sure you have."

CHAPTER NINETEEN

THE NEW FULL-TIME receptionist at Rebecca Talworth Design Ltd. sorted through the morning's post with practiced speed. Even though still at the tender age of nineteen, she had had the experience of working for a large litigation law practice in the Docklands where filing precision had been considered an essential and integral part of the firm's success. She checked each envelope first to make sure that it didn't bear a mark of confidentiality, and then, slitting it open with a letter knife, she discarded the envelope into the wastepaper bin and placed the letter in its relevant in-tray. Once she had finished, she gathered up the contents of each tray, slipped them into individual cardboard folders, twanged on the elastic retainer bands, and then, cradling the folders in her arms, she went off to deliver them to their respective recipients.

Her first port of call was to the office of Stephen Turnbull, the young and, to her mind, extremely good-looking financial director of the company. As she made to knock on the glass door of his office, he looked up and saw her, his face lighting up in a broad smile, and there was a glint in his eye that made her knees turn to jelly. She could sense immediately the involuntary flush that had been brought to her cheeks. He come-hithered her with his index finger and she entered the office.

"Good morning, Carrie," he drawled, leaning back in his chair and folding his hands behind the slicked-back hair on his head. "How are you this morning?"

"I'm well, thank you, Mr. Turnbull," Carrie replied, trying to avoid looking into his dark-brown eyes by casting a glance first at her armful of files and then out of the window behind him. A pigeon had settled down to preen itself on the rooftop of the building opposite and it was positioned in such a way that it appeared to be sitting on top of his head. She bit at her bottom lip to stop herself from laughing. "And how are you?"

"Couldn't be better." He pushed himself forward and leaned on the desk. "Listen, let's drop this 'Mr. Turnbull' bit. This is not a stuffy old law firm. Stephen'll do fine."

"All right"—Carrie felt her face colour even more—"Stephen."

"Good." He held a hand out for his file. "Anything interesting for me today?"

"Not a lot, I'm afraid," she replied, handing him the file. "Oh, there are the press cuttings from Paris. I didn't read them, though. I thought that you might like to see them first."

Stephen flicked the elastic bands off the file, and then hurriedly sifted through his mail before extracting the stapled pages of the press reports. He glanced quickly through them, dropped them on his desk, and clenched his fist into a tight ball.

"Are they good?" Carrie asked tentatively.

"They are bloody wonderful, Carrie. They are truly bloody wonderful."

Carrie lifted her shoulders in girlish glee. "Oh, that's terrific. Jackie will be delighted."

"You bet she will," Stephen replied, casting a smiling glance past the receptionist and across to the office opposite where Jackie sat at her desk. The steely glare that met him made the smile quickly disappear from his face. "Right," he said, his voice suddenly becoming brusque. "I think that will be all, thanks, Carrie. I won't hold you back. I'm sure you've got lots to do."

The young receptionist became flustered at his sudden change of tone. "Right, yes, of course I have. I'm sorry I've kept you." She hurriedly left the financial director's office and averted her eyes from his gaze as she walked along the corridor to make her next delivery.

Stephen pushed aside the file and picked up the press reports. He held them up, facing Jackie, and brushed their top edge against his mouth. She looked at him quizzically before her mouth dropped open in realization of what he was showing her. He shot three consecutive winks at her, and she immediately understood their meaning. She jumped up from her desk and ran through to his office.

"What are they like?" she asked breathlessly.

Stephen spun the press cuttings across the desk towards her. "See for yourself."

Jackie picked up the pages and flicked through them, her face becoming more animated with each one. "They're brilliant, Stephen. Every one of them is absolutely brilliant!"

Stephen laughed. "I know. And that's even with Gaultier showing at the same time."

"Has Rebecca seen these?"

"I wouldn't have thought so. She's still at home. We'll fax them through and see what she has to say about them."

"She couldn't be anything but pleased."

"I would hope so. It depends on how the mood takes her." Stephen pushed back his chair and got to his feet. "However, I think that *we* should feel extremely pleased with ourselves," he said, walking around behind her and putting his hands on her shoulders, "because it was *us* who put the whole thing together." He blew gently on her right ear.

Jackie, who had been engrossed in the press reports, suddenly realized what was happening. She pulled away from his hold and began casting furtive glances around the open-plan office. Nobody appeared to be looking in their direction. "Stephen!" she exclaimed in a laughing whisper. "For goodness' sakes, don't do that! I've told you before, we don't mix business with pleasure." She leaned back on his desk, keeping a safe distance between them, as she nonchalantly continued to read the reports.

"What a pity," Stephen replied, pushing his hands into the pockets of his trousers, "because I wouldn't mind taking you right here and now on my desk."

"Oh, wouldn't you?" Jackie asked, without shifting her eyes from the paper. "And I suppose that Carrie would be in line for the same kind of treatment."

"She's not my type. I don't go for—"

"Younger women?" Jackie cut in, lifting her head sharply to watch for his reaction.

"That was not what I was going to say." He moved towards her, made to put his arms around her, but then checked himself and instead folded them across his chest. It was he, this time, who cast a glance around at the other offices. "You know how I feel about you, Jackie. I wouldn't muck around."

Jackie let out a sigh. "Aren't we both guilty of that already, Stephen?"

Stephen grabbed the press reports out of her hand and waved them in front of her face. "Listen, we shouldn't be talking like this today. We've got great news. Rebecca Talworth is made, and all thanks to us. We should be celebrating."

Jackie smiled at him. "You're right. We should be."

Stephen let out a sigh of relief. "Jeez, I'm glad you said that. You had me worried there for a minute."

"I worry myself quite often."

"Well, don't." He gave her arm a quick squeeze. "Listen, I've got a great idea."

"And what might that be?"

"I have to head off to Milan the week after next to see if I can strike a deal over the rental of the new premises. Why don't you come with me?"

Jackie shook her head. "I can't."

"Why?"

"Because I've got something on."

"What have you got on?"

Jackie laughed. "I don't know exactly *what*. I'd have to check my diary."

"Come on, then." He grabbed her forcefully by the arm and marched her out of his office, across the corridor, and into her own. "Right, let's check it."

Having been made to hurry, Jackie now took her time, deliberately flicking through the pages of her diary. She came to the appropriate date and ran her finger down the central spine to smooth them open. "Can't do it, I'm afraid. It's Millie and Nina's half term."

Stephen detected the hint of disappointment in her voice, and sensed that all was not lost. "Surely the great and wonderful Battersea Gran could look after them?"

"God, don't talk about her. She's been a nightmare lately. I get a different lecture every time I go home." Jackie drew down the sides of her mouth as she reeled off a host of Battersea Gran's requests in a whining Cockney accent. "Why can't you make an effort to go to one of Nina's concerts? Can't you do some of the shopping for a change? It would be nice if you could *at least* be here at the weekends, so I could go back to my own place for a bit. And why don't you ever phone Dan?"

Stephen's eyes lit up. "Why don't you?"

Jackie shot him an acid look. "Don't you start as well."

"I'm not meaning it in *that* way. Why don't you call and ask if the girls can go up to stay with him and your son for half term? It would be a great adventure for them. Have they ever been to Scotland?"

"No," Jackie replied with a shrug.

"Well, there you are. There's your solution. And what's more, you'd be scoring a few Brownie points with Battersea Gran by letting her get back to her flat for a week."

Jackie pulled the arms of her chair forward and sat down, and began kneading her forehead with her fingertips.

"What's the matter?" Stephen asked.

She dropped her hands to the desk. "I don't think you quite realize how difficult all this is for me."

Stephen moved behind Jackie, leaning one hand on the back of her chair, the other on her desk. To anyone who might have witnessed this action from the corridor, it would appear as if he had just made the move to read something over her shoulder. But Stephen was close enough to see the goosebumps rise when he blew softly on the back of her neck and he could smell the heady muskiness of her perfume.

"I do understand, Jackie, believe me, I do, but I want you to be with me all the time. I *need* you to be with me all the time. And I know that you feel the same way about me. I don't want anything ever to come between us, Jackie, because if that happened, I just couldn't cope with working here anymore. We're a great partnership, my girl, not only in business, so why should we do anything to break that up?" He reached for the telephone receiver, picked it up, and held it out for her. "Go on, give Dan a call"—he leaned over and pressed his mouth to her ear—"and think about Milan!" he whispered.

Jackie took the receiver from him but made no attempt to dial. "Do you really mean that, about wanting me, Stephen?" she asked without turning her head to look at him.

"I think you know me well enough by now, don't you? When I want something badly enough, I'll go all out to get it. And once I've got it, I'll never let it out of my grasp again."

Jackie closed her eyes as she felt his breath tickle the back of her ear. "Would you mind leaving the office, then, while I make the phone call?"

Stephen glanced out at the corridor, then over to the other offices, and finally across to the reception desk. When he was sure that everyone was occupied at work, he planted a light kiss on the nape of Jackie's neck. "Of course. Good luck."

Jackie waited until he was back at his desk before punching in the quick-dial number of Dan's mobile. As it rang, she pulled in a long, settling breath, feeling herself shudder nervously as she let it out.

"Hu-llo?"

Hearing his voice again after so long sent an involuntary shockwave of guilt through her body, but it was countered by the resentment that she felt at the cheeriness of his reply.

"Dan?"

"Jackie, is that you?"

"Yes."

"Just hang on a minute, can you? I'm just going to pull over onto the side of the road." In the background, she could hear the muffled sound of the engine dying as he brought the car to a halt. "Sorry, I didn't look to see who was calling. How *are* you?"

"I'm fine."

"It's so good to hear. I haven't spoken to you for ages."

"I know. I've been really busy."

"How did Paris go?"

Jackie wished that he wouldn't be so bloody interested in everything that she did. "It went really well. The press reports were excellent."

"That's terrific. Well done, you. That's a real feather in your cap."

"Dan?"

"How's everything at home? Battersea Gran coping all right, is she?"

"Yes, she's being wonderful. Dan?"

Once again he cut across her question. "And how are Millie and Nina?" She heard him laugh. "Still watching the soaps instead of doing their homework, are they?"

Jackie grasped the opportunity. "That's what I was calling you about, Dan."

That seemed to quieten him. "There's nothing wrong, is there?" She could hear the concern in his voice.

"No, nothing at all. It's just that . . ." She glanced across to Stephen's office. He was eyeing her intently. She spun her chair round to avoid his gaze. "It's just that it's the girls' half term the week after next, and I have to go over to Milan so I won't be here."

"Right. So, can't Battersea Gran look after them?"

Jackie suddenly saw her direction. "Well, I think your mother could do with a rest. She's longing to go back to Battersea for a bit, and I'm afraid that I just haven't been able to give her the chance."

"So what are you suggesting?"

"Well, maybe that they could come up and stay with you and Josh for the week." She paused to hear Dan's reply, but none was forthcoming. "It would be an adventure for them."

Dan laughed. "You must be joking, Jackie. They'd *hate* it up here. They'd get more enjoyment going to the moon! Anyway, there's hardly enough room for Josh and me to swing a cat in the cottage, let alone have the girls come to join us."

Jackie narrowed her mouth petulantly. "So you don't want them, then?"

"That's not what I said. I would love to have them come to stay more than anything, but I don't think it's, well, very practical. Josh and I leave the house every morning at six-fifteen and we don't get back until early evening. What would they do with themselves?"

"They could look after the dogs." She regretted saying it the moment that she opened her mouth. She knew as well as Dan that the last time the girls had shown any interest in the dogs was when the Porter family, en masse, had driven to the Battersea Dog Home to collect them and Nina had given Cruise his name. "And they both have a lot of work to do, especially Millie. It would be so much better for them to be up in Scotland where there are obviously no distractions. They could just get on with it."

"I don't know, Jackie."

She could sense his resolve falter. "They really have missed both you and Josh, you know." She thought that a little friendly laugh wouldn't go amiss at that precise moment. "Not your cooking, I have to say."

"Jackie, you have to understand that we're *miles* away from the nearest McDonald's."

"Scotland's famous for its fish-and-chip shops, isn't it?"

Jackie bit at the side of a fingernail when she heard him laugh.

"That's true. Maybe I could wean them slowly onto my cooking."

"It really would be an ideal environment for them to catch up on their work, Dan."

"Yeah, I can see that."

"So could they come?"

"It would be a hell of a squash."

"They wouldn't mind that."

"They'd have to bring sleeping bags."

"They're used to kipping on the floor. You know as well as I do how many sleep-overs they go to."

Dan was silent, and Jackie sensed it as being the moment of decision.

"Oh, all right, then, but you'll have to clear it with Millie and Nina first. I don't want them coming up here and just moping around the place."

"Of course I will!" Jackie replied, stifling the urge to jump to her feet and let out a whoop of triumph. "I'll build Scotland up as *the* happening place."

Dan chuckled. "For goodness' sakes, don't do that."

"Leave it to me. I'll say all the right things. Now, how do they get up there?"

"Probably best putting them on the overnight train from Euston to Fort William. When are you thinking of sending them up?"

Jackie turned her chair around and glanced at her diary, realizing immediately that she had no idea when Stephen was planning to go to Milan. "Just hang on a moment." She caught Stephen's eye and beckoned to him frantically. He raced over to her office.

"How did you get on?" he asked as he entered, his voice reverberating around her room.

She mouthed at him to shut up and gesticulated towards the mouthpiece of her telephone before clamping her hand over it.

"Who was that?" Dan asked.

Jackie took her hand away. "Just somebody coming into my office to find out how we got on in Paris."

"Ah, right. So when are they coming up?"

"I'm still trying to find my diary." She put her hand over the mouthpiece again and glared at Stephen. "You nearly blew it then," she whispered angrily at him. "When are you wanting to go over to Milan?"

"I've booked two seats on the Tuesday morning flight out of Heathrow."

"Oh, have you? Was that before or after our little conversation just then?"

"Jackie?" Dan's voice sounded down the telephone. "Are you still there?"

Jackie took her hand away. "Yes, sorry, I've found it now. How about if I put them on the Monday night train? They'd be with you then on Tuesday morning."

"Okay. And when would they have to be back in London?"

Jackie turned the page on her diary. "The following Monday morning would be fine. They are meant to be starting back at school that day, but I'm sure they could be a little late."

"Would you meet them at the station?"

"Yes, or if not, they could always get the tube."

"No, I want you to meet them. If I'm going to have them for the week, I think you could take a bit of time off work just to do that."

"All right. Of course I'll do that. Listen, Dan, I have to go. I've got a meeting about to start. I'll text you their train times."

"You could always ring me during the day."

"I'll see. And everything's all right with you and Josh?"

"Yes, all's well. I'm just on my way back from Buckie at the minute.

Hell, Jackie, you'd have laughed. I had this contretemps with a guy down in Oban—"

"I have to go, Dan," Jackie cut in. "They're calling me into the meeting. Tell me another time."

"Oh, all right." She could hear the tone of his voice dip with disappointment. "It's been great talking to you, Jacks. You know, the other day, I was just thinking that in all the time that we've been married, I don't think that—"

"Your line's breaking up, Dan. I can't hear you very well." She put her finger on the button to end the call, and slowly replaced the telephone on its cradle.

Stephen had not bothered to return to his office, but had remained standing by her door until she finished the call. "Sorry about that," he said quietly. "I didn't know that you were still speaking to him."

"I realized that."

"So are we on for Milan?"

Jackie smiled at him and nodded.

Stephen gave her the thumbs-up. "That's wonderful. You just wait. I'll give you the time of your life."

CHAPTER TWENTY

THE STORY ABOUT Dan's little escapade in the loading yard in Oban was recounted to Patrick, with all the exaggeration of a game of Chinese Whispers, long before Dan arrived back at Auchnacerie that evening. Patrick did indeed laugh, but contrary to Ronnie Macaskill's predictions, he never managed to shift himself from his bed that day, nor for a week after. Dan's reputation, however, was given a healthy boost by his actions, and the true animosity felt against Maxwell Borthwick in the area was confirmed to Dan every time he went into a shop or a pub or a filling station. Everyone had heard the story, and everyone had heard it differently.

Also, it had helped to create a real bond in his relationship with Ronnie Macaskill, a man renowned for keeping himself to himself and having a total inability to suffer fools. Thereafter, no matter where Dan was, Ronnie would call him on his mobile every morning at ten o'clock to find out what prices Dan had been paying and with which boats he had been dealing. Ronnie relinquished to Dan every shrewd bit of knowledge in his possession about buying prawns.

Dan's own opinion of the man, however, was slightly dented the following weekend when Ronnie inveigled both him and Josh into representing Seascape in a game of *camanachd* against a rival company from Elgin.

"Played a bit of sport in your time, have you, Dan?" Ronnie had asked him during one of their morning telephone calls.

"I used to play a bit of football, yes."

"That would set you up well, then."

"Set me up for what?"

"I'm short of a few players to play *camanachd* for the company on Saturday, so I was hoping that maybe you and Josh would be good enough to take part."

"*Cama*-what? Ronnie, I can't even pronounce it, let alone play the game."

"You'll know it better as shinty, no doubt."

"Oh, right. I've got you now. That's a hell of a rough game, isn't it?"

"No, no, not at all. It's a wee bit of a mixture between hockey and lacrosse, not unlike the kind of games that you see played at girls' schools. It should be nothing more than a doddle for you."

The tinge of sardonic humour in Ronnie's voice as he imparted this information did nothing to convince Dan of its total truth.

"How long does the game go on for?"

"It would just be two halves of forty-five minutes each."

"*Ninety minutes?* Ronnie, I'd have a heart attack! I haven't taken any exercise for about eighteen months."

"That's not a worry. We're short of a goalkeeper anyway, so you won't be having to do too much running about."

"I don't know about this, Ronnie. I have a feeling that I might just let everybody down."

"Not at all. We're just a bunch of amateurs having a wee bit of a hit-around."

Having eventually agreed to play, Dan found out later from a knowledgeable, though clearly inebriated, aficionado of the sport over an evening drink in the Nevisview public bar that even those who played for the teams that made up the Marine Harvest National Premier League were of amateur status. He was also informed that, five years previously, Ronnie Macaskill, that unassuming and mild-mannered individual who had sweet-talked him into playing, had been the centre forward for Kingussie, and that during the time that he had worn their colours, the team had walked away with the prestigious Glemorangie Camanachd Cup no fewer than three times. What's more, he had represented Scotland twice in the annual Shinty Hurling International against Ireland.

It was therefore quite understandable that the following Saturday, Dan's nerves were jangling to such an extent that he was forced to have a number of unscheduled stops at the side of the road on the way from the cottage to the playing field in Fort William. As he nonchalantly viewed the beauty of the surrounding countryside while being stared at by the occupants of passing cars, he wished that he could have had a fraction of the youthful enthusiasm for the forthcoming battle displayed by his bandana-headed son who sat sucking his teeth in the car, desperate to get to the field of conflict and to get stuck in to the opposition.

Having given his team a pep talk that started with a secretive message on tactics and crescendoed into a motivational war cry, Ronnie broke free from the huddle of players and walked over to Dan, who was standing by the touchline, leaning on a *caman,* his designated weapon for the day, staring open-mouthed towards one end of the pitch.

"What the hell is *that?*" he asked, pointing his *caman* at the gigantic goal.

"That's the *tadhal*—the goal."

"But it's bigger than the bloody gates of Buckingham Palace!"

"Not quite. It measures about twelve foot by ten foot."

"Ronnie, that's one hundred and twenty square feet! How the hell am I meant to stop the ball from going in there?"

"Well, there would be three ways, actually. You can either 'cleek' it with your *caman,* slap it away, or stop it with your open hand."

Dan shook his head in desperation at Ronnie's calculated misunderstanding of his complaint. "Thanks, Ronnie."

"Oh, and you can stop the ball with your foot, if you like, but you're not allowed to swing a boot at it"—he let out a chuckle of a laugh—"nor at any of your opponents, for that matter."

Dan let out a resigned sigh. "Right, I suppose I'd better get ready, then."

Ronnie gave him an encouraging pat on the back. "Aye, a good idea, lad. Take a couple of turns around the pitch to get warmed up."

Dan narrowed his eyes at the man. "I wasn't meaning that. I meant that I should put on my protective gear."

Ronnie clicked his fingers. "Och, I was forgetting about that." He ran off into the hut at the side of the pitch and returned far too quickly holding out Dan's armour to him.

Dan ran his tongue against the top row of his teeth, wondering if it would be the last time that he would ever be able to do such a thing. "What is that?" he asked quietly, looking at the wafer-thin pair of shin pads and the soft leather gloves that Ronnie held in his hand.

Ronnie dropped the meagre collection on the ground in front of his goalkeeper. "That, Dan, is your gear."

"You have got to be joking."

Ronnie gave him a wink. "Don't worry. Those laddies will never get near your goal."

The game ended after ninety minutes of play, plus a full ten minutes of injury time, in a resounding 5–1 victory for the Seascape Camanachd Club. For Dan, however, it ended after only twenty minutes of the first half. He had been standing quite happily minding his own business in the goalmouth a good seventy yards from where the action was taking place, when the ball suddenly came looping through the air in his direction. The centre forward of the opposing side, a deceptive little devil who looked as if he trained on four pints of lager before each game but who, in truth, had the same fleetness of foot as Pegasus, covered fifty yards of the pitch at such a speed that he arrived with at least two seconds in hand at the spot where the ball was destined to make contact once more with terra firma. This fractional moment in time gave him the opportunity to steady his feet and to swing his *caman* around his head like a hammer thrower, before hitting a first-time ball absolutely fair and square in the direction of Dan.

Dan stood transfixed, like an earthling who was caught in the path of a mighty meteor from space, his eyes rooted on the cork and leather missile that flew towards him. In the last few seconds before his eternal demise, and as he found out later, much to the disgust of his fellow players, Dan took cowardly avoidance action, ducking unceremoniously and covering his head with his arms. He felt a whistling wind rush past him as the ball screamed over his quaking shoulders, immediately followed by the zing as it concaved into the back of the net. Dan unfurled himself and stared at the ball on the ground, convinced that a few wisps of smoke still rose from its leather casing. The blood in his body, which had been hitherto pumping madly somewhere about his feet, began to boil up to his head and he turned, his eyes bulging in fury, as he glared at the perpetrator of this unsportsman-like deed.

"You stupid bastard!" he yelled as he charged up the pitch, with *caman* raised, like Rob Roy leading the final charge against the Redcoats at the Battle of Killiecrankie. "You had at least a hundred square feet of fucking goal to shoot at, and you had to hit the fucking ball straight at me!"

It was now the turn of Pegasus to stand immobile, and if it had not been for the intervention of Josh who, just before the moment of contact, yelled out, "Dad, for goodness' sakes, what the *hell's* got into you?" Dan would have cleaved the man from head to foot with one blow.

Dan's reputation was therefore further enhanced by being the first Seascape Camanachd Club player ever to be red-carded from the field of play. Not that he minded much. Josh took over the goalkeeping duties thereafter and, no doubt in part due to the presence of Maria José on the touchline, performed for the rest of the game with the alacrity of a scalded cat.

CHAPTER TWENTY-ONE

Dan's heart sank the moment he woke up on the morning that the girls' train was due to pull into Fort William Station. He had become quite accustomed to lying in bed for those few precious seconds after his alarm had gone off, listening to the wind lightly blowing on the start of yet another sun-filled day. However, on this occasion, it whistled through the gap in his open window and splattered rain off the tin roof like the incessant roll of a snare drum, thus heralding the end of the long-running Indian summer.

He got out of bed and padded through to the main room, realizing as he went that the temperature in the house had dropped by about ten degrees. Having been lulled into a state of complacency by the continuance of the good weather, he had forgotten to bring in logs for the cooking stove the night before. He stuck his bare feet into a virgin pair of Wellington boots, chucked on a padded jacket, from which the price tag still hung, over his T-shirt and sports shorts, gave a short whistle to call the dogs from their bed, and ventured outside. He was back in the house no more than thirty seconds later. Having dumped the armful of logs into the wooden box by the stove, he began hopping from one foot to the other and beating his arms around his chest to get himself warm. The day was similar to the one when he had first arrived in Fort William five weeks ago, if not worse.

He was standing on the platform as the train slowly pulled into the station, the zip of his jacket done up beyond his chin, his hands thrust deep into its pockets, and a woollen hat, with *Ski Aonach Mor* emblazoned across its rim, pulled down over his ears. He looked down the length of the train at the unsynchronized motion of the doors being opened and slammed shut again, and watched as the drab-clothed mountain folk with their gaitered legs and crampon-festooned rucksacks disembarked from the carriages. And then into this fashionless scene stepped Millie and Nina, wearing such bewildered expressions and out-of-place clothes that it would seem they had just taken the wrong tube line from Notting Hill Gate.

By the time he reached them, the trailing hems of his eldest daughter's baggy jeans were already seeping up the dirty brown water that lay an inch deep on the platform, and she shivered as she pulled her miniscule army jacket around her in a vain attempt to give her bare midrift some protection against the elements. Nina, meanwhile, stood with a set of earphone wires hanging limply from her ears, moving her head from side to side like a short-circuited robot as she took in her new surroundings. Her bright yellow bell-bottomed trousers had started the same osmotic process as those of her sister, while the wooly white collar of her purple Afghan waistcoat had begun to take on the appearance, and no doubt the odour, of a miserably wet billy goat.

"Hi there, you two," Dan exclaimed enthusiastically as he opened his arms to give Millie a hug. She jumped away as if being set upon by a deranged sex maniac, her sudden movement almost displacing the pair of rain-spattered Oakley sunglasses that held back her short blonde hair.

"Dad, is that *you*?" she asked, her nose wrinkling up in disgust as she visually ingested his attire from head to foot.

"Of course it is. I haven't been away from London *that* long, have I?"

"Why are you dressed like such a prat?"

Dan snorted out a laugh, realizing now why his initial meeting with Katie at this exact venue must have seemed like the first-time encounter of ET and its young earthling mate. "Don't worry. You'll soon find out." He leaned over and gave Millie an unreciprocated kiss on each of her freezing cheeks before turning his attentions to Nina. He needn't have bothered. She could have been set upon by that deranged sex maniac without even a look of surprise flashing across her sleet-stung features.

"Ni, aren't you going to say hullo?" Dan asked, his head held to the side as he waited for some kind of reaction to their meeting.

The sideways movement of Nina's head eventually sped up to a definite shake of negativity. "This has to be the arsehole of the world," she said in a voice that would seem that she had just found herself eternally condemned to the depths of Satan's empire.

"Oh, it's not that bad," Dan retorted cheerfully, "although it is a real pity that it's raining today. We've just had a month of nothing but sun."

Nina chucked back her head. "Typical," she tutted as she bent down and heaved up her canvas bag, its sides cascading off rivulets of icy rain.

Dan swept up Millie's suitcase and relieved Nina of her load. "Come on, we'll get you back to the cottage. It's really cosy there. You'll be warm again in no time." He had taken no more than a dozen steps towards the exit of the station before the cases were once more dropped to the ground, and he stood exercising his cramped and aching fingers.

"What the hell have you brought with you? Bags of cement?"

"I wish," Millie replied morosely, tucking her hands under her armpits to keep them warm. "Mum made us bring all our schoolbooks with us. Some half term this is going to turn out to be."

They drove back to the cottage alongside the murky waters of Loch

Eil, and once again Dan wished that the Indian summer could have held out for just a week longer. The air of despondency inside the fuggy interior of Patrick's Mercedes was almost tangible, and Dan could tell that the false gaiety in his voice as he pointed out mist-shrouded landmarks was getting very close to manic level. The car, in fact, had been the only thing to date that had brought any kind of verbal comment from Nina.

"We had a car like this once, but it had leather seats and was much newer."

It got worse. As Dan pulled into the lane that led up to the cottage, Nina, who had been sitting alone in the back of the car and had been trying to stave off the slavering attention of the dogs all the way from Fort William, suddenly burst into floods of tears. Dan glanced in the rearview mirror at the collapsed face of his younger daughter. "Ni, what is it?" he asked concernedly.

"I want to go home," she choked out in long, stuttering sobs. "This is the worst place I've ever been to in my life."

"Well, you can't go home," Millie retorted with feeling. "We've been banished, remember."

"That's enough, Millie," Dan said quietly out of the side of his mouth.

"But I had two parties to go to, and Barnie was going to be at one of them."

Dan stopped the car at the top of the lane, jumped out and opened up the rear passenger door, and got in beside his daughter. He put his arm around her and gave her a hug. "It's only going to be for a week, Ni, and anyway, you'll enjoy yourself. Just wait and see."

"But what's there to *do* up here?" Nina howled.

"Well," Dan said slowly, trying desperately to think of something moderately exciting to lift his younger daughter's shattered spirits. "Quite a lot, really."

Millie, meanwhile, had decided to get into the promised warmth of the cottage as quickly as possible. Having got out of the car, she skipped from side to side up to the gate, doing her best not to get the track's now slimy mud on any part of her new silver-grey Reebok trainers. She was in the process of working out Josh's complicated but totally dog-proof latch system, when she suddenly turned and raced back to the car at the speed of an Olympic sprinter, cares for her fancy footwear cast frivolously to the biting wind. She tore the car door open, jumped in, and slammed it shut.

"My God, that thing is *terrifying!*" she screamed out melodramatically, her eyes fixed on the far corner of the cottage. "What *is* it, Dad?"

Her voice had expressed such fear and alarm that even Dan wondered momentarily whether he had been unconsciously living in the depths of Jurassic Park for the past five weeks. Then, around the edge of the wooden fence at the front of the garden, appeared the fiercely horned head of Dolly, the resident Blackface ewe, a piece of grass sticking out the side of her mouth and an expression on her face that would seem to suggest that she was deeply miffed that her welcome had been so mannerlessly rebuffed.

"Don't worry," said Dan, taking his arm from around the heaving shoulders of his younger daughter and getting out of the car. "That's just Dolly. She's as harmless as a . . ." He didn't bother to finish. He couldn't think of any happy, pleasing simile that would make any bloody difference to his daughters' miserable appraisal of their new surroundings. "Come on, you two," he sighed, "out you get. It's time to survey the Taj Mahal."

They declined the bacon and eggs that Josh had generously left for them on top of the cooking stove and breakfasted in silence on cereal and yoghurt, casting looks around the room and then at each other, lifting an eyebrow in foreboding of what they were to suffer during the course of their mid-term break. Dan whistled a merry tune as he went about his domestic chores, hoping that the false contentment that he displayed over his Spartan abode might in some way be infective enough to rub off on the girls. It was, indeed, a tall order.

"I have to go to work now," he said as he returned the dustpan and brush to the cupboard next to the sink, "so I would suggest that you just get yourselves settled in. The telly works well enough and there are a few videos on the shelf over there. All I ask is that you keep the stove going, because that does everything here—the cooking, the heating, and the hot water." He proceeded to give a demonstration on the art of replenishing the boiler that would have worked well on playschool. "You take the wood from here," he said, picking up a log from the box and holding it out to show them what a log looked like, "and then you take it to the stove and you open this door, like this, and then you put the log inside, and close the door again. Simple as that."

"Ooh, do you think that we can manage that, Nina?" Millie squeaked in a little girl's voice. "It looks *awfully* difficult."

Dan laughed. "All right. Just don't forget to do it, okay?"

"When will you be back?" Nina asked.

"No later than six o'clock."

"*Six o'clock*? You're leaving us here all by ourselves until *six o'clock*?"

"I'm sorry, but I do have to work, Ni. You'll be all right. The dogs will be with you."

Nina eyed disdainfully the two slumbering forms on the rug in front of the stove. "Thanks a bunch."

"I will have the weekend off," Dan continued, feeling a sudden guilt about his departure. "We'll all go off and do something together."

"When does Josh get back, then?" Millie asked.

"That depends."

"On what?"

"On whether he's finishing early or late at the factory and whether he's seeing Maria José. He usually gets back at—"

"Maria *what*?" Millie interjected, her eyes fixed questioningly on her father.

Dan bit at his tongue, wishing that he hadn't said anything. "Maria José."

He watched the girls' eyes sparkle as they looked at each other. "Josh doesn't have a *girlfriend,* does he?"

"Well, yes, he does, as a matter of fact."

"God, she must be blind or something," Millie scoffed.

"Or so ugly that she can't find anyone else to go out with," Nina added with a giggle.

"Or an illegal immigrant who needs to find someone to marry her so that she can stay in this country," Millie continued.

"Well, you're both completely wrong about everything. Maria José is a very beautiful and intelligent girl, and she is obviously extremely fond of Josh, otherwise she wouldn't be going out with him."

"What does she do?"

"She works in the prawn factory with Josh."

Millie let out a derisive laugh. "Come on, Dad, she couldn't be *that* intelligent if she works in a *prawn* factory!"

"And she must smell *horrible* as well," Nina remarked as she feigned a vomit. "Think of those *fingers* running through Josh's hair!"

Dan shook his head. "All right, I've had enough of you two for now. I'm going. Have you brought your mobiles with you?"

"Of course we have," said Millie. "We want *some* kind of contact with the outside world."

"Well, in that case, give me a call if you want anything. You'll have to walk up the hill at the back of the house if you want to get a signal, though. There's a small tree up there where you'll find that it works."

Nina stared fixedly at her father for a moment, then turned to her elder sister and slowly shook her head. "You see," she said miserably, "this is the arsehole of the world."

THE WEATHER DURING the next three days did nothing to disprove Nina's opinion of the place. They never ventured from the confines of their Highland prison and even suffered the self-imposed torture of being *ex-text-communicado* with their friends in London. On the first evening, while they had sat watching television, Millie had walked around the room, climbing up onto various bits of furniture, and while tottering precariously on her perch, had gazed fixedly at the screen of her mobile phone in the hope that even one blip of reception signal would appear. Eventually, the precious phone had been unlovingly discarded into her suitcase, its usefulness done, and she had flumped down onto the sofa between Nina and Josh to watch the film *Ten Things I Hate About You* for the fifth time.

There were, however, moments of diversion. On the Tuesday evening, Josh bravely took the girls with him into Fort William where they met up with Maria José for a drink in the Nevisview Inn. Neither Millie nor Nina contributed much to the flow of conversation, but instead sat picking their fingernails and staring at the dark-eyed Spanish girl, trying to find something about her that they could criticize. When Dan asked them on their return how they had got on, and whether they had liked Maria José, the girls, having been able to find a blemish neither in her character nor on her face, simply grunted and within five minutes had slipped themselves wordlessly into the comforting depths of their sleeping bags. All that Dan had done, thereafter, was to shoot a knowing wink at his son.

The following evening, they were asked over to Auchnacerie for supper. Dan had at first thought about suggesting that he should cook the meal, but then remembered that his daughters did not hold his culinary delights in such high esteem as did the Trenchard family. So he left it to Katie to produce exactly what was required—hamburgers, baked beans, and chips—and for the first time since Millie and Nina had been in Scotland, Dan watched with relief how the simple comforts of fast food brought smiles back to their faces. With a good deal of help from Josh, Patrick made it to the supper table, his face drawn and dark rings under his eyes, but his indomitable spirit still burning as fiercely as a bush fire. He teased Millie rotten over her taste in clothes, and then suggested that Nina should hang on for Max, because even though he was five years her junior, he was going to be some looker. What delighted and surprised Dan was the way in which the girls took the ribbing, and Millie even gave back as good as she got when she told Patrick that his hairstyle was at the height of fashion—for scarecrows. Sitting next to Katie at the top end of the table, Dan caught her eye during the meal and the look that passed between read only that things were surely turning for the good. By the end of the evening, a slight flush of colour had returned to Patrick's pallid features, and there seemed at last to be the beginnings of a mild acceptance by Millie and Nina that their week's sojourn in the wild, unfashionable wastes of northern Scotland wasn't going to turn out as badly as they had at first predicted.

On the Friday morning, the wind dropped and the rain clouds once more moved off eastwards over the tall stack of Ben Nevis, leaving the adjacent waters of Loch Eil and Loch Linnhe bathed by a pale autumnal sun. Before slipping quietly from the house, Dan left a note on the kitchen table for the girls saying that he felt they had done enough homework for the week, and that they should take things easy for the day. He added that they should maybe take advantage of the good weather and walk up to the tree and telephone their mother to tell her how they were getting on. However, he had little doubt in his mind that they would treat the day in similar fashion to those that had gone before, and that when he returned from work, they would still be lying prostrate on the sofas, tucked into their sleeping bags with their eyes glued to the television.

That evening, therefore, it was with considerable surprise and a certain amount of consternation that he read the note that lay alongside his own on the kitchen table. It was written in Millie's flourishing scrawl.

Dad,

It's such a beautiful day that we have decided to go up to the tree to phone Mum and then take the dogs for a walk. We'll probably be back before you get the chance to read this, but thought I should just let you know.

Love Millie

Dan dropped the note on the table and glanced out of the window. Darkness was beginning to shroud the hills opposite, and already he could make out a pair of headlights darting through the trees on the road at the other side of the loch. He shrugged his jacket back on again and walked out into the garden, feeling the night drop its invisible veil of chilling dampness over him. He hurried round to the back of the cottage and ran up the hill to the tree. There, on the ground, he found a newly discarded Hollywood chewing gum wrapper. They had definitely been there.

"Oh, for heaven's sakes! Where have you got to, you silly girls," he murmured under his breath as he pressed on up the hill. He felt beads of sweat break out on his forehead at the effort of the climb and the constant lifting of his feet to clear the tall, springy heather, but they turned cold as they trickled between his eyebrows and down the side of his nose. Just as he reached the top of the hill, he fell flat on his face in the heather, his shoe having lost its grip on a lichen-covered stone. He pushed himself back to his feet and stood motionless, looking around him.

"Oh, my God," he said slowly.

He had never ventured that far up the hill before. In the near-darkness, he could see now that nothing lay beyond its summit except total emptiness. He could walk on and never stop, and he prayed to God that that was not what Millie and Nina and the dogs had chosen to do. He yelled out their names, but his voice was lost to the rising wind. He tried to whistle in a vain attempt to attract the dogs' attention, but his mouth had gone dry, and all that came out was a pathetic exhalation of air. He turned and began to make his way clumsily down the hill, fumbling in the jacket pocket for his mobile phone. He stopped long enough to get Josh's number up onto the screen, and then continued his descent, bouncing over the heather, with the phone clamped to his ear.

"Josh?"

"Hi, Dad. How are things?"

"Where are you?"

"Just leaving work. I'm going to come straight home this evening."

"Josh, the girls have gone."

"Have they? Where?"

"I don't bloody know. They left a note for me on the kitchen table, saying that they were going off for a walk. They're not back, Josh."

"Oh, they'll be fine, Dad. Those girls have never walked farther than the length of Portobello market in their lives."

"But I found a chewing gum wrapper up by the tree."

"Ah, I see what you mean. So where are you at the minute?"

"I'm on my way back down to the cottage. Josh, if they're up on the hill, they'll never find their way back. They'll be lost, Josh."

"What do you think we should do?"

"I've no idea." Dan stopped to catch his breath. "Yes, actually, I do. Go to the police station, Josh. Tell them that your two sisters left the cottage this afternoon at about three o'clock with two dogs and that they haven't returned. Give them descriptions and anything they want to know, and tell them that we'll need to get search parties out looking for them as soon as possible."

"That's a bit serious, Dad. Do you really think it's that bad?"

"Too right, I do. I think they're in a heap of trouble."

"What are you going to do?"

"I'll take the car along to Auchnacerie to find out if they've been there. If not, I'll call you back from Trenchards' phone."

"All right." Josh paused on the line. "Dad?"

"What is it?"

"I'm sure they'll be fine. I can usually sense if something's gone wrong."

Dan silently blessed his son's ability to come out with the right words at the right time. It had been exactly that way when they had sat to-gether watching the towers of the World Trade Center crumble to the ground. "I hope you're right, Josh. I pray to God that you're right."

He burst into the kitchen at Auchnacerie without so much as a knock on the door, and found every member of the Trenchard family present, each occupied with a different project. Max lay on the sofa, fingers flicking the controls of a Play Station as he stared intently at the darting figures and flashing laser beams that filled the television screen; Sooty was at one end of the kitchen table, absorbed in yet another pictorial masterpiece; while Patrick and Katie, seated at the other end, entered data onto the laptop computer from the untidy pile of bills and receipts that Patrick had in front of him. They were immediately united by their looks of surprise and concern when Dan entered.

"Everything all right, Dan?" Patrick asked, peering over a pair of half-moon reading glasses.

"You haven't by any chance seen Millie and Nina, have you?"

Patrick looked across at his wife. She shrugged her shoulders. "No. Why? Are they not at the cottage?"

Dan let out a deep sigh of despair. "They went off for a walk at about three o'clock with the dogs and they haven't returned."

"Oh, for goodness' sakes!" Katie exclaimed, getting up from her seat and pushing her way past Sooty. "Have you any idea where they've gone?"

"No, but I've a horrible suspicion that they could have gone over the top of the hill at the back of the cottage."

Patrick began to push himself to his feet. "Kate, get on the phone to the police station in Fort William."

"Don't bother to get up, Patrick," Dan said. "I've already done that. At least, I've called Josh and asked him to go round to tell them that they're missing."

"I don't think they'll have gone very far," Max said, sending a laser beam towards a grotesque creature that exploded in a splat of computer-generated gore. "They're not the type."

"That's enough, Max," Patrick said sharply to him. "This is really quite serious, you know."

"That's all right," Dan said. "Josh said exactly the same thing. Would you mind if I called him to say that they're not here?"

Patrick gestured towards the telephone. "Of course. Go ahead."

Katie put a hand on Dan's arm as he went to pick up the receiver. "I'm sure that they'll be all right, Dan. They can't have gone that far."

"But this countryside is bloody treacherous, Katie!" Dan said vehemently, getting frustrated by their calmness. He began forcefully dialing Josh's number. "I'm always reading in the papers about people being found dead up in the bloody Highlands. I mean, they're not even prepared for the weather up here. The kind of clothes they're wearing wouldn't keep an ant warm."

Sooty sat with her pencil raised in the air, as if asking for permission to speak in a classroom. "Dan the Man?"

"You said that they had the dogs with them," Patrick stated.

"Yes."

"Well, that's good, because they've been here long enough to get their bearings. What's more, if they do have to send out the search dogs for the girls, then"—Patrick caught Katie's eye and saw from her expression that she thought he should tone it down a bit—"well, it'll help anyway."

Sooty now supported her tiring arm with a hand under the elbow. Once more she tried to get a word in. "Dan the Man?"

"Josh, it's Dad," Dan said into the receiver.

Katie turned to her daughter. "What *is* it, Sooty? Can't you see that Dan is on the phone?" She softened her voice. "We're all a bit worried, angel, because Millie and Nina have gone missing somewhere."

"I *know.*"

"So why don't you just get on with your drawing so that we can work out what best can be done to help find them?"

"But I don't think that they *need* to be found." Sooty was all at once set upon by four sets of staring eyes. She wondered what she had said wrong *now.* "Well, anyway, not up the hill," she said quietly as she got on with her drawing.

The telephone was slammed down mid-sentence and Sooty suddenly found herself hemmed in on the bench by Katie and Dan.

"What do you mean, Sooty?" Katie asked her daughter.

"I *saw* Millie and Nina out of the window there." She pointed out into the darkness. "They were on the road and I waved to them, and they waved back."

"Can you remember when this was?" Dan asked.

"When Mummy went to get Max from school. Daddy had gone to the loo, and I was sitting here by myself."

Dan looked over the top of Sooty's curly black head at Katie. "What time would that have been?"

"About quarter past four," Katie replied.

Thumping his elbows onto the table, Dan slapped his hands to his forehead and let out a long sigh of relief. "Thank goodness for that! At least they're not up on the hill." He bent over and gave Sooty a kiss on the top of her head. "Thanks, Sooty, you are a wonder girl." He jumped to his feet and went back over to the telephone and dialed Josh's number.

"Josh?"

"Have you found them?"

"No, not yet."

"Oh." Josh's voice dropped in disappointment. "I thought that when you hung up just then—"

"Sooty saw them earlier this afternoon, Josh, so they're not up the hill."

Dan heard his son let out a long sigh. "Well, that's something, anyway. Where were they heading?"

Dan looked over to where Sooty was continuing with her drawing. "Can you remember which way they were going, Sooty?"

"That way," Sooty replied, pointing the rubber on her pencil westwards. "They were going towards the bridge at the top of the loch."

"They were heading towards the main road, Josh."

"Right, I'll tell the police."

"Are you at the station?"

"Yes. They've got the Mountain Rescue Team on standby."

"Well, tell them that I don't think that we'll be needing them, but could you ask the police to check the main road between Kinlocheil and Fort William? I'll go out myself to see if I can find them. You'd better stay there just in case any word of their whereabouts comes through."

"Okay."

"Well done, Josh. And thanks."

"No worries. I was right, you see, Dad. The girls are going to be fine."

"I hope so, Josh. We've still got to find them, though."

The telephone call came through just as Dan was moving off in the car from Auchnacerie. Katie came rushing out of the house and banged on the back window to stop him.

"They've been found, Dan."

Dan jumped out of the car. "Thank heavens! Where?" he said, walking quickly ahead of Katie into the house.

"Glenfinnan."

"*Glenfinnan*? What on earth were they doing there?" He entered the kitchen and picked up the receiver from the sideboard. "Hullo?"

"Is that Mr. Dan Porter?" The man spoke with a slow, easy accent that did little to accentuate the urgency of the situation.

"Yes, it is."

"This is Constable Lamond here of the Northern Constabulary."

Dan hurried him for information. "You've found my daughters, Constable Lamond."

"That I have, sir. That I have. The two girls and their dogs are in my van at this very moment in time."

Dan blew out a relieved breath. "Thank you, Constable Lamond. I very much appreciate your trouble. They're none the worse for wear, then?"

"Aye, well, it depends on what you mean by that, sir."

"What do you mean?"

"Well, the control room at the station received a phone call from

Jimmy Maclean, the landlord at the Jacobite Inn at Glenfinnan, saying that two girls had recently left his establishment in a state that would raise a wee bit of concern."

"What do you mean? They were *drunk*?"

"Aye, well, sir, they would seem to be fairly inebriated. Jimmy Maclean feels awful ashamed and also a wee bit angry that he had been serving underage drinkers, but with all their fancy makeup, he thought that they were both of a legal age."

Dan screwed up his eyes and ran a hand over the top of his head. "Where did you pick them up?"

"On the main road, sir, about two miles out of Glenfinnan. They were heading back on the road to Fort William with a wee bit of difficulty. Certainly the dogs seemed to be making better weather of the walking than your daughters."

"What had they been drinking?"

"Ah, well, the evidence was there for all to see."

"Meaning?"

"Both were carrying packs of these Alco pop-thingies under their arms. Awful dangerous stuff, sir. Shouldn't really be allowed, passing off alcohol as lemonade."

Dan pressed his fingers to his forehead. "Oh, the *stupid* idiots!" he said quietly.

"Aye, I would agree, sir. I've already given them a good talking-to, but I don't think that a few words from yourself would go amiss."

"They'll certainly get that, Constable. I'm really sorry that you've had to deal with this. We'd better arrange a meeting point and I'll come and pick them up."

"Don't worry about that, sir. I'm on my way back to Fort William anyway, so I'll drop them off on my way past."

"Do you know where I live?"

"It'd be the cottage where Patrick Trenchard stayed, would it not?"

"Exactly."

"Well, I'll be there in about fifteen minutes."

"I'll be waiting, Constable."

The phone rang again before Dan had the time to turn round to witness the reactions of Patrick and Katie. He picked up the receiver without thinking.

"Hullo?"

It was Josh. "Dad? Have you heard the latest?"

"Have I not."

"Bloody headcases. What the hell did they think they were doing?"

"That's what I'm going to find out in about fifteen minutes."

"Well, don't go all soft on them, just because they've been missing. They won't have any idea how much trouble they've caused."

"I wouldn't think so for a minute."

"Just lay into them, Dad."

"I'll deal with it, Josh."

"Yeah, well. Listen, I don't feel like coming home right now. I'm going to give Maria José a call and meet her for a drink."

"Good idea. Sorry, Josh, about all this. To be quite honest, I have no idea what I'm going to do with them after this escapade."

"If I were you, I'd put them on the next train back to London. If they want to behave like that, they can damned well stay down there. This has done nothing for our family's reputation up here, you know."

Dan found himself grimacing at the formality of the admonishment delivered by his ex-grunge son. "I know, Josh. I do realize that, and I promise you that I'll make sure that they're fully aware of that."

"Bloody *idiots*," Josh said with a spit of animosity before ending the call.

Dan left the Trenchards' house immediately, only giving a brief account of what had taken place. Josh had been right. It was an embarrassment and he was glad to have the excuse to leave, saying that he had to get back to the cottage before the constable arrived with his wretched load.

There was no way that Dan could utter even one word of rebuke to his daughters that evening. He realized that the moment they entered the house, clinging to the arms of the constable as if being guided blindfolded along a precipitous mountain path. Even the dogs skulked off to their bed in front of the stove without giving Dan their usual rapturous welcome.

"If I were you, sir," said the tall, stern-faced policeman, "I would just get them into their beds and then have a wee word with them in the morning."

Nina's eyes tried to focus on her father, then her ashen features turned an impossible shade of green and she started to retch. Dan grabbed her and forcefully lifted her outside where she rid herself of at least some of the contents of her stomach.

As they came back into the cottage, Constable Lamond raised his eyebrows. "Aye, we've had a number of forced stops on the way home for that kind of thing, I'm afraid."

He stayed long enough to help Dan get the girls into their sleeping bags, and then, having seen him to the door with further thanks and apologies, Dan set about covering the floor around the comatose bodies of his daughters with newspapers and an assortment of receptacles that could be used in the event of further upheaval. He then sat on the sofa for the next three hours, staring at the girls, sometimes leaning forward to brush a hand against their foreheads just to make sure that they were still in the land of the living. And as he sat there, taking in the characteristics of their faces—the dimple on Millie's chin that was his, the fine blonde hair that was Jackie's, the arch of Nina's eyebrows that was his, the fullness of her mouth that was Jackie's—his heart began to ache at the thought that the evening's shenanigans could have turned out so much worse.

The girls did not wake until just before eleven o'clock the following morning. Josh had gone off to work at the normal time, which pleased Dan. He knew that his son would have had much harsher things to say to his sisters than those that Dan himself had planned. As soon as they raised their throbbing heads from their pillows, Dan handed each a glass of water and a couple of Nurofen capsules, and by the time that they had ventured out of their sleeping bags and sat down at the kitchen table, the pained furrowing of their foreheads had lessened. Not a word passed between them as Dan placed the plateful of well-done toast and mugs of hot, sweet tea in front of them. The girls glanced across the table at each other and both simultaneously burst into tears.

Even though Dan's heart yearned to comfort them, he kept up his work in silence. He picked up their sleeping bags and folded them up and put them on the sofa. He cleared the buckets and saucepans from the floor and scrumpled up the newspapers and threw them in the dustbin. And all the while, the girls kept crying and picking at their toast and drinking their tea in mouselike quantities.

It was Millie who eventually broke the silence. "We are really sorry, Dad. We really are."

"Right," said Dan, and then began to wash up his own breakfast things.

"We didn't mean to do it," said Nina, giving him full benefit of her doe-eyed meekness.

Dan turned to look at her, but his expression of displeasure never changed. "Right." He slung the dishcloth over his shoulder and began stacking away cups and plates in the cupboard next to the sink.

Millie began sobbing with renewed gusto. "We are just so *miserable,* Dad. You don't understand. We just hate it *so* much."

Dan threw the dishcloth onto the table between them with force. "It was only for a week, you know. That's all. One week. And I think that the least you could have done, for my sake, was to just make the best of it. In fact, I really thought you were. Both of you were in sparkling form the other night at the Trenchards. I was really proud of you. And then you have to go and do a stupid thing like that!"

Millie looked at him as if he had just slapped her across the face. "But—"

"There is absolutely no excuse, Millie, so don't even bother trying to wriggle your way out of this one. What you did was inexcusable. You involved a hell of a lot of people last night, and every one of us was in fear of your safety. To be honest, I couldn't give a shit about you getting drunk. I'm pretty sure that you'll be feeling the punishment for that right now. But what I can't excuse is the selfishness that you showed towards others."

Millie dipped her head and stared into her lap. "I know. I'm sorry."

"We truly are, Dad," Nina added quietly.

Dan shook his head. "Do you know something? After that night at the Trenchards, I had an idea that I might ring up your mother and ask if you could all come up here for Christmas. I thought that it would be great fun because I thought you were beginning to enjoy yourselves. But that was a stupid idea, wasn't it?" He turned and stared out the window. "You win, girls. You can get on that train on Sunday night and neither of you need ever come back to Scotland again."

"But we love it up here," Nina spluttered out, her face collapsing as only Nina's could.

"I don't think so, Nina."

"But we do," Millie continued on from her sister. "We really love being like a family again. That other night with the Trenchards was good fun. I really liked Patrick and Katie and their children. It was just . . . fun."

Dan turned and leaned against the kitchen sink, his arms folded. "Excuse me, you two, but do you think I have a memory like a sieve? No more than a minute ago, you were telling me how much you *hated* it up here?"

Millie wiped the sleeve of her T-shirt across her dripping nose as she shook her head. "Not here. School. We hate school so much, Dad. We just didn't want to go back, and that's why . . ." She didn't finish, but once more burst into tears, her action being copied to a T by her younger sister.

Dan was glad of the unscheduled break in their conversation. He suddenly realized they had been talking at cross-purposes. He pulled out a chair from the table and sat down. "Why did you not tell me?" he asked, concerned.

Millie instantly stopped crying and turned to face him with an expression of fury. "What do you mean? We are *always* telling you, Dad, but you never, ever listen. You just go on about making the best of things and that it will only be for another few years of our lives. But what you don't understand, Dad, is that every day at the place is like another year."

Dan covered his mouth with his hand. His misunderstanding of the situation went much deeper than just getting the wrong end of the stick during their recent talk. They were not the ones who were at fault here. It was he. He had been stupid, blind, and pigheaded enough to think that he could just mess around with his daughters' lives. If he had gone out and found himself a job, as Jackie had always been telling him to do, then this would never have happened. But he had to have his principles, didn't he? He had to have his own way. All that business about "being around for a family who needed him." It was all a load of crap. They hadn't needed him around. They had needed him working.

He leaned forward in his chair and sat pressing the nails of his thumbs together, not wishing to look up at his daughters' faces. "It really is that bad, is it?"

"Yes, Dad, it is," Millie said quietly. "My work is really suffering, and I know that Nina isn't being given a chance at all. And we just have no friends there, even though we've tried hard to make them."

Dan let out a long sigh and scratched his fingers at the back of his head. "This is just so stupid."

Millie's shoulders slumped despondently. "I knew that's all you would say."

"No, I didn't mean it that way. I'm going to send you both back to Alleyn's."

Millie looked up and glanced across at her sister. "But you can't. It would mean . . ."

Dan shook his head. "No. There's no alternative. You're going back to Alleyn's. I have no right to make your lives such a misery. If I wanted to give up work, that was my decision. If you wanted to stay on at Alleyn's, then that should have been yours. I should never have taken that privilege away from you." He laid his hands, palm-down, on the table. "I'll speak to your mother when she gets back from Italy, or wherever she is, and tell her what we're going to do, all right?"

"But, Dad," Nina said, her blue eyes taking on a brightness that he hadn't seen for ages, "how can we afford it?"

"That is not, and never again will be, your problem, Ni. As soon as I finish up here with Seascape, I'll come back down to London and get a job. Maybe not in the City, but I'll make sure that it pays enough to keep you both at Alleyn's for as long as you need to be there. But one thing I ask is that you never go off and do something as stupid as that ever again."

The two girls nodded solemnly, and then slid off their chairs and put their arms around his shoulders. "Thanks, Dad," Millie said, pressing her wet cheek against his neck. "You're the best."

Dan let out a self-deprecating scoff. "No, Millie, I certainly wouldn't describe myself as that."

"Dad?" Nina said from the other side.

"Yes, Ni?"

"I think I'm going to be sick again."

CHAPTER TWENTY-TWO

JOSH WAS FAIRLY disgruntled with Dan when he heard the outcome of the stern lecture that he had given his sisters. He had always had the notion that Millie and Nina could twist their father around their little fingers, and here was the proof. If he had done exactly as they had and gone off and got drunk to prove that he hated his school, the reaction from his father would have been totally different. Dan had gone soft. He had totally capitulated to them.

However, despite Josh's opinion on the worth of the talk, it seemed to have had an immediate effect on Millie. That evening, of her own volition, she went into Josh's bedroom where she spent over an hour talking with him behind closed doors. Finally, they appeared, white-faced but united, a new understanding having been forged between them. And when the two girls left on the train to London the following evening, after a successfully riotous family day-out to Mallaig, when hands had waved like octopus tentacles out of the open-topped Saab, the fondest farewell on the platform at Fort William Station was between the two eldest siblings.

After they had left, Dan tried to ring Jackie on her mobile to tell her about his plans to send the girls back to Alleyn's, but once more he found himself being patched through to her voicemail service. He felt that what he wanted to say to his wife was too long for a text, so while Josh headed off to meet up with Maria José, he went straight to the Seascape office to send her an e-mail, asking Josh to pick him up in an hour's time.

It took him time to write the e-mail. He had always found it difficult to admit that he was wrong about anything, let alone his own family, and he had never been that eloquent with the written word. He wasn't entirely content with the final draft, but nevertheless sent it off to Jackie's home e-mail address, hoping that she would get to read it before she went to meet the girls the following morning.

He still had twenty minutes to kill before Josh was due to come to pick him up, so he went onto the Internet and opened up his own mail server to see if he had any unread e-mails. There were two. The first was from Nick Jessop, giving him the latest news on how he was surviving in his new job with Broughton's.

"Things are not the same, Dan," he wrote. *"Everything has changed since 9/11. The fun seems to have gone out of the City. I sometimes wonder if I wouldn't have been better just trying to get that idea of the child's car seat off the ground. At least if I had done that, I'd have been able to spend more time with Tarquin."*

The rest of the e-mail was a running commentary on the successes of Chelsea Football Club that season. Dan wrote only a few words in reply.

"Stick to what you're doing. Tarquin will be the winner in the long run. Anyway, you would only be spending time with him in hospital if you went ahead with that damned car seat! Turning into a wild Scotsman up here. You won't be able to understand a word I say when I get back! Dan."

The other e-mail was from Debbie Leishman in New York.

"Dear Dan," she wrote. *"I really don't know how I can thank you for continuing to be such a wonderful friend. Without your support, I could never have afforded to stay off work so long with the baby. He continues to do well, and very soon I shall send you a real long update on how he is progressing and a photograph so that you can see for yourself just how like his daddy he is turning out to be. I still have wonderful memories of that weekend we had up in Maine. Oh, that we could wind back the clock and make it all happen over again. With my love, as always, Debbie."*

He wrote back, *"Dear Debbie, thanks for your e-mail. Don't give the money another thought. I'm so glad that the baby's doing well. I'll look forward to getting the progress report and the photograph. Remember to get in touch whenever you want. With love, Dan."*

The next morning, when he arrived at the Trenchards' house to pick up the Mercedes, he found a note stuck in behind the driver's windscreen wiper. It was from Katie, asking him to come into the kitchen before he left.

She rose from her customary seat in the window as he entered and pushed her arms high above her head in a long stretch. "Morning, Dan. You got my note, then."

The strain of Patrick's "bad patch" over the past few weeks had taken its toll on his wife. Her face no longer glowed with rustic health but had become pale with fatigue and worry. Yet, in a strange way, the change seemed to accentuate her attractiveness, and the vulnerability that was now displayed in one usually so capable brought out an ethereal beauty in her.

"Everything all right?" Dan asked.

"Fine. Did you get the girls onto the train all right?"

"Yes. They went off a great deal happier than when I first picked them up, at any rate."

"Maybe things needed to reach an all-time low before they got better."

"I think you're right. Talking of which, how's Patrick?"

Katie let out a laugh of frustration and shook her head. "He wants to go with you this morning."

"Really? Is he up to it?"

"*He* thinks he is, and try arguing against that."

"Do you want me to have a word with him?"

The smile slipped from Katie's face. "No, it would be no use." She closed her eyes. "If he wants to go on like that, I can't stop . . ." She faltered and Dan watched as she gulped to control her emotions. A large tear broke free from each of her tightly closed eyes.

"Hey, come on. It's all right." He moved quickly over to her and put his arms around her. She responded immediately, pressing her face against his chest and holding hard to him. "He'll be fine, Katie. I won't let him overdo it."

"I just don't know what I would do if something happened to him."

"I'll take care of him."

Katie pushed herself away from his hold. "What can you do that I haven't done already?" she snapped at him.

Dan grimaced. "Look, what I meant was . . ."

Katie sat down on the edge of the window seat and covered her face with her hands. "I know what you meant. I'm sorry, Dan. It's just that I can't control him. I've tried, but his will to keep going is just too strong."

"In that case," Dan said quietly, "maybe you just have to let him keep going."

Katie looked up at him and smiled bravely. "I know. I'm only thinking of myself, aren't I?"

"No, you're not. You're being wonderful. I don't know how the hell you cope."

"Kate!" Patrick's voice boomed along the passageway from the small downstairs bedroom. "Is Dan here yet?"

"Yes, he is," Katie called out. She walked across to the sideboard and took a wodge of kitchen towel from the roll and blew her nose. "He's just coming."

"Well, tell him to come and give me a hand, otherwise we'll be late."

Katie shrugged her shoulders. "Well, as you say, I'd better just let him keep going."

Putting his hand on her arm, Dan gave it a quick, reassuring squeeze before leaving the kitchen and heading along the passageway to Patrick's bedroom.

DID I EVER tell you about the time I bought prawns from New-foundland?" Patrick asked as they drove past the dark silhouette of Bonnie Prince Charlie's statue at Glenfinnan.

"No, I don't think so."

"What a gas. The most expensive experiment I ever tried, but by God, it was worth doing just for the thrill of it all."

"What happened?"

"I bought live prawns and chartered a plane to fly them overnight back to London. I wanted to see if I could get them into Billingsgate the next morning still crawling in their boxes."

"And did you succeed?"

Patrick shot him a challenging look. "Yes, of course I did."

"But it wasn't cost-effective."

"No, it certainly wasn't. I thought that I'd be allowed to travel with the prawns in the cargo plane, but they wouldn't let me."

"So how did you get back?"

"Well, I wanted to arrive in the UK before the cargo, so I did the only thing I could do. I caught a flight to New York, then took Concorde."

Dan glanced at him and laughed. "And that's where the profit went."

Patrick smiled. "Sort of."

Dan signalled to overtake a lorry. "You are bloody mad, Patrick," he said as he accelerated past it.

"I'd give any part of my useless body to do it all over again, though."

"What? Fly live prawns from Newfoundland?"

"No, maybe not from there." He gave Dan's arm a light nudge. "But I'm thinking about it. If the opportunity arises, then I'm off."

Dan turned to look at the man, his face seeming even more gaunt in the eerie green light that shone from the Mercedes dashboard. "How are you feeling, Patrick?"

"Shit."

"I thought so. You have to take it easy, mate. If not for your own sake, then for Katie's."

Patrick grunted out a laugh. "Have you two been conspiring against me?"

"No, we have not. I just know that she would be lost if anything happened to you."

Patrick turned and shot him a wink. "Nothing's going to happen to me, my friend. Not if I have anything to do with it."

No further word passed between them until Dan dropped his speed to drive through the village of Arisaig.

"What are your plans, Dan?"

"When I go back to London, do you mean?"

"I suppose so."

"Well, now that the girls are heading back to a fee-paying school, I don't think there's much alternative for me other than to get a proper full-time job."

"Right."

"Why do you ask?"

"No reason."

"Oh yeah?"

Patrick laughed. "I was going to ask if you would take on Seascape for me."

Their lighthearted banter was brought to a sudden halt by Patrick's request. Dan was able to feign concentration as he picked up speed, guiding the Mercedes around the tight bends in the road. In truth, he was thinking back to what Katie had said about her husband. All that bluster and bravado were just a cover. Patrick knew as well as any that there would come a time when he wouldn't be able to cope with anything much more than lifting his walking stick.

"What about the guy from Ocean Produce in Aberdeen?"

"I could put him off. Dammit, I've waited long enough for him."

"But he's got the knowledge, Patrick. I don't."

"Keep going the way you are at the minute and you'll have more knowledge than me in six months." Patrick paused, flicking his thumbnail against a knot of wood on the handle of his walking stick. "I couldn't pay you as much as you'd get in London, but it would be a decent enough salary. I'm sure it would be enough to keep the girls at that private school of theirs."

Dan noted a tone in Patrick's voice that he had never heard before. It was almost as if the man was pleading with him to stay.

"Patrick, listen, I don't think that I could have enjoyed myself more over these past few months, and I feel really lucky to have had the opportunity of working with you and getting to know you and Katie and the kids. But I can't work up here forever. I have a wife in London who would never, in a million years, consider moving to Scotland, and you've seen the girls for yourself! London is like a life-support system to them all. I can't split the family up, Patrick. I have to go back."

Patrick glanced out of the side window at the pale dawn that glowed red upon the distant wedged slope of the Isle of Eigg. Dan heard him let out a quiet laugh. "You'll be leaving the cowboy country, Dan. Can you do that?"

Dan let out a long breath. "There always comes the right time for riding off into the sunset, Patrick."

CHAPTER TWENTY-THREE

LTHOUGH THE CHRISTMAS lights in Fort William were like a pencil torch in comparison to the vast illuminations of Oxford Street, they had twinkled merrily on the snow-covered streets of the town for at least a month before Dan and Josh decided that it was time that the cottage should also be decked out in festive cheer. In his own typically enthusiastic way, Josh arrived home on the appointed evening of decoration with a Christmas tree sticking out at least four feet above the opened-top Saab. It was, of course, impossible to get it into the cottage without severe surgery. So the tree went back into the car and was chauffeured along to Auchnacerie where it was gratefully received. Consequently, the Porters were roped into helping with the decoration of the Trenchards' house under the slave-driving orchestration of Patrick, who sat at the kitchen table, pointing out misplaced baubles on the tree with his holly-bedecked walking stick. There was a moment of great consternation when the fairy for the top of the tree could not be found, so Patrick suggested that Katie had really nothing much to do for the next few weeks and could easily cope with being a stand-in. With screams of delight, Max and Sooty immediately set about winding tinsel around their mother, and it was left to Dan to hoist her onto his shoulder in a fireman's lift and climb precariously up the stepladder to put her in place. With a protesting creak of metal, the aluminium ladder gave way slowly under their combined weights, and they ended up helpless with laughter on the ground amidst the prickly branches of the fallen tree. And so the decoration process had to be started all over again.

As a result, Dan and Josh did not arrive home to their bare little cottage until two o'clock in the morning, and with a good number of Patrick's Glendurnich malts swirling around in their heads, both slept through the cacophony of their alarm calls three and a half hours later. It was only the crash of the front door opening that woke Dan from his alcoholic slumber.

He sat up in bed and rubbed at his gritty eyes, then squinted at the figure of Katie standing in the doorway of his bedroom. He glanced at his alarm clock.

"Oh, bugger!" he groaned as he threw back the bedclothes. "Sorry, Katie. Is Patrick waiting?"

"I've had to call for an ambulance, Dan. I've got to get Patrick to Inverness."

"Why?" Dan asked, looking up at her with concern as he stuck a finger down the back of his shoe to get it on. "What's happened?"

"Patrick had another collapse last night on the bathroom floor, and I didn't hear him. I found him this morning and he was having real difficulty breathing. I just pray to God he hasn't got pneumonia."

"For heaven's sakes," Dan exclaimed, standing up and banging his foot into the other shoe.

"He had a urinary infection about two years ago, and it really weakened him. The disease is so much more advanced now that this one could be a real problem."

"Have you managed to move him?"

Katie shook her head. "No. Max is sitting with him." Her voice quivered. "He can hardly speak, Dan."

Pulling on a shirt and a pair of jeans over his T-shirt and sports shorts, Dan realized that it was time for him to take control. He walked through the main room, giving Katie a quick, reassuring hug as he passed her, and banged on Josh's door. "Josh, get up! We've got a problem."

Josh had appeared in the doorway of his bedroom by the time Dan had pulled on his jacket. True to the habit of a teenage male who had just woken from his slumbers, he scratched slowly at the crotch of his boxer shorts, but desisted the moment he realized that Katie was in the room.

"What's up?" he asked, a puzzled expression on his face.

"We've got to get Patrick up to Inverness. He's had another collapse."

Josh was immediately galvanized into action by the news. He disappeared into his bedroom and started pulling on any article of clothing that came his way. "What do you want me to do?"

"Look after Max and Sooty until we get back," Dan replied as he did up the zip of his jacket. "If they want to go to school, take them. If not, just stay with them at Auchnacerie. And call Pete at the factory and tell him what's happened and that we're all out of action for the day."

They saw the ambulance turning into the drive as Katie hit the final straight to Auchnacerie at speed. By the time that she pulled the Golf into the courtyard behind the house, the paramedics already had the stretcher out of the vehicle and were standing at the back door of the house. Katie abandoned the car, leaving Dan to turn off the engine and shut her door.

He stood watching as Patrick was unceremoniously tilted from one side to the other as the paramedics negotiated the narrow doorway. Despite the oxygen mask covering his mouth and nose, his chest heaved at the effort of breathing, yet he turned his head fractionally and looked directly at Dan as he was being hoisted into the back of the ambulance. There was little movement in his facial muscles, but Dan noticed a slight wrinkling of the eyes as the stretcher was slid onto its tracks. It was the only way that Patrick could convey a smile.

"Could you follow on in my car, Dan?" Katie asked as she hurried out of the house, stuffing essentials into her canvas bag. "I'm going to travel with Patrick."

"Of course," he replied, helping one of the paramedics to close the back door of the vehicle while the other started up the engine.

As the ambulance reversed back, the Saab shot into the courtyard, immediately pulling over to one side to allow it to pass. Josh got out of the car and walked across to his father, and they stood watching as the vehicle made its way slowly down the driveway.

"What did he look like?" Josh asked.

"Not too good. He's having a real problem breathing."

"Shit," Josh said quietly. He gave his father a pat on the back. "Where are Max and Sooty?"

"I'm not sure. Probably in the kitchen."

"Right, I'll go and see how they're getting on. I don't suppose you'll have any idea when you're going to get back from Inverness?"

"No. It'll depend on what the doctors say at the hospital."

"Well, keep in touch. Have you got your mobile with you?"

"Yup, I have," Dan replied distantly, continuing to watch on after the ambulance had disappeared around the final bend in the road. "So, what do you think this time, Josh? Is everything going to be all right?"

There was a pause before Josh answered. "I don't know. All I can say is that I don't have that same feeling of total confidence about this one. But then again, this is Patrick we're talking about."

Dan let out a quiet laugh. "You're right. It is."

THE HOSPITAL WAS situated on the outskirts of Inverness, a tall, modern-looking building with every one of its windows protected from the sunlight by Venetian blinds. As the ambulance pulled into the emergency bay, Dan veered off and made his way to the car park.

He waited for an hour in the foyer of the hospital, then, having never been a great fan of the smell of medical establishments, he went out and sat in the car. With the sun on his face and still with the aftermath of a hangover, he dozed peacefully as he listened to the morning story on Radio 4.

He was awoken by the sound of the passenger door being opened. Katie got in and slumped back in the seat with a long, exhausted breath.

"How is he?" Dan asked.

"The doctor told me that he is 'stable,' whatever that means."

He reached over and patted her knee. "A lot better than 'critical,' I would think. How long do you reckon they'll keep him here?"

"No idea, but I have little doubt that as soon as Patrick kicks off the infection, he'll be yelling to get out of the place as quickly as he can."

Dan laughed. "No doubt." He reached forward and turned off the radio. "So what do you want to do?"

"I don't know. I don't think I should leave him."

"No, I agree with that."

Katie turned to Dan. "What about you? You'll be wanting to get back to Fort William."

"We only have the one car."

"Yes, we do, don't we? So what should we do?"

"Right," said Dan decisively. "If you stay here with Patrick, I'll head into Inverness. I need to do some shopping and I've also got to go to the train station to book the girls' tickets for Christmas."

"I never knew they were coming up."

"One of their last requests before they left, believe it or not."

"Is Jackie coming up too?"

Dan shook his head. "Unfortunately not. She says that Rebecca Talworth has decided to hold a charity auction on Christmas Eve, of all the times to pick, so she's not going to be able to make it. She's not an easy person to persuade otherwise, either."

"What a pity."

"I know. Anyway, I'll give Josh a call and ask him to look after Max and Sooty for the night, and then I'll see if I can find us a couple of rooms in a hotel somewhere nearby."

"I'm sorry, Dan. This is a complete nuisance for you. I should have driven up here myself, only—"

"Listen, it's no bother at all. Nothing matters except that Patrick gets better again. Seascape will survive without us all for a couple of days, and no doubt our offspring will as well."

Katie reached over and gave him a long kiss on his cheek. "You have been an absolute star over the past four months, Dan the Man, and I don't think I have ever thanked you for all you've done for my family."

"It's been a pleasure, Katie. I really mean that. You helped me get out of a rut too, remember?"

Katie put a hand on his arm and sat back, staring at him quizzically. "Tell me, what would you rather have done? Run Vagabonds or work with Patrick?"

Dan laughed. "I don't think you need to ask that question, Mrs. Trenchard."

"You're right. I don't believe I do." She opened up the car door. "What time will you be back?"

"Say six o'clock this evening?"

"All right. I'll be waiting for you in the foyer."

She closed the door and Dan watched in the rearview mirror as she ran across the car park, a small, brave figure in a pair of multipanelled tartan trousers.

CHAPTER TWENTY-FOUR

THE OFFICES OF the Business Development Department of the Highland Regional Council took up two small, fluorescent-lit rooms on the third floor of an ugly Victorian building on Bridge Street in Inverness. There were two desks in each room, and in order to get behind them, it was necessary to squeeze past the bank of filing cabinets that lined the high, cream-coloured walls. This posed an almost insurmountable problem for the well-built figure of Maxwell Borthwick every time that he had to take a seat at his desk.

Hemmed in by these permanent reminders of just how boring his job was, Maxwell sat reading through a thick, acetate-covered business plan that had been placed on his desk that afternoon by the weasly faced director of business development, Cyril Bentwood.

"Could you have a quick glance at that for me, please, Maxwell?" he had asked, as he had taken his sheepskin car coat and ghastly porkpie hat from the chrome coat stand. "And I would appreciate your thoughts on it first thing tomorrow morning."

"Of course, Cyril," Maxwell had replied, sticking up a middle finger at his boss as he turned and left the room, his work finished for the day at five o'clock precisely.

Maxwell detested Cyril Bentwood at the best of times, but his sentiments towards him had become even more acidic now that the little Englishman had been given the opportunity to tighten his control over Maxwell's geographical movements. And that had all come about due to the incident in Oban when that bastard from Seascape had hoisted his beloved BMW up onto those pallets.

It had taken a full six hours and a hefty £50 backhander before he had managed to persuade the obtuse forklift driver to bring the car down, and even though he had driven like the wind back up to Inverness, he had still missed out on a full day's worth of work. Cyril, of course, had reveled in it all. "One has to be trustworthy as a civil servant, Maxwell," he had said. "We are funded by taxpayers' money, and, as such, it is our duty to honour our work commitment. I am disappointed that you do not feel ready to respect this. Of course, I shall overlook your unscheduled absence from the office on this occasion, but if there happens to be a reoccurrence, I'm afraid that I will be left with no alternative other than to recommend that you be moved to some lesser office in the Council."

It had taken all Maxwell's self-control to stop himself from reaching over the desk, picking up the man, and hanging him up on the coat stand alongside his car coat and porkpie hat. What the hell did he mean, a "lesser office in the Council"? What on earth did he think he was running? The bloody Bank of England?

But he had taken the telling-off. He had had no alternative, and now Cyril Bentwood was making sure that he curbed Maxwell's wandering instincts by getting out of him as many work-hours as he possibly could.

Maxwell leaned back in his chair and linked his podgy fingers behind his head. It was going to be a long evening. He had been reading the wretched document for nearly two hours now and he hadn't even reached the end of the background report. His mind was far too active for this kind of work. That was his problem. He was better suited to the realms of nationwide administration, applying his brainpower to the running of his beloved country. It was he who should be throwing documents onto the desks of insignificant little pricks like Cyril Bentwood to read.

He got up from his chair and picked up the electric kettle from on top of a filing cabinet and gave it a shake. He reckoned that there was enough water in it for one small cup of instant coffee. He certainly wasn't going to be bothered to go through the rigmarole of contorting his way out of the office just for a half-pint of water. He pressed the switch on the kettle, and then, pushing his chair hard into the footwell of the desk, he walked across to the tall, dirt-smeared window and looked down onto the crowded street.

With Christmas just two weeks away, the shops in Inverness were remaining open every night until eight. He loved the atmosphere of the bustling crowds, yet it was not so much that it put him in the joyous spirit of Christmas, but more that it resembled what he had always imagined that living in a big city, like Edinburgh or Glasgow, would be like. And that, above all, was what he yearned for.

He pulled a silk handkerchief from his trouser pocket and wiped away a bead of sweat from his enormous brow, a late reminder of the delicious tangy heat of the vindaloo curry that he had enjoyed at lunchtime. He stopped suddenly, his handkerchief pressed to his face, and stared down at the two figures that picked their way, side by side, through the crowds on the pavement. Well, speak of the devil, he thought to himself. Look who's turned up in Inverness. Seascape's own bloody Dan Porter. Maxwell cupped his hands against the glass to get a clearer view of his companion. He knew that he recognized her. Yes, of course, it was Trenchard's wife. He was sure of it. What on earth were they doing together so far from home at this time of the day?

He reached up and undid the catch on the window and managed to slide it open on the third attempt. He leaned out onto the sill and managed to catch sight of them again just as they cut across the flow of pedestrians at the bottom of the street and entered the brightly lit foyer of the Caledonia Hotel.

Maxwell pulled his bulk back into the room and shut the window. He turned, a broad smile of satisfaction puckering up his flabby cheeks. "Oh-ho-ho!" he said out loud, "now what do we have going on here?"

He took his jacket from the back of the chair and, as quickly as possible, squeezed his way to the door of the office, flicking off the switch of the kettle as he passed. He glanced momentarily at the document on his desk before killing the fluorescent lights and closing the door behind him.

CAN I HELP you, sir?" asked the bright-faced receptionist of the Caledonia Hotel.

"Yes, I do believe you can," Maxwell replied cheerfully, as he glanced quickly over to the seating area in the foyer, just to make sure that the two persons in question were not present. "You wouldn't, by any chance, have a Mr. Dan Porter staying here at the minute, would you?"

"If you could wait a moment, sir, I'll just check for you." The girl typed quickly on the keyboard of her computer and then ran her finger down the screen. "Yes, we do, sir." She put a hand on the receiver of her telephone. "Would you like me to put you through to his room?"

Maxwell waved a hand dismissively. "No, don't worry. I think I'll just surprise him. I'm an old friend of both Mr. Porter and Mrs. Trenchard. I take it that she's staying here as well?"

The girl consulted her computer once more. "Yes, she is."

"Oh, that's wonderful. I haven't seen either of them for so long." He leaned forward on the top of the high reception desk and smiled conspiringly at the girl. "I know it's probably against company policy, but you wouldn't just give me their room number, so that I could go up and give them a bit of a surprise."

The girl bit at her lip. "I'm not supposed to, sir."

Maxwell stood away from the desk. "Of course. I quite understand." He made sure the girl saw that he was pondering the dilemma. "Would it be possible then to buy a bottle of champagne for them, so that I could send it up to their room?"

"Of course it is," the girl replied with a smile before looking back down at her computer screen. It was she who leaned across the desk this time. "Their room numbers are three twenty-one and three twenty-two," she whispered to him.

Maxwell felt disappointed that they were in different rooms, but he managed not to make it apparent to the girl. "Thank you. I very much appreciate it," he replied in an equally secretive tone. He turned and made his way towards the lift.

"What about the champagne, sir?" the girl called after him.

Maxwell turned and shot her a wink. "Let's leave that until later, shall we? One surprise at a time."

FOR THE REST of the evening, Maxwell became their shadow. He was desperate not to let this opportunity go a-begging because he knew that his chances to get even with Porter were going to be few and far between. Having found an open service room on their corridor, he kept watch through the barely open door until they eventually left their rooms together about half an hour later. He had never had to make his way down three flights of stairs so fast in all his life, but he managed to reach the ground floor just as they were walking out of the hotel. As luck would have it, they had parked in the car park down by the river, about three rows away from where his BMW sat.

He followed them at a safe distance as they made their way out of town, and for a heart-stopping moment, he thought they were heading for the A9, the main road that linked Inverness with the rest of the world. But just before the slip road, they signalled to the left and pulled into the car park of Raigmore Hospital.

He waited for them for an hour, killing time by listening to a Runrig album on the minidisc system that he had had recently installed in the BMW. When they reappeared through the glass doors of the hospital, he stabbed at the OFF switch and slumped down into his seat. He watched them get into the Golf, reverse out of their parking slot, and move off towards the exit. He started his own car, but did not move. He wanted to see which way they turned at the bottom of the road. The indicator light flashed to the right, and he knew that they were heading back into Inverness.

Cutting the engine once more, he got out of the car and walked across to the hospital entrance. He had a pretty shrewd idea of what was going on, but he just had to make sure. He only had to ask a few words of the woman at the reception desk to have his thoughts confirmed, and he left the hospital with a smile on his face and a jaunty bounce to his step. He heaved himself into the BMW and let out a long, slow laugh. So Patrick Trenchard was in the High Dependency Unit, was he? He started up the car and reversed back at speed. Right, Maxwell, he thought to himself, let's see how we can turn this to our advantage.

CHAPTER TWENTY-FIVE

IT HAD BEEN Dan's decision not to eat in the hotel dining room that evening. He had glanced into its dazzlingly bright interior and seen the young shirtsleeved businessmen seated at the tables, their mobile phones clustered around them as if they were an integral part of the dinner service, and he felt that he didn't want to be part of them. He also had a suspicion that the superior-looking headwaiter might take unkindly to the scruffy clothes that he had hastily thrown on that morning. So he and Katie left the hotel and walked across the street to a cheery-looking establishment called Buchan's Steak Bar. They sat opposite each other at a small table tucked away into the corner of the restaurant, next to the door that led to the gents' lavatory. They had been lucky enough to get a seat at all, as the place was seething with feasting late-night shoppers, and every square inch of the floor space was taken up with enormous shopping bags and parcels of every size and shape. Yet although the room was filled with the general clamour of pre-Christmas merriment, the mood at their table was solemn.

Dan placed his knife and fork down on his plate. "Are you sure you don't feel like eating anything?"

Katie shook her head and took another drink from her wineglass. "I had a ham roll at the hospital. That'll do me."

"You've eaten nothing else all day, though."

"For goodness' sakes, please stop worrying about me, Dan. I'm fine."

Dan flicked his head to the side. "Okay."

Katie let out a long sigh. "I'm sorry. That was rude. I'm just so . . . keyed up about Patrick."

Dan finished off a mouthful of steak, and then pushed the plate to one side. "You don't have to apologize. I can imagine how you're feeling."

"It just goes on and on, and I know that there'll be no respite for me, until . . ."—she bit at her bottom lip—"until something pretty final happens to Patrick." She paused to take another drink of wine. "No, I don't think you can ever imagine how I'm feeling. Patrick has been my protection, my rock, ever since we were married. I was never cut out to take over that role from him. He knows it too and that's one of the reasons he feels that he has to keep going. But sometimes, it just makes me feel very vulnerable and very lonely, and I long for him to be whole again." She gazed at her wineglass as she spun it around in her fingers. "The worst are the nights. I lie in that huge double bed by myself and listen to him moving restlessly about in that poky little room downstairs. I long to just get up and go to him and lie down beside him and let him wrap me in those big powerful arms of his and hear him say, 'Don't worry, Kate. I'll look after you.' But, of course, I can't." She let out a hopeless laugh. "The bed's too narrow and his arms are too weak." The unhappy smile slid from her face. "And then, the following morning, I'm supposed to leap out of bed and be strong and resolute and supportive of my family." She shook her head as she took another sip of wine. "I can't really describe it, Dan, but I do know that you can never imagine how I'm feeling."

"No, you're right. I don't think I probably can."

Katie rocked back in her chair and threw her hands up in the air. "But this is so unfair. I shouldn't be saying that kind of thing to you.

All you've done is help us, Dan. Both you and Josh came out of the blue and you've been our . . . saviours. We could never have survived these last few months without you. So what gives me the right to come out and say something like that?"

Dan leaned forward on the table and rubbed at the two-day's worth of stubble on his chin. "I hope it's because I'm a friend."

Katie smiled and reached over and gripped his forearm. "You are, Dan. A very dear friend, both to Patrick and to me." She pushed back from the table and pressed her fingers against her eyes. "I am just feeling so tired. I didn't sleep a wink last night, and all I really want to do is to crash out for about twelve hours without interruption." She picked up her canvas bag from the floor. "Would you mind if I went back to the hotel now?"

"Not at all. I'll come over with you," Dan replied, catching the eye of a waitress and signalling for the bill. He then glanced at his watch. It was just before nine o'clock. He smiled across the table at Katie. "If we're quick, you should just about make your twelve hours."

THANK GOD HOTELS cater for unprepared travelers, Dan thought, as he made use of the disposable razor that he had found, neatly packaged, in the bathroom cabinet. He had already had a deep, luxurious bath and the empty sachets in the soap tray were testament to the fact that he had used every freebie that the hotel supplied. Throwing the razor into the waste bin, he toweled off what was left of the shaving soap on his face, and feeling clean and revitalized, he walked naked from the bathroom, flopped down on the bed, and rang the house in Clapham.

It was Jackie who answered. He had hoped that his decision to send the girls back to Alleyn's might have helped solve some of their differences, but he only managed a stilted conversation with her before she handed him over to Millie. Talking to his elder daughter was the complete antithesis. Over the telephone, Millie sounded loving and buoyant in spirit, and he had to hold the receiver away from his ear at her reaction to the news that he had bought their train tickets for Christmas. The call lasted a further ten minutes, during which time Dan hardly uttered a word.

He began to watch a film on the television but it wasn't long before the events of the day caught up with him as well. During a lengthy and deeply meaningful conversation between the two main actors, stuck in a wind-blown bivouac somewhere high up in the Himalayas, his head slumped on the pillow and he fell into a deep sleep.

It was the long, continuous beep of the empty screen that woke him. He fumbled for the remote, eventually finding it on the floor beside the bed, and turned off the television. He glanced at his watch before pulling the bedclothes over him, plumping up his pillow, and settling himself for the rest of the night. He angled his wristwatch to catch the glare of the streetlights coming in through the window. It was two o'clock in the morning. He had at least another six hours' undisturbed sleep to enjoy.

As he became accustomed to the quiet, he heard what he thought was the sound of someone talking in hushed tones in one of the adjoining bedrooms. He switched on the bedside light and sat up, and turned his head one way and then the other, trying to work out from which side of the room the voice was coming. He threw back the bedclothes and got to his feet and walked across to the wall that separated his room from Katie's. The sound was coming from her room. He pressed his ear against the wall, and then immediately took a couple of paces back. He stood, scratching a finger thoughtfully down the side of his face as he fixed his eyes on the spot where his ear had been. Katie wasn't talking. She was crying.

He sat for a full quarter of an hour on the edge of his bed, listening to her intermittent sobs and wondering whether he should do anything about it. Maybe she was still asleep. Maybe she would wake up in the morning and she wouldn't know anything about it. Then he heard a definite change to the pattern. He stood up and went back to the wall and listened. The volume was fluctuating, sometimes distant, sometimes close to the wall that separated them. He knew then that Katie was awake and was moving about in the room.

He went into the bathroom and took one of the white toweling dressing gowns from the back of the door. He put it on and walked out of his bedroom into the corridor, knotting the tie on the dressing gown as he went. He stood outside Katie's door, listening intently, his knuckle raised to knock. He thought for a moment that she had stopped, and he was about to turn and go back to his room when he heard her sobs of despair much clearer than he had done before. He gave two quiet taps on the door.

"Katie?" he whispered.

There was no reply.

"Kate, it's Dan." He knew as soon as he had said it that he shouldn't have done so. He had only called her Kate because it sounded softer and less likely to disturb the other hotel guests. But it was Patrick who called her that. No one else.

The door flew open and Katie appeared and she threw her arms around him. The action opened up the top half of his dressing gown and she pushed her spiky brown hair against his bare chest.

"Oh, Dan! Oh, Dan!" she said in a voice that echoed down the corridor.

Dan glanced around him. "Ssh, Katie. You'll wake everyone up."

She reached a hand behind his neck and pulled his face down towards her and kissed him on the mouth and he felt her tongue trying to prise open his mouth. He flinched away.

"Stop it, Katie. Don't do that. It's not the answer." He looked down at her tear-stained face, and his eyes settled unwillingly on the curve of her breasts, exposed by her half-open pyjama top.

"I'm Kate," she sobbed, "I'm Kate." She turned her head and kissed his chest, and then pushing back the front of his dressing gown, her mouth sought out one of his nipples.

"For God's sakes, Katie, don't do this," Dan exclaimed, trying to push her away from him. "We'll only regret it later."

Katie stood back from him, her eyes flamed with defiance. "No, I never will. I never will."

She took hold of his hand and tried to pull him into her room. Dan used his strength to disengage himself from her grip. "We're not going to do this, Katie."

She stood watching him, a bewildered, hurt expression on her face, and then she slowly raised her fingers to the front of her pyjama top and undid the three remaining buttons before letting it slip to the ground. "My name is Kate, and I want to be held, and I want to be loved again." She reached out and took his hand once more, and with a shake of his head, Dan allowed himself to be led into her room.

And while Katie began to take from him the long-lost sensation of physical comfort, a large figure appeared from the service room in the corridor and stretched out his aching limbs before setting off with heavy, tiptoe steps towards the lift.

CHAPTER TWENTY-SIX

WHY DID YOU leave?" Katie asked as she walked quickly past Dan into his bedroom the following morning. "There was no need to."

Dan scratched at the back of his head and closed the door. "Katie, we shouldn't have done that last night."

"Oh, and why not? It was my decision. You have no reason to reproach yourself for what happened."

Dan pushed his hands into the pockets of the dressing gown. "We're both married, Katie. That's why." He let out a long sigh. "Patrick also happens to be one of the best friends I have ever had. And I have just slept with his wife."

Katie raised her eyebrows. "Well, bully for you," she said quietly.

"Come on, Katie, can't you understand what—"

"No, Dan," Katie interjected. "It's *you* who has to understand. I'm not one of those women who can be comforted with a few kind words and a little friendly hug and a pat on the top of my head. I boil up inside every time that happens. I want to grab whoever's said it and tell them that I am bursting with anger and frustration and all I want to do is—shout at them, 'Don't give me your . . . kindly condolences. Give me back my husband!' " She sat down heavily on the edge of his bed. "You gave me, Dan, the one thing that could give me any small comfort at all, and that was physical love and physical protection. So don't start trying to envelop me in your own guilt."

Walking over to the window, Dan swept his hands through his hair and linked them behind his head. "Oh, Katie, I don't know what the hell I'm meant to say about all this."

"You don't have to say anything."

"But what *about* Patrick?"

"Patrick need never know it happened, and if it's any small comfort to you, it won't ever happen again." She got up and went to stand beside him, and put a hand on his shoulder. "But I needed it, Dan. I feel . . . different this morning. I feel able to cope with what's to come. And that's your doing, so I thank you from the bottom of my heart for helping me."

Dan shook his head slowly. "But it has changed everything, Katie."

"Why?"

"Because I can't stay up here now."

"Why not?"

"Because I couldn't face Patrick again."

"Oh, come *on,* Dan!"

He spun round to look at her. "No, Katie, *you* listen this time. I am not a liar. I am physically incapable of keeping something like this under wraps. Okay, I played games with the reality of situations in the City, but the truth behind them was plain for all to see, if they bothered to work it out. If a trader saw through a deal that I was trying to push onto him, I'd just give him a wink and say something like 'Oh well, it was worth a go.' Don't you see, Katie? I've always had to have people trusting me, otherwise I would never have been able to succeed in my job."

Katie dropped her hand from his shoulder. "I'm sorry," she said quietly.

"Oh, Katie, don't feel sorry. Listen, it takes two to tango. Maybe I should pretend that I didn't enjoy it, but that would be way too far from the truth. Yet it has changed everything."

Katie walked slowly over to the bed and sat down again. "So what are you going to do?"

Dan turned and leaned against the window sill. "I've found out that there's a bus leaving for Fort William at ten o'clock. Once I'm there, I'll have a word with Pete and tell him that I have to go. It's only another couple of weeks before the chap from Ocean Produce starts, so I'm sure he can cope until then. After that, I'll get Josh to take me back to the cottage to pick up my gear."

"What will you tell them both?"

"The first of my lies. That I have been called back to London to start a new job."

"Will Josh go with you?"

"That's up to him." Dan let out a short laugh. "I doubt it, though. Everything he loves is up here. His job, Marie José, and, of course, the Trenchard family."

Dan saw a tear trickle slowly down Katie's cheek. "What do I say to Patrick?"

"I would suggest that you say exactly the same to him and to Max and to Sooty as I'm going to say to Pete and Josh. The trouble with subterfuge is that stories always have to match exactly."

"He'll miss you so much, Dan."

"As I will him."

She looked up at him, a pleading look in her eyes. "Could you not just see him for a moment before you go?"

Dan shook his head. "No, Katie. We are pretty much alike, Patrick and I. He would be able to tell immediately that something had happened. We must never give him any reason not to get well again."

She stood up and hurried towards him and encircled his waist with her arms. This time, Dan responded without reservation. He placed his arms around her neck, and leaning forward, he kissed the top of her spiky head. They stood holding each other for a minute before he turned her around to face the door. "Now, go and see your husband, Katie. He needs you as much as you need him."

K ATIE WALKED OUT of the doors of the hospital and stood beneath the canopy, looking up at the cold grey skies. She had noticed the first flurries of snow out of the window when she was sitting beside Patrick's bed. Yet, despite the bleakness of the weather, she felt contented, almost happy. Once more, Patrick was fighting back, and whilst in the presence of the doctor, he had slid the oxygen mask off his mouth and said in a laboured voice that he wanted to get the hell out of that bloody mausoleum as fast as he possibly could. The doctor, who had overheard every word, simply smiled at her and said that Patrick had progressed well enough to move him out of the High Depency Unit and that he would discharge him into Katie's care as soon as possible.

She pulled her coat around her and clutched the collar closed at the neck, then ran across the car park to the Golf. As she reversed out of her parking space, she took care not to clip the rear bumper of the red BMW that was parked beside her.

It had been pure devilment on Maxwell Borthwick's part to slot his car into the parking space next to the Golf. There were many other spaces available in the car park, but as soon as he saw her arriving, he moved his car adjacent to hers so that he could see her close up before he ruined her life forever.

He watched as the Golf turned out onto the main road, then he got out of the car, and wrapping his blue serge overcoat around him, he walked delicately across to the entrance door, taking care not to slip on the newly fallen snow. He approached the reception desk with a friendly smile on his face.

"Good morning," he said in a bright, cheery voice. "I wonder if you could direct me to the ward where I might find Patrick Trenchard."

The woman clattered speedily on her keyboard, and then picked up the telephone and dialed an extension number. "Hullo, this is reception," she said. "Could I speak to Staff Nurse, please?" She smiled at Maxwell as she waited for the staff nurse to come to the telephone. "Hullo, yes, this is reception here. Do you still have Patrick Trenchard with you? . . . Right, I see. And how long will that be? . . . Right." She cupped her hand over the receiver. "They are in the process of moving Mr. Trenchard from the High Dependency Unit into a day ward. He won't be ready for visitors for about half an hour."

Maxwell slapped his hands down on the desk. "Not to worry." He turned and pointed to an empty bench in the foyer. "I'll just go and have a seat over there. Maybe you could let me know when he is ready."

He walked over to the bench and sat down, and immediately let out a long, shuddering yawn. He hadn't had a moment's sleep all night. As soon as he had left the hotel in the early hours of the morning, he had gone back to the office to write the report for Cyril Bentwood. It had been a difficult task, because his mind had kept imagining with relish the conversation he was going to have with Patrick Trenchard later on in the day. But at seven o'clock on the dot, he had placed the report on Bentwood's desk, and at that point he had sworn to himself that, once he had disposed of Trenchard, he would then turn his attentions to the wretched little man with the sheepskin car coat and the porkpie hat.

It was a full hour before the receptionist walked over to him and woke him gently with a tap on his shoulder. "That's Mr. Trenchard ready for visitors now."

Maxwell pushed himself to his feet. "Thank you. Which way do I go?"

The receptionist gave him directions and he set off hurriedly along the corridor towards the ward. Not only was he desperate to see Trenchard's reaction to his revelations, but he was also keen to get back to the office before Bentwood saw fit to move him to a "lesser" office.

The staff nurse waylaid him at the entrance to the ward. "The doctor has requested that only family should be visiting Mr. Trenchard for the time being," she said.

"I quite understand that. It's just that I'm a very old friend and I was just passing through Inverness on my way up north. I promise that I'll only stay for a couple of minutes."

The staff nurse smiled and led him to Patrick's bed.

Maxwell was delighted to see just how ill Patrick Trenchard was. He lay prostrate on the bed, his mouth and nose covered by an oxygen mask, and his eyes flickered open and shut in synchronisation with the effort of his breathing. He was a mere shadow of the loud-mouthed braggart with whom Maxwell had had dealings in the past. He leaned over Patrick and grinned into his face. He saw a stirring of recognition in the wrinkles on his forehead.

"I bet you're surprised to see me, aren't you, Trenchard?" he said in a quiet voice.

He detected a slight narrowing of Patrick's eyes.

"I am really sorry to see you like this, Trenchard. Never mind, you'll soon be up and about, won't you?"

Patrick turned his head slowly as if trying to look for the bell.

"No, no, we don't want to call the nurse, do we? Not yet anyway." Maxwell looked around and saw a chair against the wall opposite. He went over and picked it up and brought it over to Patrick's bedside and sat down.

"So how is your friend Dan Porter? Been stacking any more cars recently, has he?"

He witnessed a slight stretching to Patrick's mouth.

"Oh you think it's funny, do you? Well, let's see if this wipes that pathetic smile off your face." He moved his chair in closer to Patrick's bed and leaned over so that his mouth was inches from Patrick's ear. "You see, I just *happened* to be in the Caledonia Hotel last night, and lo and behold, who should be staying there but your wife and your good friend Dan Porter. Now, I thought it was a bit odd that they seemed to be getting on rather *too* well, so I took it upon myself to do a bit of . . ."—he sucked loudly on his blubbery bottom lip—"yes, a bit of 'sleuthing,' and I think that you'll be rather grateful that I did." He cast a glance around the ward for dramatic effect. "You see, at about two o'clock this morning, I was sitting, rather uncomfortably I might add, in a service room on the third floor of the hotel, watching their rooms. I could hardly believe my eyes when I saw what happened next. Do you want to know what I saw?"

Patrick stared fixedly at the man.

"I'll take that as a yes, then. Well, what happened was that your friend Porter came out of his bedroom and knocked on your wife's door, and in the blink of an eye, the door opened and your wife threw herself—no, maybe catapulted might be a more appropriate word—into Porter's arms. There was a moment when they just held each other, right there in the corridor, before your wife, very deliberately, undid the buttons on her sexy little pyjama top and let it fall to the ground. Well, I have to say, Trenchard, that I was sincerely impressed. She certainly has a good pair of paps, that wife of yours. And they were certainly good enough to get Porter jumping into that room." Maxwell's face took on a serious expression. "Well, now, I'm a man of integrity, and I did nothing untoward like listen at the door for the sound of heaving bedsprings, but I left in the knowledge that I could do you a great favour in letting you know what happened." He sat back with a sigh and slapped his knees with his hands. "Well, that's just about it. My story is told." He leaned forward again. "So what do you think of that, Trenchard?"

Watching carefully for Patrick's reaction, he was amazed, and somewhat perturbed when, beneath the clear plastic of the oxygen mask, he saw Patrick's mouth stretch into a grin. He saw Patrick's hand rise from the bed and a finger slowly beckon to him. Maxwell got to his feet and leaned over Patrick, watching him as he lifted the oxygen mask from his face. His voice was slow, but perfectly clear and perfectly precise.

"Why—don't—you—mind—your—own—fucking—business, you—fat—bastard."

Maxwell jumped back from the bed as if Patrick had just poured boiling water into his ear. He watched with a shocked expression as Patrick let the mask plop back onto his face and then moved his hand slowly, but without faltering, towards the bell. He pressed the button and the buzzer sounded noisily around the ward. The staff nurse was at his bedside in a matter of moments. She could tell by the flick of Patrick's hand that visiting time was over. As she led Maxwell to the exit, he turned and glanced once more over to where Patrick lay. He was staring at the ceiling, and although most of his face was hidden beneath the oxygen mask, Maxwell could tell by the wrinkling of his eyes that he wore a smile of utter contentment. It was almost as if he had just been informed that his illness had been vanquished and that a full recovery was now a certainty.

CHAPTER TWENTY-SEVEN

As Dan had suspected, Josh had no wish to leave Fort William. They had talked about it as they drove back to the cottage, and Josh had made it plain that he never wanted to live in London again. His new life was in Scotland with friends the like of which he could never possibly meet in the seething mass of the metropolis. And so Dan had left him, with the dogs and with the Saab, and headed back to London on the overnight sleeper alone.

The taxi dropped him outside the house in Clapham at ten o'clock the next morning. Having paid the cabbie, Dan stood on the pavement, staring at the stained-glass front door and wondering if he was pleased to be back. And then he heard the sound of Mrs. Watt coming out of her house and he made a bolt for the gate to avoid meeting her. He let himself into the house and slammed the door shut, dropping his suitcase to the floor. He leaned his back against the stained glass and shut his eyes, taking in the familiar smell of his own home. Yet, this time, it seemed alien. In the past it had given him comfort and a sense of security, but now it just seemed old and stale. It was as if he didn't really belong to the house anymore.

But it *was* his home, and it *was* his family, and he had made a commitment to the girls to let them finish their schooling at Alleyn's. He had to be thankful for everything he had achieved because, by God, it could have turned out so differently. He could have been stuck in Tottenham Hale with Sharon or Janice or Kathleen, and their one child, working in that bloody fabrication shed. But he had made it to here, to this fine house in Clapham, where he lived with his wife Jackie, their three wonderful children, and two deranged dogs. He was, indeed, a lucky man.

He walked through to the kitchen and realized as he entered the room that he had hardly ever done so without being greeted by the appalling smell of one of Biggles's misdeeds. He thought of the dogs, and then he thought of Josh, and then he thought of Patrick and Katie, and he yearned to be back with them all. He had only been away from them for a matter of hours, and already he missed the intuitive wisdom and boundless enthusiasm of Josh, the drive and the sense of humour and the fight in Patrick, and the quiet resilience and strength of character in Katie. And last night, on the train, as he tossed and turned on his narrow bunk, he missed having her body curled in next to his. He would never forget that night, as long as he lived, when he lay on top of her, absorbing her pain and sorrow into his very being.

He filled up the electric kettle and turned it on, and then saw the four piles of mail sitting on the shelf next to the telephone. He thumbed through the first one, sorting out the junk from the readable, and he was about to open a letter from Broughton's, the company for which Nick Jessop worked, when he heard the sound of footsteps coming down the stairs.

"Millie? Is that you?" It was Jackie's voice.

"No, it's me—Dan."

He heard the footsteps stop, and then ascend the stairs at speed. He flicked his head back dismissively and continued with the opening of the letter. It was a brief five-liner.

Dear Dan,

I have been told by one of my colleagues, Nick Jessop, that you might be interested in seeking a job with Broughton's. I am, of course, familiar with your past achievements in the City and therefore was hoping that we might meet for lunch in the near future. I know that you are in Scotland at present, but on your return, do please e-mail me at j.burrows@broughtons.com to let me know if you want to take this further.

Yours sincerely

Good old Nick, he thought to himself. He doesn't give up, does he? He fluttered the letter down onto the kitchen table and then heard the sound of Jackie's footsteps coming down the stairs once more. She entered the kitchen and stood in the doorway, wearing a pair of jeans and a T-shirt. She made no move to come towards him to greet him.

"Hi," he said, smiling at her. "This is a bit of a surprise. I didn't expect to find you here." He walked over to her and made to give her a kiss on the mouth, but she turned her face so that it landed on her cheek. He put his arms around her and gave her a hug. It was like holding a lump of wood.

"I was going to say exactly the same thing myself," Jackie said, pushing him away. "What are you doing back? I thought you were going to be up in Scotland until mid-January."

"I know," Dan replied, walking over to the sideboard and unhooking two mugs. "Do you want a cup of coffee?"

"No thanks."

"How are the girls?"

"Fine. They both spent last night at Jessica Napier's house." She bit at the side of her mouth. "So why are you back?"

Dan spooned coffee into the mug. "My contract finished early," he said, realizing that he had just told Lie No. 2. "So I thought that I would just come back and see if I could find myself a job." He flicked his head over to where the letter lay on the table. "Things look prom-ising, as well. I've been asked to meet some guy from Broughton's."

"But what about Christmas? The girls are meant to be joining you and Josh in Scotland."

"I know. I've been thinking about that." Dan poured water into the coffee cup, and then took a spoon from the drawer and gave it a stir. "I made a bit of money with Seascape. Not a huge amount, but I never spent anything, so I thought that I might check out the Internet for a cheap skiing holiday somewhere."

"What about Josh?"

"Josh didn't want to move out of Scotland. He's totally settled up there. I left him with the dogs and the car, and he's as happy as Larry." He dropped the spoon into the sink. "But you can come skiing if you want."

Jackie shook her head. "You know I can't. Rebecca's got this charity auction, and I have to be there."

"Of course." Dan took a sip of coffee. "So, tell me, what's been the news with you? Are you taking a bit of a break at the minute?"

Jackie leaned her shoulder against the doorpost and fixed him with a steely glare. "Dan, I want to ask you something."

"Go ahead."

"How long have you been having an affair?"

The mug jigged in Dan's hand and boiling coffee spilled over his wrist. "What?" he exclaimed, transferring the mug to the other hand and flicking his wrist to cool down the scald.

"You heard me. How long have you been having an affair?"

"I don't know what the hell you're talking about."

Jackie pushed herself away from the doorpost and pulled a chair out from the table and sat down. "Dan, I know that you've been having an affair. You're not a very good liar, you know. You never were. Your face has gone beetroot, and so has your hand, thanks to that coffee."

Dan bit at the inside of his cheek as he stared at his wife. I know I'm not a very good liar, he thought to himself. That's what I told

Katie. "I have not been having an affair, Jackie," he said in a voice that was as controlled as he could make it.

Jackie slammed her hand hard down on the table. "Come *on,* Dan. Let's at least be adult about this! Why don't you just admit it to my face? On the other hand, why do I need that kind of proof? Your actions speak well enough for you."

Dan kept staring at her. How the hell could she have known? There was no way anyone could have told her, because nobody *knew* about it except Katie and himself.

"Did you not know, Dan, that the best way to express guilt is through silence?"

Dan heaved out a long sigh. He could not be bothered with telling Lie No. 3, because it would only lead on to Lie No. 4, and then Lie No. 5.

"It was only one night, Jackie."

Jackie drummed her fingers hard on the table. "One night. Well, at least that's a start." She got up and walked towards him. "But the trouble is that I don't believe you, you rotten bastard. I reckon that it was going on for a lot longer than one night."

"It was not," Dan replied, moving back from the threatening presence of his wife.

Jackie stopped inches away from him and glared into his eyes. "And to think that you've made me feel so *guilty* about everything over the past few months. How *dare* you make me feel that way when you've been carrying on with another woman."

Dan frowned at her, having absolutely no understanding of how she had found out about Katie and what she was talking about right now. "What do you mean, I've made you feel guilty? Guilty about what?"

Jackie hit back. "So what was it like screwing her, Dan? Was she *so* much better than me?"

"Oh, come on, Jackie. It was only one night, I promise you. That's all. Her husband was—"

"I know!" she interjected. "I know everything! Her husband was killed on the eleventh of September two thousand and one in New York, and you, the kindhearted friend, stepped in with your solace and your compassion, and you made love to her and you got her pregnant."

"What *are* you talking about?"

Jackie marched over to the sideboard and opened a drawer, and pulled out a fistful of papers. She held them up in her hand and Dan could make out in the corner of the topmost sheet the black horse logo of Lloyd's Bank. "Every month, from your bank account, there is a transfer of two hundred and fifty pounds into Debbie Leishman's account in New York."

Dan put down the mug of coffee on the sideboard and covered his face with his hands. Oh my God, he thought to himself, it's all been a bloody misunderstanding. I've just admitted to sleeping with a woman, and Jackie had absolutely no idea about it.

"Oh, yes," Jackie continued, "you do that! You cover your face, Dan Porter, because I've found you out. And do you know how I did that?" She turned and pulled another piece of paper from the drawer. "Do you know what this is?"

"No, Jackie, I have no idea," Dan replied resignedly.

"It's an e-mail from your Debbie bloody Leishman. When I got back from Milan, I went to check my e-mails and of course you know as well as I do what pops up onto the screen when the computer is switched on. Your wretched in-box!" She held the piece of paper up in front of her as if she were about to sing an aria. *"Dear Dan, I really don't know how I can thank you for continuing to be such a wonderful friend."* She read it in a whining American drawl. *"Without your support, I could never have afforded to stay off work so long with the baby. He continues to do well, and very soon I shall send you a real long update on how he is progressing and a photograph so that you can see for yourself just how like his daddy he is turning out to be. I still have wonderful memories of that weekend we had up in Maine. Oh, that we could wind back the clock and make it all happen over again. With my love, as always, Debbie."*

She scrumpled up the piece of paper and lobbed it over her shoulder.

"So, Dan Porter, you are a father four times over. What a stud you are!"

Dan slowly shook his head. "Are you quite finished?"

Jackie let out a short laugh. "What do you mean, 'quite finished'? I'm barely started, Dan."

"The father of that baby, Jackie, was John Fricker, and for your information, he and Debbie were *not* married. They had, however, been living together for about three months before he was killed in the World Trade Center. And because they weren't married, Debbie was not eligible for compensation. She was a working girl and she wasn't dependent on John. She didn't even know she was pregnant when he died. Anyway, after the baby was born, I took it upon myself to help her in the only way I could."

Jackie's mouth was set hard and her eyes narrowed with contempt. It was the first time ever that Dan had seen her look ugly. "So what's all this about 'the wonderful weekend that *we* spent together in Maine'?" Her voice changed once more to the sugary American accent.

"That was John, Debbie, and myself. If I remember right, it was after that weekend that they became a couple."

Jackie had had her direction planned from the start, but she knew now that it had been a false trail. She backtracked through their conversation to seek out her next point of attack, her head quivering with the effort. "So, who *did* you have an affair with?" she eventually blurted out.

Dan flopped a hand dismissively at her. "I've had enough of this witch-hunt, Jackie." He poured the remainder of his coffee into the sink. "I'm not telling you." He turned to face her. "Anyway, what's all this business of me making *you* feel guilty?"

Jackie bit hard on her bottom lip. "I'm leaving you, Dan."

"I beg your pardon?"

"I'm leaving you."

"For heaven's sakes, Jackie. Don't be so bloody ridiculous. You can't leave. We've got a marriage. We've got children. You can't just turn your back on twenty years of accumulation." He leaned a hand against the sink. "Jackie, it was only one night."

Without speaking, Jackie turned and walked over to the door. She opened it and cast a glance over her shoulder at him. "Goodbye, Dan."

"Jackie, you are being totally irrational."

But she had closed the door behind her before he had finished the sentence.

Dan leaned his bottom against the kitchen sink and crossed his arms and looked out at the bare little garden at the back of the house. Better to leave her for a bit. It was just another of their rows. Admittedly, she had every reason to feel hurt and angry, but they would be able to sort it out. They had always been able to do so in the past. He heard her moving around upstairs, going from one room to the other, and then her footsteps began to descend the stairs once more. They sounded denser this time, and it occurred to Dan that she could well be carrying something of considerable weight.

He pushed himself away from the sink and walked quickly over to the door and opened it. He had been right. Jackie was standing in the hallway with a suitcase at her side. She glanced at him briefly and then up the stairwell, a worried expression creasing her brow. And then Dan heard a second set of footsteps descend the stairs.

He was a young man, maybe thirty years old, dressed in a pair of dark blue chinos, a black polo-necked sweater, and a blazer, and he was carrying another suitcase that Dan recognized as being Jackie's. By the time that he had reached the bottom of the stairs, Jackie had already opened the front door and placed her suitcase against it to keep it open. She took hold of the man's arm and ushered him quickly towards the door.

"Who is this, Jackie?" Dan asked, walking slowly up the two steps from the kitchen and along the passage towards them.

"Come on, Stephen, for God's sakes, let's go," Jackie murmured urgently at the man.

Dan heard every word. "Stephen. Oh, for heaven's sakes, it's the wonderboy Stephen."

Stephen turned and gave Dan an uncertain smile.

Dan let out a long whistle as everything became clear in his mind. "So, Jackie, this is your reason for feeling so guilty, is it? The wonderboy Stephen." Dan looked hard at the man. "Tell me, Stephen, how long have you been bonking my wife in my own house?" The smile slid from Stephen's face and he turned to look at Jackie for support.

"I'll be back for the rest of my things later, Dan."

"Oh, will you? Well, you'd better get yourself a bloody great van, because you can take our bed with you as well. I would hate to deprive Stephen here of his *shagpit!*" He spat out the words only inches from the young man's face, and he noticed with pleasure that he flinched as spittle shot into his eye. Dan shook his head. "Well, at least you had the decency to send the girls away so that they didn't have to listen to you rogering each other all night."

Jackie took hold of Stephen's arm once more and guided him out of the house. "Come on, Stephen, let's get out of here before he gets violent."

But strangely enough, Dan had not one instinct towards physical violence. He just felt sad and tired and pretty much emotionally drained. He simply watched as Jackie and Stephen pushed and jostled each other awkwardly down the short path. They opened the gate and turned out onto the street, and Dan stood listening to the fast tap-tapping of Jackie's high-heeled shoes and the clattering wheels of her pull-along suitcase on the pavement as she hurried away to put the greatest possible distance between herself and her husband and her home.

CHAPTER TWENTY-EIGHT

Despite the emotional turmoil and heartbreak that had been caused by Jackie's departure, Dan did take Millie and Nina skiing at Christmas, having managed to pick up a cheap deal on a cancelled holiday in Andorra. It was the best thing he could have done. They were up on the slopes every morning at nine-thirty and they skied hard all day, thumping out their anger and frustration on the mogul fields until they heard the hooter sound out for the final cable car to take them down the mountain. And when they returned to the empty house in Clapham on New Year's Eve, the excitement of a party at Rebecca Napier's house that evening and the prospect of returning to Alleyn's in just a few weeks' time helped to keep the spirits of Millie and Nina buoyant.

The hallway floor was scattered with Christmas cards when they entered the house, and Dan simply collected them together and placed them on the hall table. He didn't particularly feel like opening any of them. He knew that Jackie's name would be written on every one. So they remained there until that evening when he stood on the front step, waving the girls off to their party. He shut the door, picked up the pile, and took them through to the kitchen. He took a beer from the fridge, sat down at the table, and began to open them. After the fifth one, he pushed the pile aside and took a long drink from his can of beer.

His eye was caught by one envelope that was not the lurid pink or Caribbean blue of a Christmas card. He reached forward and slid it out of the disordered pile and immediately saw the Seascape logo in the top left-hand corner. It was addressed to him in type. He waved the envelope around in front of his eyes, wondering if he wanted to open this one any more than he did the Christmas cards. Blowing out a breath of trepidation, he broke the seal with his forefinger and took out the letter. He took another large swig of his beer before opening it up and reading it.

Dear Dan,

I'm dictating this letter to Betty in the office, because my handwriting now looks as if an inebriated spider has fallen into an inkwell and then crawled across the paper. For this reason, you will probably find not one of my usual expletives written down, because Betty is a very good editor. (Patrick wants me to write here that that is not what he said, but I am not going to type that kind of a word. By the way, I hope that you are well and keeping your spirits up.)

I was sorry not to have had the chance to say goodbye, but Kate told me about the job and I am delighted for you, although I am sure that it would have tasted a good deal sweeter if you had not been faced with such a devastating domestic crisis on your return. I do hope that you and the girls are being able to cope all right. Anyway, Kate and I keep sending huge amounts of love and strength to all three of you down the airwaves!

We had Josh for Christmas and he was obviously quite subdued after learning about it all, but the children loved having him with us. I think that he's heading off to Edinburgh for New Year with Maria José, so that should cheer him up a bit. I decided that he needed a bit of a boost just before Christmas so I sent him down to Oban for a couple of days to get a bit of work experience with Ronnie Macaskill. Ronnie kept him for a week! He said that the boy is a natural buyer and has 'a good eye for a prawn'! Definitely his father's son, Ronnie said. He also asked me to send on his best wishes to you, and said that if you're ever wanting another game of shinty, all you have to do is pick up the phone!

Your dogs seem to have taken up permanent residence at Auchnacerie. The kids think they're wonderful, although Biggles was definitely 'persona non grata' over Christmas, having grabbed the stuffing off the kitchen table before Kate had the chance to ram it into the turkey!

I managed to get out of hospital a week after you left. Can't stand those places. I'm not much good at the minute, though. That wretched chest infection rather took its toll, so the walking sticks have been retired and I'm on wheels all the time now. But I'm still live and kicking, and Pete Jackson and Bob Murray, the guy who joined us from Ocean Produce, are managing to keep the business up and running.

But, Dan, what I really wanted to say in this letter was how much I have appreciated your help and your friendship over these past few months. I don't think I have ever enjoyed a time in my life more. I will remember with great fondness our trips together to Mallaig and all the laughs that you gave me. Talking of which, remember that dreadful man, Maxwell Borthwick? (BMW and forklift truck ring a bell!?) Well, I think that I managed to deflate his ego once and for all. I won't bore you with the details, but it was a wonderfully enjoyable experience!

Most of all, though, I want to thank you for the support that you gave Kate when I was in hospital in Inverness. This illness is a bugger (He made me put that—Betty) and sometimes it has been extremely hard for me to give the kind of support that Kate is in most need of. (Bad English—won't let me change it!) You are a good, compassionate man, Dan Porter, and I feel blessed in knowing that it was you who was at Kate's side when she needed most the strength and understanding of a true friend. And that's exactly what you are—to all the Trenchard family.

Keep well, Dan, and I hope that very soon you saddle up your horse and ride back into Cowboy Country. We'll have the steaks sizzling and the coffee pot on the stove when you do!

With very best wishes,
Patrick

Dan had to read it through three times before fully understanding the code that Patrick had adopted in his letter. He was now permanently in a wheelchair. He couldn't write himself. Pete Jackson and Bob Murray were coping with the running of the business, yet he went to all the trouble of going into the office so that Betty could type him out a letter. Why? Because he didn't want Katie to type it. He didn't want her to find out what he knew.

Dan tilted back the wooden chair and linked his hands behind his head. He knew now that he had made the right decision to return to London. Patrick had known instinctively what had taken place between him and Katie. He should have known that there was never the need to tell Lie No. 1 in the first place.

ALTHOUGH HAVING BEEN in constant contact with his mother since his return to London, Dan had never actually gone to see her. He knew that he had to tell her face-to-face about his marriage split-up, and he was just putting off the fateful day. However, he had always promised that he would bring in the New Year with her and her friends in Cavendish Rise, and it was therefore with a certain amount of foreboding that he let himself into her flat at nine o'clock that evening.

Looking up as he entered the stiflingly hot little sitting room, Battersea Gran levered herself out of the armchair from where she had been watching her television with the volume shut off.

"Hullo, love," she said as he bent down to give her a kiss on either cheek. "Well, let's have a look at you." She stood back and studied him with as much pleasure as she might have done having just won the star prize on the Wheel of Fortune. "My word, that skiing holiday has done you the world of good. You've certainly got wonderful colour in your cheeks."

"We were lucky. The sun shone every day," Dan replied.

"Well, I'm sure that you'll really be feeling the cold now," she said, stepping forward and rubbing the arm of his leather jacket between her fingers to gauge its thermal qualities. "You know, Dan, you're of an age now when you shouldn't be bothering about dressing up in trendy gear. You should go and buy yourself a good cardy. That's what your father always wore, and he hardly had a day's illness in his life."

Dan burst out laughing and grabbed his mother and gave her a long hug. "It's great to see you, Mum. I really have missed you."

"And I've missed you too, son."

Dan took off his jacket and glanced at the television screen. "So what are you watching?"

"I think it's the build-up to the big party in Edinburgh." She smiled up at him. "I kept the volume down so that I could hear you arriving."

"Josh is going to be there."

"Is he?" Battersea Gran exclaimed, walking across to the screen and peering at it. "Do you think we'd be able to see him?"

"I doubt it. There are hundreds of thousands of people there. It's the largest New Year's party in the world, you know."

"Really? I do hope he'll be all right," she said, continuing to squint at the screen. "It looks awfully cold up there. I hope he's wearing lots of clothes."

Dan raised his eyebrows behind her back. "Come on, Mum, let's get settled in to watch it, then. Did you buy some drink?"

"Oh, yes, of course," she said, breaking away from the television and hurrying off towards the door.

"I'll get it. You sit down."

"All right, then. I got some cans of lager for you, and because you've been in Scotland, I bought you a bottle of whisky. It was on offer at the local supermarket for nine pounds. It's all on the kitchen table."

"What about you?"

"I'll just have a glass of sherry, please, dear."

Dan went through to the kitchen and returned a moment later with a can of beer and the glass of sherry.

"Don't you want a tumbler for that?" she asked as he handed her the sherry.

"No, this is fine."

"You'll get germs drinking it like that. You don't know who's been handling that can."

"I think I'll survive." Dan sat down on the sofa, and leaning back against the white lace antimacassar, pulled the ring off the can. "Mum, I noticed that there were only two glasses laid out on the kitchen table. I thought you were having a few people round tonight."

His mother stared at the silent television without answering.

"Mum? I said that I thought there were others coming in to spend New Year with us."

His mother turned to look at him, and he could see from the way that her lipsticked mouth drooped at the corners that there was something wrong.

"What's happened?" he asked quietly.

"Nothing really, dear. Just a small misunderstanding."

"About what?"

"About the residents' committee."

"Tell me about it."

"Well, dear . . ."—she placed her glass of sherry on the occasional table next to her and settled her elbows on the arm of the chair—"when I got back from looking after Millie and Nina, I went around to the flat of the chairman of the residents' committee, and asked him when the next meeting was going to be, and he said that I didn't need to bother attending it. I said to him that of course I had to be there because it was my job to make the tea and the scones and everything. And he said to me that because I had been away for so long, they had decided to appoint someone else to that position. And do you know who they have chosen instead of me?"

Dan shook his head. "Who?"

"It's that dreadful woman Nancy Smith in flat 5F4. I mean, Dan, she can't even butter bread, let alone make a scone, and"—she waggled a finger at him to emphasise her point—"and she has only been in her flat for six months." She threw herself back in her armchair and shot a purse-mouthed expression at him. "Now what do you think of that? It's a blooming scandal, that's what it is." She pulled a handkerchief from the sleeve of her jersey and dabbed at her eyes. "I have been usurped, Dan."

"It sounds like it."

"And now nobody will speak to me."

"I'm sure they will, Mum. It'll all blow over in time."

"It certainly will not, Dan, my boy. It's gone way beyond 'blowing over,' as you put it."

"Why?"

His mother did not reply, but instead crossed her arms and pouted her mouth.

"What did you do, Mum?" Dan asked, trying to suppress a laugh.

"I took the one course that was left open to me."

"Which was what?"

"I demonstrated."

This time, Dan couldn't help but laugh. "You demonstrated?"

Battersea Gran leaned forward on the arm of her chair again, a conspiratorial glint in her eye. "Yes, and I have to say, Dan, that I made a very good demonstrator."

"What did you do?"

"Well, I went down to the local shop and I bought one of those magic marker thingies, and then I made up this banner on a dishtowel that your Auntie Vi once gave me. I've never used it."

"What did you write?"

"UNFAIR DISMISSAL. MAKING TEA WAS MY JOB in big black letters. Actually, I got the size of the letters wrong, so I had to write MY JOB on the other side and then keep turning it around."

"So when did you demonstrate?"

"At the next residents' meeting. I arrived in the hall just at the right
time, between Item Three on the agenda—the foyer flower rota, and
Item Four—the sanitation of the dustbin area."

"And what did you do?"

"I walked in, without so much as an invitation, sat down on the
floor in front of the committee, and started turning my dishcloth this
way and that and chanting, 'Unfair dismissal. Making tea was my job.
Unfair dismissal. Making tea was my job.' " She grinned excitedly at
Dan. "It's got a good ring to it, hasn't it?"

"And did they take any notice?"

"They certainly did. I disrupted the whole meeting."

"Well done, you, Mum. I'm really proud of you."

She dabbed at her eyes with the handerkerchief once more. "But
then, I can hardly bring myself to tell you what happened next, Dan."

"Well, if you can, I would very much appreciate it."

She took in a deep breath. "I was evicted."

"Oh, dear."

"Thrown out I was, Dan. Like an intruder in my own block of
flats."

"And who was brave enough to carry out the eviction?"

"Stan Beardsley from the Fabric Committee. Dan, he used to be a
commissionaire at the Hyde Park Hotel. I didn't stand a chance. I mean,
it was like calling in the professionals. He lifted me bodily from the
floor and put me down in the corridor." Her face crumpled, and in
that instant, Dan realized where Nina had inherited her aptitude for
looking totally miserable. "And I haven't spoken to anyone since. I
have been sitting in my little flat over the past four weeks without so
much as one knock on the door."

Dan looked at her, a frown creasing his forehead. "What do you
mean, the past four weeks? Haven't you been staying at Clapham?"

"No, dear, I have not."

"But who's been looking after Millie and Nina?"

"I suppose Jackie," she replied tartly.

"But Jackie works, Mum."

"I know she does, dear, but she said"—she faltered—"she said that she could manage without me."

"She never did."

"She said that she never wanted me in the house again." Battersea Gran wrung her handkerchief in her plump little hands. "I'm sorry, Dan, I didn't mean to tell you that. I know that she's your wife, but we just had our differences, and try as I might, I could never seem to do or say the right thing."

Dan put his head in his hands. "Oh, Mum, I'm so sorry."

"No, dear, it was probably my fault all along."

"No, it certainly wasn't." He dropped his hands onto the sofa and turned to look at her. "Listen, Mum, this is not very easy to tell you, but . . . Jackie has left me."

His mother's face expressed such immediate compassion that he felt like jumping to his feet and kneeling down in front of her and burying his head in her huge, pink-sweatered bosom. "Oh, Dan. What an awful thing to happen. And you did love her so much."

Dan shook his head. "You're right. But I'm afraid 'did' is probably the operative word."

She leaned across and held onto his arm. "Had she been playing around, dear?"

Dan nodded.

"I had my suspicions, I have to say."

"Yes. I reckon you would have done." Dan leaned forward on the sofa and looked at his mother. "Are you happy here, Mum?"

"What, here in the flat, do you mean?"

"Yes."

"No, I'm bloody miserable, if you will pardon my French."

"Well, I wondered if you might like to come to live with me and the girls in Clapham."

"Oh, no, dear, I could never impose myself on you like that."

"Mum, you would not be imposing yourself. Right now, I don't think there is anyone we would rather have in the house."

"Do you really mean that, Dan?"

"Yes, I really mean it. As you know, the girls are going back to Alleyn's, so if we sell this place, it would certainly help me with the finances." He took a drink of beer from his can. "At least please think about it, Mum."

His mother smiled at him. "I don't need to think about it, dear. I can't think of anything I would rather do."

"Good." He raised his can towards her. "Let's toast ourselves an early Happy New Year then, shall we?" He clinked his can against her glass. "Cheers, Mum."

"Chin-chin, love."

Battersea Gran picked up the remote for her television and turned it up to almost full volume. The roar of the crowd in Edinburgh filled the room. "Now let's see if we can spot Josh," she yelled across the three-foot gap between herself and her son.

CHAPTER TWENTY-NINE

W HAT? NO TARQUIN today?" Dan asked as he placed his pint of beer down on the table in the King's Head pub.

"Not today," Nick Jessop replied, folding up the business supplement of *The Sunday Times* and discarding it onto the pile of newspapers that lay beside him on the bench. "Laura has taken him off to some fancy-dress party this afternoon. It was quite incongruous to see a pirate with a pacifier in his mouth." He took a gulp of beer. "So what have you done with your family today?"

Dan took off his leather jacket and hung it on the back of the chair before sitting down. "They're all out of the house. Battersea Gran headed off to church on the bus this morning, and then rang to say that she's going to have lunch with a friend. And the girls have gone round to see Jackie."

"Ah. So contact has been reestablished."

"Not really. It's mostly through the lawyers. One good thing, though, is that I had a phone call from her lawyer on Friday, saying that I could stay in the house for as long as the girls were in full-time education. That should give me time to build up enough capital to buy a flat somewhere."

"That sounds a decent enough arrangement. How are the girls getting on at Alleyn's?"

"Loving it." Dan took a drink of beer. "I should never have taken them away in the first place."

"C'est la vie," Nick said, raising his glass. "So it's back to the old times, then."

"Almost."

Nick leaned his elbows on the table. "I've really enjoyed working with you again, Dan. It's been great having you in the office over the past few months. It's given the whole place a boost."

"Well, I have you to thank for getting me the job."

"Think nothing of it. By the way"—he picked up the business supplement and leafed quickly through it and then folded it twice— "you've got your name in the papers again." He handed it over to Dan.

Dan read quickly through the short article about the proposed merger between Broughton's and Carswell Asset Management and then lobbed the supplement back onto the bench. He noticed in the pile of newspapers the gaudy red title page of the *News of the World*. He scoffed and shook his head. "Honestly, Nick, I don't know why you bother reading all that crap."

Nick glanced down at his newspapers. "To which publication are you referring in such disparaging terms?"

"The *News of the World*, Nick. It's a load of rubbish."

"It is not!" Nick retorted, pulling the paper out from below the pile. "I think it's great. The *News of the World* is the master of the pun." He opened up the broadsheet and began scanning its pages. "This, for instance. 'Tellers a Story about Williams Bonk.' Now *tellers* is spelt t-e-l-l-e-r-s. What do you think that's about?"

"I have no idea."

"Two tellers were caught on the security camera of Williams Bank having it off in the safe."

"That's very good. I wonder why I didn't guess."

"Right. I'll try another one on you." Nick turned the page and sought out his next tacky headline. "Okay, this one. 'Strip Cartoon in Leicester Square Keeps Abreast with Technology.' Any idea?"

Dan let out a sigh. "Well, it's got to be something to do with breasts."

"Yes?" Nick said, slanting his eyes at Dan, wanting him to go into a little more depth.

"I have no idea, Nick."

Nick sucked his teeth. "You're hopeless. *'Belinda Carter (24), a secretary from Bromley, Kent, gave everyone a thrill in Leicester Square on Friday night. Returning from a Cartoon Character party, held in the Planet Hollywood restaurant, she divested herself of every last stitch of her Minnie Mouse outfit and danced naked on a bench in the square. The crowd that gathered around to watch were not only captivated by her dance routine, but also by the enormity of her breasts. "I'm very proud of them," she told the policeman who had covered her indiscretions with his jacket before leading her away. "It cost me six months' wages to get these silicon implants and I like to display them." '* How about that, then?"

"Thank you, Nick. I am enlightened. Now, do you think that you could put that paper down so that we could have a normal conversation?"

"One more."

"Oh, for heaven's sakes."

"Just a quick one." He turned the page. "Right, you should get this one." He quickly read through the story. "And you'll be pleased to hear that it's not even smutty. Are you ready?"

Dan didn't even bother to reply. He just nodded his head.

" 'Prawn to Stay Alive.' "

"No idea."

"Not even going to hazard a guess?"

"No."

Nick looked disappointed. "All right then. *'When a rescue team reached the wreckage of a light aircraft that had crashed into a fog-bound hillside in remote Wester Ross, they were amazed to find that its cargo of prawns were still alive and crawling around on the ground. "It was amazing that anything survived that kind of an impact," said Hughie McLeish of the Lochaber Mountain Rescue Team. "They must be tough little creatures." The pilot of the plane, Dick Freeman (52) of Inverness, was killed outright along with his passenger, Patrick Trenchard (45) of Fort Will—' "*

"Oh for God's sake!" exclaimed Dan, grabbing the paper from Nick.

"What's the matter? What are you objecting to now?"

Dan held up a hand as he continued to read the article.

Patrick Trenchard of Fort William. The plane, a Piper Aztec, had been chartered by Mr. Trenchard, who owns Seascape, the Fort William–based prawn factory, to fly a shipment of prawns from the Outer Hebrides back to the mainland. "I stuck a load of the prawns in a plastic bag and put them in my haversack," continued Hughie. "The wife and I had them for our tea and they were delicious!"

Dan tossed the paper back onto the table. "I have to go, Nick."

"Why?"

Dan got up and flipped his jacket off the back of the chair. "I'll tell you later." He hurried off towards the door of the pub, and then stopped and went back to the table. "Listen, Nick, I might not be at work tomorrow. I don't know yet, but just be prepared if I don't show up."

"Why? Come on, Dan, you've got to give me some idea of what's happened."

Dan pointed at the *News of the World* on the table. "Patrick Trenchard was the chap Josh and I worked for up in Scotland. He was a great friend of mine."

"Oh, God. I'm really sorry, Dan, I had no idea."

"No, you did me a favour. I'm not quite sure why Josh has never rung to tell me. So would you be able to cover for me if I do go AWOL?"

"Of course."

"I'll keep in touch just in case there's any development on the Carswell merger."

"How long do you reckon you'll be away?"

"Not long. I promise you that I won't leave you in the lurch, though."

As Dan ran back to the house in Haleridge Road, he cursed himself for not having brought his mobile phone with him. He made it there in ten minutes flat. He opened the front door and went straight through to the kitchen and picked up the telephone receiver. He dialed Josh's mobile number.

"Come on, Josh," he muttered under his breath. "Answer it, for God's sake."

The mobile was redirected to Josh's voicemail service, and Dan ended the call without leaving a message. Josh must have been out of range, no doubt at the cottage. He thought about ringing the factory, but being a Sunday, the switchboard would probably not be manned. Anyway, the place would more than likely be closed following Patrick's death.

That left him only one option. Auchnacerie.

For a moment, his hand hovered above the dialing keyboard before he punched in the number. As soon as the call was connected, it was answered by his son.

"Josh?"

"Dad, where the hell have you been? I've been trying to get in touch with you all morning. Dad, I've got some really bad news—"

"I know, Josh. I've just read about it in the Sunday papers. When did it happen?"

"Friday night."

"Why didn't you contact me?"

"Because I only heard about it last night when I got back from Barcelona."

"What were you doing there?"

"Patrick sent me and Maria José over on a sales trip."

"Right." Even though Dan was eager for information, he still experienced a swell of pride at Josh's obvious rise in status. "So why are you at Auchnacerie?"

"Maria José and I are looking after Max and Sooty. Katie's had to go up to Inverness to have a meeting in the coroner's office. There has to be an enquiry."

"How are the children?"

"They seem to be bearing up all right. Max is here with me, and Maria José and Sooty have taken the dogs for a walk."

"Did you see Katie before she left?"

"Yes, I did."

"How is she taking it?"

"She's obviously pretty upset, but, on the other hand, she seems to be quite calm about it all. Maybe that's what comes from living with illness for so long. She's a pretty tough person."

"I know she is."

"Just before she left for Inverness, she told me that Patrick had been planning this trip for ages, and that he had been so excited about it. She said that he would have wanted to end his days doing something completely madcap like that, rather than fester away in a wheelchair."

"I think that's very true." Dan suddenly had a vision of Patrick, eyes glinting with excitement and intrigue, staring out of the plane windscreen into the all-enveloping fog. He shook his head to clear it from his mind. "I don't suppose any arrangements have been made for the funeral?"

"Not yet. Katie reckons that there'll be a postmortem."

"Of course."

"Are you coming up, Dad?"

Dan ran a hand through his hair. "I've got to work it out, Josh. I'll have to have a word with Battersea Gran and the girls before I make a decision." He bit at his bottom lip. "What's your gut feeling, Josh? You always seem to know."

There was a brief silence on the line. "I think you should come up immediately, Dad," Josh said quietly. "Katie needs your support. That's my gut feeling."

Dan smiled. "I'm glad you said that, Josh."

"So will you come?"

"I'll try to get on the train tonight. Can I get hold of you at Auchnacerie?"

"Yes. Maria José and I are staying here until Katie gets back."

"In that case, I'll make some plans and then give you a call. I'll just stay at the cottage."

"All right, then," Josh replied, "and Dad, you'd better bring some warm clothes. It's bloody freezing up here."

CHAPTER THIRTY

T HERE WAS NO need for you all to come, you know," Dan said
to his mother as he walked with her and Millie and Nina along
the platform at Euston Station.

"No bother at all, dear," puffed Battersea Gran. "Sunday night telly
has never been quite the same since *Monarch of the Glen* finished. Anyway, I've always rather liked railway stations. There's such an air of
excitement about them!"

Dan found his carriage and put his suitcase in through the door. He
had taken notice of what Josh had said about the weather and now
turned to face his farewell committee wearing his padded jacket and
fawn-coloured corduroy trousers. "I'll be back as soon as I can," he
said, bending down and giving his mother a kiss on the cheek. "I'll let
you know when."

Battersea Gran put her hand on the sleeve of his jacket and her eyes
brightened when she felt its soft, downy texture. "Now that's what I
call clothing. At last you've come to your senses."

The girls began laughing behind her back. Dan shot them a wink
before moving over to Nina and giving a kiss and a long hug. Then he

put his arms around Millie's neck. "You be in charge," he whispered into her ear. "Give me a call if anything goes haywire."

"All right, Dad," Millie said, giving him a smacking kiss on the side of his neck. "Even though you're dressed like a prat, I still love ya."

Dan laughed. "I'm glad to hear it."

"Give my love to everyone up there."

"I will do." He broke away from Millie's embrace. "Right, you lot, I think you should get away home. There's no point waiting until the train leaves."

He stood watching them until they had reached the gate at the top of the platform. They turned and gave him an enthusiastic wave before disappearing into the crowded terminus. He shook his head slowly. What a difference, he thought to himself. Six months ago, those girls would hardly have acknowledged his existence, yet now they could not be more close to him. He tilted back his head and gazed up at the cavernous glass roof of the station. Six months ago, he had been precisely here, on his way up to Scotland on some whimsical jaunt, without one iota of realization that his selfish, insular existence had led his family into crisis. And what a price he had had to pay for it.

He turned and walked over to the carriage door, then glanced back to where he had last seen Battersea Gran and Millie and Nina. He could never afford to make that mistake again. Two families now depended on it. He knew that he owed that much to Patrick.

And as he boarded the train, he thought of Katie and he grinned as her shrewd advice came to mind. He took his wallet from the inside pocket of his jacket, and extracting a ten-pound note, he went off in search of the car attendant.